Praise for the Patrick Melrose novels

'From the very first lines I was completely hooked . . . By turns witty, moving and an intense social comedy, I wept at the end but wouldn't dream of giving away the totally unexpected reason'   Antonia Fraser, *Sunday Telegraph*

'St Aubyn conveys the chaos of emotion, the confusion of heightened sensation, and the daunting contradictions of intellectual endeavour with a force and subtlety that have an exhilarating, almost therapeutic effect'
                                Francis Wyndham, *New York Review of Books*

'Wonderful caustic wit . . . Perhaps the very sprightliness of the prose – its lapidary concision and moral certitude – represents the cure for which the characters yearn. So much good writing is in itself a form of health'   Edmund White, *Guardian*

'Vicious and hilarious, with a steely integrity. St Aubyn is unbelievably good at describing the way one talks in the privacy of one's own head'   Mark Haddon, *The Times*

'The act of investigative self-repair has all along been the underlying project of these extraordinary novels. It is the source of their urgent emotional intensity, and the determining principle of their construction . . . A terrifying, spectacularly entertaining saga'   James Lasdun, *Guardian*

'Humour, pathos, razor-sharp judgement, pain, joy and everything in between. The Melrose novels are a masterwork for the twenty-first century'   Alice Sebold

'A humane meditation on lives blighted by the sins of the previous generation. St Aubyn remains among the cream of British novelists'   *Sunday Times*

D0167971

'The Patrick Melrose novels can be read as the navigational charts of a mariner desperate not to end up in the wretched harbor from which he embarked on a voyage that has led in and out of heroin addiction, alcoholism, marital infidelity and a range of behaviors for which the term "self-destructive" is the mildest of euphemisms. Some of the most perceptive, elegantly written and hilarious novels of our era . . . Remarkable'

Francine Prose, *New York Times*

'The main joy of a St Aubyn novel is the exquisite clarity of his prose, the almost uncanny sense he gives that, in language as in mathematical formulae, precision and beauty invariably point to truth . . . Characters in St Aubyn novels are hyper-articulate, and the witty dialogue is here, as ever, one of the chief joys'

Suzi Feay, *Financial Times*

'The Melrose sequence is now clearly one of the major achievements of contemporary British fiction'   *Evening Standard*

'The darkest possible comedy about the cruelty of the old to the young, vicious and excruciatingly honest. It opened my eyes to a whole realm of experience I have never seen written about. That's the mark of a masterpiece'   *The Times*

'Edward St Aubyn, like Proust, has created a world in which no one in their right mind would like to live but which feels real and vivid and hilariously and dangerously vacuous. Who better than he to turn to if your faith in the future of literary fiction is wavering'   Alan Taylor, *Herald*

'The bravura quality of St Aubyn's performance is irresistible. Brilliant'   *Sunday Telegraph*

'St Aubyn's Melrose novels now deserve to be thought of as an important roman-fleuve'

Henry Hitchings, *Times Literary Supplement*

'St Aubyn's Melrose series slices and dices morality with prose so chiselled and a narrative so intense that the hairs on the back of your neck stand up'   Geordie Greig, *Evening Standard*

'Blackly comic, superbly written fiction . . . His style is crisp and light; his similes exhilarating in their accuracy . . . St Aubyn writes with luminous tenderness of Patrick's love for his sons'

Caroline Moore, *Sunday Telegraph*

'His prose has an easy charm that masks a ferocious, searching intellect. As a sketcher of character, his wit – whether turned against pointless members of the aristocracy or hopeless crack dealers – is ticklingly wicked. As an analyser of broken minds and tired hearts he is as energetic, careful and creative as the perfect shrink. And when it comes to spinning a good yarn, whether over the grand scale or within a single page of anecdote, he has a natural talent for keeping you on the edge of your seat'   Melissa Katsoulis, *The Times*

'A masterpiece. Edward St Aubyn is a writer of immense gifts'

Patrick McGrath

'Irony courses through these pages like adrenaline . . . Patrick's intelligence processes his predicaments into elegant, lucid, dispassionate, near-aphoristic formulations . . . Brimming with witty flair, sardonic perceptiveness and literary finesse'

Peter Kemp, *Sunday Times*

PATRICK MELROSE VOLUME 1

EDWARD ST AUBYN was born in London
in 1960. His superbly acclaimed Melrose novels
are *Never Mind*, *Bad News*, *Some Hope*, *Mother's Milk*
(shortlisted for the Man Booker Prize 2006) and *At Last*.
He is also the author of the novels *A Clue to the Exit*,
On the Edge and *Lost for Words*.

EDWARD ST AUBYN

PATRICK MELROSE

VOLUME 1

NEVER MIND   BAD NEWS   SOME HOPE

PICADOR

First published 2018 by Picador
an imprint of Pan Macmillan
20 New Wharf Road, London N1 9RR
Associated companies throughout the world
www.panmacmillan.com

ISBN 978-1-5098-9768-1

Never Mind and *Bad News* first published 1992 by
William Heinemann. First published in paperback 1998 as
part of *The Patrick Melrose Trilogy* by Vintage. First published by
Picador in paperback 2007 as part of *Some Hope: A Trilogy*.
Some Hope first published 1994 by William Heinemann.

Printed and bound by CPI Group (UK) Ltd, Croydon, CR0 4YY

Visit www.picador.com to read more about all our books
and to buy them. You will also find features, author interviews and
news of any author events, and you can sign up for e-newsletters
so that you're always first to hear about our new releases.

Contents

NEVER MIND

For Ana

1

At half-past seven in the morning, carrying the laundry she had ironed the night before, Yvette came down the drive on her way to the house. Her sandal made a faint slapping sound as she clenched her toes to prevent it from falling off, and its broken strap made her walk unsteadily over the stony, rutted ground. Over the wall, below the line of cypresses that ran along the edge of the drive, she saw the doctor standing in the garden.

In his blue dressing gown, and already wearing dark glasses although it was still too early for the September sun to have risen above the limestone mountain, he directed a heavy stream of water from the hose he held in his left hand onto the column of ants moving busily through the gravel at his feet. His technique was well established: he would let the survivors struggle over the wet stones, and regain their dignity for a while, before bringing the thundering water down on them again. With his free hand he removed a cigar from his mouth, its smoke drifting up through the brown and grey curls that covered the jutting bones of his forehead. He then narrowed the jet of water with his thumb to batter more effectively an ant on whose death he was wholly bent.

Yvette had only to pass the fig tree and she could slip into the house without Dr Melrose knowing she had arrived. His habit, though, was to call her without looking up from the ground just when she thought she was screened by the tree.

Yesterday he had talked to her for long enough to exhaust her arms, but not for so long that she might drop the linen. He gauged such things very precisely. He had started by asking her opinion of the mistral, with exaggerated respect for her native knowledge of Provence. By the time he was kind enough to show an interest in her son's job at the shipyard, the pain had spread to her shoulders and started to make sharp forays into her neck. She had been determined to defy him, even when he asked about her husband's back pains and whether they might prevent him from driving the tractor during the harvest. Today he did not call out with the '*Bonjour, chère Yvette*' which inaugurated these solicitous morning chats, and she stooped under the low branches of the fig tree to enter the house.

The chateau, as Yvette called what the Melroses called an old farmhouse, was built on a slope so that the drive was level with the upper floor of the house. A wide flight of steps led down one side of the house to a terrace in front of the drawing room.

Another flight skirted the other side of the house down to a small chapel which was used to hide the dustbins. In winter, water gurgled down the slope through a series of pools, but the gutter which ran beside the fig tree was silent by this time of year, and clogged with squashed and broken figs that stained the ground where they had fallen.

Yvette walked into the high dark room and put down the laundry. She switched on the light and began to divide the towels from the sheets and the sheets from the tablecloths. There were ten tall cupboards piled high with neatly folded linen, none of it now used. Yvette sometimes opened these cupboards to admire this protected collection. Some of the tablecloths had laurel branches and bunches of grapes woven into them in a way that only showed when they were held at certain angles. She would run her finger over the monograms embroidered on the smooth white sheets, and over the coronets encircling the letter 'V' in the corner of the napkins. Her favourite was the unicorn that stood over a ribbon of foreign words on some of the oldest sheets but these too were never used, and Mrs Melrose insisted that Yvette recycle the same poor pile of plain linen from the smaller cupboard by the door.

Eleanor Melrose stormed her way up the shallow steps from the kitchen to the drive. Had she walked more slowly, she might have tottered, stopped, and sat down in despair on the low wall that ran along the side of the steps. She felt defiantly sick in a way she dared not challenge with food and had already aggravated with a cigarette. She had brushed her teeth after vomiting but the bilious taste was still in her mouth. She had brushed her teeth before vomiting as well, never able to utterly crush the optimistic streak in her nature. The mornings had grown cooler since the beginning of September and the air already smelt of autumn, but this hardly mattered to Eleanor who was sweating through the thick layers of powder on her forehead. With each step she pushed her hands against her knees to help her forward, staring down through huge dark glasses at the white canvas shoes on her pale feet, her dark pink raw-silk trousers like hot peppers clinging to her legs.

She imagined vodka poured over ice and all the cubes that had been frosted turning clear and collapsing in the glass and the ice cracking, like a spine in the hands of a confident osteopath. All the sticky, awkward cubes of ice floating together, tinkling, their frost thrown off to the side of the glass, and the vodka cold and unctuous in her mouth.

The drive rose sharply to the left of the steps to a circle of flat ground where her maroon Buick was parked under an umbrella pine. It looked preposterous, stretched out on its white-walled tyres against the terraced vines and olive groves behind it, but to Eleanor her car was like a consulate in a strange city, and she moved towards it with the urgency of a robbed tourist.

Globules of translucent resin were stuck to the Buick's bonnet. One splash of resin with a dead pine needle inside it was glued to the base of the windscreen. She tried to pick it off, but only smeared the windscreen more and made the tips of her fingers sticky. She wanted to get into the car very much, but she went on scratching compulsively at the resin, blackening her fingernails. The reason that Eleanor liked her Buick so much was that David never drove it, or even sat in it. She owned the house and the land, she paid for the servants and the drink, but only this car was really in her possession.

When she had first met David twelve years ago, she had been fascinated by his looks. The expression that men feel entitled to wear when they stare out of a cold English drawing room onto their own land had grown stubborn over five centuries and perfected itself in David's face. It was never quite clear to Eleanor why the English thought it was so distinguished to have done nothing for a long time in the same place, but David left her in no doubt that they did. He was also descended from Charles II through a prostitute. 'I'd keep quiet about that, if I were you,' she had joked when he first told her. Instead of smiling, he had turned his profile towards her in a way she had grown to loathe, thrusting out his underlip and looking as if he were exercising great tolerance by not saying something crushing.

There had been a time when she admired the way that David became a doctor. When he had told his father of his intention, General Melrose had immediately cut off his annuity, preferring to use the money to rear pheasants. Shooting men and animals were the occupations of a gentle-

8

man, tending their wounds the business of middle-class quacks. That was the General's view, and he was able to enjoy more shooting as a consequence of holding it. General Melrose did not find it difficult to treat his son coldly. The first time he had taken an interest in him was when David left Eton, and his father asked him what he wanted to do. David stammered, 'I'm afraid I don't know, sir,' not daring to admit that he wanted to compose music. It had not escaped the General's attention that his son fooled about on the piano, and he rightly judged that a career in the army would put a curb on this effeminate impulse. 'Better join the army,' he said, offering his son a cigar with awkward camaraderie.

And yet, to Eleanor, David had seemed so different from the tribe of minor English snobs and distant cousins who hung around, ready for an emergency, or for a weekend, full of memories that were not even their own, memories of the way their grandfathers had lived, which was not in fact how their grandfathers had lived. When she had met David, she thought that he was the first person who really understood her. Now he was the last person she would go to for understanding. It was hard to explain this change and she tried to resist the temptation of thinking that he had been waiting all along for her money to subsidize his fantasies of how he deserved to live. Perhaps, on the contrary, it was her money that had cheapened him. He had stopped his medical practice soon after their marriage. At the beginning, there had been talk of using some of her money to start a home for alcoholics. In a sense they had succeeded.

The thought of running into David struck Eleanor again. She tore herself away from the pine resin on the windscreen, clambered into the car and drove the unwieldy Buick past the steps and along the dusty drive, only stopping when she was halfway down the hill. She was on her way over to Victor Eisen's so she could make an early start for the airport with

Anne, but first she had to straighten herself out. Folded in a cushion under the driver's seat was a half-bottle of Bisquit brandy. In her bag she had the yellow pills for keeping her alert and the white ones for taking away the dread and panic that alertness brought with it. With the long drive ahead of her she took four instead of two of the yellow pills and then, worrying that the double dose might make her jumpy, she took two of the white ones, and drank about half the bottle of brandy to help the pills down. At first she shuddered violently, and then before it even reached her bloodstream, she felt the sharp click of alcohol, filling her with gratitude and warmth.

She subsided into the seat on which she had only been perched, recognizing herself in the mirror for the first time that day. She settled into her body, like a sleepwalker who climbs back into bed after a dangerous expedition. Silent through the sealed windows, she saw black and white magpies burst from the vines, and the needles of the pine trees standing out sharply against the pale sky, swept clean by two days of strong wind. She started the engine again and drove off, steering vaguely along the steep and narrow lanes.

David Melrose, tired of drowning ants, abandoned watering the garden. As soon as the sport lost a narrow focus, it filled him with despair. There was always another nest, another terrace of nests. He pronounced ants 'aunts', and it added zest to his murderous pursuits if he bore in mind his mother's seven haughty sisters, high-minded and selfish women to whom he had displayed his talent on the piano when he was a child.

David dropped the hose on the gravel path, thinking how useless to him Eleanor had become. She had been rigid with terror for too long. It was like trying to palpate a patient's swollen liver when one had already proved that it hurt. She could only be persuaded to relax so often.

He remembered an evening twelve years before, when he had asked her to dinner at his flat. How trusting she was in those days! They had already slept together, but Eleanor still treated him shyly. She wore a rather shapeless white dress with large black polka dots. She was twenty-eight but seemed younger because of the simple cut of her lank blonde hair. He found her pretty in a bewildered, washed-out way, but it was her restlessness that aroused him, the quiet exasperation of a woman who longs to throw herself into something significant, but cannot find what it is.

He had cooked a Moroccan dish of pigeon stuffed with almonds. He served it to her on a bed of saffron rice and then drew back the plate. 'Will you do something for me?' he asked.

'Of course,' she said. 'What?'

He put the plate on the floor behind her chair and said, 'Would you eat your food without using a knife and fork, or your hands, just eat it off the plate?'

'Like a dog, you mean?' she asked.

'Like a girl pretending to be a dog.'

'But why?'

'Because I want you to.'

He enjoyed the risk he was taking. She might have said no and left. If she stayed and did what he wanted, he would capture her. The odd thing was that neither of them thought of laughing.

A submission, even an absurd one, was a real temptation to Eleanor. She would be sacrificing things she did not want to believe in – table manners, dignity, pride – for something she did want to believe in: the spirit of sacrifice. The emptiness of the gesture, the fact that it did not help anybody, made it seem more pure at the time. She knelt down on all fours on the threadbare Persian rug, her hands flattened either side of the plate. Her elbows jutted out as she lowered herself and picked up a piece of pigeon between her teeth. She felt the strain at the base of her spine.

She sat back, her hands resting on her knees, and chewed quietly. The pigeon tasted strange. She looked up a little and saw David's shoes, one pointing towards her along the floor, the other dangling close to her in the air. She looked no higher than the knees of his crossed legs, but bowed down again, eating more eagerly this time, rooting about in the mound of rice to catch an almond with her lips and shaking her head gently to loosen some pigeon from the bone. When she looked up at him at last, one of her cheeks was glazed with gravy and some grains of the yellow rice were stuck to her mouth and nose. All the bewilderment was gone from her face.

For a few moments David had adored her for doing what he had asked. He extended his foot and ran the edge of his shoe gently along her cheek. He was completely captivated by the trust she showed him, but he did not know what to do with it, since it had already achieved its purpose, which was to demonstrate that he could elicit her submission.

The next day he told Nicholas Pratt what had happened. It was one of those days when he made his secretary say that he was busy, and sat drinking in his club, beyond the reach of fevered children and women who pretended their hangovers were migraines. He liked to drink under the blue and gold ceiling of the morning room, where there was always a ripple left by the passage of important men. Dull, dissolute, and obscure members felt buoyed up by this atmosphere of power, as little dinghies bob up and down on their moorings when a big yacht sails out of the harbour they have shared.

'Why did you make her do it?' asked Nicholas, hovering between mischief and aversion.

'Her conversation is so limited, don't you find?' said David.

Nicholas did not respond. He felt that he was being forced to conspire, just as Eleanor had been forced to eat.

'Did she make better conversation from the floor?' he asked.

'I'm not a magician,' said David, 'I couldn't make her amusing, but I did at least keep her quiet. I was dreading having another talk about the agonies of being rich. I know so little about them, and she knows so little about anything else.'

Nicholas chuckled and David showed his teeth. Whatever one felt about David wasting his talents, thought Nicholas, he had never been any good at smiling.

David walked up the right side of the double staircase that led from the garden to the terrace. Although he was now sixty, his hair was still thick and a little wild. His face was astonishingly handsome. Its faultlessness was its only flaw; it was the blueprint of a face and had an uninhabited feeling to it, as if no trace of how its owner had lived could modify the perfection of the lines. People who knew David well watched for signs of decay, but his mask grew more noble each year. Behind his dark glasses, however rigidly he held his neck, his eyes flickered unobserved, assessing the weaknesses in people. Diagnosis had been his most intoxicating skill as a doctor and after exhibiting it he had often lost interest in his patients, unless something about their suffering intrigued him. Without his dark glasses, he wore an inattentive expression, until he spotted another person's vulnerability. Then the look in his eyes hardened like a flexed muscle.

He paused at the top of the stairs. His cigar had gone out and he flung it over the wall into the vines below. Opposite him, the ivy that covered the south side of the house was already streaked with red. He admired the colour. It was a gesture of defiance towards decay, like a man spitting in the face of his torturer. He had seen Eleanor hurrying away early in her ridiculous car. He had even seen Yvette trying to steal into the house without drawing attention to herself. Who could blame them?

He knew that his unkindness to Eleanor was effective only if he alternated it with displays of concern and elaborate apologies for his destructive nature, but he had abandoned these variations because his disappointment in her was boundless. He knew that she could not help him unravel the knot of inarticulacy that he carried inside him. Instead, he could feel it tightening, like a promise of suffocation that shadowed every breath he took.

It was absurd; but all summer long he had been obsessed by the memory of a mute cripple he had seen in Athens airport. This man, trying to sell tiny bags of pistachio nuts by tossing printed advertisements into the laps of waiting passengers, had heaved himself forward, stamping the ground with uncontrollable feet, his head lolling and his eyes rolling upwards. Each time David had looked at the man's mouth twisting silently, like a gasping fish on a river bank, he had felt a kind of vertigo.

David listened to the swishing sound his yellow slippers made as he walked up the last flight of steps to the door that led from the terrace into the drawing room. Yvette had not yet opened the curtains, which saved him the trouble of closing them again. He liked the drawing room to look dim and valuable. A dark red and heavily gilded chair that Eleanor's American grandmother had prised from an old Venetian family on one of her acquisitive sweeps through Europe gleamed against the opposite wall of the room. He enjoyed the scandal connected with its acquisition and, knowing that it ought to be carefully preserved in a museum, he made a point of sitting on it as often as possible. Sometimes, when he was alone, he sat in the Doge's chair, as it was always called, leaning forward on the edge of the seat, his right hand clasping one of the intricately carved arms, striking a pose he remembered from the *Illustrated History of England* he had been given at prep school. The picture portrayed Henry V's superb anger when he was sent a present of tennis balls by the insolent King of France.

David was surrounded by the spoils of Eleanor's matriarchal American family. Drawings by Guardi and Tiepolo, Piazetta and Novelli hung thickly over the walls. An eighteenth-century French screen, crowded with greyish-brown monkeys and pink roses, divided the long room in half. Partially hidden behind it, from where David stood, was a black Chinese cabinet, its top crowded with neat rows of bottles, and its inner shelves filled with their reinforcements. As he poured himself a drink, David thought about his dead father-in-law, Dudley Craig, a charming, drunken Scotsman who had been dismissed by Eleanor's mother, Mary, when he became too expensive to keep.

After Dudley Craig, Mary had married Jean de Valençay, feeling that if she was going to keep a man, he might as well be a duke. Eleanor had been brought up in a string of houses where every object seemed to have been owned by a king or an emperor. The houses were wonderful, but guests left them with relief, conscious that they were not quite good enough, in the duchess's eyes, for the chairs on which they had sat.

David walked towards the tall window at the end of the room. The only one with its curtain open, it gave a view onto the mountain opposite. He often stared at the bare outcrops of lacerated limestone. They looked to him like models of human brains dumped on the dark green mountainside, or at other times, like a single brain, bursting from dozens of incisions. He sat on the sofa beside the window and looked out, trying to work up a primitive sense of awe.

2

Patrick walked towards the well. In his hand he carried a grey plastic sword with a gold handle, and swished it at the pink flowers of the valerian plants that grew out of the terrace wall. When there was a snail on one of the fennel stems, he sliced his sword down the stalk and made it fall off. If he killed a snail he had to stamp on it quickly and then run away, because it went all squishy like blowing your nose. Then he would go back and have a look at the broken brown shell stuck in the soft grey flesh, and would wish he hadn't done it. It wasn't fair to squash the snails after it rained because they came out to play, bathing in the pools under the dripping leaves and stretching out their horns. When he touched their horns they darted back and his hand darted back as well. For snails he was like a grown-up.

One day, when he was not intending to go there, he had been surprised to find himself next to the well and so he decided that the route he had discovered was a secret short cut. Now he always went that way when he was alone. He walked through a terrace of olive trees where yesterday the wind had made the leaves flick from green to grey and grey to green, like running his fingers back and forth over velvet, making it turn pale and dark again.

He had shown Andrew Bunnill the secret short cut and Andrew said it was longer than the other way, and so he told Andrew he was going to throw him down the well. Andrew was feeble and had started to cry. When Andrew flew back to London, Patrick said he would throw him out of the plane. Blub, blub, blub. Patrick wasn't even on the plane, but he told Andrew he would be hiding under the floor and would saw a circle around his chair. Andrew's nanny said that Patrick was a nasty little boy, and Patrick said it was just because Andrew was so wet.

Patrick's own nanny was dead. A friend of his mother's said she had gone to heaven, but Patrick had been there and knew perfectly well that they had put her in a wooden box and dropped her in a hole. Heaven was the other direction and so the woman was lying, unless it was like sending a parcel. His mother cried a lot when nanny was put in the box, she said it was because of her own nanny. That was stupid, because her own nanny was still alive and in fact they had to go and visit her on the train, and it was the most boring thing ever. She had horrible cake with only a tiny bit of jam in the middle and millions of miles of fluff on either side. She always said, 'I know you like this,' which was a lie, because he had told her he didn't the last time. It was called sponge cake and so he had asked was it for having a bath with and his mother's nanny had laughed and laughed and hugged him for ages. It was disgusting because she pressed her cheek next to his and her skin hung down loosely, like that chicken's neck he had seen hanging over the edge of the table in the kitchen.

Why did his mother have to have a nanny anyway? He didn't have one anymore and he was only five. His father said he was a little man now. He remembered going to England when he was three. It was winter and he saw snow for the first time. He could remember standing on the road by a stone bridge and the road was covered in frost and the fields were covered in snow and the sky was shining and the road and the hedges were blazing and he had blue woollen gloves on and his nanny held his hand and they stood still for ages looking at the bridge. He used to think of that often, and the time they were in the back of the car and he had his head in her lap and he looked up at her and she smiled and the sky behind her head was very wide and blue, and he had fallen asleep.

Patrick walked up a steep bank on a path that ran beside a bay tree and emerged next to the well. He was forbidden to play by the well. It was his favourite place to play. Sometimes he climbed onto the rotten cover and jumped up and down, pretending it was a trampoline. Nobody could stop him, nor did they often try. The wood was black where the blistered pink paint had peeled off. It creaked dangerously and made his heart beat faster. He was not strong enough to lift the cover himself, but when it was left open he collected stones and clumps of earth to throw down the shaft. They hit the water with a deep reverberating splash and broke into the blackness.

Patrick raised his sword in triumph as he reached the top of the path. He could see that the cover of the well was pushed back. He started to search about for a good stone, the biggest one he could lift and the roundest he could find. He hunted in the surrounding field and unearthed a reddish stone which he needed both hands to carry. He placed it on the flat surface next to the opening of the well shaft and hoisted himself up until his legs no longer touched the ground and, leaning over as far as he could, looked down at the darkness where he knew the water was hiding. Holding on with his left hand, he pushed the stone over the edge and heard the plunging sound it made and watched the surface break and the disturbed water catch the light of the sky and gleam back at it unreliably. So heavy and black it was more like oil. He shouted down the shaft where the dry bricks turned green and then black. If he leaned over far enough he could hear a damp echo of his own voice.

Patrick decided to climb up the side of the well. His scuffed blue sandals fitted in the gaps between the rocks. He wanted to stand on the ledge beside the open well shaft. He had done it once before, for a dare, when Andrew was staying. Andrew had stood beside the well saying, 'Please don't, Patrick, please come down, *please* don't.' Patrick wasn't scared then, although Andrew was, but now that he was alone he felt dizzy, squatting on the ledge, with his back to the water. He stood up very slowly and as he straightened, he felt the invitation of the emptiness behind him, pulling him backwards. He was convinced that his feet would slip if he moved, and he tried to stop wobbling by clenching his fists and his toes and looking down very seriously at the hard ground around the well. His sword was still resting on the ledge and he wanted to retrieve it in order to make his conquest complete, and so he leaned over carefully, with an enormous effort of will, defying the fear that tried to arrest his limbs, and picked up the sword by its scratched and dented grey blade. Once he got hold of the sword, he bent his knees hesitantly and jumped over the edge, landing on the ground, shouting hooray and making the noise of clashing metal as he slashed about him at imaginary enemies. He whacked a bay leaf with the flat of his sword and then stabbed the air underneath it with a morbid groan, clutching his side at the same time. He liked to imagine an ambushed Roman army about to be smashed to bits by the barbarians, when he arrived, the commander of the special soldiers with purple cloaks, and he was braver than anybody and saved the day from unthinkable defeat.

When he went for a walk in the woods he often thought about Ivanhoe, the hero of one of his favourite comics, who cut down the trees on either side of him as he passed. Patrick had to walk around the pine trees, but he imagined he had the power to carve his own path, striding majestically through the small wood at the end of the terrace on which he stood, felling with a single blow each tree to his right and left. He read things in books and then he thought about them lots. He had read about rainbows in a soppy picture book, but then he had started to see them in the streets in London after it rained, when the petrol from the cars stained the tarmac and the water fanned out in broken purple, blue, and yellow rings.

He didn't feel like going into the wood today and so he decided to jump down all the terraces. It was like flying, but some of the walls were too high and he had to sit on the edge, throw his sword down, and lower himself as far as he could before he dropped. His shoes filled with the dry soil around the vines and he had to take them off twice and hold them upside down to shake out the earth and the pebbles. Nearer the bottom of the valley the terraces became wider and shallower and he could leap over the edge of all the walls. He gathered his breath for the final flight.

Sometimes he managed to jump so far that he felt like Superman practically, and at other times he made himself run faster by thinking about the Alsatian dog that chased him down the beach on that windy day when they had gone to lunch at George's. He had begged his mother to let him go for a walk, because he loved looking at the wind when it exploded the sea, like smashing bottles against rocks. Everyone said not to go too far, but he wanted to be nearer the rocks. There was a sandy path leading to the beach and while he was walking down it a fat, long-haired Alsatian appeared at the top of the hill, barking at him. When he saw it move closer, he started to run, following the twists in the path at first and then jumping straight down the soft slope, faster and faster, until he was taking giant strides, his arms spread out against the wind, rushing down the hill onto the half circle of sand between the rocks, right up to the edge of the highest wave. When he looked up the dog was miles away up on the hill, and he knew it could never catch him because he was so fast. Later he wondered if it had tried.

Patrick arrived panting at the dried-up river bed. He climbed onto a big rock between two clumps of pale green bamboo. When he had taken Andrew there they had played a game that Patrick invented. They both had to stand on the rock and try to push each other off, and on one side they pretended there was a pit full of broken razor blades and on the other there was a tank full of honey. And if you fell to one side you were cut to death in a million places, and on the other you drowned, exhausted by a heavy golden swim. Andrew fell over every time, because he was so utterly wet.

Andrew's father was wet too, in a way. Patrick had been to Andrew's birthday party in London, and there was a huge box in the middle of the drawing room, full of presents for the other children. They all queued up and took a present out of the box and then ran around comparing what they'd got. Unlike them, Patrick hid his present under an armchair and went back to get another one. When he was leaning over the box, fishing out another shiny package, Andrew's father squatted down next to him and said, 'You've already had one haven't you, Patrick?' – not angrily, but in a voice like he was offering Patrick a sweet. 'It isn't fair on the other children if you take their presents, is it?' Patrick looked at him defiantly and said, 'I haven't got one already,' and Andrew's father just looked all sad and utterly wet and said, 'Very well, Patrick, but I don't want to see you taking another one.' And so Patrick got two presents, but he hated Andrew's father because he wanted more.

Patrick had to play the rock game on his own now, jumping from one side of the rock to another, challenging his sense of balance with wild gestures. When he fell over, he pretended it had not happened, although he knew that was cheating.

Patrick looked doubtfully at the rope François had tied for him to one of the nearby trees so that he could swing over the river bed. He felt thirsty and started to climb back up to the house along the path where the tractor worked its way among the vines. His sword had become a burden and he carried it under his arm resentfully. He had heard his father use a funny expression once. He said to George, 'Give him enough rope and he'll hang himself.' Patrick did not know what that meant at first, but he became convinced, with a flash of terror and shame, that they were talking about the rope that François had tied to the tree. That night he dreamt that the rope had turned into one of the tentacles of an octopus and wrapped itself around his throat. He tried to cut it, but he could not because his sword was only a toy. His mother cried a lot when they found him dangling from the tree.

Even when you were awake it was hard to know what grown-ups meant when they said things. One day he had worked out a way of guessing what they were going to do: no meant no, maybe meant perhaps, yes meant maybe and perhaps meant no, but the system did not work, and he decided that maybe everything meant perhaps.

Tomorrow the terraces would be crowded with grape-pickers filling their buckets with bunches of grapes. Last year François had taken him on the tractor. His hands were very strong and hard like wood. François was married to Yvette who had gold teeth you could see when she smiled. One day Patrick was going to have all his teeth made of gold, not just two or three. He sometimes sat in the kitchen with Yvette and she let him taste the things she was cooking. She came up to him with spoons full of tomato and meat and soup and said, '*Ça te plaît?*' And he could see her gold teeth when he nodded. Last year François told him to sit in the corner of the trailer next to two big barrels of grapes. Sometimes when the road was rough and steep he turned around and said, '*Ça va?*' And Patrick shouted back, '*Oui, merci*,' over the noise of the engine and the bumping and squealing of the trailer and the brakes. When they got to the place where the wine was made, Patrick was very excited. It was dark and cool in there, the floor was hosed with water, and there was a sharp smell of juice turning into wine. The room was vast and François took him up a ladder to a high ramp that ran above the wine press and all of the vats. The ramp was made of metal with holes in it and it was a funny feeling being so high up with holes under his feet.

When they got to the wine press Patrick looked down and saw two steel rollers turning in opposite directions with no space in between them. Stained with grape juice, they pressed against each other, spinning loudly. The lower railing of the ramp only came up to Patrick's chin and he felt very close to the wine press. And looking at it, he felt that his eyes were like the grapes, made of the same soft translucent jelly and that they might fall out of his head and get crushed between the two rollers.

As Patrick approached the house, climbing as usual the right-hand flight of the double staircase because it was luckier, he turned into the garden to see if he could find the frog that lived in the fig tree. Seeing the tree frog was very lucky indeed. Its bright green skin was even smoother against the smooth grey skin of the fig tree, and it was hard to find it among the fig leaves which were almost the same colour as itself. In fact, Patrick had only seen the tree frog twice, but he had stood still for ages staring at its sharp skeleton and bulging eyes, like the beads on his mother's yellow necklace, and at the suckers on its front feet that held it motionless against the trunk and, above all, at the swelling sides which enlivened a body as delicate as jewellery, but greedier for breath. The second time he saw the frog, Patrick stretched out his hand and carefully touched its head with the tip of his index finger, and it did not move and he felt that it trusted him.

The frog was not there today and so he climbed wearily up the last flight of steps, pushing against his knees with his hands. He walked around the house to the kitchen entrance and reached up to open the squealing door. He had expected to find Yvette in the kitchen, but she was not there. Bottles of white wine and champagne jostled and clinked as he opened the refrigerator door. He turned back into the larder, where he found two warm bottles of chocolate milk in the corner of the lower shelf. After several attempts he opened one and drank the soothing liquid straight from the bottle, something Yvette had told him not to do. Immediately after drinking he felt violently sad and sat for several minutes on the kitchen counter staring down at his dangling shoes.

He could hear the piano music, muted by distance and closed doors, but he did not pay any attention to it, until he recognized the tune his father had composed for him. He jumped off the counter and ran down the corridor that led to the hall, crossed the hall, and broke into a kind of cantering motion as he entered the drawing room and danced to his father's tune. It was wild music with harsh flurries of high notes superimposed on a rumbling military march. Patrick hopped and skipped between the tables and chairs and around the edge of the piano, only coming to rest when his father ceased to play.

'How are you today, Mr Master Man?' asked his father, staring at him intently.

'All right, thank you,' said Patrick, wondering if it was a trick question. He was out of breath, but he knew he must concentrate because he was with his father. When he had asked what was the most important thing in the world, his father had said, 'Observe everything.' Patrick often forgot about this instruction, but in his father's presence he looked at things carefully, without being sure what he was looking for. He had watched his father's eyes behind their dark glasses. They moved from object to object and person to person, pausing for a moment on each and seeming to steal something vital from them, with a quick adhesive glance, like the flickering of a gecko's tongue. When he was with his father, Patrick looked at everything seriously, hoping he looked serious to anyone who might watch his eyes, as he had watched his father's.

'Come here,' said his father. Patrick stepped closer.

'Shall I pick you up by the ears?'

'No,' shouted Patrick. It was a sort of game they played. His father reached out and clasped Patrick's ears between his forefingers and thumbs. Patrick put his hands around his father's wrists and his father pretended to pick him up by his ears, but Patrick really took the strain with his arms. His father stood up and lifted Patrick until their eyes were level.

'Let go with your hands,' he said.

'No,' shouted Patrick.

'Let go and I'll drop you at the same time,' said his father persuasively.

Patrick released his father's wrists, but his father continued to pinch his ears. For a moment the whole weight of his body was supported by his ears. He quickly caught his father's wrists again.

'Ouch,' he said, 'you said you were going to drop me. *Please* let go of my ears.'

His father still held him dangling in the air. 'You've learned something very useful today,' he said. 'Always think for yourself. Never let other people make important decisions for you.'

'Please let go,' said Patrick. 'Please.' He felt that he was going to cry, but he pushed back his sense of desperation. His arms were exhausted, but if he relaxed them he felt as if his ears were going to be torn off, like the gold foil from a pot of cream, just ripped off the side of his head.

'You *said*,' he yelled, 'you said.'

His father dropped him. 'Don't whimper,' he said in a bored voice, 'it's very unattractive.' He sat down at the piano and started playing the march again, but Patrick did not dance.

He ran from the room, through the hall, out of the kitchen, over the terrace, along the olive grove and into the pine wood. He found the thorn bush, ducked underneath it, and slid down a small slope into his most secret hiding place. Under a canopy of bushes, wedged up against a pine tree which was surrounded by thickets on every side, he sat down and tried to stop the sobs, like hiccups, that snarled his throat.

Nobody can find me here, he thought. He could not control the spasms that caught his breath as he tried to inhale. It was like being caught in sweaters, when he plunged his head in and couldn't find the neck of the sweater and he tried to get out through the arm and it all got twisted and he thought he would never get out and he couldn't breathe.

Why did his father do that? Nobody should do that to anybody else, he thought, nobody should do that to anybody else.

In winter when there was ice on the puddles, you could see the bubbles trapped underneath and the air couldn't breathe: it had been ducked by the ice and held under, and he hated that because it was so unfair and so he always smashed the ice to let the air go free.

Nobody can find me here, he thought. And then he thought, what if nobody can find me here?

3

Victor was still asleep in his room downstairs and Anne wanted him to stay asleep. After less than a year together they now slept in separate rooms because Victor's snoring, and nothing else about him, kept her awake at night. She walked barefoot down the steep and narrow staircase running the tips of her fingers along the curve of the whitewashed walls. In the kitchen she removed the whistle from the spout of the chipped enamel kettle, and made coffee as silently as possible.

There was a tired ebullience about Victor's kitchen, with its bright orange plates and watermelon slices grinning facetiously from the tea towels. It was a harbour of cheap gaiety built up by Victor's ex-wife, Elaine, and Victor had been torn between protesting against her bad taste and the fear that it might be in bad taste to protest. After all, did one notice the kitchen things? Did they matter? Wasn't indifference more dignified? He had always admired David Melrose's certainty that beyond good taste lay the confidence to make mistakes because they were one's own. It was at this point that Victor often wavered. Sometimes he opted for a few days, or a few minutes, of assertive impertinence, but he always returned to his careful impersonation of a gentleman; it was all very well to *épater les bourgeois*, but the excitement was double-edged if you were also one of them. Victor knew that he could never acquire David Melrose's conviction that success was somehow vulgar. Though sometimes he was tempted to believe that David's languor and contempt masked regret for his failed life, this simple idea dissolved in David's overbearing presence.

What amazed Anne was that a man as clever as Victor could be caught with such small hooks. Pouring herself some coffee she felt a strange sympathy for Elaine. They had never met, but she had come to understand what had driven Victor's wife to seek refuge in a full set of Snoopy mugs.

When Anne Moore had been sent by the London bureau of the *New York Times* to interview the eminent philosopher Sir Victor Eisen, he had seemed a little old-fashioned. He had just returned from lunch at the Athenaeum, and his felt hat, darkened by rain, lay on the hall table. He pulled his watch out of his waistcoat pocket with what struck Anne as an archaic gesture.

'Ah, exactly on time,' he said. 'I admire punctuality.'

'Oh, good,' she answered, 'a lot of people don't.'

The interview had gone well, so well in fact that later in the afternoon it moved into his bedroom. From that point on Anne had willingly interpreted the almost Edwardian clothes, the pretentious house and the claret-stained anecdotes as part of the camouflage that a Jewish intellectual would have had to take on, along with a knighthood, in order to blend into the landscape of conventional English life.

During the months that followed she lived with Victor in London, ignoring any evidence that made this mild interpretation look optimistic. Those interminable weekends, for instance, which started with briefings on Wednesday night: how many acres, how many centuries, how many servants. Thursday evening was given over to speculation: he hoped, he really hoped, that the Chancellor wouldn't be there this time; could Gerald still be shooting now that he was in a wheelchair? The warnings came on Friday, during the drive down: '*Don't* unpack your own bags in this house.' '*Don't* keep asking people what they do.' '*Don't* ask the butler how he *feels*, as you did last time.' The weekends only ended on Tuesday when the stalks and skins of Saturday and Sunday were pressed again for their last few drops of sour juice.

In London, she met Victor's clever friends but at weekends the people they stayed with were rich and often stupid. Victor was *their* clever friend. He purred appreciatively at their wine and pictures and they started many of their sentences by saying, 'Victor will be able to tell us . . .' She watched them trying to make him say something clever and she watched him straining himself to be more like them, even reiterating the local pieties: wasn't it splendid that Gerald *hadn't* given up shooting? Wasn't Gerald's mother amazing? Bright as a button and still beavering away in the garden at ninety-two. 'She completely wears me out,' he gasped.

If Victor sang for his supper, at least he enjoyed eating it. What was harder to discount was his London house. He had bought the fifteen-year lease on this surprisingly large white stucco house in a Knightsbridge crescent after selling his slightly smaller but freehold house at a less fashionable address. The lease now had only seven years to run. Anne stoutly ascribed this insane transaction to the absent-mindedness for which philosophers are famous.

Only when she had come down here to Lacoste in July and seen Victor's relationship with David had her loyalty begun to wear away. She started to wonder how high a price in wasted time Victor was prepared to pay for social acceptance, and why on earth he wanted to pay it to David.

According to Victor, they had been 'exact contemporaries', a term he used for anyone of vaguely his own age who had not noticed him at school. 'I knew him at Eton' too often meant that he had been ruthlessly mocked by someone. He said of only two other scholars that they were friends of his at school, and he no longer saw either of them. One was the head of a Cambridge college and the other a civil servant who was widely thought to be a spy because his job sounded too dull to exist.

She could picture Victor in those days, an anxious schoolboy whose parents had left Austria after the First World War, settled in Hampstead, and later helped a friend find a house for Freud. Her images of David Melrose had been formed by a mixture of Victor's stories and her American vision of English privilege. She pictured him, a demigod from the big house, opening the batting against the village cricket team, or lounging about in a funny waistcoat he was allowed to wear because he was in Pop, a club Victor never got into. It was hard to take this Pop thing seriously but somehow Victor managed. As far as she could make out it was like being a college football hero, but instead of making out with the cheerleaders, you got to beat young boys for burning your toast.

When she had met David, at the end of the long red carpet unrolled by Victor's stories, she spotted the arrogance but decided that she was just too American to buy into the glamour of David's lost promise and failure. He struck her as a fraud and she had said so to Victor. Victor had been solemn and disapproving, arguing that on the contrary David suffered from the clarity with which he saw his own situation. 'You mean he *knows* he's a pain in the ass?' she had asked.

Anne moved back towards the stairs, warming her hands with a steaming orange mug covered in purple hearts of various sizes. She would have liked to spend the day reading in the hammock that hung between the plane trees in front of the house, but she had agreed to go to the airport with Eleanor. This American Girls' Outing had been imposed on her by Victor's unquenchable desire to be associated with the Melroses. The only Melrose Anne really liked was Patrick. At five years old he was still capable of a little enthusiasm.

If at first she had been touched by Eleanor's vulnerability, Anne was now exasperated by her drunkenness. Besides, Anne had to guard against her wish to save people, as well as her habit of pointing out their moral deficiencies, especially as she knew that nothing put the English more on edge than a woman having definite opinions, except a woman who went on to defend them. It was as if every time she played the ace of spades, it was beaten by a small trump. Trumps could be pieces of gossip, or insincere remarks, or irrelevant puns, or anything that dispelled the possibility of seriousness. She was tired of the deadly smile on the faces of people whose victory was assured by their silliness.

Having learned this, it had been relatively easy to play along with the tax-exiled English duke, George Watford, who came up from the coast for weekends with the Melroses, wearing shoes that tapered to a quite impossible thinness. His rather wooden face was covered in the thinnest cracks, like the varnish on the Old Masters he had 'shocked the nation' by selling. The English didn't ask much of their dukes in Anne's opinion. All they had to do was hang on to their possessions, at least the very well-known ones, and then they got to be guardians of what other people called 'our heritage'. She was disappointed that this character with a face like a cobweb had not even managed the small task of leaving his Rembrandts on the wall where he found them.

Anne continued to play along until the arrival of Vijay Shah. Only an acquaintance, not a friend of Victor's, they had met ten years before when Vijay, as head of the Debating Society, had invited Victor down to Eton to defend the 'relevance' of philosophy. Since then Vijay had cultivated the connection with a barrage of arty postcards and they had occasionally met at parties in London. Like Victor, Vijay had been an Eton scholar, but unlike Victor he was also very rich.

Anne felt guilty at first that she reacted so badly to Vijay's appearance. His oyster-coloured complexion and the thick jowls that looked like a permanent attack of mumps were the unhappy setting for a large hooked nose with tufts of intractable hair about the nostrils. His glasses were thick and square but, without them, the raw dents on the bridge of his nose and the weak eyes peering out from the darker grey of their sockets looked worse. His hair was blow-dried until it rose and stiffened like a black meringue on top of his skull. His clothes did nothing to compensate for these natural disadvantages. If Vijay's favourite flared green trousers were a mistake, it was a trivial one compared to his range of lightweight jackets in chaotic tartan patterns, with flapless pockets sewn onto the outside. Still, any clothes were preferable to the sight of him in a bathing suit. Anne remembered with horror his narrow shoulders and their white pustules struggling to break through a thick pelt of wiry black hair.

Had Vijay's character been more attractive his appearance might have elicited pity or even indifference, but spending just a few days with him convinced Anne that each hideous feature had been moulded by internal malevolence. His wide, grinning mouth was at once crude and cruel. When he tried to smile, his purplish lips could only curl and twist like a rotting leaf thrown onto a fire. Obsequious and giggly with older and more powerful people, he turned savage at the smell of weakness, and would attack only easy prey. His voice seemed to be designed exclusively for simpering and yet when they had argued on the night before he left, it had achieved the shrill astringency of a betrayed schoolmaster. Like many flatterers, he was not aware that he irritated the people he flattered. When he had met the Wooden Duke he had poured himself out in a rich gurgling rush of compliments, like an overturned bottle of syrup. She overheard George complaining afterwards to David, 'Perfectly ghastly man your friend Victor brought over. Kept telling me about the plaster-work at Richfield. Thought he must want a job as a guide.' George grunted disdainfully and David grunted disdainfully back.

A little Indian guy being sneered at by monsters of English privilege would normally have unleashed the full weight of Anne's loyalty to underdogs, but this time it was wiped out by Vijay's enormous desire to be a monster of English privilege himself. 'I can't bear going to Calcutta,' he giggled, 'the people, my dear, and the noise.' He paused to let everyone appreciate this nonchalant remark made by an English soldier at the Somme.

The memory of Vijay's ingratiating purr died away as Anne tried to push open her bedroom door, which always stuck on a bulge in the quaintly uneven floor. This was another relic of Elaine, who had refused to change what she called 'the authentic feel of the house'. Now the hexagonal tiles were worn to a paler terracotta where the door scraped them each time it was opened. Afraid of spilling her coffee she let the door stay stuck and edged sideways into the room. Her breasts brushed the cupboard as she passed.

Anne put her coffee mug down on the round marble-topped table with black metal legs which Elaine had carried back in triumph from some junk store in Apt and cunningly used as a bedside table. It was far too high and Anne often pulled the wrong book from the pile of unseen titles above her. Suetonius' *Twelve Caesars*, which David had lent her way back at the beginning of August, kept turning up like a reproach. She had glanced at one or two chapters, but the fact that David had recommended the book made her reluctant to become intimate with it. She knew she really ought to read a bit more of it before dinner so as to have something intelligent to say when she gave it back to him tonight. All she remembered was that Caligula had planned to torture his wife to find out why he was so devoted to her. What was David's excuse, she wondered.

Anne lit a cigarette. Lying on a pile of pillows and smaller cushions, slurping her coffee and playing with her cigarette smoke, she felt briefly that her thoughts were growing more subtle and expansive. The only thing that compromised her pleasure was the sound of running water in Victor's bathroom.

First, he would shave and wipe the remnants of the shaving cream on a clean towel. Then he would plaster his hair as flat as he could, walk to the foot of the stairs and shout, 'Darling.' After a brief pause he would shout it again in his let's-not-play-foolish-games voice. If she still did not appear he would call out, 'Breakfast.'

Anne had teased him about it just the other day, and said, 'Oh, darling, you shouldn't have.'

'Have what?'

'Made breakfast.'

'I haven't.'

'Oh, I thought when you shouted, "Breakfast," you meant it was ready.'

'No, I meant that I was ready for breakfast.'

Anne had not been far wrong, Victor was indeed in his bathroom downstairs brushing his hair vigorously. But, as always, a few seconds after he stopped the wave of hair which had tormented him since childhood sprang up again.

His pair of ivory hairbrushes had no handles. They were quite inconvenient, but very traditional, like the wooden bowl of shaving soap, which never thickened as satisfactorily as foam from a can. Victor was fifty-seven, but looked younger.

Only a drooping in his flesh, a loss of tension around the jaw and the mouth and the tremendous depth of the horizontal lines in his forehead, revealed his age. His teeth were neat and strong and yellow. Though he longed for something more aerodynamic his nose was bulbous and friendly. Women always praised his eyes because their pale grey looked luminous against his slightly pitted olive-brown skin. All in all, strangers were surprised when a rapid and rather fruity lisp emerged from a face which could well have belonged to an overdressed prizefighter.

In pink pyjamas from New & Lingwood, a silk dressing gown, and a pair of red slippers, Victor felt almost sleek. He had walked out of the bathroom, through his simple whitewashed bedroom with its green mosquito netting held in place over the windows by drawing pins, and out into the kitchen, where he hovered, not yet daring to call Anne.

While Victor hesitated in the kitchen, Eleanor arrived. The Buick was too long to twist its way up Victor's narrow drive and she'd had to park it on the edge of a small pine wood at the bottom of the hill. This land did not belong to Victor but his neighbours, the Fauberts, well known in Lacoste for their eccentric way of life. They still used a mule to plough their fields, they had no electricity, and in their large dilapidated farmhouse they lived in just one room. The rest of the house was crowded with barrels of wine, jars of olive oil, sacks of animal feed, and piles of almonds and lavender. The Fauberts had not altered anything since old Madame Faubert died, and she had never changed anything since she arrived as a young bride, half a century before, bearing a glass bowl and a clock.

Eleanor was intrigued by these people. She imagined their austere and fruitful life like a stained-glass window in a medieval church – labourers in the vineyard with grape-filled baskets on their backs. She had seen one of the Fauberts in the Crédit Agricole and he had the sullen air of a man who looks forward to strangling poultry. Nevertheless, she treasured the idea that the Fauberts were connected to the earth in some wholesome way that the rest of us had forgotten. She had certainly forgotten about being wholesomely connected with the earth herself. Perhaps you had to be a Red Indian, or something.

She tried to walk more slowly up the hill. God, her mind was racing, racing in neutral, she was pouring with sweat and getting flashes of dread through the exhilaration. Balance was so elusive: either it was like this, too fast, or there was the heavy thing like wading through a swamp to get to the end of a sentence. When there were cicadas earlier in the summer it was good. Their singing was like blood rushing in her ears. It was one of those outside inside things.

Just before the top of the hill she stopped, breathed deeply, and tried to muster her scattered sense of calm, like a bride checking her veil in the last mirror before the aisle. The feeling of solemnity deserted her almost immediately and a few yards further on her legs began to shake. The muscles in her cheeks twitched back like stage curtains, and her heart tried to somersault its way out of her chest. She must remember not to take so many of those yellow pills at once. What on earth had happened to the tranquillizers? They seemed to have been drowned by the floodtide of Dexedrine. Oh, my God, there was Victor in the kitchen, dressed like an advertisement as usual. She gave him a breezy and confident wave through the window.

Victor had finally summoned the courage to call Anne, when he heard the sound of feet on the gravel outside and saw Eleanor waving at him eagerly. Jumping up and down, crossing and uncrossing her arms above her head, her lank blonde hair bobbing from side to side, she looked like a wounded marine trying to attract a helicopter.

She formed the word 'Hello' silently and with great exaggeration as if she were speaking to a deaf foreigner.

'It's open,' Victor called.

One really has to admire her stamina, he thought, moving towards the front door.

Anne, primed to hear the cry of 'Breakfast', was surprised to hear 'It's open' instead. She got out of bed and ran downstairs to greet Eleanor.

'How are you? I'm not even dressed yet.'

'I'm wide awake,' said Eleanor.

'Hello, darling, why don't you make a pot of tea,' said Victor. 'Would you like some, Eleanor?'

'No, thanks.'

After making the tea, Anne went up to dress, pleased that Eleanor had arrived early. Nevertheless, having seen her frenzied air and the sweat-streaked face powder, Anne did not look forward to being driven by her, and she tried to think of some way to do the driving herself.

In the kitchen, with a cigarette dangling from her mouth, Eleanor rummaged about in her handbag for a lighter. She still had her dark glasses on and it was hard to make out the objects in the murky chaos of her bag. Five or six caramel-coloured plastic tubs of pills swirled around with spare packets of Player's cigarettes, a blue leather telephone book, pencils, lipstick, a gold powder compact, a small silver hip-flask full of Fernet-Branca, and a dry-cleaning ticket from Jeeves in Pont Street. Her anxious hands dredged up every object in her bag, except the red plastic lighter she knew was in there somewhere. 'God. I must be going mad,' she muttered.

'I thought I'd take Anne to Signes for lunch,' she said brightly.

'Signes? That's rather out of your way, isn't it?'

'Not the way we're going.' Eleanor had not meant to sound facetious.

'Quite,' Victor smiled tolerantly. 'The way you're going it couldn't be closer, but isn't it rather a long route?'

'Yes, only Nicholas's plane doesn't get in until three and the cork forests are so pretty.' It was unbelievable, there was the dry-cleaning ticket again. There must be more than one. 'And there's that monastery to see, but I don't suppose there'll be time. Patrick always wants to go to the Wild West funfair when we drive that way to the airport. We could stop there too.' Rummage, rummage, rummage, pills, pills, pills. 'I must take him one day. Ah, there's my lighter. How's the book going, Victor?'

'Oh, you know,' said Victor archly, 'identity is a big subject.'

'Does Freud come into it?'

Victor had had this conversation before and if anything made him want to write his book it was the desire not to have it again. 'I'm not dealing with the subject from a psychoanalytical point of view.'

'Oh,' said Eleanor, who had lit her cigarette and was prepared to be fascinated for a while, 'I would have thought it was – what's the word? – well, terribly psychological. I mean, if anything's in the mind, it's who you are.'

'I may quote you on that,' said Victor. 'But remind me, Eleanor, is the woman Nicholas is bringing this time his fourth or fifth wife?'

It was no use. She felt stupid again. She always felt stupid with David and his friends, even when she knew it was they who were being stupid. 'She's not his wife,' she said. 'He's left Georgina who was number three, but he hasn't married this one yet. She's called Bridget. I think we met in London, but she didn't make a very strong impression on me.' Anne came downstairs wearing a white cotton dress almost indistinguishable from the white cotton nightgown she had taken off. Victor reflected with satisfaction that she still looked young enough to get away with such a girlish dress. White dresses deepened the deceptive serenity which her wide face and high cheekbones and calm black eyes already gave to her appearance. She stepped lightly into the room. By contrast, Eleanor made Victor think of Lady Wishfort's remark, 'Why I am arrantly flayed; I look like an old peeled wall.'

'OK,' said Anne, 'I guess we can leave whenever you like.

'Will you be all right for lunch?' she asked Victor.

'You know what philosophers are like, we don't notice that kind of thing. And I can always go down to the Cauquière for a rack of lamb with *sauce Béarnaise*.'

'*Béarnaise*? With lamb?' said Anne.

'Of course. The dish which left the poor Duc de Guermantes so famished that he had no time to chat with the dying Swann's dubious daughter before hurrying off to dinner.'

Anne smiled at Eleanor and asked, 'Do you get Proust for breakfast round at your house?'

'No, but we get him for dinner fairly often,' Eleanor replied.

After the two women had said goodbye, Victor turned towards the refrigerator. He had the whole day free to get on with his work and suddenly felt tremendously hungry.

4

'God, I feel awful,' groaned Nicholas, switching on his bed-side table lamp.

'Poor squirrel,' said Bridget sleepily.

'What are we doing today? I can't remember.'

'Going to the South of France.'

'Oh yes. What a nightmare. What time's the plane?'

'Twelve something. It arrives at three something. I think there's an hour difference, or something.'

'For Christ sake, stop saying "something".'

'Sorry.'

'God knows why we stayed so late last night. That woman on my right was utterly appalling. I suppose somebody told her long ago that she had a pretty chin, and so she decided to get another one, and another, and another. You know, she used to be married to George Watford.'

'To who?' asked Bridget.

'The one you saw in Peter's photograph album last weekend with a face like a crème brûlée after the first blow of the spoon, all covered in little cracks.'

'Not everyone can have a lover who's rich *and* beautiful,' said Bridget, sliding through the sheets towards him.

'Oaw, give over, luv, give over,' said Nicholas in what he imagined to be a Geordie accent. He rolled out of bed and, moaning, 'Death and destruction,' crawled histrionically across the crimson carpet towards the open door of the bathroom.

Bridget looked critically at Nicholas's body as he clambered to his feet. He had got a lot fatter in the past year. Maybe older men were not the answer. Twenty-three years was a big difference and at twenty, Bridget had not yet caught the marriage fever that tormented the older Watson-Scott sisters as they galloped towards the thirtieth year of their scatterbrained lives. All Nicholas's friends were such wrinklies and some of them were a real yawn. You couldn't exactly drop acid with Nicholas. Well, you could; in fact, she had, but it wasn't the same as with Barry. Nicholas didn't have the right music, the right clothes, the right attitude. She felt quite bad about Barry, but a girl had to keep her options open.

The thing about Nicholas was that he really was rich and beautiful *and* he was a baronet, which was nice and sort of Jane Austeny. Still, it wouldn't be long before people started saying, 'You can tell he used to be good-looking,' and someone else would intervene charitably with, 'Oh, no, he still is.' In the end she would probably marry him and she would be the fourth Lady Pratt. Then she could divorce him and get half a million pounds, or whatever, and keep Barry as her sex slave and still call herself Lady Pratt in shops. God, sometimes she was so cynical it was frightening.

She knew that Nicholas thought it was the sex that kept them together. It was certainly what had got them together at the party where they first met. Nicholas had been quite drunk and asked her if she was a 'natural blonde'. Yawn, yawn, *what* a tacky question. Still, Barry was in Glastonbury and she'd been feeling a bit restless and so she gave him this heavy look and said, 'Why don't you find out for yourself?' as she slipped out of the room. He thought he *had* found out, but what he didn't know was that she dyed *all* her hair. If you do something cosmetic, you might as well do it thoroughly, that was her motto.

In the bathroom, Nicholas stuck out his tongue and admired its thickly coated surface, still tinged with blackish purple from last night's coffee and red wine. It was all very well to make jokes about Sarah Watford's double chins, but the truth was that unless he held his head up like a Guardsman on parade he had one himself. He couldn't face shaving, but he dabbed on a little of Bridget's make-up. One didn't want to look like the old queen in *Death in Venice*, with rouge trickling down cholera-fevered cheeks, but without a little light powder he had what people called 'a distinctly unhealthy pallor'. Bridget's make-up was rather basic, like her sometimes truly appalling clothes. Whatever one said about Fiona (and one had said some thoroughly unpleasant things in one's time) she did have the most amazing creams and masks sent over from Paris. He sometimes wondered if Bridget might not be (one had to slip into the softening nuances of the French tongue) *insortable*. Last weekend at Peter's she had spent the whole of Sunday lunch giggling like a fourteen-year-old.

And then there was her background. He did not know when the house of Watson and the house of Scott had seen fit to unite their fortunes, but he could tell at a glance that the Watson-Scotts were Old Vicarage material who would kill to have their daughter's engagement in *Country Life*. The father was fond of the races and when Nicholas had taken him and his keen-on-roses wife to *Le Nozze di Figaro* at Covent Garden, Roddy Watson-Scott had said, 'They're under starter's orders,' as the conductor mounted the podium. If the Watson-Scotts were just a little too obscure, at least everyone was agreed that Bridget was flavour of the month and he was a lucky dog to have her.

If he married again he would not choose a girl like Bridget.

Apart from anything else, she was completely ignorant. She had 'done' *Emma* for A-level, but since then, as far as he could make out, she only read illustrated magazines called *Oz* or *The Furry Freak Brothers* supplied to her by a seamy character called Barry. She spent hours poring over pictures of spiralling eyeballs and exploding intestines and policemen with the faces of Doberman pinschers. His own intestines were in a state of bitter confusion and he wanted to clear Bridget out of the bedroom before *they* exploded.

'Darling!' he shouted, or rather tried to shout. The sound came out as a croak. He cleared his throat and spat in the basin.

'You couldn't be an angel and get my glass of orange juice from the dining room, could you? And a cup of tea?'

'Oh, all right.'

Bridget had been lying on her stomach, playing with herself lazily. She rolled out of bed with an exaggerated sigh. God, Nicholas was boring. What was the point of having servants? He treated them better than he treated her. She slouched off to the dining room.

Nicholas sat down heavily on the teak lavatory seat. The thrill of educating Bridget socially and sexually had begun to pall when he had stopped thinking about how wonderfully good he was at it and noticed how little she was willing to learn. After this trip to France he would have to go to Asprey's to get her a going-away present. And yet he did not feel ready for that girl from the Old Masters department of Christie's – a simple string of pearls about her woolly blue neck – who longed to exhaust herself helping a chap to keep his estate intact; a general's daughter used to an atmosphere of discipline. A girl, his thoughts expanded gloomily, who would enjoy the damp little hills of Shropshire's Welsh border, something he had yet to achieve himself despite owning so very many of them and having 'farmer' next to his still unsuccessful candidature for Pratt's club. The Wits never tired of saying, 'But, Nicholas, I thought you owned the place.' He'd made too many enemies to get himself elected.

Nicholas's bowels exploded. He sat there sweating miserably like one of the paranoid wrecks in Bridget's favourite cartoon strips. He could imagine Fattie Poole squealing, 'The man's an absolute cunt, and if they let him in here, I shall have to spend the rest of my life at the Turf.' It had been a mistake to get David Melrose to propose him, but David had been one of his father's best friends, and ten years ago he'd not been as misanthropic or unpopular as he was now, nor had he spent so much time in Lacoste.

The route from Clabon Mews to Heathrow was too familiar to register on Nicholas's senses. He had moved into the soporific phase of his hangover, and felt slightly nauseous. Very tired, he slouched in the corner of the taxi. Bridget was less jaded about foreign travel. Nicholas had taken her to Greece in July and Tuscany in August, and she still liked the idea of how glamorous her life had become.

She disliked Nicholas's English Abroad outfits, particularly the panama hat he had on today and wore tilted over his face to show that he was not in the mood to talk. Nor did she like his off-white wild-silk jacket and the yellow corduroy trousers. She was embarrassed by the shirt with very narrow dark red stripes and a stiff white rounded collar, and by his highly polished shoes. He was a complete freak about shoes. He had fifty pairs, all made for him, and *literally* identical, except for silly details which he treated as world-shatteringly important.

On the other hand, she knew that her own clothes were devastatingly sexy. What could be more sexy than a purple miniskirt and black suede cowboy jacket with tassels hanging all along the arms and across the back? Under the jacket you could see her nipples through the black T-shirt. Her black and purple cowboy boots took half an hour to get off, but they were well worth it, because everybody noticed them.

Since half the time she didn't get the point of one's stories at all, Nicholas wondered whether to tell Bridget about the figs. In any case, he was not sure he wanted her to get the point of the fig story. It had happened about ten years ago, just after David persuaded Eleanor to buy the house in Lacoste. They hadn't married because of Eleanor's mother trying to stop them, and David's father threatening to disinherit him.

Nicholas tipped the brim of his hat. 'Have I ever told you what happened the first time I went to Lacoste?' To make sure the story did not fall flat, he added, 'The place we're going today.'

'No,' said Bridget dully. More stories about people she didn't know, most of them taking place before she was born. Yawn, yawn.

'Well, Eleanor – whom you met at Annabel's, you probably don't remember.'

'The drunk one.'

'Yes!' Nicholas was delighted by these signs of recognition. 'At any rate, Eleanor – who wasn't drunk in those days, just very shy and nervous – had recently bought the house in Lacoste, and she complained to David about the terrible waste of figs that fell from the tree and rotted on the terrace. She mentioned them again the next day when the three of us were sitting outside. I saw a cold look come over David's face. He stuck his lower lip out – always a bad sign, half brutal and half pouting – and said, "Come with me." It felt like following the headmaster to his study. He marched us towards the fig tree with great long strides, Eleanor and I stumbling along behind. When we got there we saw figs scattered all over the stone paving. Some of them were old and squashed, others had broken open, with wasps dancing around the wound or gnawing at the sticky red and white flesh. It was a huge tree and there were a *lot* of figs on the ground. And, then David did this amazing thing. *He told Eleanor to get on all fours and eat all the figs off the terrace.*'

'What, in front of you?' said Bridget, round-eyed.

'Quite. Eleanor *did* look rather confused and I suppose the word is betrayed. She didn't protest, though, just got on with this rather unappetizing task. David wouldn't let her leave a single one. She did once look up pleadingly and say, "I've had enough now, David," but he put his foot on her back and said, "Eat them up. We don't want them going to waste, do we?"'

'Kink-ky,' said Bridget.

Nicholas was rather pleased with the effect his story was having on Bridget. A hit, a palpable hit, he thought to himself.

'What did you do?' asked Bridget.

'I watched,' said Nicholas. 'You don't cross David when he's in that sort of mood. After a while Eleanor looked a little sick and so then I did suggest we collect the rest of the figs in a basket. "You mustn't interfere," said David. "Eleanor can't bear to see the figs wasted when there are starving people in the world. Can you, darling? And so she's going to eat them all up on her own." He grinned at me, and added, "Anyway, she's far too picky about her food, don't you think?"'

'Wow!' said Bridget. 'And you still go and stay with these people?'

The taxi drew up outside the terminal and Nicholas was able to avoid the question. A porter in a brown uniform spotted him immediately and hurried to collect the bags. Nicholas stood transfixed for a moment, like a man under a warm shower, between the grateful cabbie and the assiduous porter, both calling him 'Guv' simultaneously. He always gave larger tips to people who called him 'Guv'. He knew it, and they knew it, it was what was called a 'civilized arrangement'.

Bridget's concentration span was enormously improved by the story about the figs. Even when they had boarded the plane and found their seats, she could still remember what it was she'd wanted him to explain.

'Why do you like this guy anyway? I mean, does he sort of make a habit of ritual humiliation or something?'

'Well, I'm told, although I didn't witness this myself, that he used to make Eleanor take lessons from a prostitute.'

'You're kidding,' said Bridget admiringly. She swivelled round in her seat. 'Kink-ky.'

An air hostess brought two glasses of champagne, apologizing for the slight delay. She had blue eyes and freckles and smiled ingratiatingly at Nicholas. He preferred these vaguely pretty girls on Air France to the absurd ginger-haired stewards and frumpish nannies on English aeroplanes. He felt another wave of tiredness from the processed air, the slight pressure on his ears and eyelids, the deserts of biscuit-coloured plastic around him and the dry acid taste of the champagne.

The excitement radiating from Bridget revived him a little, and yet he had still not explained what attracted him to David. Nor was it a question he particularly wanted to look into. David was simply part of the world that counted for Nicholas. One might not like him, but he was impressive. By marrying Eleanor he had obliterated the poverty which constituted his great social weakness. Until recently the Melroses had given some of the best parties in London.

Nicholas lifted his chin from the cushion of his neck. He wanted to feed Bridget's ingenuous appetite for the atmosphere of perversion. Her reaction to the story about the figs had opened up possibilities he would not know how to exploit, but even the possibilities were stimulating.

'You see,' he said to Bridget, 'David was a younger friend of my father's, and I'm a younger friend of his. He used to come down to see me at school and take me to Sunday lunch at the Compleat Angler.' Nicholas could feel Bridget's interest slipping away in the face of this sentimental portrait. 'But what I think fascinated me was the air of doom he carried around with him. As a boy he played the piano brilliantly and then he developed rheumatism and couldn't play,' said Nicholas. 'He won a scholarship to Balliol but left after a month. His father made him join the army and he left that too. He qualified as a doctor but didn't bother to practise. As you can see, he suffers from an almost heroic restlessness.'

'Sounds like a real drag,' said Bridget.

The plane edged slowly towards the runway, while the cabin crew mimed the inflation of life jackets.

'Even their son is the product of rape.' Nicholas watched for her reaction. 'Although you mustn't tell anyone that. I only know because Eleanor told me one evening, when she was very drunk and weepy. She'd been refusing to go to bed with David for ages because she couldn't bear to be touched by him, and then one evening he rugby tackled her on the stairs and wedged her head between the banisters. In law, of course, there is no such thing as marital rape, but David is a law to himself.'

The engines started to roar. 'You'll find in the course of your life,' boomed Nicholas, and then, realizing that he sounded pompous, he put on his funny pompous voice, 'as I have found in the course of mine, that such people, though perhaps destructive and cruel towards those who are closest to them, often possess a vitality that makes other people seem dull by comparison.'

'Oh, God, gimme a break,' said Bridget. The plane gathered speed and shuddered into the pasty English sky.

5

As Eleanor's Buick drifted along the slow back roads to
Signes the sky was almost clear except for a straggling cloud
dissolving in front of the sun. Through the tinted border of
the windscreen, Anne saw the cloud's edges curling and
melting in the heat. The car had already been caught behind
an orange tractor, its trailer loaded with dusty purple grapes;
the driver had waved them on magnanimously. Inside the
car, the air conditioning gently refrigerated the atmosphere.
Anne had tried to prise the keys from her, but Eleanor said
that nobody else ever drove her car. Now the soft suspension
and streams of cold air made the dangers of her driving seem
more remote.

It was still only eleven o'clock and Anne was not looking
forward to the long day ahead. There had been an awkward,
stale silence since she'd made the mistake of asking how
Patrick was. Anne felt a maternal instinct towards him, which
was more than she could say for his mother. Eleanor had
snapped at her, 'Why do people think they are likely to please
me by asking how Patrick is, or how David is? I don't know
how they are, only they know.'

Anne was stunned. A long time went by before Anne tried
again. 'What did you think of Vijay?'

'Not much.'

'Me neither. Luckily he had to leave earlier than expected.'
Anne still did not know how much to reveal about the row

49

with Vijay. 'He was going to stay with that old man they all worship, Jonathan somebody, who writes those awful books with the crazy titles, like *Anemones and Enemies* or *Antics and Antiques*. You know the one I mean?'

'Oh, him, Jesus, he's awful. He used to come to my mother's house in Rome. He would always say things like, "The streets are pullulating with beggars," which made me really angry when I was sixteen. But is that Vijay man rich? He kept talking as if he must be, but he didn't look as if he ever spent any money – not on his clothes anyhow?'

'Oh, yeah,' said Anne, 'he is *so* rich: he is factory-rich, bank-rich. He keeps polo ponies in Calcutta, but he doesn't like polo and never goes to Calcutta. Now that's what I call rich.'

Eleanor was silent for a while. It was a subject in which she felt quietly competitive. She did not want to agree too readily that neglecting polo ponies in Calcutta was what she called rich.

'But stingy as hell,' said Anne to cover the silence. 'That was one of the reasons we had a row.' She was longing to tell the truth now, but she was still unsure. 'Every evening he rang home, which is Switzerland, to chat in Gujarati to his aged mother, and if there was no answer, he'd show up in the kitchen with a black shawl around his frail shoulders, looking like an old woman himself. Finally I had to ask him for some money for the phone calls.'

'And did he pay you?'

'Only after I lost my temper.'

'Didn't Victor help?' asked Eleanor.

'Victor shies away from crass things like money.'

The road had cut into cork forests, and trees with old or fresh wounds where belts of bark had been stripped from their trunks grew thickly on both sides.

'Has Victor been doing much writing this summer?' asked Eleanor.

'Hardly any. And it's not as if he does anything else when he's at home,' Anne replied. 'You know, he's been coming down here for what? Eight years? And he's never even been over to say hello to those farmers next door.'

'The Fauberts?'

'Right. Not once. They live three hundred yards away in that old farmhouse, with the two cypresses out front. Victor's garden practically belongs to them, but they've never exchanged a word. "We haven't been introduced," is his excuse,' said Anne.

'He's terribly English for an Austrian, isn't he?' smiled Eleanor. 'Oh look, we're coming up to Signes. I hope I can find that funny restaurant. It's in a square opposite one of those fountains that's turned into a mound of wet moss with ferns growing out of it. And inside there are heads of wild boars with polished yellow tusks all over the walls. Their mouths are painted red, so it looks as if they could still charge out from behind the wall.'

'God, how terrifying,' said Anne, drily.

'When the Germans left here,' Eleanor continued, 'at the end of the war, they shot every man in the village, except for Marcel – the one who owns the restaurant. He was away when it happened.'

Anne was silenced by Eleanor's air of crazed empathy. Once they'd found the restaurant, she was at once relieved and a little disappointed that the dark watery square was not more redolent of sacrifice and retribution. The walls of the restaurant were made of blonde plastic moulded to look like planks of pine and there were in fact only two boars' heads in the rather empty room, which was harshly lit by bare fluorescent tubes. After the first course of tiny thrushes full of lead shot and trussed up on pieces of greasy toast,

Anne could only toy with the dark depressing stew, loaded onto a pile of overcooked noodles. The red wine was cold and raw and came in old green bottles with no label.

'Great place, isn't it?' said Eleanor.

'It's certainly got atmosphere,' said Anne.

'Look, there's Marcel,' said Eleanor desperately.

'*Ah, Madame Melrose, je ne vous ai pas vue,*' he said, pretending to notice Eleanor for the first time. He hurried round the end of the bar with quick small steps, wiping his hands on the stained white apron. Anne noticed his drooping moustache and the extraordinary bags under his eyes.

Immediately, he offered Eleanor and Anne some cognac. Anne refused despite his claim that it would do her good, but Eleanor accepted, and then returned the offer. They drank another and chatted about the grape harvest while Anne, who could only understand a little of his *midi* accent, regretted even more that she was not allowed to drive.

By the time they got back to the car, the cognac and tranquillizers had come into their own and Eleanor felt her blood tumbling like ball bearings through the veins under her numbed skin. Her head was as heavy as a sack of coins and she closed her eyes slowly, slowly, completely in control.

'Hey,' said Anne, 'wake up.'

'I am awake,' said Eleanor grumpily and then more serenely, 'I'm awake.' Her eyes remained closed.

'Please let me drive.' Anne was ready to argue the point.

'Sure,' said Eleanor. She opened her eyes, which suddenly seemed intensely blue against the pinkish tinge of frayed blood vessels. 'I trust you.'

Eleanor slept for about half an hour while Anne drove up and down the twisting roads from Signes to Marseilles.

When Eleanor woke up, she was lucid again and said, 'Goodness that stew was awfully rich, I did feel a little weighed down after lunch.' The high from the Dexedrine was back; like the theme from *The Valkyrie*, it could not be kept down for long, even if it took a more muted and disguised form than before.

'What's Le Wild Ouest?' said Anne. 'I keep passing pictures of cowboys with arrows through their hats.'

'Oh, we must go, we must go,' said Eleanor in a childish voice. 'It's a funfair but the whole thing is made to look like Dodge City. I've never actually been in, but I'd really like to—'

'Have we got time?' asked Anne sceptically.

'Oh, yes, it's only one-thirty, look, and the airport is only forty-five minutes away. Oh, let's. Just for half an hour. Pl-ea-se?'

Another billboard announced Le Wild Ouest at four hundred metres. Soaring above the tops of the dark pine trees were miniature imitation stagecoaches in brightly coloured plastic hanging from a stationary Ferris wheel.

'This can't be for real,' said Anne. 'Isn't it fantastic? We have to go in.'

They walked through the giant saloon doors of Le Wild Ouest. On either side, the flags of many nations drooped on a circle of white poles.

'Gosh, it's exciting,' said Eleanor. It was hard for her to decide which of the wonderful rides to take first. In the end she chose to go on the stagecoach Ferris wheel. 'I want a yellow one,' she said.

The wheel edged forward as each stagecoach was filled. Eventually, theirs rose above the level of the highest pines.

'Look! There's our car,' squealed Eleanor.

'Does Patrick like this place?' asked Anne.

'He's never been,' said Eleanor.

'You'd better take him soon, or he'll be too old. People grow out of this sort of thing, you know.' Anne smiled.

Eleanor looked massively gloomy for a moment. The wheel

started to turn, generating a little breeze. On the upward curve, Eleanor felt her stomach tighten. Instead of giving her a better view of the funfair and the surrounding woods, the motion of the wheel made her feel sick and she stared grimly at the white tips of her knuckles, longing for the ride to be over.

Anne saw that Eleanor's mood had snapped and that she was again in the company of an older, richer, drunker woman.

They got off the ride, and walked through a street of shooting arcades. 'Let's get out of this fucking place,' said Eleanor. 'It's time to collect Nicholas anyhow.'

'So tell me about Nicholas,' said Anne, trying to keep up. 'Oh, you'll find out soon enough.'

6

'So this Eleanor woman is a real victim, right?' said Bridget. She had fallen asleep after smoking a joint in the loo and she wanted to compensate with a burst of belated curiosity.

'Is every woman who chooses to live with a difficult man a victim?'

Nicholas undid his seatbelt as soon as the plane landed. They were in the second row and could easily get off ahead of the other passengers if, just for once, Bridget did not unsheathe her compact from its blue velvet pouch and admire herself in its powdery little mirror.

'Shall we go,' sighed Nicholas.

'The seatbelt sign is still on.'

'Signs are for sheep.'

'Bahaha-a-a,' bleated Bridget at the mirror, 'I'm a sheep.'

This woman is intolerable, thought Nicholas.

'Well, I'm a shepherd,' he said out loud, 'and don't make me put on my wolf's clothing.'

'Oh, my,' said Bridget, cowering in the corner of her seat, 'what big teeth you have.'

'All the better to bite your head off.'

'I don't think you're my granny at all,' she said with real disappointment.

The plane stopped its creeping progress and there was a general clicking of opening buckles and discarded seatbelts.

'Come on,' said Nicholas, now all businesslike. He very

much disliked joining the struggling tourists as they jostled each other down the aisle.

They arrived at the open door of the plane, pale and over-dressed, and started to clank their way down a flight of metal steps, caught between the air crew who pretended to be sorry at their departure and the ground crew who pretended to be pleased by their arrival. As she went down the steps, Bridget felt slightly nauseous from the heat and the smell of spent fuel.

Nicholas looked across the tarmac at the long queue of Arabs slowly climbing on board an Air France plane. He thought of the Algerian crisis in '62 and the threat of betrayed colonists parachuting into Paris. The thought petered out as he imagined how far back he would have to begin in order to explain it to Bridget. She probably thought that Algeria was an Italian dress designer. He felt a familiar longing for a well-informed woman in her early thirties who had read history at Oxford; the fact that he had divorced two of them already made little difference to his immediate enthusiasm. Their flesh might hang more loosely on the bone, but the memory of intelligent conversation tormented him like the smell of succulent cooking wafting into a forgotten prison cell. Why was the centre of his desire always in a place he had just deserted? He knew that the memory of Bridget's flesh would betray him with the same easy poignancy if he were now climbing on to the bus with a woman whose con-versation he could bear. Theoretically, of course, there were women – he had even had affairs with them – who combined the qualities which he threw into unnecessary competition, but he knew that something inside him would always scatter his appreciation and divide his loyalties.

The doors folded shut and the bus jerked into motion. Bridget sat opposite Nicholas. Under her absurd skirt, her legs were slim and bare and golden. He detached them pornographically from the rest of her body, and found he was still excited by the idea of their availability. He crossed his legs and loosened his entangled boxer shorts through the stiff ridges of his corduroy trousers.

It was only when he considered to whom these golden legs belonged that his fleeting erection seemed a small and inconvenient reward for a state of almost permanent irritation. In fact, scanning the figure above the waist, along the fringed sleeve of her black suede jacket, and up towards the bored and stubborn expression on her face, he felt a spasm of revulsion and estrangement. Why was he taking this ludicrous creature to stay with David Melrose who was, after all, a man of some discernment, not to say a merciless snob?

The terminal building smelled of disinfectant. A woman in blue overalls drifted across the glaring floor, the circular pads of her polishing machine humming as she swung it gently back and forth across the black and brown translucent pebbles trapped in cheap white marble. Still stoned, Bridget lost herself in the flakes of colour as if they were the flint and quartz stars of a white sky.

'What are you staring at?' snapped Nicholas.

'This floor is something else,' said Bridget.

At passport control she could not find her passport but Nicholas refused to start a scene just when they were about to meet Eleanor.

'Rather eccentrically, in this airport one crosses the main lobby before collecting one's luggage,' said Nicholas. 'That's probably where Eleanor will be waiting for us.'

'Wow!' said Bridget. 'If I was a smuggler,' she paused, hoping Nicholas might challenge her, 'this would be my dream airport. I mean, there's this whole lobby where you could slip someone your hand luggage, full of goodies, and then go and fetch your legal luggage for Customs.'

'That's what I admire about you,' said Nicholas, 'your

creative thinking. You might have had a brilliant career in advertising; although I think as far as smuggling goes the Marseilles authorities have more pressing problems to wrestle with than any "goodies" you might import in your handbag. I don't know if you're aware of it but . . .'

Bridget had stopped listening. Nicholas was being a wanker again. He always got like this when he was uptight; in fact he was like this all the time except when he was in bed, or with people he wanted to charm. Lagging behind, she stuck her tongue out at him. Nyah, nyah, nyah . . . boring, boring, boring.

Bridget covered her ears and looked down at her dragging feet, while Nicholas strode on alone, pouring sarcasm on ideas increasingly remote from Bridget's tame remarks about smuggling.

Looking up again, Bridget saw a familiar figure. It was Barry leaning against the pillar next to the newsstand. Barry could always sense when he was being looked at and, depending on his mood, attributed this to 'paranoia' or 'ESP'.

'Bridge! Incredible!'

'Barry! All you need is love,' said Bridget, reading out loud the words on Barry's T-shirt and laughing.

'This really is incredible,' said Barry, running his fingers through his long black hair. 'You know I was thinking about you this morning.'

Barry thought about Bridget every morning, but it still struck him as further evidence of mind control that he had not only thought about her today but run into her at the airport as well.

'We're going to Arles for the Progressive Jazz Festival,' said Barry. 'Hey, why don't you come along? It's going to be really fantastic. Bux Millerman is playing.'

'Wow,' breathed Bridget.

'Hey, listen,' said Barry, 'take Etienne's number anyway.

That's where I'll be staying and maybe we can like meet up.'

'Yeah,' said Bridget, 'great.'

Barry pulled out a giant Rizla rolling paper and scribbled a number on it. 'Don't smoke it,' he said humorously, 'or we'll never get in touch.'

Bridget gave him the Melrose number because she knew he would not use it, and that this whole meeting-up thing was not going to happen. 'How long have you been here?' she asked.

'Ten days roughly and the only piece of advice I can give you is *don't drink the pink*. That wine is full of chemical shit and the hangover is worse than the comedown off a sulphate binge.'

Nicholas's voice burst in on them. 'What the hell do you think you're doing?' He glared at her. 'You're really pushing your luck, swanning off in the middle of an airport without any warning. I've been dragging round these fucking cases looking for you for the last quarter of an hour.'

'You should get a trolley,' said Barry.

Nicholas stared straight ahead of him as if nobody had spoken. 'Don't ever do this again or I'll snap you like . . . Ah, there's Eleanor!'

'Nicholas, I'm so sorry. We got caught on the Ferris wheel at a funfair and instead of letting us off they sent it round a second time. Can you imagine?'

'So like you, Eleanor, always getting more fun than you bargained for.'

'Well, I'm here now.' Eleanor greeted Nicholas and Bridget with a flat circular wave, like someone polishing a window-pane. 'And this is Anne Moore.'

'Hi,' said Anne.

'How do you do?' said Nicholas, and introduced Bridget.

Eleanor led them towards the car park and Bridget blew a kiss over her shoulder in Barry's direction.

'*Ciao*,' said Barry, jabbing his finger at the confident words on his T-shirt. 'Don't forget.'

'Who was that fascinating-looking man your girlfriend was talking to?' asked Eleanor.

'Oh, just somebody on the plane,' said Nicholas. He was annoyed to find Barry at the airport and for a moment he thought that Bridget might have arranged the meeting. The idea was absurd, but he could not shake it off, and as soon as they were all settled in the car, he hissed at her, 'What were you talking to that chap about?'

'Barry isn't a chap,' said Bridget, 'that's what I like about him, but if you really want to know, he said, "Don't drink the pink, it's full of chemical shit and the hangover is worse than a comedown off a speed binge."'

Nicholas swivelled round and gave her a deadly look.

'He's absolutely right, of course,' said Eleanor. 'Perhaps we should have asked him to dinner.'

7

After hanging Patrick from his ears and watching him escape from the library, David shrugged, sat down at the piano, and started to improvise a fugue. His rheumatic hands protested at every key he touched. A glass of pastis, like a trapped cloud, stood on top of the piano. His body ached all day long and the pain woke him at night every time he shifted position. Nightmares often woke him as well and made him whimper and scream so loudly that his insomnia overflowed into neighbouring bedrooms. His lungs, also, were shot away and when his asthma flared up he wheezed and rattled, his face swollen by the cortisone he used to appease his constricted chest. Gasping, he would pause at the top of the stairs, unable to speak, his eyes roaming over the ground as if he were searching for the air he desperately needed.

At the age of fifteen his musical talent had attracted the interest of the great piano teacher Shapiro, who took on only one pupil at a time. Unfortunately, within a week, David had contracted rheumatic fever and spent the next six months in bed with hands too stiff and clumsy to practise on the piano. The illness wiped out his chances of becoming a serious pianist and, although pregnant with musical ideas, from then on he claimed to be bored by composition and those 'hordes of little tadpoles' one had to use to record music on paper. Instead, he had hordes of admirers who pleaded with him to play after dinner. They always clamoured for the tune they had heard last time, which he could not remember, until they heard the one he played now, which he soon forgot. His compulsion to amuse others and the arrogance with which he displayed his talent combined to disperse the musical ideas he had once guarded so closely and secretly.

Even while he drank in the flattery he knew that underneath this flamboyant frittering away of his talent he had never overcome his reliance on pastiche, his fear of mediocrity, and the rankling suspicion that the first attack of fever was somehow self-induced. This insight was useless to him; to know the causes of his failure did not diminish the failure, but it did make his self-hatred a little more convoluted and a little more lucid than it would have been in a state of plain ignorance.

As the fugue developed, David attacked its main theme with frustrated repetitions, burying the initial melody under a mudslide of rumbling bass notes, and spoiling its progress with violent bursts of dissonance. At the piano he could sometimes abandon the ironic tactics which saturated his speech, and visitors whom he had bullied and teased to the point of exasperation found themselves moved by the piercing sadness of the music in the library. On the other hand, he could turn the piano on them like a machine gun and concentrate a hostility into his music that made them long for the more conventional unkindness of his conversation. Even then, his playing would haunt the people who most wanted to resist his influence.

David stopped playing abruptly and closed the lid over the keyboard. He took a gulp of pastis and started to massage his left palm with his right thumb. This massage made the pain a little worse, but gave him the same psychological pleasure as tearing at scabs, probing abscesses and mouth ulcers with his tongue, and fingering bruises.

When a couple of stabs from his thumb had converted

the dull ache in his palm into a sharper sensation, he leaned over and picked up a half-smoked Montecristo cigar. One was 'supposed' to remove the paper band from the cigar, and so David left it on. To break even the smallest rules by which others convinced themselves that they were behaving correctly gave him great pleasure. His disdain for vulgarity included the vulgarity of wanting to avoid the appearance of being vulgar. In this more esoteric game, he recognized only a handful of players, Nicholas Pratt and George Watford among them, and he could just as easily despise a man for leaving the band *on* his cigar. He enjoyed watching Victor Eisen, the great thinker, thrashing about in these shallow waters, more firmly hooked each time he tried to cross the line that separated him from the class he yearned to belong to.

David brushed the soft flakes of cigar ash from his blue woollen dressing gown. Every time he smoked he thought of the emphysema that had killed his father, and felt annoyed by the prospect of dying in the same manner.

Under the dressing gown he wore a pair of very faded and much darned pyjamas that had become his on the day his father was buried. The burial had taken place conveniently close to his father's house, in the little churchyard he had spent the last few months of his life staring at through the window of his study. Wearing the oxygen mask which he humorously called his 'gas mask', and unable to negotiate the 'stair drill', he slept in his study, which he renamed the 'departure lounge', on an old Crimean campaign bed left to him by his uncle.

David attended the damp and conventional funeral without enthusiasm; he already knew he had been disinherited. As the coffin was lowered into the ground, he reflected how much of his father's life had been spent in a trench of one sort or another, shooting at birds or men, and how it was really the best place for him.

After the funeral, when the guests had left, David's mother came up to his old bedroom for a moment of private mourning with her son. She said, in her sublime voice, 'I know he would have wanted you to have these,' and placed a pair of carefully folded pyjamas on the bed. When David did not reply, she pressed his hand and closed her faintly blue eyelids for a moment, to show that such things lay too deep for words, but that she knew how much he would prize the little pile of white and yellow flannel from a shop in Bond Street which had gone out of business before the First World War.

It was the same yellow and white flannel that had now grown too hot. David got up from the piano stool and paced about with his dressing gown open, puffing on his cigar. There was no doubt that he was angry with Patrick for running away. It had spoiled his fun. He granted that he had perhaps miscalculated the amount of discomfort he could safely inflict on Patrick.

David's methods of education rested on the claim that childhood was a romantic myth which he was too clear-sighted to encourage. Children were weak and ignorant miniature adults who should be given every incentive to correct their weakness and their ignorance. Like King Chaka, the great Zulu warrior, who made his troops stamp thorn bushes into the ground in order to harden their feet, a training some of them may well have resented at the time, he was determined to harden the calluses of disappointment and develop the skill of detachment in his son. After all, what else did he have to offer him?

For a moment he was winded by a sense of absurdity and impotence; he felt like a farmer watching a flock of crows settle complacently on his favourite scarecrow.

But he pushed on bravely with his original line of thought. No, it was no use expecting gratitude from Patrick, although one day he might realize, like one of Chaka's men running over flinty ground on indifferent feet, how much he owed to his father's uncompromising principles.

When Patrick was born David had been worried that he might become a refuge or an inspiration to Eleanor, and he had jealously set about ensuring that this did not happen. Eleanor eventually resigned herself to a vague and luminous faith in Patrick's 'wisdom', a quality she attributed to him some time before he had learned to control his bowels. She thrust him downstream in this paper boat and collapsed back, exhausted by terror and guilt. Even more important to David than the very natural worry that his wife and his son might grow fond of one another was the intoxicating feeling that he had a blank consciousness to work with, and it gave him great pleasure to knead this yielding clay with his artistic thumbs.

As he walked upstairs to get dressed, even David, who spent most of his day angry or at least irritated, and who made a point of not letting things surprise him, was surprised by the burst of rage that swept over him. What had started as indignation at Patrick's escape turned now into a fury he could no longer control. He strode into his bedroom with his underlip pushed out petulantly and his fists clenched, but he felt at the same time a strong desire to escape his own atmosphere, like a crouching man hurrying to get away from the whirling blades of the helicopter in which he has just landed.

The bedroom he entered had a mock-monastic look, large and white, with bare dark-brown tiles miraculously warm in winter when the underfloor heating was turned on. The only painting on the wall was a picture of Christ wearing the crown of thorns, one of which pierced his pale brow.

A trickle of still fresh blood ran down his smooth forehead towards his swimming eyes, which looked up diffidently at this extraordinary headgear as if to ask, 'But is it really *me*?' The painting was a Correggio and easily the most valuable object in the house, but David had insisted on hanging it in his bedroom, saying sweetly that he would ask for nothing else.

The brown and gold bedhead, bought by Eleanor's mother, who was by then the Duchesse de Valençay, from a dealer who assured her that Napoleon's head had rested against it on at least one occasion, further compromised the austerity of the room, as did the dark-green silk Fortuny bedspread, covered in phoenixes floating up from the fires beneath them. Curtains of the same fabric hung from a simple wooden pole, at windows which opened onto a balcony with a wrought-iron balustrade.

David opened these windows impatiently and stepped onto the balcony. He looked at the tidy rows of vines, the rectangular fields of lavender, the patches of pine-wood, and beyond to the villages of Bécasse and St-Crau draped over the lower hills. 'Like a couple of ill-fitting skull-caps,' as he liked to say to Jewish friends.

He shifted his gaze upward and scanned the long curved ridge of the mountain which, on a clear day like this, seemed so close and so wild. Searching for something in the landscape that would receive his mood and answer it, he could only think again, as he had so often before, how easy it would be to dominate the whole valley with a single machine gun riveted to the rail which he now gripped with both hands.

He was turning back restlessly towards the bedroom when a movement below the balcony caught the corner of his eye.

Patrick had stayed in his hiding place for as long as he could, but it was cold in there out of the sun and so he scrambled from under the bush and, with theatrical reluctance, started to walk back home through the tall dry grass. To sulk alone was difficult. He felt the need for a wider audience but he wished he didn't. He dared not punish anyone with his absence, because he was not sure that his absence would be noticed.

He walked along slowly, then curved back to the edge of the wall and stopped to stare at the big mountain on the other side of the valley. The massive formations up on the crest and the smaller ones dotted over its sides yielded shapes and faces as he willed them to appear. An eagle's head. A grotesque nose. A party of dwarfs. A bearded old man. A rocket ship, and countless leprous and obese profiles with cavernous eye sockets formed out of the smoky fluidity his concentration gave to the stone. After a while, he no longer recognized what he was thinking and, just as a shop window sometimes prevents the onlooker from seeing the objects behind the glass and folds him instead in a narcissistic embrace, his mind ignored the flow of impressions from the outside world and locked him into a daydream he could not have subsequently described.

The thought of lunch dragged him back into the present with a strong sense of anxiety. What was the time? Was he too late? Would Yvette still be there to talk to him? Would he have to eat alone with his father? He always recovered from his mental truancy with disappointment. He enjoyed the feeling of blankness, but it frightened him afterwards when he came out of it and could not remember what he had been thinking.

Patrick broke into a run. He was convinced that he had missed lunch. It was always at a quarter to two and normally Yvette would come out and call him, but hiding in the bushes he might not have heard.

When he arrived outside the kitchen, Patrick could see Yvette through the open door, washing lettuce in the sink. He had a stitch in his side from running, and now that he could tell that lunch was some way off he felt embarrassed by his desperate haste. Yvette waved to him from the sink, but he did not want to look hurried, so he just waved back and strolled past the door, as if he had business of his own to attend to. He decided to check once more whether he could find the lucky tree frog before doubling back to the kitchen to sit with Yvette.

Around the corner of the house, Patrick climbed up onto the low wall at the outer edge of the terrace and, a fifteen-foot drop to his left, he balanced his way along with arms spread out. He walked the whole length of the wall and then jumped down again. He was at the top of the garden steps with the fig tree in sight, when he heard his father's voice shouting, *'Don't let me ever see you do that again!'*

Patrick was startled. Where was the voice coming from? Was it shouting at him? He spun around and looked behind him. His heart was beating hard. He often overheard his father shouting at other people, especially his mother, and it terrified him and made him want to run away. But this time he had to stand still and listen because he wanted to understand what was wrong and whether he was to blame.

'Come up here immediately!'

Now Patrick knew where the voice was coming from. He looked up and saw his father leaning over the balcony.

'What have I done wrong?' he asked, but too quietly to be heard. His father looked so furious that Patrick lost all conviction of his own innocence. With growing alarm he tried to work backward from his father's rage to what his own crime might be.

By the time he had climbed the steep stairs to his father's

bedroom, Patrick was ready to apologize for anything, but still felt a lingering desire to know what he was apologizing for. In the doorway he stopped and asked again, audibly this time, 'What have I done wrong?'

'Close the door behind you,' said his father. 'And come over here.' He sounded disgusted by the obligation the child had thrust upon him.

As Patrick slowly crossed the floor he tried to think of some way to placate his father. Maybe if he said something clever he'd be forgiven, but he felt extraordinarily stupid and could only think over and over: two times two equals four, two times two equals four. He tried to remember something he had noticed that morning, or anything, anything at all that might persuade his father that he had been 'observing everything'. But his mind was eclipsed by the shadow of his father's presence.

He stood by the bed and stared down at the green bedspread with the bonfire birds on it. His father sounded rather weary when he spoke.

'I'm going to have to beat you.'

'*But what have I done wrong?*'

'You know perfectly well what you have done,' his father said in a cold, annihilating voice that Patrick found overwhelmingly persuasive. He was suddenly ashamed of all the things he had done wrong. His whole existence seemed to be contaminated by failure.

Moving quickly, his father grabbed Patrick's shirt collar. He sat down on the bed, hoisted Patrick over his right thigh, and removed the yellow slipper from his left foot. Such rapid manoeuvres would normally have made David wince with pain, but he was able to regain his youthful agility in the service of such a good cause. He pulled down Patrick's trousers and underpants and raised the slipper surprisingly high for a man who had trouble with his right shoulder.

The first blow was astonishingly painful. Patrick tried to take the attitude of stoic misery admired by dentists. He tried to be brave but, during the beating, although he at last realized that his father wanted to hurt him as much as possible, he refused to believe it.

The harder he struggled, the harder he was hit. Longing to move but afraid to move, he was split in half by this incomprehensible violence. Horror closed in on him and crushed his body like the jaws of a dog. After the beating, his father dropped him like a dead thing onto the bed.

And he still could not get away. Pushing his palm against Patrick's right shoulder blade, his father was holding him down. Patrick twisted his head around anxiously, but could only see the blue of his father's dressing gown.

'What are you doing?' he asked, but his father did not answer and Patrick was too scared to repeat the question. His father's hand was pushing down on him and, his face squashed into the folds of the bedspread, he could hardly breathe. He stared fixedly up at the curtain pole and the top of the open windows. He could not understand what form the punishment was now taking, but he knew that his father must be very angry with him to be hurting him so much. He could not stand the helplessness that washed over him. He could not stand the unfairness. He did not know who this man was, it could not be his father who was crushing him like this.

From the curtain pole, if he could get up on the curtain pole, he could have sat looking down on the whole scene, just as his father was looking down on him. For a moment, Patrick felt he was up there watching with detachment the punishment inflicted by a strange man on a small boy. As hard as he could Patrick concentrated on the curtain pole and this time it lasted longer, he was sitting up there, his arms folded, leaning back against the wall.

Then he was back down on the bed again feeling a kind of blankness and bearing the weight of not knowing what was happening. He could hear his father wheezing, and the bedhead bumping against the wall. From behind the curtains with the green birds, he saw a gecko emerge and cling motionlessly to the corner of the wall beside the open window. Patrick lanced himself towards it. Tightening his fists and concentrating until his concentration was like a telephone wire stretched between them, Patrick disappeared into the lizard's body.

The gecko understood, because at that very instant it dashed round the corner of the window and out onto the wall. Below he could see the drop to the terrace and the leaves of the Virginia creeper, red and green and yellow, and from up there, close against the wall, he could hold on with suckered feet and hang upside down safely from the eaves of the roof. He scurried onto the old roof tiles which were covered in grey and orange lichen, and then into the trough between the tiles, all the way up to the ridge of the roof. He moved fast down the other slope, and was far away, and nobody would ever find him again, because they wouldn't know where to look, and couldn't know that he was coiled up in the body of a gecko.

'Stay here,' said David, standing up and adjusting his yellow and white pyjamas.

Patrick could not have done anything else. He recognized, dully at first and then more vividly, the humiliation of his position. Face down on the bed, with his trousers bunched around his knees and a strange, worrying wetness at the base of his spine. It made him think he was bleeding. That, somehow, his father had stabbed him in the back.

His father went to the bathroom and came back. With a handful of lavatory paper he wiped away the increasingly cold pool of slime that had started to trickle between Patrick's buttocks.

'You can get up now,' he said.

Patrick could not in fact get up. The memory of voluntary action was too remote and complicated. Impatiently, his father pulled up Patrick's trousers and lifted him off the bed. Patrick stood beside the bed while his father clasped his shoulders, ostensibly to straighten his stance, but it made Patrick think that his father was going to pin his shoulders back and force them together until he was turned inside out and his lungs and heart burst out of his chest.

Instead, David leaned over and said, 'Don't ever tell your mother or anyone else what happened today, or you'll be *very* severely punished. Do you understand?'

Patrick nodded.

'Are you hungry?'

Patrick shook his head.

'Well, I'm starving,' said David chattily. 'You really should eat more, you know. Build up your strength.'

'Can I go now?'

'All right, if you don't want any lunch, you can go.' David was irritated again.

Patrick walked down the drive and as he stared at the toes of his scuffed sandals he saw, instead, the top of his head as if from ten or twelve feet in the air, and he felt an uncomfortable curiosity about the boy he was watching. It was not quite personal, like the accident they saw on the road last year and his mother said not to look.

Back down again, Patrick felt utter defeat. There was no flash of purple cloaks. No special soldiers. No gecko. Nothing. He tried to take to the air again, the way seabirds do when a wave breaks over the rock where they were standing. But he had lost the power to move and stayed behind, drowning.

8

During lunch David felt that he had perhaps pushed his disdain for middle-class prudery a little too far. Even at the bar of the Cavalry and Guards Club one couldn't boast about homosexual, paedophiliac incest with any confidence of a favourable reception. Who could he tell that he had raped his five-year-old son? He could not think of a single person who would not prefer to change the subject – and some would behave far worse than that. The experience itself had been short and brutish, but not altogether nasty. He smiled at Yvette, said how ravenous he was, and helped himself to the brochette of lamb and flageolets.

'Monsieur has been playing the piano all morning.'

'And playing with Patrick,' David added piously.

Yvette said they were so exhausting at that age.

'Exhausting!' David agreed.

Yvette left the room and David poured another glass of the Romanée-Conti that he had taken from the cellar for dinner, but had decided to drink on his own. There were always more bottles and it went so well with lamb. 'Nothing but the best, or go without': that was the code he lived by, as long as the 'go without' didn't actually happen. There was no doubt about it, he was a sensualist, and as to this latest episode, he hadn't done anything medically dangerous, just a little rubbing between the buttocks, nothing that would not happen to the boy at school in due course. If he had committed any crime, it was to set about his son's education too assiduously. He was conscious of already being sixty, there was so much to teach him and so little time.

He rang the little bell beside his plate and Yvette came back into the dining room.

'Excellent lamb,' said David.

'Would Monsieur like the tarte Tatin?'

He had no room left, alas, for tarte Tatin. Perhaps she could tempt Patrick to have some for tea. He just wanted coffee. Could she bring it to the drawing room? Of course she could.

David's legs had stiffened and when he rose from his chair he staggered for a couple of steps, drawing in his breath sharply through his teeth. 'God damn,' he said out loud. He had suddenly lost all tolerance for his rheumatic pains and decided to go upstairs to Eleanor's bathroom, a pharmaceutical paradise. He very seldom used painkillers, preferring a steady flow of alcohol and the consciousness of his own heroism.

Opening the cupboard under Eleanor's basin he was struck by the splendour and variety of the tubes and bottles: clear ones and yellow ones and dark ones, orange ones with green caps, in plastic and glass, from half a dozen countries, all urging the consumer not to exceed the stated dose. There were even envelopes marked Seconal and Mandrax, stolen, he imagined, from other people's bathroom cabinets. Rummaging about among the barbiturates and stimulants and antidepressants and hypnotics, he found surprisingly few painkillers. He had turned up only a bottle of codeine, a few diconol and some distalgesics, when he discovered, at the back of the cupboard, a bottle of sugar-coated opium pellets he had prescribed just two years before, for his mother-in-law, to ease the uncontrollable diarrhoea which accompanied her intestinal cancer. This last act of Hippocratic mercy, long after the end of his brief medical practice, filled him with nostalgia for the healer's art.

On a charmingly quaint label from Harris's in St James's Street, was written: 'The Opium (B.P. 0.6 grains)' and under that, 'Duchesse de Valençay' and finally, 'To be taken as required.' Since there were several dozen pellets left, his mother-in-law must have died before developing an opium habit. A merciful release, he reflected, popping the bottle into the pocket of his houndstooth jacket. It would have been too tiresome if she had been an opium addict on top of everything else.

David poured his coffee into a thin round eighteenth-century china cup, decorated with gold and orange cockerels fighting one another under a gold and orange tree. He took the bottle from his pocket, shook three white pellets into his hand and swallowed them with a gulp of coffee. Excited by the idea of resting comfortably under the influence of opium, he celebrated with some brandy made in the year of his birth, a present to himself which, as he told Eleanor when she paid for a case of it, reconciled him to growing old. To complete the portrait of his contentment he lit a cigar and sat in a deep chair beside the window with a battered copy of Surtees's *Jorrocks' Jaunts and Jollities*. He read the first sentence with familiar pleasure, 'What truebred city sportsman has not in his day put off the most urgent business – perhaps his marriage, or even the interment of his rib – that he might "Brave the morn" with that renowned pack, the Surrey Subscription Fox Hounds?'

When David woke up a couple of hours later, he felt tied down to a turbulent sleep by thousands of small elastic strings. He looked up slowly from the ridges and the valleys of his trousers and focused on his coffee cup. It seemed to have a thin luminous band around its edges and to be slightly raised above the surface of the small round table it lay on. He was disturbed but fascinated when he noticed that one of the gold and orange cockerels was very slowly pecking out the eye of the other. He had not expected to hallucinate. Although extraordinarily free from pain, he was worried by the loss of control that hallucination entailed.

The armchair felt like a cheese fondue as he dragged himself out of it, and walking across the floor reminded him of climbing a sand dune. He poured two glasses of cold coffee and drank them straight down, hoping they would sober him up before Eleanor returned with Nicholas and that girl of his.

He wanted to go for a brisk walk, but could not help stopping to admire the luxurious glow of his surroundings. He became particularly engrossed in the black Chinese cabinet and the colourful figures embossed on its lacquered surface. The palanquin in which an important mandarin lounged shifted forward, and the parasol held above his head by servants in shallow straw hats started to revolve hesitatingly.

David tore himself away from this animated scene and went outside. Before he could find out whether fresh air would dispel his nausea and give him back the control he wanted, he heard the sound of Eleanor's car coming down the drive. He doubled back, grabbed his copy of Surtees, and retreated into the library.

After Anne had been dropped off at Victor's, Nicholas took her place in the front passenger seat. Bridget sprawled in the back sleepily. Eleanor and Nicholas had been talking about people she didn't know.

'I'd almost forgotten how wonderful it is here,' said Nicholas, as they approached the house.

'I've completely forgotten,' said Eleanor, 'and I live here.'

'Oh, Eleanor, what a sad thing to say,' said Nicholas. 'Tell me it isn't true quickly, or I won't enjoy my tea.'

'OK,' said Eleanor, lowering the electric window to flick a cigarette out, 'it isn't true.'

'Good girl,' said Nicholas.

Bridget couldn't think of anything to say about her new surroundings. Through the car window she could see wide steps sweeping down beside a large house with pale blue shutters. Wisteria and honeysuckle climbed and tumbled at various points along the side of the house to break the monotony of the stone. She felt she had seen it all before, and for her it had only the slim reality of a photograph in the flicked pages of a magazine. The dope had made her feel sexy. She was longing to masturbate and felt remote from the chatter going on around her.

'François should come to fetch your bags,' said Eleanor. 'Leave them in the car and he'll bring them later.'

'Oh, it's all right, I can manage the bags,' said Nicholas. He wanted to get Bridget alone in their room for a moment and tell her to 'buck up'.

'No, really, let François do it, he's had nothing to do all day,' said Eleanor, who didn't want to be left alone with David.

Nicholas had to content himself with beaming his unspoken disapproval towards Bridget, who wandered down the steps trying to avoid the cracks between the paving stones, and did not even glance in his direction.

When they arrived in the hall, Eleanor was delighted by David's absence. Perhaps he had drowned in the bath. It was too much to hope. She sent Nicholas and Bridget out onto the terrace and went to the kitchen to ask Yvette for some tea. On the way she drank a glass of brandy.

'Could you bear to make a little light conversation now and again?' said Nicholas as soon as he was alone with Bridget. 'You haven't yet addressed a word to Eleanor.'

'OK, darling,' said Bridget, still trying not to walk on the cracks. She turned towards Nicholas and said in a loud whisper, 'Is this the one?'

'What?'

'The fig tree where he made her eat on all fours.'

Nicholas looked up at the windows above him, remembering the conversations he had overheard from his bedroom the last time he was staying. He nodded, putting his fingers to his lips.

Figs littered the ground underneath the tree. Some were reduced to a black stain and a few pips, but a number had not yet decayed and their purple skins, covered in a dusty white film, were still unbroken. Bridget knelt down like a dog on the ground.

'For God's sake,' snarled Nicholas, leaping over to her side. At that moment the drawing room door opened and Yvette came out, carrying a tray of cakes and cups. She only glimpsed what was going on, but it confirmed her suspicion that rich English people had a strange relationship with the animal kingdom. Bridget rose, smirking.

'*Ah, fantastique de vous revoir, Yvette,*' said Nicholas.

'*Bonjour, Monsieur.*'

'*Bonjour,*' said Bridget prettily.

'*Bonjour, Madame,*' said Yvette stoutly, though she knew that Bridget was not married.

'David!' roared Nicholas over Yvette's head. 'Where have you been hiding?'

David waved his cigar at Nicholas. 'Got lost in Surtees,' he said, stepping through the doorway. He wore his dark glasses to protect him from surprises. 'Hello, my dear,' he said to Bridget, whose name he had forgotten. 'Have either of you seen Eleanor? I caught a glimpse of some pink trousers rounding a corner, but they didn't answer to her name.'

'That's certainly what she was last seen wearing,' said Nicholas.

'Pink suits her so well, don't you think?' said David to Bridget. 'It matches the colour of her eyes.'

'Wouldn't some tea be delicious?' said Nicholas quickly.

Bridget poured the tea, while David went to sit on a low wall, a few feet away from Nicholas. As he tapped his cigar gently and let the ash fall at his feet, he noticed a trail of ants working their way along the side of the wall and into their nest in the corner.

Bridget carried cups of tea over to the two men, and as she turned to fetch her own cup, David held the burning tip of his cigar close to the ants and ran it along in both directions as far as he could conveniently reach. The ants twisted, excruciated by the heat, and dropped down onto the terrace. Some, before they fell, reared up, their stitching legs trying helplessly to repair their ruined bodies.

'What a civilized life you have here,' Bridget sang out as she sank back into a dark-blue deckchair. Nicholas rolled his eyeballs and wondered why the hell he had told her to make light conversation. To cover the silence he remarked to David that he had been to Jonathan Croyden's memorial service the day before.

'Do you find that you go to more memorial services, or more weddings these days?' David asked.

'I still get more wedding invitations, but I find I enjoy the memorials more.'

'Because you don't have to bring a present?'

'Well, that helps a great deal, but mainly because one gets a better crowd when someone really distinguished dies.'

'Unless all his friends have died before him.'

'That, of course, is intolerable,' said Nicholas categorically.

'Ruins the party.'

'Absolutely.'

'I'm afraid I don't approve of memorial services,' said

David, taking another puff on his cigar. 'Not merely because I cannot imagine anything in most men's lives that deserves to be celebrated, but also because the delay between the funeral and the memorial service is usually so long that, far from rekindling the spirit of a lost friend, it only shows how easily one can live without him.' David blew on the tip of his cigar and it glowed brightly. The opium made him feel that he was listening to another man speak.

'The dead are dead,' he went on, 'and the truth is that one forgets about people when they stop coming to dinner. There are exceptions, of course – namely, the people one forgets *during* dinner.'

With his cigar he caught a stray ant which was escaping with singed antennae from his last incendiary raid. 'If you really miss someone, you are better off doing something you both enjoyed doing together, which is unlikely to mean, except in the most bizarre cases, standing around in a draughty church, wearing a black overcoat and singing hymns.'

The ant ran away with astonishing speed and was about to reach the far side of the wall when David, stretching a little, touched it lightly with a surgeon's precision. Its skin blistered and it squirmed violently as it died.

'One should only go to an enemy's memorial service. Quite apart from the pleasure of outlasting him, it is an opportunity for a truce. Forgiveness is so important, don't you think?'

'Gosh, yes,' said Bridget, 'especially getting other people to forgive you.'

David smiled at her encouragingly, until he saw Eleanor step through the doorway.

'Ah, Eleanor,' grinned Nicholas with exaggerated pleasure, 'we were just talking about Jonathan Croyden's memorial.'

'I guess it's the end of an era,' said Eleanor.

'He *was* the last man alive to have gone to one of Evelyn Waugh's parties in drag,' said Nicholas. 'He was said to dress much better as a woman than as a man. He was an inspiration to a whole generation of Englishmen. Which reminds me, after the memorial I met a very tiresome, smarmy Indian who claimed to have visited you just before staying with Jonathan at Cap Ferrat.'

'It must have been Vijay,' said Eleanor. 'Victor brought him over.'

'That's the one,' Nicholas nodded. 'He seemed to know that I was coming here. Perfectly extraordinary as I'd never set eyes on him before.'

'He's desperately fashionable,' explained David, 'and consequently knows more about people he has never met than he does about anything else.'

Eleanor perched on a frail white chair with a faded blue cushion on its circular seat. She rose again immediately and dragged the chair further towards the shade of the fig tree.

'Watch out,' said Bridget, 'you might squash some of the figs.'

Eleanor made no reply.

'It seems a pity to waste them,' said Bridget innocently, leaning over to pick a fig off the ground. 'This one is perfect.' She brought it close to her mouth. 'Isn't it weird the way their skin is purple and white at the same time.'

'Like a drunk with emphysema,' said David, smiling at Eleanor.

Bridget opened her mouth, rounded her lips and pushed the fig inside. She suddenly felt what she later described to Barry as a 'very heavy vibe' from David, 'as if he was pushing his fist into my womb'. Bridget swallowed the fig, but she felt a physical need to get out of the deckchair and move further away from David.

She walked beside the edge of the wall above the garden terrace and, wanting to explain her sudden action, she stretched out her arms, embraced the view, and said, 'What a perfect day.' Nobody replied. Scanning the landscape for something else to say, she glimpsed a slight movement at the far end of the garden. At first she thought it was an animal crouched under the pear tree, but when it got up she saw that it was a child. 'Is that your son?' she asked. 'In the red trousers.'

Eleanor walked over to her side. 'Yes, it's Patrick. Patrick!' she shouted. 'Do you want some tea, darling?'

There was no answer. 'Maybe he can't hear you,' said Bridget.

'Of course he can,' said David. 'He's just being tiresome.'

'Maybe we can't hear him,' said Eleanor. 'Patrick!' she shouted again. 'Why don't you come and have some tea with us?'

'He's shaking his head,' said Bridget.

'He's probably had tea two or three times already,' said Nicholas; 'you know what they're like at that age.'

'God, children are so *sweet*,' said Bridget, smiling at Eleanor. 'Eleanor,' she said in the same tone, as if her request should be granted as a reward for finding children sweet, 'could you tell me which room I'm in because I'd quite like to go up and have a bath and unpack.'

'Of course. Let me show you,' said Eleanor.

Eleanor led Bridget into the house.

'Your girlfriend is very, I believe the word is "vivacious",' said David.

'Oh, she'll do for now,' said Nicholas.

'No need to apologize, she's absolutely charming. Shall we have a real drink?'

'Good idea.'

'Champagne?'

'Perfect.'

David fetched the champagne and reappeared tearing the golden lead from the neck of a clear bottle.

'Cristal,' said Nicholas dutifully.

'Nothing but the best, or go without,' said David.

'It reminds me of Charles Pewsey,' said Nicholas. 'We were drinking a bottle of that stuff at Wilton's last week and I asked him if he remembered Gunter, Jonathan Croyden's unspeakable amanuensis. And Charles roared – you know how deaf he is – "Amanuensis? Bumboy, you mean: *unspeakable bumboy*." Everyone turned round and stared at us.'

'They always do when one's with Charles.' David grinned. It was so typical of Charles, one had to know Charles to appreciate how funny it was.

The bedroom Bridget had been put in was all flowery chintz, with engravings of Roman ruins on every wall. Beside the bed was a copy of Lady Mosley's *A Life of Contrasts*, on top of which Bridget had thrown *Valley of the Dolls*, her current reading. She sat by the window smoking a joint, and watched the smoke drift through the tiny holes in the mosquito net. From below, she could hear Nicholas shout '*unspeakable bumboy*'. They must be reminiscing about their school days. Boys will be boys.

Bridget lifted one foot onto the windowsill. She still held the joint in her left hand, although it would burn her fingers with the next toke. She slipped her right hand between her legs and started to masturbate.

'It just goes to show that being an amanuensis doesn't matter as long as you have the butler on your side,' said Nicholas.

David picked up his cue. 'It's always the same thing in life,' he chanted. 'It's not what you do, it's who you know.'

To find such a ludicrous example of this important maxim made the two men laugh.

Bridget moved over to the bed and spread herself out face down on the yellow bedcover. As she closed her eyes and resumed masturbating, the thought of David flashed over her like a static shock, but she forced herself to focus loyally on the memory of Barry's stirring presence.

9

When Victor was in trouble with his writing he had a nervous habit of flicking open his pocket watch and clicking it closed again. Distracted by the noise of other human activities he found it helpful to make a noise of his own. During the contemplative passages of his daydreams he flicked and clicked more slowly, but as he pressed up against his sense of frustration the pace increased.

Dressed this morning in the flecked and bulky sweater he had hunted down ruthlessly for an occasion on which clothes simply didn't matter, he fully intended to begin his essay on the necessary and sufficient conditions of personal identity. He sat at a slightly wobbly wooden table under a yellowing plane tree in front of the house, and as the temperature rose he stripped down to his shirtsleeves. By lunchtime he had recorded only one thought, 'I have written books which I have had to write, but I have not yet written a book which others have to read.' He punished himself by improvising a sandwich for lunch, instead of walking down to La Coquière and eating three courses in the garden, under the blue and red and yellow parasol of the Ricard Pastis company.

Despite himself he kept thinking of Eleanor's puzzled little contribution that morning, 'Gosh, I mean, if anything is in the mind, it's who you are.' If anything is in the mind it's who you are: it was silly, it was unhelpful, but it whined about him like a mosquito in the dark.

Just as a novelist may sometimes wonder why he invents characters who do not exist and makes them do things which do not matter, so a philosopher may wonder why he invents cases that cannot occur in order to determine what must be the case. After a long neglect of his subject, Victor was not as thoroughly convinced that impossibility was the best route to necessity as he might have been had he recently reconsidered Stolkin's extreme case in which 'scientists destroy my brain and body, and then make out of new matter, a replica of Greta Garbo'. How could one help agreeing with Stolkin that 'there would be no connection between me and the resulting person'?

Nevertheless, to think one knew what would happen to a person's sense of identity if his brain was cut in half and distributed between identical twins seemed, just for now, before he had thrown himself back into the torrent of philosophical debate, a poor substitute for an intelligent description of what it is to know who you are.

Victor went indoors to fetch the familiar tube of Bisodol indigestion tablets. As usual he had eaten his sandwich too fast, pushing it down his throat like a sword-swallower. He thought with renewed appreciation of William James's remark that the self consists mainly of 'peculiar motions in the head and between the head and throat', although the peculiar motions somewhat lower down in his stomach and bowels felt at least as personal.

When Victor sat down again he pictured himself thinking, and tried to superimpose this picture on his inner vacancy. If he was essentially a thinking machine, then he needed to be serviced. It was not the problems of philosophy but the problem *with* philosophy that preoccupied him that afternoon. And yet how often the two became indistinguishable. Wittgenstein had said that the philosopher's treatment of a question was like the treatment of a disease. But which treatment? Purging? Leeches? Antibiotics against the infections of language? Indigestion tablets, thought Victor, belching softly, to help break down the doughy bulk of sensation?

We ascribe thoughts to thinkers because this is the way we speak, but persons need not be claimed to be the thinkers of these thoughts. Still, thought Victor lazily, why not bow down to popular demand on this occasion? As to brains and minds, was there really any problem about two categorically different phenomena, brain process and consciousness, occurring simultaneously? Or was the problem with the categories?

From down the hill Victor heard a car door slam. It must be Eleanor dropping Anne at the bottom of the drive. Victor flicked open his watch, checked the time, and snapped it closed again. What had he achieved? Almost nothing. It was not one of those unproductive days when he was confused by abundance and starved, like Buridan's ass, between two equally nourishing bales of hay. His lack of progress today was more profound.

He watched Anne rounding the last corner of the drive, painfully bright in her white dress.

'Hi,' she said.

'Hello,' said Victor with boyish gloom.

'How's it going?'

'Oh, it's been a fairly futile exercise, but I suppose it's good to get any exercise at all.'

'Don't knock that futile exercise,' said Anne, 'it's big business. Bicycles that don't go anyplace, a long walk to nowhere on a rubber treadmill, heavy things you don't even *need* to pick up.'

Victor remained silent, staring down at his one sentence. Anne rested her hands on his shoulders. 'So there's no major news on who we are?'

'Afraid not. Personal identity, of course, is a fiction, a pure fiction. But I've reached this conclusion by the wrong method.'

'What was that?'

'Not thinking about it.'

'But that's what the English mean, isn't it, when they say, "He was very philosophical about it"? They mean that someone stopped thinking about something.' Anne lit a cigarette.

'Still,' said Victor in a quiet voice, 'my thinking today reminds me of a belligerent undergraduate I once taught, who said that our tutorials had "failed to pass the So What Test".'

Anne sat down on the edge of Victor's table and eased off one of her canvas shoes with the toe of the other. She liked to see Victor working again, however unsuccessfully. Placing her bare foot on his knee, she said, 'Tell me, Professor, is this *my* foot?'

'Well, some philosophers would say that under certain circumstances,' said Victor, lifting her foot in his cupped hands, 'this would be determined by whether the foot is in pain.'

'What's wrong with the foot being in pleasure?'

'Well,' said Victor, solemnly considering this absurd question, 'in philosophy as in life, pleasure is more likely to be an hallucination. Pain is the key to possession.' He opened his mouth wide, like a hungry man approaching a hamburger, but closed it again, and gently kissed each toe.

Victor released her foot and Anne kicked off the other shoe. 'I'll be back in a moment,' she said, walking out carefully over the warm sharp gravel to the kitchen door.

Victor reflected with satisfaction that in ancient Chinese society the little game he had played with Anne's foot would have been considered almost intolerably familiar. An unbound foot represented for the Chinese a degree of abandon which genitals could never achieve. He was stimulated by the thought of how intense his desire would have been at another time, in another place. He thought of the lines from *The Jew of Malta*, 'Thou hast committed Fornication: but that was in another country, and besides the wench is dead.' In the past he had been a Utilitarian seducer, aiming to increase the sum of *general* pleasure, but since starting his affair with Anne he had been unprecedentedly faithful. Never physically alluring, he had always relied on his cleverness to seduce women. As he grew uglier and more famous, so the instrument of seduction, his speech, and the instrument of gratification, his body, grew into an increasingly inglorious contrast. The routine of fresh seductions highlighted this aspect of the mind–body problem more harshly than intimacy, and he had decided that perhaps it was time to be in the same country with a living wench. The challenge was not to substitute a mental absence for a physical one.

Anne came out of the house carrying two glasses of orange juice. She gave one to Victor.

'What were you thinking?' she asked.

'Whether you would be the same person in another body,' lied Victor.

'Well, ask yourself, would you be nibbling my toes if I looked like a Canadian lumberjack?'

'If I knew it was *you* inside,' said Victor loyally.

'Inside the steel-capped boots?'

'Exactly.'

They smiled at each other. Victor took a gulp of orange juice. 'But tell me,' he said, 'how was your expedition with Eleanor?'

'On the way back I found myself thinking that everybody who is meeting for dinner tonight will probably have said something unkind about everybody else. I know you'll think it's very primitive and American of me, but why do people spend the evening with people they've spent the day insulting?'

'So as to have something insulting to say about them tomorrow.'

'Why, of course,' gasped Anne. '*Tomorrow is another day.* So different and yet so similar,' she added.

Victor looked uneasy. 'Were you insulting each other in the car, or just attacking David and me?'

'Neither, but the way that everyone else was insulted I knew that we would break off into smaller and smaller combinations, until everyone had been dealt with by everyone else.'

'But that's what charm is: being malicious about everybody except the person you are with, who then glows with the privilege of exemption.'

'If that's what charm is,' said Anne, 'it broke down on this occasion, because I felt that none of us was exempt.'

'Do you wish to confirm your own theory by saying something nasty about one of your fellow dinner guests?'

'Well, now that you mention it,' said Anne, laughing, 'I thought that Nicholas Pratt was a total creep.'

'I know what you mean. His problem is that he wanted to go into politics,' Victor explained, 'but was destroyed by what passed for a sex scandal some years ago and would probably now be called an "open marriage". Most people wait until they've become ministers to ruin their political careers with a sex scandal, but Nicholas managed to do it when he was still trying to impress Central Office by contesting a by-election in a safe Labour seat.'

'Precocious, huh,' said Anne. 'What exactly did he do to deserve his exile from paradise?'

'He was found in bed with two women he was not married to by the woman he was married to, and she decided not to "stand by his side".'

'Sounds like there wasn't any room,' said Anne, 'but like you say, it was bad timing. Back in those days you

couldn't go on television and say how it was a "really liber-
ating experience".'

'There may still be,' said Victor with mock astonishment, joining the tips of his fingers pedagogically, to form
an arc with his hands, 'certain rural backwaters of Tory
England where, even today, group sex is not practised by *all*
the matrons on the Selection Committee.'

Anne sat down on Victor's knee. 'Victor, do two people
make a group?'

'Only part of a group, I'm afraid.'

'You mean,' said Anne with horror, 'we've been having
part-of-a-group sex?' She got up again, ruffling Victor's hair.
'That's awful.'

'I think,' Victor continued calmly, 'that when his political
ambitions were ruined so early, Nicholas became rather indifferent to a career and fell back on his large inheritance.'

'He still doesn't make it on to my casualty list,' said Anne.
'Being found in bed with two girls isn't the shower room in
Auschwitz.'

'You have high standards.'

'I do and I don't. No pain is too small if it hurts, but any
pain is too small if it's cherished,' Anne said. 'Anyhow, he
isn't suffering that badly, he's got a stoned schoolgirl with
him. She was being moody in the back of the car. Two like
her isn't enough, he'll have to graduate to triplets.'

'What's she called?'

'Bridget something. One of those not very convincing
English names like Hop-Scotch.'

Anne moved on quickly, she was determined not to let
Victor get lost in ruminations about where Bridget might
'fit in'. 'The oddest thing about the day was our visit to
Le Wild Ouest.'

'Why on earth did you go there?'

'As far as I could make out we were there because Patrick wants to go, but Eleanor gets priority.'

'You don't think she might have just been checking whether it was an amusing place to take her son?'

'In the Dodge City of arrested development, you gotta be quick on the draw,' said Anne, whipping out an imaginary gun.

'You seem to have entered into the spirit of the place,' said Victor drily.

'If she wanted to take her son there,' Anne resumed, 'he could have come with us. And if she wanted to find out whether it was an "amusing place", Patrick could have told her.'

Victor did not want to argue with Anne. She often had strong opinions about human situations which did not really matter to him, unless they illustrated a principle or yielded an anecdote, and he preferred to concede this stony ground to her, with whatever show of leniency his mood required. 'There isn't anyone at dinner tonight left for us to disparage,' he said, 'except David, and we know what you think of him.'

'That reminds me, I must read at least a chapter of *The Twelve Caesars* so I can give it back to him this evening.'

'Read the chapters on Nero and Caligula,' Victor suggested, 'I'm sure they're David's favourites. One illustrates what happens when you combine a mediocre artistic talent with absolute power. The other shows how nearly inevitable it is for those who have been terrified to become terrifying, once they have the opportunity.'

'But isn't that the key to a great education? You spend your adolescence being promoted from terrified to terrifier, without any women around to distract you.'

Victor decided to ignore this latest demonstration of Anne's rather tiresome attitude towards English public schools. 'The interesting thing about Caligula,' he went on patiently, 'is that he intended to be a model emperor, and for the first few months of his reign he was praised for his magnanimity. But the compulsion to repeat what one has experienced is like gravity, and it takes special equipment to break away from it.'

Anne was amused to hear Victor make such an overtly psychological generalization. Perhaps if people had been dead long enough they came alive for him.

'Nero I dislike for having driven Seneca to suicide,' Victor droned on. 'Although I'm well aware of the hostility that can arise between a pupil and his tutor, it is just as well to keep it within limits,' he chuckled.

'Didn't Nero commit suicide himself, or was that just in *Nero, the Movie?*'

'When it came to suicide he showed less enthusiasm than he had done for driving other people to it. He sat around for a long time wondering which part of his "pustular and malodorous" body to puncture, wailing, "Dead and so great an artist!"'

'You sound like you were there.'

'You know how it is with the books one reads in one's youth.'

'Yeah, that's kinda how I feel about *Francis the Talking Mule*,' said Anne.

She got up from the creaking wicker chair. 'I guess I'd better catch up on "one's youth" before dinner.' She moved over to Victor's side. 'Write me one sentence before we have to go,' she said gently. 'You can do that, can't you?'

Victor enjoyed being coaxed. He looked up at her like an obedient child. 'I'll try,' he said modestly.

Anne walked through the gloom of the kitchen and climbed the twisting stairs. She felt a cool pleasure at being alone for the first time since the early morning and wanted to have a bath straight away. Victor liked to wallow in the tub, controlling the taps with his big toe, and she knew how irrationally disappointed he became if the steaming water ran out during this important ceremony. Besides, if she bathed now she could lie on her bed and read for a couple of hours before going out to dinner.

On top of the books by her bed was *Goodbye to Berlin* and Anne thought how much more fun it would be to reread that rather than dip into the grisly Caesars. From the thought of pre-war Berlin her mind jumped back to the remark she had made about the shower room in Auschwitz. Was she, she wondered, giving in to that English need to be facetious? She felt tainted and exhausted by a summer of burning up her moral resources for the sake of small conversational effects. She felt she had been subtly perverted by slick and lazy English manners, the craving for the prophylactic of irony, the terrible fear of being 'a bore', and the boredom of the ways they relentlessly and narrowly evaded this fate.

Above all it was Victor's ambivalence towards these values that was wearing her down. She could no longer tell whether he was working as a double agent, a serious writer pretending to the Folks on the Hill – of which the Melroses were only rather a tarnished example – that he was a devoted admirer of the effortless nullity of their lives. Or perhaps he was a triple agent, pretending to her that he had not accepted the bribe of being admitted to the periphery of their world.

Defiantly, Anne picked up *Goodbye to Berlin* and headed towards the bathroom.

The sun disappeared early behind the roof of the tall, narrow house. At his table under the plane tree Victor put his sweater back on. He felt safe in the bulk of his sweater with the distant sound of Anne running her bath. He wrote a sentence in his spidery hand, and then another.

10

If David had awarded himself the most important painting in the house, at least Eleanor had secured the largest bedroom. At the far end of the corridor, its curtains were closed all day to protect a host of frail Italian drawings from the draining power of the sun.

Patrick hesitated in the doorway of his mother's bedroom, waiting to be noticed. The dimness of the room made it seem even larger, especially when a breeze stirred the curtains and an unsteady light spread shadows over the stretching walls. Eleanor sat at her desk with her back to Patrick, writing a cheque to the Save the Children Fund, her favourite charity. She did not hear her son come into the room until he stood beside her chair.

'Hello, darling,' she said, with a desperate affection that sounded like a long-distance telephone call. 'What did you do today?'

'Nothing,' said Patrick, looking down at the floor.

'Did you go for a walk with Daddy?' asked Eleanor bravely. She felt the inadequacy of her questions, but could not overcome the dread of having them scantily answered.

Patrick shook his head. A branch swayed outside the window, and he watched the shadow of its leaves flickering above the curtain pole. The curtains billowed feebly and collapsed again, like defeated lungs. Down the corridor a door slammed. Patrick looked at the clutter on his mother's desk.

It was covered in letters, envelopes, paper clips, rubber bands, pencils, and a profusion of different-coloured chequebooks. An empty champagne glass stood beside a full ashtray.

'Shall I take the glass down?' he asked.

'What a thoughtful boy you are,' gushed Eleanor. 'You could take it down and give it to Yvette. That would be very kind.'

Patrick nodded solemnly and picked up the glass. Eleanor marvelled at how well her son had turned out. Perhaps people were just born one way or another and the main thing was not to interfere too much.

'Thank you, darling,' she said huskily, wondering what she was meant to have done, as she watched him walk out of the room, gripping the stem of the glass tightly in his right hand.

As Patrick was going down the staircase, he overheard his father and Nicholas talking at the other end of the corridor. Suddenly afraid of falling, he started to walk down the way he used to when he was little, leading with one foot, and then bringing the other down firmly beside it on the same step. He had to hurry in case his father caught up with him, but if he hurried he might fall. He heard his father saying, 'We'll put it to him at dinner, I'm sure he'll agree.'

Patrick froze on the stairs. They were talking about him. They were going to make him agree. Squeezing the stem of the glass fiercely in his hand, he felt a rush of shame and terror. He looked up at the painting hanging on the stairs and imagined its frame hurtling through the air and embedding its sharp corner in his father's chest; and another painting whistling down the corridor and chopping Nicholas's head off.

'I'll see you downstairs in an hour or two,' said Nicholas.

'Right-ho,' said his father.

Patrick heard Nicholas's door close, and he listened

intently to his father's footsteps coming down the corridor. Was he going to his bedroom, or coming down the stairs? Patrick wanted to move, but the power to move had deserted him again. He held his breath as the footsteps stopped.

In the corridor David was torn between visiting Eleanor, with whom he was always furious on principle, and going to have a bath. The opium which had taken the edge off the perpetual ache in his body now weakened his desire to insult his wife. After a few moments spent considering the choice he went into his bedroom.

Patrick knew he was not visible from the top of the stairs, but when he heard the footsteps pause he had tried to push back the idea of his father with concentration like a flamethrower. For a long time after David had gone into his bedroom, Patrick did not accept that the danger was over. When he relaxed his grip on the glass, the base and half the stem slipped out of his hand and broke on the step below him. Patrick couldn't understand how the glass had snapped. Removing the rest of the glass from his hand, he saw a small cut in the middle of his palm. Only when he saw it bleed did he understand what had happened and, knowing that he must be in pain, he at last felt the sharp sting of the cut.

He was terrified of being punished for dropping the glass. It had fallen apart in his hand, but they would never believe that, they would say that he'd dropped it. He stepped carefully among the scattered pieces of glass on the steps below and got to the bottom of the stairs, but he did not know what to do with the half glass in his hand, and so he climbed back up three of the steps and decided to jump. He threw himself forward as hard as he could, but tripped as he landed, letting the rest of the glass fly from his hand and shatter against the wall. He lay splayed and shocked on the floor.

When she heard Patrick's screams, Yvette put down the soup ladle, wiped her hands quickly on her apron, and hurried into the hall.

'Ooh-la-la,' she said reproachfully, '*tu vas te casser la figure un de ces jours.*' She was alarmed by Patrick's helplessness, but as she drew closer she asked him more gently, '*Où est-ce que ça te fait mal, pauvre petit?*'

Patrick still felt the shock of being winded and pointed to his chest where he had taken the brunt of the fall. Yvette picked him up, murmuring, '*Allez, c'est pas grave,*' and kissed him on the cheek. He went on crying, but less desperately. A tangled sensation of sweat and gold teeth and garlic mingled with the pleasure of being held, but when Yvette started to rub his back, he squirmed in her arms and broke free.

At her desk Eleanor thought, 'Oh God, he's fallen downstairs and cut himself on the glass I gave him. It's my fault again.' Patrick's screaming impaled her on her chair like a javelin, while she considered the horror of her position.

Still dominated by guilt and the fear of David's reprisals, she summoned up the courage to go out onto the landing. At the bottom of the stairs she found Yvette sitting beside Patrick.

'*Rien de cassé, Madame,*' said Yvette. '*Il a eu peur en tombant, c'est tout.*'

'*Merci, Yvette,*' said Eleanor.

It wasn't practical to drink as much as she did, thought Yvette, going to fetch a dustpan and brush.

Eleanor sat down beside Patrick, but a fragment of glass cut into her bottom. 'Ouch,' she exclaimed, and got up again to brush the back of her dress.

'Mummy sat on a piece of glass,' she said to Patrick. He looked at her glumly. 'But never mind about that, tell me about your terrible fall.'

'I jumped down from very high up.'

'With a glass in your hand, darling? That could have been very dangerous.'

'It was dangerous,' said Patrick angrily.

'Oh, I'm sure it was,' said Eleanor, reaching out self-consciously to brush back the fringe of light brown hair from his forehead. 'I'll tell you what we could do,' she said, proud of herself for remembering, 'we could go to the funfair tomorrow, to Le Wild Ouest, would you like that? I went there today with Anne to see if you would like it, and there were lots of cowboys and Indians and rides. Shall we go tomorrow?'

'I want to go away,' said Patrick.

Up in his monk's suite, David hurried next door and turned the bath taps to their full volume, until the thundering water drowned the uncongenial sound of his son. He sprinkled bath salts into the water from a porcelain shell and thought how intolerable it was having no nanny this summer to keep the boy quiet in the evenings. Eleanor hadn't the least idea of how to bring up a child.

After Patrick's nanny had died, there had been a dim procession of foreign girls through the London house. Homesick vandals, they left in tears after a few months, sometimes pregnant, never any more fluent in the English they had come to learn. In the end Patrick was often entrusted to Carmen, the morose Spanish maid who could not be bothered to refuse him anything. She lived in the basement, her varicose veins protesting at every step of the five storeys she seldom climbed to the nursery. In a sense one had to be grateful that this lugubrious peasant had had so little influence on Patrick. Still, it was very tiresome to find him on the stairs night after night, escaped from behind his wooden gate, waiting for Eleanor.

They so often returned late from Annabel's that Patrick had once asked anxiously, 'Who is Annabels?' Everyone in the room had laughed and David could remember Bunny Warren saying, with that simple-hearted tactlessness for which he was almost universally adored, 'She's a very lovely young girl your parents are exceptionally fond of.' Nicholas had seen his chance and said, 'I sospect ze child is experienzing ze sibling rivalry.'

When David came in late at night and found Patrick sitting on the stairs, he would order him back to the nursery, but after he had gone to bed he sometimes heard the floorboards creak on the landing. He knew that Patrick crept into his mother's room to try to extract some consolation from her stupefied back, as she lay curled up and unconscious on the edge of her mattress. He had seen them in the morning like refugees in an expensive waiting room.

David turned off the taps and found that the screaming had stopped. Screaming that only lasted as long as it took to fill a bath could not be taken seriously. David tested the water with a foot. It was far too hot, but he pushed his leg down deeper until the water covered his hairless shin, and started to scald him. Every nerve in his body urged him to step out of the steaming bath, but he called up his deep resources of contempt and kept his leg immersed to prove his mastery over the pain.

He straddled the bath; one foot burning, the other cool against the cork floor. It took no effort for him to revive the fury he had felt an hour earlier when he glimpsed Bridget kneeling under the tree. Nicholas had obviously told that silly bitch about the figs.

Oh, happy days, he sighed, where had they fled? Days when his now bedraggled wife, still freshly submissive and eager to please, had grazed so peacefully among the rotting figs.

David hoisted his other leg over the side of the bath and plunged it into the water, in the hope that the additional pain would stimulate him to think of the right revenge to take on Nicholas during dinner.

'Why the hell did you have to do that? I'm sure David saw you,' Nicholas snapped at Bridget, as soon as he had heard David's bedroom door close.

'Saw what?'

'You, down on all fours.'

'I didn't have to,' said Bridget sleepily from the bed. 'I only did it because you were so keen to tell me the story, and I thought it might turn you on. It obviously did the first time.'

'Don't be so absurd.' Nicholas stood with his hands on his hips, a picture of disapproval. 'As to your effusive remarks – "What a perfect life you have here",' he simpered, '"What a wonderful view" – they made you sound even more vulgar and stupid than you are.'

Bridget still had trouble in taking Nicholas's rudeness seriously.

'If you're going to be horrid,' she said, 'I'll elope with Barry.'

'And that's another thing,' gasped Nicholas, removing his silk jacket. There were dark sweat rings under the arms of his shirt. 'What was going through your mind – if mind is the right word – when you gave that yob the telephone number here?'

'When I said that we must keep in touch, he asked me for the number of the house I was staying in.'

'You could have lied, you know,' yelped Nicholas. 'There's such a thing as dishonesty.' He paced up and down shaking his head. 'Such a thing as a broken promise.'

Bridget rolled off the bed and crossed the room. 'Just fuck

off,' she said, slamming the bathroom door and locking it. She sat on the edge of the bath and remembered that her copy of *Tatler* and, worse, her make-up were in the room next door.

'Open the door, you stupid bitch,' said Nicholas swivelling the doorknob.

'Fuck off,' she repeated. At least she could prevent Nicholas from using the bathroom for as long as possible, even if she only had a bubble bath to amuse her.

11

While he was locked out of the bathroom Nicholas unpacked and filled the most convenient shelves with his shirts; in the cupboard his suits took up rather more than half the space. The biography of F. E. Smith that he had already carried with him to half a dozen houses that summer was placed again on the table on the right-hand side of the bed. When he was finally allowed access to the bathroom, he distributed his possessions around the basin in a familiar order, his badger brush to one side and his rose mouthwash to the other.

Bridget refused to unpack properly. She pulled out a frail-looking dress of dark-red crushed velvet for tonight, tossed it on the bed, and abandoned her suitcase in the middle of the floor. Nicholas could not resist kicking it over, but he said nothing, conscious that if he was rude to her again straight away she might cause him difficulties during dinner.

Silently, Nicholas put on a dark-blue silk suit and an old pale-yellow shirt, the most conventional one he had been able to find at Mr Fish, and was now ready to go downstairs. His hair smelt faintly of something made up for him by Trumper's, and his cheeks of a very simple extract of lime he considered clean and manly.

Bridget sat at the dressing table, very slowly applying too much black eyeliner.

'We must get downstairs, or we'll be late,' said Nicholas.

'You always say that and then there's nobody there.'

'David is even more punctual than I am.'

'So go down without me.'

'I would rather we went down together,' said Nicholas, with menacing weariness.

Bridget continued to admire herself in the inadequately lit mirror, while Nicholas sat on the edge of the bed and gave his shirtsleeves a little tug to reveal more of his royal cufflinks. Made of thick gold and engraved with the initials E.R., they might have been contemporary, but had in fact been a present to his rakish grandfather, the Sir Nicholas Pratt of his day and a loyal courtier of Edward VII's. Unable to think how he could further embellish his appearance, he got up and wandered around. He drifted back into the bathroom and stole another glance at himself in the mirror. The softening contours of his chin, where the flab was beginning to build up, would undoubtedly profit from yet another suntan. He dabbed a little more lime extract behind his ears.

'I'm ready,' said Bridget.

Nicholas came over to the dressing table and quickly pressed Bridget's powder puff to his cheekbones, and ran it coyly over the bridge of his nose. As they left the room, he glanced at Bridget critically, unable to approve fully of the red velvet dress he had once praised. It carried with it the aura of an antique stall in Kensington Market, and showed up its cheapness glaringly in the presence of other antiques. The red emphasized her blonde hair, and the velvet brought out the glassy blue of her eyes, but the design of the dress, which seemed to have been made for a medieval witch, and the evidence of amateur repairs in the worn material struck him as less amusing than the first time he had seen Bridget in this same dress. It had been at a half Bohemian party in Chelsea given by an ambitious Peruvian. Nicholas and the other social peaks that the host was trying to scale stood together at one end of the room insulting the mountaineer as he scrambled about them attentively. When they had nothing better to do they allowed him to bribe them with his hospitality, on the understanding he would be swept away by an avalanche of invective if he ever treated them with familiarity at a party given by people who really mattered.

Sometimes it was great festivals of privilege, and at other times it was the cringing and envy of others that confirmed one's sense of being at the top. Sometimes it was the seduction of a pretty girl that accomplished this important task and at other times it was down to one's swanky cufflinks.

'All roads lead to Rome,' murmured Nicholas complacently, but Bridget was not curious to know why.

As she had predicted, there was nobody waiting for them in the drawing room. With its curtains drawn, and lit only by pools of urine-coloured light splashed under the dark-yellow lampshades, the room looked both dim and rich. Like so many of one's friends, reflected Nicholas.

'Ah, *Extraits de Plantes Marines*,' he said, sniffing the burning essence loudly, 'you know it's impossible to get it now.' Bridget did not answer.

He moved over to the black cabinet and lifted a bottle of Russian vodka out of a silver bucket full of ice cubes. He poured the cold viscous fluid into a small tumbler. 'They used to sell it with copper rings which sometimes overheated and spat burning essence onto the light bulbs. One evening, Monsieur et Madame de Quelque Chose were changing for dinner when the bulb in their dining room exploded, the lampshade caught fire, and the curtains burst into flames. After that, it was taken off the market.'

Bridget showed no surprise or interest. In the distance the telephone rang faintly. Eleanor so disliked the noise of telephones that there was only one in the house, at a small desk under the back stairs.

'Can I get you a drink?' asked Nicholas, knocking back

his vodka in what he considered the correct Russian manner.

'Just a Coke,' said Bridget. She didn't really like alcohol, it was such a crude high. At least that was what Barry said. Nicholas opened a bottle of Coke and poured himself some more vodka, this time in a tall glass packed with ice.

There was a clicking of high heels on the tiles and Eleanor came in shyly, wearing a long purple dress.

'There's a phone call for you,' she said, smiling at Bridget, whose name she had somehow forgotten between the telephone and the drawing room.

'Oh, wow,' said Bridget, 'for me?' She got up, making sure not to look at Nicholas. Eleanor described the route to the phone, and Bridget eventually arrived at the desk under the back stairs. 'Hello,' she said, '*hello*?' There was no answer.

By the time she returned to the drawing room Nicholas was saying, 'Well, one evening, the Marquis and Marquise de Quelque Chose were upstairs changing for a big party they were giving, when a lampshade caught fire and their drawing room was completely gutted.'

'How marvellous,' said Eleanor, with not the faintest idea of what Nicholas had been talking about. Recovering from one of those blank patches in which she could not have said what was going on around her, she knew only that there had been an interval since she was last conscious. 'Did you get through all right?' she said to Bridget.

'No. It's really weird, there was no one there. He must have run out of money.'

The phone rang again, more loudly this time through all the doors that Bridget had left open. She doubled back eagerly.

'Imagine wanting to talk to someone on the phone,' said Eleanor. 'I dread it.'

'Youth,' said Nicholas tolerantly.

'I dreaded it even more in my youth, if that's possible.'

Eleanor poured herself some whisky. She felt exhausted

and restless at the same time. It was the feeling she knew better than any other. She returned to her usual seat, a low footstool wedged into the lampless corner beside the screen. As a child, when the screen had belonged to her mother, she had often squatted under its monkey-crowded branches pretending to be invisible.

Nicholas, who had been sitting tentatively on the edge of the Doge's chair, rose again nervously. 'This is David's favourite seat, isn't it?'

'I guess he won't sit in it if you're in it already,' said Eleanor.

'That's just what I'm not so sure of,' said Nicholas. 'You know how fond he is of having his own way.'

'Tell me about it,' said Eleanor flatly.

Nicholas moved to a nearby sofa and sucked another mouthful of vodka from his glass. It had taken on the taste of melted ice, which he disliked, but he rolled it around his mouth, having nothing in particular to say to Eleanor. Annoyed by Bridget's absence and apprehensive about David's arrival, he waited to see which would come through the door. He felt let down when Anne and Victor arrived first.

Anne had replaced her simple white dress with a simple black one and she already held a lighted cigarette. Victor had conquered his anxiety about what to wear and still had on the thick speckled sweater.

'Hi,' said Anne to Eleanor, and kissed her with real affection.

When the greetings were over, Nicholas could not help remarking on Victor's appearance. 'My dear chap, you look as if you're about to go mackerel fishing in the Hebrides.'

'In fact, the last time I wore this sweater,' said Victor, turning around and handing a glass to Anne, 'was when I had to see a student who was floundering badly with his D.Phil. It was called "Abelard, Nietzsche, Sade, and Beckett", which gives you some idea of the difficulties he was running into.'

Does it? thought Eleanor.

'Really, people will stop at nothing to get a doctorate these days.' Victor was warming up for the role he felt was required of him during dinner.

'But how did *your* writing go today?' asked Eleanor. 'I've been thinking all day of you taking a non-psychological approach to identity,' she lied. 'Have I got that right?'

'Absolutely,' said Victor. 'Indeed, I was so haunted by your remark, that if anything is in the mind it's who you are, that I was unable to think of anything else.'

Eleanor blushed. She felt she was being mocked. 'It sounds to me as if Eleanor is quite right,' said Nicholas gallantly. 'How can you separate who we are from who we think we are?'

'Oh, I dare say you can't,' replied Victor, 'once you have decided to consider things in that fashion. But I'm not attempting psychoanalysis, an activity, incidentally, which will seem as quaint as medieval map-making when we have an accurate picture of how the brain works.'

'Nothing a don likes more than bashing another chap's discipline,' said Nicholas, afraid that Victor was going to be a crashing bore during dinner.

'If you can call it a discipline,' chuckled Victor. 'The Unconscious, which we can only discuss when it *ceases* to be unconscious, is another medieval instrument of enquiry which enables the analyst to treat denial as evidence of its opposite. Under these rules we hang a man who denies that he is a murderer, and congratulate him if he says he is one.'

'Are you rejecting the idea that there is an unconscious?' said Anne.

'Are you rejecting the idea that there is an unconscious?' simpered Nicholas to himself in his hysterical American female voice.

'I am saying,' said Victor, 'that if we are controlled by forces we do not understand, the term for that state of affairs is ignorance. What I object to is that we turn ignorance into an inner landscape and pretend that this allegorical enterprise, which might be harmless or even charming, if it weren't so expensive and influential, amounts to a science.'

'But it helps people,' said Anne.

'Ah, the therapeutic promise,' said Victor wisely.

Standing in the doorway, David had been observing them for some time, unnoticed by anyone, except Eleanor.

'Oh, hello, David,' said Victor.

'Hi,' said Anne.

'My dear, so lovely to see you as always,' David answered, turning away from her instantly and saying to Victor, 'Do tell us more about the therapeutic promise.'

'But why don't *you* tell us?' said Victor. 'You're the doctor.'

'In my rather brief medical practice,' said David modestly, 'I found that people spend their whole lives imagining they are about to die. Their only consolation is that one day they're right. All that stands between them and this mental torture is a doctor's authority. And that is the only therapeutic promise that works.'

Nicholas was relieved to be ignored by David, whereas Anne watched with detachment the theatrical way the man set about dominating the room. Like a slave in a swamp full of bloodhounds, Eleanor longed to disappear and she cowered still closer to the screen.

David strode majestically across the room, sat in the Doge's chair and leaned towards Anne. 'Tell me, my dear,' he said, giving a little tug on the stiff silk of his dark-red trousers and crossing his legs, 'have you recovered from your quite unnecessary sacrifice, in going to the airport with Eleanor?'

'It wasn't a sacrifice, it was a pleasure,' said Anne innocently.

'And that reminds me, I've also had the pleasure of bringing back *The Twelve Caesars*. What I mean is that I had the pleasure of reading it and now you have the pleasure of getting it back.'

'So much pleasure in one day,' said David, letting one of the yellow slippers dangle from his foot.

'Right,' said Anne. 'Our cup overfloweth.'

'I've had a delightful day as well,' said David, 'there must be magic in the air.'

Nicholas glimpsed an opportunity to join the conversation without provoking David. 'So what did you think of *The Twelve Caesars*?' he asked Anne.

'Together they would have made a great jury,' said Anne, 'if you like your trials fast.' She turned her thumb towards the floor.

David let out an abrupt, 'Ha,' which showed he was amused. 'They'd have to take turns,' he said, pointing his thumbs down too.

'Absolutely,' said Anne. 'Imagine what would happen if they tried to choose a foreman.'

'And think of the Imperial Thumbache,' said David, twisting his aching thumbs up and down with childish enjoyment.

This happy vein of fantasy was interrupted by Bridget's return. After talking to Barry on the phone, Bridget had smoked another little joint and the colours around her had become very vivid. '*Love* those kinky yellow slippers,' she said to David brightly.

Nicholas winced.

'Do you really like them?' asked David, fixing her genially. 'I'm so pleased.'

David knew intuitively that Bridget would be embarrassed by discussing her phone call, but he had no time to interrogate her now because Yvette came in to announce dinner.

Never mind, thought David, I can get her later. In the pursuit of knowledge, there was no point in killing the rabbit before one found out whether its eyes were allergic to shampoo, or its skin inflamed by mascara. It was ridiculous to 'break a butterfly upon a wheel'. The proper instrument for a butterfly was a pin. Stimulated by these consoling thoughts, David rose from his chair and said expansively, 'Let's have dinner.'

Disturbed by a draught from the opening door, the candles in the dining room flickered and animated the painted panels around the walls. A procession of grateful peasants, much appreciated by David, edged a little further along the twisting road that led to the castle gates, only to slip back again as the flames shifted the other way. The wheels of a cart which had been stuck in a roadside ditch, seemed to creak forward, and for a moment the donkey pulling it swelled with dark new muscles.

On the table Yvette had laid out two bowls of rouille for the fish soup, and a sweating green bottle of Blanc de Blancs stood at either end of the table.

On the way from the drawing room to the dining room, Nicholas made one last attempt to extort some enthusiasm for his beleaguered anecdote. It now took place in the residence of the Prince et Princesse de Quelque Chose. 'Whoosh!' he shouted at Anne with an explosive gesture. 'The fifteenth-century tapestries burst into flame and their *hôtel particulier* BURNED TO THE GROUND. The reception had to be cancelled. There was a national scandal, and every bottle of Plantes Marines was banned *worldwide*.'

'As if it wasn't tough enough already being called Quelque Chose,' said Anne.

'But now you can't get it anywhere,' cried Nicholas, exhausted by his efforts.

'Sounds like the right decision. I mean, who wants their peculiar hotel burnt to the ground? Not me!'

Everyone waited to be seated and looked enquiringly at Eleanor. Although there seemed to be no room for doubt, with the women next to David and the men next to her and the couples mixed, she felt a dreadful conviction that she would make a mistake and unleash David's fury. Flustered, she stood there saying, 'Anne . . . would you . . . no, you go there . . . no, I'm sorry . . .'

'Thank God we're only six,' David said in a loud whisper to Nicholas. 'There's some chance she'll crack the problem before the soup gets cold.' Nicholas smirked obediently.

God, I hate grown-up dinner parties, thought Bridget, as Yvette brought in the steaming soup.

'Tell me, my dear, what did you make of the Emperor Galba?' said David to Anne, leaning courteously towards her, to emphasize his indifference to Bridget.

This was the line that Anne had hoped the conversation would not take. Who? she thought, but said, 'Ah, what a character! What *really* interested me, though, was the character of Caligula. Why do you think he was so obsessed with his sisters?'

'Well, you know what they say,' David grinned, 'vice is nice, but incest is best.'

'But what . . .' asked Anne, pretending to be fascinated, 'what's the psychology of a situation like that? Was it a kind of narcissism? The nearest thing to seducing himself?'

'More, I think, the conviction that only a member of his own family could have suffered as he had done. You know, of course, that Tiberius killed almost all of their relations, and so he and Drusilla were survivors of the same terror. Only she could really understand him.'

As David paused to drink some wine, Anne resumed her impersonation of an eager student. 'Something else I'd love to know is why Caligula thought that torturing his wife would reveal the reason he was so devoted to her?'

'To discover witchcraft was the official explanation, but presumably he was suspicious of affection which was divorced from the threat of death.'

'And, on a larger scale, he had the same suspicion about Roman people. Right?' asked Anne.

'Up to a point, Lord Copper,' said David. He looked as if there were things he knew, but would never divulge. So these were the benefits of a classical education, thought Anne, who had often heard David and Victor talk about them.

Victor had been eating his soup silently and very fast while Nicholas told him about Jonathan Croyden's memorial service. Eleanor had abandoned her soup and lit a cigarette; the extra Dexedrine had put her off her food. Bridget day-dreamed resolutely.

'I'm afraid I don't approve of memorial services,' said Victor, pursing his lips for a moment to savour the insincerity of what he was about to say, 'they are just excuses for a party.'

'What's wrong with them,' David corrected him, 'is that they are excuses for such bad parties. I suppose you were talking about Croyden.'

'That's right,' said Victor. 'They say he spoke better than he wrote. There was certainly room for improvement.'

David bared his teeth to acknowledge this little malice. 'Did Nicholas tell you that your friend Vijay was there?'

'No,' said Victor.

'Oh,' said David, turning to Anne persuasively, 'and you never told us why he left so suddenly.' Anne had refused to answer this question on several occasions, and David liked to tease her by bringing it up whenever they met.

'Didn't I?' said Anne, playing along.

'He wasn't incontinent?' asked David.

'No,' said Anne.

'Or worse, in his case, flirtatious?'

'Absolutely not.'

'He was just being himself,' Nicholas suggested.

'That might have done it,' said Anne, 'but it was more than that.'

'The desire to pass on information is like a hunger, and sometimes it is the curiosity, sometimes the indifference, of others that arouses it,' said Victor pompously.

'OK, OK,' said Anne, to save Victor from the silence that might well follow his pronouncement. 'Now it's not going to seem like that big a deal to you sophisticated types,' she added demurely. 'But when I took a clean shirt of his up to his room, I found a bunch of terrible magazines. Not just pornography, much much worse. Of course I wasn't going to ask him to leave. What he reads is his own affair, but he came back and was so rude about my being in his room, when I was only there to take back his lousy shirt, that I kind of lost my temper.'

'Good for you,' said Eleanor timidly.

'What sort of magazines exactly?' asked Nicholas, sitting back and crossing his legs.

'I wish you'd confiscated them,' giggled Bridget.

'Oh, just awful,' said Anne. 'Crucifixion. All kinds of animal stuff.'

'God, how hilarious,' said Nicholas. 'Vijay rises in my estimation.'

'Oh, yeah?' said Anne. 'Well, you should have seen the look on the poor pig's face.'

Victor was a little uneasy. 'The obscure ethics of our relations to the animal kingdom,' he chuckled.

'We kill them when we feel like it,' said David crisply, 'nothing very obscure about that.'

'Ethics is not the study of what we do, my dear David, but what we ought to do,' said Victor.

'That's why it's such a waste of time, old boy,' said Nicholas cheerfully.

'Why do you think it's superior to be amoral?' Anne asked Nicholas.

'It's not a question of being superior,' he said, exposing his cavernous nostrils to Anne, 'it just springs from a desire not to be a bore or a prig.'

'Everything about Nicholas is superior,' said David, 'and even if he *were* a bore or a prig, I'm sure he would be a superior one.'

'Thank you, David,' said Nicholas with determined complacency.

'Only in the English language,' said Victor, 'can one be "a bore", like being a lawyer or a pastry cook, making boredom into a profession – in other languages a person is simply boring, a temporary state of affairs. The question is, I suppose, whether this points to a greater intolerance towards boring people, or an especially intense quality of boredom among the English.'

It's because you're such a bunch of boring old farts, thought Bridget.

Yvette took away the soup plates and closed the door behind her. The candles flickered, and the painted peasants came alive again for a moment.

'What one aims for,' said David, 'is ennui.'

'Of course,' said Anne, 'it's more than just French for our old friend boredom. It's boredom plus money, or boredom plus arrogance. It's I-find-everything-boring, therefore I'm fascinating. But it doesn't seem to occur to people that you can't have a world picture and then not be part of it.'

There was a moment of silence while Yvette came back carrying a large platter of roast veal and vegetables.

'Darling,' said David to Eleanor, 'what a marvellous memory you have to be able to duplicate the dinner you gave Anne and Victor last time they were here.'

'Oh, God, how awful,' said Eleanor. 'I'm so sorry.'

'Talking of animal ethics,' said Nicholas, 'I gather that Gerald Frogmore shot more birds last year than anyone in England. Not bad for a chap in a wheelchair.'

'Maybe he doesn't like to see things move about freely,' said Anne. She immediately felt the excitement of half wishing she had not made this remark.

'You're not anti-blood sports?' asked Nicholas, with an unspoken 'on top of everything else'.

'How could I be?' asked Anne. 'It's a middle-class prejudice based on envy. Have I got that right?'

'Well, I wasn't going to say so,' said Nicholas, 'but you put it so much better than I could possibly hope to . . .'

'Do you despise people from the middle classes?' Anne asked.

'I don't despise people *from* the middle classes, on the contrary, the further from them, the better,' said Nicholas, shooting one of his cuffs. 'It's people *in* the middle classes that disgust me.'

'Can middle-class people be from the middle class in your sense?'

'Oh, yes,' said Nicholas generously, 'Victor is an outstanding case.'

Victor smiled to show that he was enjoying himself.

'It's easier for girls, of course,' Nicholas continued. 'Marriage is such a blessing, hoisting women from dreary backgrounds into a wider world.' He glanced at Bridget. 'All a chap can really do, unless he's the sort of queer who spends his whole time writing postcards to people who might need a spare man, is to toe the line. And be thoroughly charming and well informed,' he added, with a reassuring smile for Victor.

'Nicholas, of course, is an expert,' David intervened, 'having personally raised several women from the gutter.'

'At considerable expense,' Nicholas agreed.

'The cost of being dragged into the gutter was even higher, wouldn't you say, Nicholas?' said David, reminding Nicholas of his political humiliation. 'Either way, the gutter seems to be where you feel at home.'

'Cor blimey, guv,' said Nicholas in his comical cockney voice. 'When you've gorn down the drain like wot I 'ave, the gutter looks like a bed o' roses.'

Eleanor still found it inexplicable that the best English manners contained such a high proportion of outright rudeness and gladiatorial combat. She knew that David abused this licence, but she also knew how 'boring' it was to interfere with the exercise of unkindness. When David reminded someone of their weaknesses and failures she was torn between a desire to save the victim, whose feelings she adopted as her own, and an equally strong desire not to be accused of spoiling a game. The more she thought about this conflict, the more tightly it trapped her. She would never know what to say because whatever she said would be wrong.

Eleanor thought about her stepfather barking at her mother across the wastes of English silver, French furniture, and Chinese vases that helped to prevent him from becoming physically violent. This dwarfish and impotent French duke had dedicated his life to the idea that civilization had died in 1789. He nonetheless accepted a ten per cent cut from the dealers who sold pre-revolutionary antiques to his wife. He had forced Mary to sell her mother's Monets and Bonnards on the ground that they were examples of a decadent art that would never really matter. To him, Mary was the least valuable object in the fastidious museums they inhabited, and when eventually he bullied her to death he felt that he had eliminated the last trace of modernity from his life except, of course, for the enormous income that now came to him from the sales of a dry-cleaning fluid made in Ohio.

Eleanor had watched her mother's persecution with the

same vivid silence as she experienced in the face of her own gradual disintegration tonight. Although she was not a cruel person, she remembered being helpless with laughter watching her stepfather, by then suffering from Parkinson's disease, lift a forkful of peas, only to find the fork empty by the time it reached his mouth. Yet she had never told him how much she hated him. She had not spoken then, and she would not speak now.

'Look at Eleanor,' said David, 'she has that expression she only puts on when she is thinking of her dear rich dead mother. I'm right, aren't I, darling?' he cajoled her. 'Aren't I?'

'Yes, you are,' she admitted.

'Eleanor's mother and aunt,' said David in the tone of a man reading *Little Red Riding Hood* to a gullible child, 'thought that they could buy human antiques. The moth-eaten bearers of ancient titles were reupholstered with thick wads of dollars, but,' he concluded with a warm banality which could not altogether conceal his humorous intentions, 'you just can't treat human beings like things.'

'Definitely,' said Bridget, amazed to hear herself speak.

'You agree with me?' said David, suddenly attentive.

'Definitely,' said Bridget, who appeared to have broken her silence on somewhat limited terms.

'Maybe the human antiques wanted to be bought,' Anne suggested.

'Nobody doubts that,' said David, 'I'm sure they were licking the windowpane. What's so shocking is that after being saved, they dared to rear up on their spindly Louis Quinze legs and start giving orders. The *ingratitude*!'

'Cor!' said Nicholas. 'Wot I wouldn't give for some o' 'em Looey Can's legs – they must be wurf a bob or two.'

Victor was embarrassed on Eleanor's behalf. After all, she was paying for dinner.

Bridget was confused by David. She agreed wholeheartedly

with what he had said about people not being things. In fact, once she'd been tripping and had realized with overwhelming clarity that what was wrong with the world was people treating each other like things. It was such a big idea that it was hard to hold on to, but she had felt very strongly about it at the time, and she thought David was trying to say the same thing. She also admired him for being the only person who frightened Nicholas. On the other hand, she could see why he frightened Nicholas.

Anne had had enough. She felt a combination of boredom and rebelliousness which reminded her of adolescence. She could take no more of David's mood, and the way he baited Eleanor, tormented Nicholas, silenced Bridget, and even diminished Victor.

'Sorry,' she murmured to Eleanor, 'I'll be right back.'

In the dim hallway, she pulled a cigarette out of her bag and lit it. The flaming match was reflected in all the mirrors around the hall, and made a sliver of glass shine momentarily at the foot of the stairs. Stooping down to pick up the glass with the tip of her index finger, Anne suddenly knew that she was being watched and, looking up, she saw Patrick sitting on the widest step where the staircase curved. He wore flannel pyjamas with blue elephants on them, but his face looked downcast.

'Hi, Patrick,' said Anne, 'you look so grim. Can't you get to sleep?'

He did not answer or move. 'I just have to get rid of this piece of glass,' said Anne. 'I guess something broke here earlier?'

'It was me,' said Patrick.

'Hang on one second,' she said.

She's lying, thought Patrick, she won't come back.

There was no wastepaper basket in the hall, but she

brushed the glass off her finger into a porcelain umbrella stand that bristled with David's collection of exotic canes.

She hurried back to Patrick and sat on the step beneath him. 'Did you cut yourself on that glass?' she asked tenderly, putting her hand on his arm.

He pulled away from her and said, 'Leave me alone.'

'Do you want me to get your mother?' asked Anne.

'All right,' said Patrick.

'OK. I'll go get her right away,' said Anne. Back in the dining room, she heard Nicholas saying to Victor, 'David and I were meaning to ask you before dinner whether John Locke really said that a man who forgot his crimes should not be punished for them.'

'Yes, indeed,' said Victor. 'He maintained that personal identity depended on continuity of memory. In the case of a forgotten crime one would be punishing the wrong person.'

'I'll drink to that,' said Nicholas.

Anne leaned over to Eleanor and said to her quietly, 'I think you ought to go and see Patrick. He was sitting on the stairs asking for you.'

'Thank you,' whispered Eleanor.

'Perhaps it should be the other way round,' said David. 'A man who remembers his crimes can usually be relied upon to punish himself, whereas the law should punish the person who is irresponsible enough to forget.'

'D'you believe in capital punishment?' piped up Bridget.

'Not since it ceased to be a public occasion,' said David. 'In the eighteenth century a hanging was a really good day's outing.'

'Everybody enjoyed themselves: even the man who was being hanged,' added Nicholas.

'Fun for all the family,' David went on. 'Isn't that the phrase everybody uses nowadays? God knows, it's always what *I* aim for, but an occasional trip to Tyburn must have made the task easier.'

Nicholas giggled. Bridget wondered what Tyburn was. Eleanor smiled feebly, and pushed her chair back.

'Not leaving us I hope, darling,' said David.

'I have to . . . I'll be back in a moment,' Eleanor mumbled.

'I didn't quite catch that: you have to be back in a moment?'

'There's something I have to do.'

'Well, hurry, hurry, hurry,' said David gallantly, 'we'll be lost without your conversation.'

Eleanor walked to the door at the same time as Yvette opened it carrying a silver coffee pot.

'I found Patrick on the stairs,' Anne said. 'He seemed kind of sad.'

David's eyes darted towards Eleanor's back as she slipped past Yvette. 'Darling,' he said, and then more peremptorily, 'Eleanor.'

She turned, her teeth locked onto a thumbnail, trying to get a grip that would hold. She often tore at the stunted nails when she was not smoking. 'Yes?' she said.

'I thought that we'd agreed that you wouldn't rush to Patrick each time he whines and blubbers.'

'But he fell down earlier and he may have hurt himself.'

'In that case,' said David with sudden seriousness, 'he may need a doctor.' He rested the palms of his hands on the top of the table, as if to rise.

'Oh, I don't think he's hurt,' said Anne, to restrain David. She had a strong feeling that she would not be keeping her promise to Patrick if she sent him his father rather than his mother. 'He just wants to be comforted.'

'You see, darling,' said David, 'he isn't hurt, and so it is just a sentimental question: does one indulge the self-pity of a child, or not? Does one allow oneself to be blackmailed, or not? Come and sit down – we can at least discuss it.'

Eleanor edged her way back to her chair reluctantly. She knew she would be pinned down by a conversation that would defeat her, but not persuade her.

'The proposition I want to make,' said David, 'is that education should be something of which a child can later say: if I survived that, I can survive anything.'

'That's crazy and wrong,' said Anne, 'and you know it.'

'I certainly think that children should be stretched to the limit of their abilities,' said Victor, 'but I'm equally certain they can't be if they're intensely miserable.'

'Nobody wants to make anybody miserable,' said Nicholas, puffing out his cheeks incredulously. 'We're just saying that it doesn't do the child any good to be molly-coddled. I may be a frightful reactionary, but I think that all you have to do for children is hire a reasonable nanny and put them down for Eton.'

'What, the nannies?' said Bridget giggling. 'Anyway, what if you have a girl?'

Nicholas looked at her sternly.

'I guess that putting things down is your speciality,' said Anne to Nicholas.

'Oh, I know it's an unfashionable view to hold these days,' Nicholas went on complacently, 'but in my opinion nothing that happens to you as a child really matters.'

'If we're getting down to things that don't really matter,' said Anne, 'you're top of my list.'

'Oh, my word,' said Nicholas, in his sports commentator's voice, 'a ferocious backhand from the young American woman, but the line judge rules it out.'

'From what you've told me,' said Bridget, still elated by the thought of nannies in tailcoats, 'nothing much that happened in *your* childhood did matter: you just did what everyone expected.' Feeling a vague pressure on her right thigh, she glanced round at David, but he seemed to be staring ahead, organizing a sceptical expression on his face. The pressure stopped. On her other side, Victor peeled a nectarine with hurried precision.

'It's true,' said Nicholas, making a visible effort at equanimity, 'that my childhood was uneventful. People never remember happiness with the care that they lavish on preserving every detail of their suffering. I remember stroking my cheek against the velvet collar of my overcoat. Asking my grandfather for pennies to throw into that golden pool at the Ritz. Big lawns. Buckets and spades. That sort of thing.'

Bridget could not concentrate on what Nicholas was saying. She felt cold metal against her knee. Looking down, she saw David lifting the edge of her dress with a small silver knife and running it along her thigh. What the fuck did he think he was doing? She frowned at him reproachfully. He merely pressed the point a little more firmly into her thigh, without looking at her.

Victor wiped the tips of his fingers with his napkin, while answering a question which Bridget had missed. He sounded a little bored and not surprisingly, when she heard what he had to say. 'Certainly if the degree of psychological connectedness and psychological continuity have become sufficiently weakened, it would be true to say that a person should look upon his childhood with no more than charitable curiosity.'

Bridget's mind flashed back to her father's foolish conjuring tricks, and her mother's ghastly floral-print dresses, but charitable curiosity was not what she felt.

'Would you like one of these?' said David, lifting a fig from the bowl in the middle of the table. 'They're at their best at this time of year.'

'No, thanks,' she said.

David pinched the fig firmly between his fingers and

pushed it towards Bridget's mouth, 'Come on,' he said, 'I know how much you like them.'

Bridget opened her mouth obediently and took the fig between her teeth. She blushed because the table had fallen silent and she knew that everyone was watching her. As soon as she could she took the fig from her mouth and asked David if she could borrow his knife to peel it with. David admired her for the speed and stealth of this tactic and handed over the knife.

Eleanor watched Bridget take the fig with a familiar sense of doom. She could never see David impose his will on anyone without considering how often he had imposed it on her.

At the root of her dread was the fragmented memory of the night when Patrick was conceived. Against her will, she pictured the Cornish house on its narrow headland, always damp, always grey, more Atlantic than earth. He had pushed the hollow base of her skull against the corner of the marble table. When she had broken free he had punched the back of her knees and made her fall on the stairs and raped her there, with her arms twisted back. She had hated him like a stranger and hated him like a traitor. God, how she had loathed him, but when she had become pregnant she had said she would stay if he never, *never* touched her again.

Bridget chewed the fig unenthusiastically. As Anne watched her, she could not help thinking of the age-old question which every woman asks herself at some time or other: do I have to swallow it? She wondered whether to picture Bridget as a collared slave draped over the feet of an oriental bully, or as a rebellious schoolgirl being forced to eat the apple pie she tried to leave behind at lunch. She suddenly felt quite detached from the company around her.

Nicholas struck Anne as more pathetic than he had before. He was just one of those Englishmen who was always saying silly things to sound less pompous, and pompous things to sound less silly. They turned into self-parodies without going to the trouble of acquiring a self first. David, who thought he was the Creature from the Black Lagoon, was just a higher species of this involuted failure. She looked at Victor slumped round-shouldered over the remains of his nectarine. He had not kept up the half-clever banter which he usually felt it his duty to provide. She could remember him earlier in the summer saying, 'I may spend my days doubting doubting, but when it comes to gossip I like *hard* facts.' From then on it had been nothing but hard facts. Today he was different. Perhaps he really wanted to do some work again.

Eleanor's crushed expression no longer moved her either. The only thing that made Anne's detachment falter was the thought of Patrick waiting on the stairs, his disappointment widening as he waited, but it only spurred her on to the same conclusion: that she wanted nothing more to do with these people, that it was time to leave, even if Victor would be embarrassed by leaving early. She looked over to Victor, raising her eyebrows and darting her eyes towards the door. Instead of the little frown she had expected from him, Victor nodded his head discreetly as if agreeing with the pepper mill. Anne let a few moments go by then leaned over to Eleanor and said, 'It's sad, but I think we really must leave. It's been a long day, you must be tired too.'

'Yes,' said Victor firmly, 'I must get up early tomorrow morning and make some progress with my work.' He heaved himself up and started to thank Eleanor and David before they had time to organize the usual protests.

In fact, David hardly looked up. He continued to run his thumbnail around the sealed end of his cigar, 'You know the way out,' he said, in response to their thanks, 'I hope you'll forgive me for not coming to wave goodbye.'

'Never,' said Anne, more seriously than she had intended.

Eleanor knew there was a formula everybody used in

these situations, but she searched for it in vain. Whenever she thought of what she was meant to say, it seemed to dash around the corner, and lose itself in the crowd of things she should not say. The most successful fugitives were often the dullest, the sentences that nobody notices until they are not spoken: 'How nice to see you . . . won't you stay a little longer . . . what a good idea . . .'

Victor closed the dining room door behind him carefully, like a man who does not want to wake a sleeping sentry. He smiled at Anne and she smiled back, and they were suddenly conscious of how relieved they were to be leaving the Melroses. They started to laugh silently and to tiptoe towards the hall.

'I'll just check if Patrick is still here,' Anne whispered.

'Why are we whispering?' Victor whispered.

'I don't know,' Anne whispered back. She looked up the staircase. It was empty. He had obviously grown tired of waiting and gone back to bed. 'I guess he's asleep,' she said to Victor.

They went out of the front door and up the wide steps towards their car. The moon was bruised by thin cloud and surrounded by a ring of dispersed light.

'You can't say I didn't try,' said Anne, 'I was hanging right in there until Nicholas and David started outlining their educational programme. If some big-deal friend of theirs, like George, was feeling sad and lonely they would fly back to England and *personally* mix the dry martinis and load the shotguns, but when David's own son is feeling sad and lonely in the room next door, they fight every attempt to make him less miserable.'

'You're right,' said Victor, opening the car door, 'in the end one must oppose cruelty, at the very least by refusing to take part in it.'

'Underneath that New and Lingwood shirt,' said Anne, 'beats a heart of gold.'

Must you leave so soon? thought Eleanor. *That* was the phrase. She had remembered it. Better late than never was another phrase, not really true in this case. Sometimes things were too late, too late the very moment they happened. Other people knew what they were meant to say, knew what they were meant to mean, and other people still – otherer people – knew what the other people meant when they said it. God, she was drunk. When her eyes watered, the candle flames looked like a liqueur advertisement, splintering into mahogany-coloured spines of light. Not drunk enough to stop the half-thoughts from sputtering on into the night, keeping her from any rest. Maybe she could go to Patrick now. Whatshername had slipped off cunningly just after Victor and Anne left. Maybe they would let her go too. But what if they didn't? She could not stand another failure, she could not bow down another time. And so she did nothing for a little longer.

'If nothing matters, you're top of my list,' Nicholas quoted, with a little yelp of delight. 'One has to admire Victor, who tries so hard to be conventional, for never having an entirely conventional girlfriend.'

'Almost nothing is as entertaining as the contortions of a clever Jewish snob,' said David.

'Very broad-minded of you to have him in your house,' said Nicholas, in his judge's voice. 'Some members of the jury may feel that it is *too* broad-minded, but that is not for me to say,' he boomed, adjusting an imaginary wig. 'The openness of English society has always been its great strength: the entrepreneurs and arrivistes of yesterday – the Cecils, for example – become the guardians of stability in a mere three or four hundred years. Nevertheless, there is no principle, however laudable in itself, which cannot be perverted. Whether the openness and the generosity of what the press chooses to call "the establishment" has been abused on this occasion, by welcoming into its midst a dangerous intellectual of murky Semitic origins is for you, and for you alone, to judge.'

David grinned. He was in the mood for fun. After all, what redeemed life from complete horror was the almost unlimited number of things to be nasty about. All he needed now was to ditch Eleanor, who was twitching silently like a beetle on its back, get a bottle of brandy, and settle down to gossip with Nicholas. It was too perfect. 'Let's go into the drawing room,' he said.

'Fine,' said Nicholas, who knew that he had won David over and did not want to lose this privilege by paying any attention to Eleanor. He got up, drained his glass of wine, and followed David to the drawing room.

Eleanor remained frozen in her chair, unable to believe how lucky she was to be completely alone. Her mind rushed ahead to a tender reconciliation with Patrick, but she stayed slumped in front of the debris of dinner. The door opened and Eleanor jumped. It was only Yvette.

'*Oh, pardon, Madame, je ne savais pas que vous étiez toujours là.*'

'*Non, non, je vais justement partir,*' said Eleanor apologetically. She went through the kitchen and up the back stairs to avoid Nicholas and David, walking the whole length of the corridor to see whether Patrick was still waiting for her on the staircase. He was not there. Instead of being grateful that he had already gone to bed, she felt even more guilty that she had not come to console him earlier.

She opened the door to his room gently, excruciated by the whining of the hinge. Patrick was asleep in his bed. Rather than disturb him, she tiptoed back out of the room.

Patrick lay awake. His heart was pounding. He knew it was his mother, but she had come too late. He would not call to her again. When he had still been waiting on the stairs and the door of the hall opened, he stayed to see if it was his mother, and he hid in case it was his father. But it was only that woman who had lied to him. Everybody used his name but they did not know who he was. One day he would play football with the heads of his enemies.

Who the fuck did he think he was? How dare he poke a knife up her dress? Bridget pictured herself strangling David as he sat in his dining-room chair, her thumbs pressing into his windpipe. And then, confusingly, she imagined that she had fallen into his lap, while she was strangling him, and she could feel that he had a huge erection. 'Gross out,' she said aloud, 'totally gross.' At least David was intense, intensely gross, but intense. Unlike Nicholas, who turned out to be a complete cringer, really pathetic. And the others were so boring. How was she meant to spend another second in this house?

Bridget wanted a joint to take the edge off her indignation. She opened her suitcase and took a plastic bag out of the toe of her back-up pair of cowboy boots. The bag contained some dark green grass that she had already taken the seeds and stalks out of, and a packet of orange Rizlas. She sat down at an amusing Gothic desk fitted between the bedroom's two round windows. Sheaves of engraved writing paper were housed under its tallest arch, with envelopes in the smaller arches either side. On the desk's open flap was a black leather pad holding a large piece of blotting paper. She rolled a small joint above it and then brushed the escaped leaves carefully back into her bag.

Turning off the light to create a more ceremonial and private atmosphere, Bridget sat down in the curved windowsill and lit her joint. The moon had risen above the thin clouds and cast deep shadows on the terrace. She sucked a thick curl of smoke appreciatively into her lungs and held it in, noticing how the dull glow of the fig leaves made them look as if they were cut out of old pewter. As she blew the smoke slowly through the little holes in the mosquito net she heard the door open beneath her window.

'Why are blazers so common?' she heard Nicholas ask.

'Because they're worn by ghastly people like him,' David answered.

God, didn't they ever grow tired of bitching about people? thought Bridget. Or, at least, about people she didn't know. Or did she know him? With a little flash of shame and paranoia Bridget remembered that her father wore blazers. Perhaps they were trying to humiliate her. She held her breath and sat absolutely still. She could see them now, both smoking their cigars. They started to walk down the terrace, their conversation fading as they headed towards the far end. She took another toke on her joint; it had almost gone out, but she got it going again. The bastards were probably talking about her, but she might just be thinking that because she was stoned. Well, she *was* stoned and she did think that. Bridget smiled. She wished she had someone to be silly with. Licking her finger she doused down the side of the joint that was burning too fast. They were pacing back now and she could hear again what they were saying.

'I suppose I would have to answer that,' Nicholas said, 'with the remark that Croyden made – not quoted, incidentally, in his memorial service – when he was found emerging from a notorious public lavatory in Hackney.' Nicholas's voice rose an octave, '"I have pursued beauty wherever it has led me, even to the most unbeautiful places."'

'Not a bad policy,' said David, 'if a little fruitily expressed.'

12

When they got back home, Anne was in a good mood. She flopped down on the brown sofa, kicked off her shoes, and lit a cigarette. 'Everybody knows you've got a great mind,' she said to Victor, 'but what interests me is your slightly less well-known body.'

Victor laughed a little nervously and walked across the room to pour himself a glass of whisky. 'Reputation isn't everything,' he said.

'Come over here,' Anne ordered softly.

'Drink?' asked Victor.

Anne shook her head. She watched Victor drop a couple of ice cubes into his glass.

He walked over to the sofa and sat down beside her, smiling benignly.

When she leaned forward to kiss him, he fished one of the ice cubes out of the glass and, with unexpected swiftness, slipped it down the front of her dress.

'Oh, God,' gasped Anne, trying to keep her composure, 'that's deliciously cool and refreshing. And wet,' she added, wriggling and pushing the ice cube further down under her black dress.

Victor put his hand under her dress and retrieved the ice cube expertly, putting it in his mouth and sucking it before letting it slip from his mouth back into the glass. 'I thought you needed cooling off,' he said, putting his palms firmly on each of her knees.

'Oh, my,' Anne purred, in a southern drawl, 'despite outward appearances, I can see you're a man of strong appetites.' She lifted one of her feet onto the sofa and reached out her hand at the same time to run her fingers through the thick waves of Victor's hair. She pulled his head gently towards the stretched tendon of her raised thigh. Victor kissed the white cotton of her underwear and grazed it like a man catching a grape between his teeth.

Unable to sleep, Eleanor put on a Japanese dressing gown and retreated to her car. She felt strangely elated in the white leather interior of the Buick, with her packet of Player's and the bottle of cognac she retrieved from under the driving seat. Her happiness was complete when she turned on Radio Monte Carlo and found that it was playing one of her favourite songs: 'I Got Plenty o' Nuttin'' from *Porgy and Bess*. She mouthed the words silently, 'And nuttin's plenty for me,' dipping her head from side to side, almost in time with the music.

When she saw Bridget hobbling along in the moonlight with a suitcase banging against her knee, Eleanor thought, not for the first time, that she must be hallucinating. What on earth was the girl doing? Well, it was really very obvious. She was leaving. The simplicity of the act horrified Eleanor. After years of dreaming about how to tunnel under the guardroom undetected, she was amazed to see a newcomer walk out through the open gate. Just going down the drive as if she were free.

Bridget swung her suitcase from one hand to another. She wasn't sure it would fit on the back of Barry's bike. The whole thing was a total freakout. She had left Nicholas in bed, snoring as usual, like an old pig with terminal flu. The idea was to dump her suitcase at the bottom of the drive and go back to fetch it once she had met up with Barry. She swapped hands again. The lure of the Open Road definitely lost some of its appeal if you took any luggage with you.

Two-thirty by the village church, that's what Barry had said on the phone before dinner. She dropped her suitcase into a clump of rosemary, letting out a petulant sigh to show herself she was more irritated than frightened. What if the village didn't have a church? What if her suitcase was stolen? How far was it to the village anyway? God, life was so complicated. She had run away from home once when she was nine, but doubled back because she couldn't bear to think what her parents might say while she was away.

As she joined the small road that led down to the village, Bridget found herself walled in by pines. The shadows thickened until the moonlight no longer shone on the road. A light wind animated the branches of the tall trees. Full of dread, Bridget suddenly came to a stop. Was Barry really a fun person when it came down to it? After making their appointment he had said, 'Be there or be square!' At the time she was so infatuated by the idea of escaping Nicholas and the Melroses that she had forgotten to be annoyed, but now she realized just how annoying it was.

Eleanor was wondering whether to get another bottle of cognac (cognac was for the car because it was so stimulating), or go back to bed and drink whisky. Either way she had to return to the house. When she was about to open the car door she saw Bridget again. This time she was staggering up the drive, dragging her suitcase. Eleanor felt cool and detached. She decided that nothing could surprise her any longer. Perhaps Bridget did this every evening for the exercise. Or maybe she wanted a lift somewhere. Eleanor preferred to watch her than to get involved, so long as Bridget got back into the house quickly.

Bridget thought she heard the sound of a radio, but she lost it again amid the rustle of leaves. She was shaken and rather embarrassed by her escapade. Plus her arms were about to drop off. Well, never mind, at least she had asserted herself, sort of. She opened the door of the house. It squeaked. Luckily, she could rely on Nicholas to be sleeping like a drugged elephant, so that no sound could possibly reach him. But what if she woke David? *Freak-ee*. Another squeak and she closed the door behind her. As she crept down the corridor she could hear a sort of moaning and then a yelping shout, like a cry of pain.

David woke up with a shout of fear. Why the hell did people say, 'It's *only* a dream'? His dreams exhausted and dismembered him. They seemed to open onto a deeper layer of insomnia, as if he was only lulled to sleep in order to be shown that he could not rest. Tonight he had dreamed that he was the cripple in Athens airport. He could feel his limbs twisted like vine stumps, his wobbling head burrowing this way and that as he tried to throw himself forward, and his unfriendly hands slapping his own face. In the waiting room at the airport all the passengers were people he knew: the barman from the Central in Lacoste, George, Bridget, people from decades of London parties, all talking and reading books. And there he was, heaving himself across the room one leg dragging behind him, trying to say, 'Hello, it's David Melrose, I hope you aren't deceived by this absurd disguise,' but he only managed to moan, or as he grew more desperate, to squeal, while he tossed advertisements for roasted nuts at them with upsetting inaccuracy. He could see the embarrassment in some of their faces, and feigned blankness in others. And he heard George say to his neighbour, 'What a perfectly ghastly man.'

David turned on the light and fumbled for his copy of *Jorrocks Rides Again*. He wondered whether Patrick would remember. There was always repression, of course, although it didn't seem to work very well on his own desires. He must *try* not to do it again, that really would be tempting fate. David could not help smiling at his own audacity.

Patrick did not wake up from his dream, although he could feel a needle slip under his shoulder blade and push out through his chest. The thick thread was sewing his lungs up like an old sack until he could not breathe. Panic like wasps hovering about his face, ducking and twisting and beating the air.

He saw the Alsatian that had chased him in the woods, and he felt he was running through the rattling yellow leaves again with wider and wider strides. As the dog drew closer and was about to get him, Patrick started adding up numbers out loud, and at the last moment his body lifted off the ground until he was looking down on the tops of the trees, as if at seaweed over the side of a boat. He knew that he must never allow himself to fall asleep. Below him the Alsatian scrambled to a halt in a flurry of dry leaves and picked up a dead branch in its mouth.

BAD NEWS

For Dee

1

Patrick pretended to sleep, hoping the seat next to him would remain empty, but he soon heard a briefcase sliding into the overhead compartment. Opening his eyes reluctantly, he saw a tall snub-nosed man.

'Hi, I'm Earl Hammer,' said the man, extending a big freckled hand covered in thick blond hair, 'I guess I'm your seating companion.'

'Patrick Melrose,' said Patrick mechanically, offering a clammy and slightly shaking hand to Mr Hammer.

Early the previous evening, George Watford had telephoned Patrick from New York.

'Patrick, my dear,' he said in a strained and drawling voice, slightly delayed by its Atlantic crossing, 'I'm afraid I have the most awful news for you: your father died the night before last in his hotel room. I've been quite unable to get hold of either you or your mother – I believe she's in Chad with the Save the Children Fund – but I need hardly tell you how I feel; I adored your father, as you know. Oddly enough, he was supposed to be having lunch with me at the Key Club on the day that he died, but of course he never turned up; I remember thinking how unlike him it was. It must be the most awful shock for you. Everybody liked him, you know, Patrick. I've told some of the members there and some of the servants, and they were *very* sorry to hear about his death.'

'Where is he now?' asked Patrick coldly.

'At Frank E. MacDonald's in Madison Avenue: it's the place everyone uses over here, I believe it's awfully good.'

Patrick promised that as soon as he arrived in New York he would call George.

'I'm sorry to be the bringer of such bad news,' said George. 'You're going to need all your courage during this difficult time.'

'Thanks for calling,' said Patrick, 'I'll see you tomorrow.'

'Goodbye, my dear.'

Patrick put down the syringe he had been flushing out, and sat beside the phone without moving. Was it bad news? Perhaps he would need all his courage not to dance in the street, not to smile too broadly. Sunlight poured in through the blurred and caked windowpanes of his flat. Outside, in Ennismore Gardens, the leaves of the plane trees were painfully bright.

He suddenly leaped out of his chair. 'You're not going to get away with this,' he muttered vindictively. The sleeve of his shirt rolled forward and absorbed the trickle of blood on his arm.

'You know, Paddy,' said Earl, regardless of the fact that nobody called Patrick 'Paddy', 'I've made a hell of a lot of money, and I figured it was time to enjoy some of the good things in life.'

It was half an hour into the flight and Paddy was already Earl's good buddy.

'How sensible of you,' gasped Patrick.

'I've rented an apartment by the beach in Monte Carlo, and a house in the hills behind Monaco. *Just a beautiful house*,' said Earl, shaking his head incredulously. 'I've got an English butler: he tells me what sports jacket to wear –

can you believe that? And I've got the leisure time to read the *Wall Street Journal* from cover to cover.'

'A heady freedom,' said Patrick.

'It's *great*. And I'm also reading a real interesting book at the moment, called *Megatrends*. *And* a Chinese classic on the art of war. Are you interested in war at all?'

'Not madly,' said Patrick.

'I guess I'm biased: I was in Vietnam,' said Earl, staring at the horizon through the tiny window of the plane.

'You liked it?'

'Sure did,' Earl smiled.

'Didn't you have any reservations?'

'I'll tell you, Paddy, the only reservations I had about Vietnam were the target restrictions. Flying over some of those ports and seeing tankers deliver oil you *knew* was for the Viet Cong, and not being able to strike them – that was one of the most frustrating experiences of my life.' Earl, who seemed to be in an almost perpetual state of amazement at the things he said, shook his head again.

Patrick turned towards the aisle, suddenly assailed by the sound of his father's music, as clear and loud as breaking glass, but this aural hallucination was soon swamped by the vitality of his neighbour.

'Have you ever been to the Tahiti Club in St Tropez, Paddy? That's a hell of a place! I met a couple of dancers there.' His voice dropped half an octave to match the new tone of male camaraderie. 'I got to tell you,' he said confidentially, 'I love to screw. God, I *love* it,' he shouted. 'But a great body is not enough, you know what I mean? You gotta have that *mental thing*. I was screwing these two dancers: they were *fantastic* women, great bodies, just beautiful, but I couldn't come. You know why?'

'You didn't have that mental thing,' suggested Patrick.

'That's right! I didn't have that *mental thing*,' said Earl.

*

Perhaps it was that mental thing that was missing with Debbie. He had called her last night to tell her about his father's death.

'Oh, God, that's appalling,' she stammered, 'I'll come over straight away.'

Patrick could hear the nervous tension in Debbie's voice, the inherited anxiety about the correct thing to say. With parents like hers, it was not surprising that embarrassment had become the strongest emotion in her life. Debbie's father, an Australian painter called Peter Hickmann, was a notorious bore. Patrick once heard him introduce an anecdote with the words, 'That reminds me of my best bouillabaisse story.' Half an hour later, Patrick could only count himself lucky that he was not listening to Peter's second-best bouillabaisse story.

Debbie's mother, whose neurotic resources made her resemble a battery-operated stick insect, had social ambitions which were not in her power to fulfil while Peter stood at her side telling his bouillabaisse stories. A well-known professional party planner, she was foolish enough to take her own advice. The brittle perfection of her entertainments turned to dust when human beings were introduced into the airless arena of her drawing room. Like a mountaineer expiring at base camp, she passed on her boots to Debbie, and with them the awesome responsibility: *to climb*. Mrs Hickmann was inclined to forgive Patrick the apparent purposelessness of his life and the sinister pallor of his complexion, when she considered that he had an income of one hundred thousand pounds a year, and came from a family which, although it had done nothing since, had seen the Norman invasion from the winning side. It was not perfect, but it would do. After all, Patrick was only twenty-two.

Meanwhile, Peter continued to weave life into anecdote and to describe grand incidents in his daughter's life to the fast-emptying bar of the Travellers Club where, after forty years of stiff opposition, he had been elected in a moment of weakness which all the members who had since been irradiated by his conversation bitterly regretted.

After Patrick had discouraged Debbie from coming round to see him, he set out for a walk through Hyde Park, tears stinging his eyes. It was a hot dry evening, full of pollen and dust. Sweat trickled down his ribs and broke out on his forehead. Over the Serpentine, a wisp of cloud dissolved in front of the sun, which sank, swollen and red, through a bruise of pollution. On the scintillating water yellow and blue boats bobbed up and down. Patrick stood still and watched a police car drive very fast along the path behind the boathouses. He vowed he would take no more heroin. This was the most important moment in his life and he must get it right. He had to get it right.

Patrick lit a Turkish cigarette and asked the stewardess for another glass of brandy. He was beginning to feel a little jumpy without any smack. The four Valiums he had stolen from Kay had helped him face breakfast, but now he could feel the onset of withdrawal, like a litter of drowning kittens in the sack of his stomach.

Kay was the American girl he had been having an affair with. Last night when he had wanted to bury himself in a woman's body, to affirm that, unlike his father, he was alive, he had chosen to see Kay. Debbie was beautiful (everybody said so), and she was clever (she said so herself), but he could imagine her clicking anxiously across the room, like a pair of chopsticks, and just then he needed a softer embrace.

Kay lived in a rented flat on the outskirts of Oxford, where she played the violin, kept cats, and worked on her Kafka thesis. She took a less complacent attitude towards Patrick's idleness than anyone else he knew. 'You have to sell yourself,' she used to say, 'just to get rid of the damned thing.'

Patrick disliked everything about Kay's flat. He knew she had not put the gold cherubs against the William Morris-styled wallpaper; on the other hand, she had not taken them down. In the dark corridor, Kay had come up to him, her thick brown hair falling on one shoulder, and her body draped in heavy grey silk. She had kissed him slowly, while her jealous cats scratched at the kitchen door.

Patrick had drunk the whisky and taken the Valium she had given him. Kay told him about her own dying parents. 'You have to start looking after them badly before you've got over the shock of how badly they looked after you,' she said. 'I had to drive my parents across the States last summer. My dad was dying of emphysema and my mother, who used to be a ferocious woman, was like a child after her stroke. I was barrelling along at eighty through Utah, looking for a bottle of oxygen, while my mother kept saying with her impoverished vocabulary, "Oh dear, oh my, Papa's not well. Oh my." '

Patrick imagined Kay's father sunk in the back of the car, his eyes glazed over with exhaustion and his lungs, like torn fishing nets, trawling vainly for air. How had his own father died? He had forgotten to ask.

Since his luminous remarks about 'that mental thing', Earl had been speaking about his 'whole variety of holdings' and his love for his family. His divorce had been 'hard on the kids', but he concluded with a chuckle, 'I've been diversifying, and I don't just mean in the business field.'

Patrick was grateful to be flying on Concorde. Not only would he be fresh for the ordeal of seeing his father's corpse, before it was cremated the next day, but he was also halving his conversation time with Earl. They ought to advertise. A simpering voiceover popped into his mind: 'It's because we care, not just for your physical comfort, but for your mental health, that we shorten your conversation with people like Earl Hammer.'

'You see, Paddy,' said Earl, 'I've made very considerable – I mean *big* – contributions to the Republican Party, and I could get just about any embassy I want. But I'm not interested in London or Paris: that's just social shit.'

Patrick drank his brandy in one gulp.

'What I want is a small Latin American or Central American country where the ambassador has control of the CIA on the ground.'

'On the ground,' echoed Patrick.

'That's right,' said Earl. 'But I have a dilemma at this point; a real hard one.' He was solemn again. 'My daughter is trying to make the national volleyball team and she has a series of real important games over the next year. Hell, I don't know whether to go for the embassy or root for my daughter.'

'Earl,' said Patrick earnestly, 'I don't think there's anything more important than being a good dad.'

Earl was visibly moved. 'I appreciate that advice, Paddy, I really do.'

The flight was coming to an end. Earl made some remarks about how you always met 'high-quality' people on Concorde. At the airport terminal Earl took the US citizens' channel, and Patrick headed for the Aliens'.

'Goodbye, friend,' shouted Earl with a big wave, 'see you around!'

'Every parting,' snarled Patrick under his breath, 'is a little death.'

2

'What is the purpose of your visit, sir? Business or pleasure?'

'Neither.'

'I'm sorry?' She was a pear-shaped, slug-coloured, short-haired woman wearing big glasses and a dark blue uniform.

'I'm here to collect my father's corpse,' mumbled Patrick.

'I'm sorry, sir, I didn't catch that,' she said with official exasperation.

'*I'm here to collect my father's corpse,*' Patrick shouted slowly.

She handed back his passport. 'Have a nice day.'

The rage that Patrick had felt after passing through passport control eclipsed his usual terror of Customs (What if they stripped him? What if they saw his arms?).

And so here he was again, slumped in the back of a cab, in a seat often repaired with black masking tape, but still opening occasionally onto small craters of yellow foam, back in a nation that was dieting its way to immortality, while he still dieted his way in the opposite direction.

As his taxi bounced and squeaked along the freeway, Patrick started to register reluctantly the sensations of re-entry into New York. There was of course a driver who spoke no English, and whose lugubrious photograph confirmed the suicidal gloom which the back of his neck could only hint at. The neighbouring lanes bore witness to the usual combination of excess and decay. Enormous battered cars with sloppy engines, and black-windowed limos, swarmed into the city, like flies on their favourite food. Patrick stared at the dented hubcap of an old white station wagon. It had seen so much, he reflected, and remembered nothing, like a slick amnesiac reeling in thousands of images and rejecting them instantly, spinning out its empty life under a paler wider sky.

The thought that had obsessed him the night before cut into his trance. It was intolerable: his father had cheated him again. The bastard had deprived him of the chance to transform his ancient terror and his unwilling admiration into contemptuous pity for the boring and toothless old man he had become. And yet Patrick found himself sucked towards his father's death by a stronger habit of emulation than he could reasonably bear. Death was always, of course, a *temptation*; but now it seemed like a temptation to obey. On top of its power to strike a decadent or defiant posture in the endless vaudeville of youth, on top of the familiar lure of raw violence and self-destruction, it had taken on the aspect of conformity, like going into the family business. Really, it had all the options covered.

Acre after acre of tombstones stretched out beside the freeway. Patrick thought of his favourite lines of poetry: 'Dead, long dead, / Long dead!' (How could you beat that?) 'And my heart is a handful of dust, / And the wheels go over my head, / And my bones are shaken with pain, / For into a shallow grave they are thrust, / Only a yard beneath the street,' something, something, 'enough to drive one mad.'

The slippery humming metal of the Williamsburg Bridge reawakened him to his surroundings, but not for long. He felt queasy and nervous. Another withdrawal in a foreign hotel room; he knew the routine. Except that this was going to be the last time. Or *among* the last times. He laughed nervously. No, the bastards weren't going to get him. Concentration like a flamethrower. No prisoners!

The trouble was that he always wanted smack, like wanting to get out of a wheelchair when the room was on fire. If you thought about it that much you might as well take it. His right leg twitched up and down rapidly. He folded his arms across his stomach and pinched the collar of his overcoat together. 'Fuck off,' he said out loud, 'just fuck off.'

Into the gorgeous streets. Blocks of light and shadow. Down the avenue, lights turned green all the way. Light and shadow, ticking like a metronome, as they surged over the curve of the earth.

It was late May, it was hot, and he really ought to take off his overcoat, but his overcoat was his defence against the thin shards of glass that passers-by slipped casually under his skin, not to mention the slow-motion explosion of shop windows, the bone-rattling thunder of subway trains, and the heartbreaking passage of each second, like a grain of sand trickling through the hourglass of his body. No, he would not take off his overcoat. Do you ask a lobster to disrobe?

He glanced up and saw that he was on Sixth Avenue. Forty-second Street, Forty-third Street, row after Mies van der Rohe. Who had said that? He couldn't remember. Other people's words drifted through his mind, like the tumbleweed across a windy desert in the opening shots of *They Came from Outer Space*.

And what about all the characters who inhabited him, as if he was a cheap hotel: Gift o' the Gab O'Connor and the Fat Man, and Mrs Garsington, and all the rest of them, longing to push him aside and have their say. Sometimes he felt like a television on which somebody else was changing the channels impatiently and very fast. Well, they could just fuck off as well. This time he was going to fall apart *silently*.

They were getting near the Pierre now. The land of the static electric shock. Doorknobs and lift buttons spitting sparks at a body which had generated its way through miles of thick carpet before forgetting to earth itself. It was here that he had begun his delirious decline on his last visit to New York. From a suite with as much chinoiserie as a person could be expected to take, and a view of the Park from far above the cry of traffic, he had slipped down, via the world-famous seediness of the Chelsea Hotel, and landed in a coffin-sized room at the bottom of a garbage-filled well shaft on Eighth Street, between C and D. From this vantage he had looked back with nostalgia on the hotel he had despised only a few weeks earlier for having a rat in its fridge.

Still, throughout this decline in his accommodation, Patrick had never spent less than five thousand dollars a week on heroin and cocaine. Ninety per cent of the drugs were for him and ten per cent for Natasha, a woman who remained an impenetrable mystery to him during the six months they lived together. The only thing he felt certain about was that she irritated him; but then, who didn't? He continually longed for an uncontaminated solitude, and when he got it he longed for it to stop.

'Hotel,' said the driver.

'About fucking time,' mumbled Patrick.

A grey-coated doorman lifted his cap and held out his hand, while a bellboy hurried out to fetch Patrick's bags. One welcome and two tips later Patrick was stalking sweatily through the long corridor which led to the reception. The tables in the Oval Room were occupied by pairs of lunching women, toying with plates of different-coloured lettuces and ignoring glasses of mineral water. Patrick caught sight of himself in a large gilt mirror, and noticed that, as usual, he looked rather overdressed and extremely ill. There was a disturbing contrast between the care with which the clothes had been assembled and the ease with which the face looked as if it might fall apart. His very long black overcoat, dark blue suit, and thin black and silver tie (bought by his father in the early sixties) seemed to be unrelated to the chaotic tangle of brown hair which surrounded his dead-white and shiny face. The face itself was in a spasm of contradiction. The full lips were pinched inward, the eyes reduced to narrow slits, the nose, which was permanently blocked, forced him to breathe through his open mouth and made him look rather imbecilic; and a frown concentrated his forehead into a vertical crease directly above the nose.

After he had registered, Patrick braced himself to clear as quickly as possible the long gauntlet of welcomes and tips that still lay between him and having a drink in his room. Someone took him to the lift, someone took him up in the lift (that long stale suspense, watching the numbers flicker up to thirty-nine), someone showed him how to turn on the television, someone put his suitcase down on the rack, someone pointed out the bathroom light, someone gave him his room key, and, at last, someone brought him a bottle of Jack Daniel's and a black bucket of frail ice cubes, and four glasses.

He poured himself a full glass over a few cubes of ice. The smell of the bourbon seemed to him infinitely subtle and poignant, and as he gulped down the first burning mouthful, standing by the window, looking out over Central Park, leafy and hot under a paler wider sky, he wanted to cry. It was so fucking beautiful. He felt his sadness and exhaustion fuse with the dissolving and sentimental embrace of the bourbon. It was a moment of catastrophic charm. How could he ever hope to give up drugs? They filled him with such intense emotion. The sense of power they gave him was, admittedly, rather subjective (ruling the world from under the bedcovers, until the milkman arrived and you thought he was a platoon of stormtroopers come to steal your drugs and splatter your brains across the wall), but then again, *life* was so subjective.

He really ought to go to the funeral parlour now, it would be appalling to miss the chance of seeing his father's corpse (perhaps he could rest his foot on it). Patrick giggled and put down his empty glass on the windowsill. He was not going to take any smack. 'I want to make that *absolutely* clear,' he squealed in the voice of Mr Muffet, his old chemistry teacher from school. Walk tall, that was his philosophy, *but get some downers first*. Nobody could give up everything at once, especially (sob, sob) at a time like this. He must go down into that pulsing, burgeoning, monstrous mass of vegetation, the Park, and score. The gaggle of black and Hispanic dealers who hung around the entrance to Central Park opposite his hotel recognized Patrick as a potential customer from some way off.

'Uppers! Downers! Check it out,' said a tall, bruised-looking black man. Patrick walked on.

A hollow-cheeked Hispanic with a scrawny beard jerked his jaw forward and said, 'Wot canna du for ju, my friend?'

'I got goo-ood stuff,' said another black man, wearing shades. '*Check it out.*'

'Have you got any Quaaludes?' drawled Patrick.

'Sure, I got some Quaaludes. I got Lemon 714s – how many you want?'

'How much?'

'Five dollars.'

'I'll take six. And maybe some speed,' Patrick added. This was what they called impulse shopping. Speed was the last thing he wanted, but he didn't like to buy a drug unless he had the capacity to contradict it.

'I got some Beauties, they're phar-ma-ceu-ti-cal.'

'You mean you made them yourself.'

'No, man, pharmaceutical mean they're goo-ood shit.'

'Three of those.'

'Ten dollars each.'

Patrick handed over sixty dollars and took the pills. By this time the other dealers had gathered round, impressed by the easy way that Patrick parted with money.

'Ju English, right?' said the Hispanic.

'Don't bother the man,' said Shades.

'Yes,' said Patrick, knowing what was coming next.

'You got free heroin over there, right?' said the bruised-looking black man.

'That's right,' said Patrick patriotically.

'One day I'm going to come over to Britain and get me some of that free smack,' the bruised-looking man said, looking relieved for a few seconds.

'You do that,' said Patrick, heading back up the steps to Fifth Avenue. 'Bye now.'

'You come back here tomorrow,' said Shades possessively.

'Yeah,' mumbled Patrick, running up the steps. He put the Quaalude in his mouth, summoned a little saliva, and managed to force the pill down. It was an important skill to be able to swallow a pill without anything to drink. People who needed a drink were intolerable, he reflected, hailing a cab.

'Madison Avenue and Eighty-second Street,' he said, realizing that the Quaalude, which was after all a large pill, was stuck halfway down his throat. As the cab sped up Madison Avenue, Patrick twisted his neck into various positions in an attempt to get the pill all the way down.

By the time they reached Frank E. MacDonald's, Patrick was stretched out with his neck craned backwards and sideways over the edge of the seat, his hair touching the black rubber floor mat while he squeezed as much saliva as he could from the sides of his dry cheeks and swallowed furiously. The driver looked in the rear-view mirror. Another weirdo.

Patrick eventually dislodged the Quaalude from the ledge

it had found just under his Adam's apple, and walked through the tall oak doors of the funeral parlour, dread and absurdity competing inside him. The young woman behind the curved oak counter with Doric half-columns set at either end of its inner panel wore a blue jacket and a grey silk blouse, like an air hostess for a flight into the Afterlife.

'I've come to see the corpse of David Melrose,' said Patrick coldly. She told him to step right into the elevator and go 'straight on up' to the third floor, as if he might be tempted to stop off and see some other corpses on the way.

The lift was a homage to French tapestry-making. Above the buttoned leather bench, on which the bereaved could pause before facing the corpse of their loved one, was an Arcadia of petit point where a courtier pretending to be a shepherd played a flute to a courtier pretending to be a shepherdess.

This was it, the big moment: the corpse of his chief enemy, the ruins of his creator, the body of his dead father; the great weight of all that was unsaid and would never have been said; the pressure to say it now, when there was nobody to hear, and to speak also on his father's behalf, in an act of self-division that might fissure the world and turn his body into a jigsaw puzzle. *This was it*.

The sound that greeted Patrick as the doors of the lift slid open made him wonder if George had organized a surprise party, but the idea was too grotesque, given the difficulty of procuring more than half a dozen people *worldwide* who knew his father at all well and still liked him. He stepped out onto the landing and saw, beyond two Corinthian pillars, a panelled room full of gaily dressed elderly strangers. Men in every variety of lightweight tartan, and women in big white and yellow hats, were drinking cocktails and clutching each other's arms. At the back of the room, into which he wandered uncomprehendingly, was an open tilted coffin lined with white satin, and containing a punctiliously dressed, diminutive man with a diamond tie pin, snow-white hair, and a black suit. On a table beside him Patrick saw a stack of cards saying, 'In Loving Memory of Hermann Newton.' Death was no doubt an overwhelming experience, but it must be even more powerful than he had imagined if it could transform his father into a small Jew with so many amusing new friends.

Patrick's heart thudded into action. He spun round and stormed back to the lift, where he received a static electric shock when he pushed the call button. 'I can't fucking believe it,' he snarled, kicking a Louis XV-styled chair. The lift doors opened to reveal a fat old man with sagging grey flesh, wearing a pair of extra-ordinary Bermuda shorts and a yellow T-shirt. Hermann had obviously left a No Mourning clause in his will. Or maybe people were just happy to see him dead, thought Patrick. Beside the fat man stood his blowsy wife, also in beachwear, and next to her was the young woman from the reception desk.

'Wrong fucking corpse,' said Patrick, glaring at her.

'Oh, ho. Whoa there,' said the fat man, as if Patrick was overstating his case.

'Try again,' said Patrick, ignoring the old couple as they waddled past.

He gave the receptionist his special melt-down-and-die stare, with eyebeams as heavy as scaffolding shooting across the space between them and pouring radioactivity into her brain. She seemed unperturbed.

'I'm certain we don't have another party in the building at the moment,' she said.

'I don't want to go to a party,' said Patrick. 'I want to see my father.'

When they had reached the ground floor, the receptionist walked over to the counter where Patrick had first seen her and showed him her list of 'parties' in the building. 'There isn't any name on here except Mr Newton's,' she said smugly, 'that's why I sent you to the Cedar Suite.'

'Perhaps my father isn't dead at all,' said Patrick, leaning towards her; 'that really would be a shock. Maybe it was just a cry for help, what do you think?'

'I'd better go check with our director,' she said, retreating. 'Excuse me just one moment.' She opened a door concealed in one of the panels and slipped behind it.

Patrick leaned against the counter, breathless with rage, among the black and white marble diamonds of the lobby floor. Just like the floor of that hall in Eaton Square. He had only been as high as the old lady's hand. She had clutched her cane, her prominent blue veins flowing down her fingers into a sapphire ring. Blood arrested and clarified. The old lady talked to his mother about their committee, while Patrick got lost in the feeling that he was making the resemblance happen. Now there were days when everything resembled everything else, and the smallest excuse for comparison made one object consume another in a bulimic feast.

What the fuck was going on? Why were his father's *remains* so hard to find? He had no trouble in discovering them in himself, it was only Frank E. MacDonald that was experiencing this difficulty. While Patrick cackled hysterically at this thought, a bald homosexual with a moustache, and a strong sense of the restrained flair he brought with him into the mortuary business, emerged from the panelled door and clicked his way across the black and white diamonds of the lobby floor. Without apology, he told Patrick to step right this way and led him back into the elevator. He pressed the button for the second floor, less near to heaven than Mr Newton, but without the sound of a cocktail party. In the silence of that discreetly lit corridor, the director mincing ahead of him, Patrick began to realize that he had wasted his defences on an impostor and, exhausted by the farce of Mr Newton's wake, he was now dangerously vulnerable to the impact of his father's corpse.

'This is the room,' said the director, playing with his cuff. 'I'll leave you to be alone with him,' he purred.

Patrick glanced into the small, richly carpeted room. *Fucking hell.* What was his father doing in a coffin? He nodded to the director and waited outside the room, feeling a wave of madness rise up inside him. What did it mean that he was about to see his father's corpse? What was it meant to mean? He hovered in the doorway. His father's head was lying towards him and he could not yet see the face, just the grey curls of his hair. They had covered the body with tissue paper. It lay in the coffin, like a present someone had put down halfway through unwrapping.

'It's Dad!' muttered Patrick incredulously, clasping his hands together and turning to an imaginary friend. 'You *shouldn't* have!'

He stepped into the room, filled with dread again, but driven by curiosity. The face, alas, had not been covered in tissue, and Patrick was amazed by the nobility of his father's countenance. Those looks, which had deceived so many people because they were disconnected from his father's personality, were all the more impertinent now that the disconnection was complete. His father looked as if death was an enthusiasm he did not share, but with which he had been surrounded like a priest at a boxing match.

Those bruised, flickering eyes that assessed every weakness, like a teller's fingers counting a stack of banknotes, were now closed. That underlip, so often thrust out before a burst of anger, now contradicted the proud expression into which his features had relaxed. It had been torn open (he must have still been wearing his false teeth) by rage and protest and the consciousness of death.

However closely he tracked his father's life – and he felt the influence of this habit like a pollution in his bloodstream, a poison he had not put there himself, impossible to purge or leech without draining the patient – however closely he tried to imagine the lethal combination of pride and cruelty and sadness which had dominated his father's life, and however much he longed for it not to dominate his own life, Patrick could never follow him into that final moment when he had known he was about to die and he had been right. Patrick had known he was about to die often enough, but he had always been wrong.

Patrick felt a strong desire to take his father's lip in both hands and tear it like a piece of paper, along the gash already made by his teeth.

No, not that. He would not have that thought. The obscene necessity of going over the curtain pole. Not that, he would not have that thought. Nobody should do that to anybody else. He could not be that person. Bastard.

Patrick growled, his teeth bared and clenched. He punched the side of the coffin with his knuckles to bring him round. How should he play this scene from the movie of his life? He straightened himself and smiled contemptuously.

'Dad,' he said in his most cloying American accent, 'you were so fucking sad, man, and now you're trying to make me sad too.' He choked insincerely. 'Well,' he added in his own voice, 'bad luck.'

3

Anne Eisen turned into her building, carrying a box of cakes from Le Vrai Pâtisserie. If it had been La Vraie Pâtisserie, as Victor never tired of pointing out, it would have been even *vraie*-er, or *plus vraie*, she thought, smiling at Fred the doorman. Fred looked like a boy who had inherited his older brother's school uniform. The gold-braided sleeves of his brown coat hung down to the knuckles of his big pale hands, whereas his trousers, defeated by the bulk of his buttocks and thighs, flapped high above the pale blue nylon socks that clung to his ankles.

'Hi, Fred,' said Anne.

'Hello, Mrs Eisen. Can I help you with your packages?' said Fred, waddling over.

'Thanks,' said Anne, stooping theatrically, 'but I can still manage two millefeuilles and a pain aux raisins. Say, Fred,' she added, 'I have a friend coming over round four o'clock. He's young and sort of ill-looking. Be gentle with him, his father just died.'

'Oh, gee, I'm sorry,' said Fred.

'I don't think *he* is,' said Anne, 'although he may not know that yet.'

Fred tried to look as if he hadn't heard. Mrs Eisen was a real nice lady, but sometimes she said the weirdest things.

Anne got into the lift and pressed the button for the eleventh floor. In a few weeks it would all be over. No more eleventh floor, no more of Professor Wilson's cane chairs and his African masks and his big abstract I-think-it's-good-but-his-work-never-really-caught-on painting in the drawing room.

Jim Wilson, whose rich wife enabled him to exhibit his rather old-fashioned liberal wares on Park Avenue, no less, had been 'visiting' Oxford since October, while Victor visited Columbia in exchange. Every time Anne and Victor went to a party – and they almost never stopped – she'd needle him about being the visiting professor. Anne and Victor had an 'open' marriage. 'Open', as in 'open wound' or 'open rebellion' or indeed 'open marriage', was not always a good thing, but now that Victor was seventy-six it hardly seemed worth divorcing him. Besides, somebody had to look after him.

Anne got out of the lift and opened the door to apartment 11E, reaching for the light switch, next to the Red Indian blanket that hung in the hall. What the hell was she going to say to Patrick? Although he had turned into a surly and malicious adolescent, and was now a drug-addled twenty-two-year-old, she could still remember him sitting on the stairs at Lacoste when he was five, and she still felt responsible – she knew it was absurd – for not managing to get his mother away from that gruesome dinner party.

Oddly enough, the delusions which had enabled her to marry Victor had really started on that evening. During the next few months Victor immersed himself in the creation of his new book, *Being, Knowing, and Judging*, so easily (and yet so wrongly!) confused with its predecessor, *Thinking, Knowing, and Judging*. Victor's claim that he wanted to keep his students 'on their toes' by giving his books such similar titles had not altogether extinguished Anne's doubts or those of his publisher. Nevertheless, like a masterful broom, his new book had scattered the dust long settled on the subject of identity, and swept it into exciting new piles.

At the end of this creative surge Victor had proposed to Anne. She had been thirty-four and, although she didn't know it at the time, her admiration for Victor was at its peak. She had accepted him, not only because he was imbued with that mild celebrity which is all a living philosopher can hope for, but also because she believed that Victor was a good man.

What the hell was she going to say to Patrick, she wondered as she took a spinach-green majolica plate from Barbara's fabulous collection and arranged the cakes on its irregularly glazed surface.

It was no use pretending to Patrick that she had liked David Melrose. Even after his divorce from Eleanor, when he was poor and ill, David had been no more endearing than a chained Alsatian. His life was an unblemished failure and his isolation terrifying to imagine, but he still had a smile like a knife; and if he had tried to learn (talk about a mature student!) how to please people, his efforts were faintly repulsive to anyone who knew his real nature.

As she leaned over an annoyingly low Moroccan table in the drawing room, Anne felt her dark glasses slip from the top of her head. Perhaps her yellow cotton dress was a little too upbeat for the occasion, but what the hell? Patrick had not seen her recently enough to tell that she had dyed her hair. No doubt Barbara Wilson would have let it go naturally grey, but Anne had to appear on television tomorrow night to talk about 'The New Woman'. While she had been trying to find out what on earth a New Woman might be, she had got a New hairstyle and bought a New dress. It was research and she wanted expenses.

Twenty to four. Dead time until he arrived. Time to light a lethal, cancer-causing cigarette, time to fly in the face of the Surgeon General's advice – as if you could trust a man who was a surgeon and a general at the same time. She called that working both sides of the street. There was no disguising it, though, she *did* feel guilty, but then she felt guilty putting three drops of bath essence into the water instead of two. So what the hell?

Anne had barely lit her mild, light, mentholated, almost entirely pointless cigarette, when the buzzer rang from downstairs.

'Hi, Fred.'

'Oh, hello, Mrs Eisen: Mr Melrose is here.'

'Well, I guess you'd better send him up,' she said, wondering if there wasn't some way they could ever vary this conversation.

Anne went into the kitchen, switched on the kettle, and sprinkled some tea leaves into the Japanese teapot with the wobbly overarching rattan handle.

The doorbell interrupted her and she hurried out of the kitchen to open the front door. Patrick was standing with his back to her in a long black overcoat.

'Hello, Patrick,' she said.

'Hello,' he mumbled, trying to squeeze past her. But she took him by the shoulders and embraced him warmly.

'I'm so sorry,' she said.

Patrick would not yield to this embrace, but slid away like a wrestler breaking an opponent's grip.

'I'm sorry too,' he said, bowing slightly. 'Being late is a bore, but arriving early is unforgivable. Punctuality is one of the smaller vices I've inherited from my father; it means I'll never really be chic.' He paced up and down the drawing room with his hands in his overcoat pockets. '*Unlike* this apartment,' he sneered. 'Who was lucky enough to swap this place for your nice house in London?'

'Victor's opposite number at Columbia, Jim Wilson.'

'God, imagine having an opposite number instead of always being one's own opposite number,' said Patrick.

'Do you want some tea?' asked Anne with a sympathetic sigh.

'Hum,' said Patrick. 'I wonder if I could have a real drink as well? For me it's already nine in the evening.'

'For you it's always nine in the evening,' said Anne. 'What do you want? I'll fix it for you.'

'No, I'll do it,' he said, 'you won't make it strong enough.'

'OK,' said Anne, turning towards the kitchen, 'the drinks are on the Mexican millstone.'

The millstone was engraved with feathered warriors, but it was the bottle of Wild Turkey which commanded Patrick's attention. He poured some into a tall glass and knocked back another Quaalude with the first gulp, refilling the glass immediately. After seeing his father's corpse, he had gone to the Forty-fourth Street branch of the Morgan Guaranty Bank and collected three thousand dollars in cash which now bulged inside an orange-brown envelope in his pocket.

He checked the pills again (lower right pocket) and then the envelope (inside left) and then the credit cards (outer left). This nervous action, which he sometimes performed every few minutes, was like a man crossing himself before an altar – the Drugs; the Cash; and the Holy Ghost of Credit.

He had already taken a second Quaalude after the visit to the bank, but he still felt groundless and desperate and overwrought. Perhaps a third one was overdoing it, but over-doing it was his occupation.

'Does this happen to you?' asked Patrick, striding into the kitchen with renewed energy. 'You see a millstone, and the words "round my neck" ring up like the price on an old cash register. Isn't it humiliating,' he said, taking some ice cubes, 'God, I love these ice machines, they're the best thing about America so far – humiliating that one's thoughts have all been prepared in advance by these idiotic mechanisms?'

'The idiotic ones aren't good,' Anne agreed, 'but there's

no need for the cash register to come up with something cheap.'

'If your mind works like a cash register, anything you come up with is bound to be cheap.'

'You obviously don't shop at Le Vrai Pâtisserie,' said Anne, carrying the cakes and tea into the drawing room.

'If we can't control our conscious responses, what chance do we have against the influences we haven't recognized?'

'None at all,' said Anne cheerfully, handing him a cup of tea.

Patrick let loose a curt laugh. He felt detached from what he had been saying. Perhaps the Quaaludes were beginning to make a difference.

'Do you want a cake?' said Anne. 'I bought them to remind us of Lacoste. They're as French as . . . as French letters.'

'That French,' gasped Patrick, taking one of the mille-feuilles out of politeness. As he picked it up, the cake oozed cream from its flanks, like pus dribbling from a wound. Christ, he thought, this cake is completely *out of control*.

'It's *alive*!' he said out loud, squeezing the millefeuille rather too hard. Cream spurted out and dropped on to the elaborate brass surface of the Moroccan table. His fingers were sticky with icing. 'Oh, I'm sorry,' he mumbled, putting the cake down.

Anne handed him a napkin. She noticed that Patrick was becoming increasingly clumsy and slurred. Before he had arrived she was dreading the inevitable conversation about his father; now she was worried that it might not take place.

'Have you been to see your father yet?' she asked outright.

'I did see him,' said Patrick without hesitation. 'I thought he was at his best in a coffin – so much less difficult than usual.' He grinned at her disarmingly.

Anne smiled at him faintly, but Patrick needed no encouragement.

'When I was young,' he said, 'my father used to take us to restaurants. I say "restaurants" in the plural, because we never stormed in and out of less than three. Either the menu took too long to arrive, or a waiter struck my father as intolerably stupid, or the wine list disappointed him. I remember he once held a bottle of red wine upside down while the contents gurgled out onto the carpet. "How dare you bring me this filth?" he shouted. The waiter was so frightened that instead of throwing him out, he brought more wine.'

'So you liked being with him in a place he didn't complain about.'

'Exactly,' said Patrick. 'I couldn't believe my luck, and for a while I expected him to sit up in his coffin, like a vampire at sunset, and say, "The service here is intolerable." Then we would have had to go to three or four other funeral parlours. Mind you, the service *was* intolerable. They sent me to the wrong corpse.'

'The wrong corpse!' exclaimed Anne.

'Yes, I wound up at a jaunty Jewish cocktail party given for a Mr Hermann Newton. I wish I could have stayed; they seemed to be having such fun . . .'

'What an appalling story,' said Anne, lighting a cigarette. 'I'll bet they give courses in Bereavement Counselling.'

'Of course,' said Patrick, letting out another quick hollow laugh and sinking back into his armchair. He could definitely feel the influence of the Quaaludes now. The alcohol had brought out the best in them, like the sun coaxing open the petals of a flower, he reflected tenderly.

'I'm sorry?' he said. He had not heard Anne's last question.

'Is he being cremated?' she repeated.

'Yes, that's right,' said Patrick. 'I gather that when people are cremated one never really gets their ashes, just some communal rakings from the bottom of the oven. As you can imagine, I regard that as good news. Ideally, *all* the ashes would belong to somebody else, but we don't live in a perfect world.'

Anne had given up wondering whether he was sorry about his father's death, and had started wishing he was a little sorrier. His venomous remarks, although they could not affect David, made Patrick look so ill he might have been waiting to die from a snakebite.

Patrick closed his eyes slowly and, after a very long time, slowly opened them again. The whole operation took about half an hour. Another half an hour elapsed while he licked his dry and fascinatingly sore lips. He was really getting something off that last Quaalude. His blood was hissing like a television screen after closedown. His hands were like dumbbells, like dumbbells in his hands. Everything folding inward and growing heavier.

'Hello there!' Anne called.

'I'm so sorry,' said Patrick, leaning forward with what he imagined was a charming smile. 'I'm awfully tired.'

'Maybe you ought to go to bed.'

'No, no, no. Let's not exaggerate.'

'You could lie down for a few hours,' Anne suggested, 'and then have dinner with Victor and me. We're going to a party afterward, given by some ghastly Long Island Anglophiles. Just your kind of thing.'

'It's sweet of you, but I really can't face too many strangers at the moment,' said Patrick, playing his bereavement card a little too late to convince Anne.

'You should come along,' she coaxed. 'I'm sure it will be an example of "unashamed luxury".'

'I can't imagine what that means,' said Patrick sleepily.

'Let me give you the address anyhow,' Anne insisted. 'I don't like the idea of your being alone too much.'

'Fine. Write it down for me before I go.'

He knew he had to take some speed soon or involuntarily take up Anne's offer to 'lie down for a few hours'. He did not want to swallow a whole Beauty, because it would take him on a fifteen-hour megalomaniac odyssey, and he didn't want to be that conscious. On the other hand, he had to get rid of the feeling that he had been dropped into a pool of slowly drying concrete.

'Where's the loo?'

Anne told him how to get there, and Patrick waded across the carpet in the direction she had indicated. Once he had locked the bathroom door Patrick felt a familiar sense of security. Inside a bathroom he could give in to the obsession with his own physical and mental state which was so often compromised by the presence of other people or the absence of a well-lit mirror. Most of the 'quality time' in his life had been spent in a bathroom. Injecting, snorting, swallowing, stealing, overdosing; examining his pupils, his arms, his tongue, his stash.

'O bathrooms!' he intoned, spreading out his arms in front of the mirror. 'Thy medicine cabinets pleaseth me mightily! Thy towels moppeth up the rivers of my blood . . .' He petered out as he took the Black Beauty from his pocket. He was just going to take enough to function, just enough to . . . what had he been about to say? He couldn't remember. My God, it was short-term memory loss again, the Professor Moriarty of drug abuse, interrupting and then obliterating the precious sensations one went to such trouble to secure.

'Inhuman fiend,' he muttered.

The black capsule eventually came apart and he emptied half the contents onto one of the Portuguese tiles around the basin. Taking out one of his new hundred-dollar notes, he rolled it into a tight tube and sniffed up the small heap of white powder from the tile.

His nose stung and his eyes watered slightly but, refusing to be distracted, Patrick resealed the capsule, wrapped it in a Klecnex, put it back in his pocket and then, for no reason he could identify, almost against his will, he took it out again, emptied the rest of the powder onto a tile and sniffed it up as well. The effects wouldn't last so long this way, he argued, inhaling deeply through his nose. It was too sordid to take half of anything. Anyhow, his father had just died and he was entitled to be confused. The main thing, the heroic feat, the proof of his seriousness and his samurai status in the war against drugs, was that he hadn't taken any heroin.

Patrick leaned forward and checked his pupils in the mirror. They had definitely dilated. His heartbeat had accelerated. He felt invigorated, he felt refreshed, in fact he felt rather aggressive. It was as if he had never taken a drink or a drug, he was back in complete control, the lighthouse beams of speed cutting through the thick night of the Quaaludes and the alcohol and the jet lag.

'And,' he said, clasping his lapels with mayoral solemnity, 'last but not least, through the dark shadow, if I might put it thus, of our grief for the passing away of David Melrose.'

How long had he been in the bathroom? It seemed like a lifetime. The fire brigade would probably be forcing the door down soon. Patrick started to clear up hastily. He didn't want to put the shell of the Black Beauty into the waste-paper basket (paranoia!) and so he forced the two halves of the empty capsule down the basin plughole. How was he going to explain his reanimated state to Anne? He splashed some cold water on his face and left it ostentatiously dripping. There was only one thing left to do: that authentic-sounding flush with which every junkie leaves a bathroom, hoping to deceive the audience that crowds his imagination.

'For God's sake,' said Anne when he got back to the drawing room, 'why don't you dry your face?'

'I was just reviving myself with a little cold water.'

'Oh yeah?' said Anne. 'What kind of water was that?'

'Very refreshing water,' he said, wiping his sweaty palms on his trousers as he sat down. 'Which reminds me,' he said, getting up immediately, 'I'd love another drink if I may.'

'Sure,' said Anne resignedly. 'By the way, I forgot to ask, how is Debbie?'

The question filled Patrick with the horror which assailed him when he was asked to consider another person's feelings. How was Debbie? How the fuck should he know? It was hard enough to rescue himself from the avalanche of his own feelings, without allowing the gloomy St Bernard of his attention to wander into other fields. On the other hand the amphetamines had given him an urgent desire to talk and he couldn't ignore the question entirely.

'Well,' he said from the other side of the room, 'she's following in her mother's footsteps, and writing an article about great hostesses. Teresa Hickmann's footsteps, invisible to most people, glow in the dark for her dutiful daughter. Still, we should be grateful that she hasn't modelled her conversational style on her father's.'

Patrick was momentarily lost again in the contemplation of his psychological state. He felt lucid, but not about anything, except his own lucidity. His thoughts, anticipating themselves hopelessly, stuttered in the starting blocks, and brought his feeling of fluency dangerously close to silence. 'But you haven't told me,' he said, tearing himself away from this intriguing mental stammer and at the same time taking his revenge on Anne for asking him about Debbie, 'how is Victor?'

'Oh, fine. He's a grand old man now, a role he's been training for all his life. He gets a lot of attention and he's lecturing on Identity, which, as he says, he can do with his eyes closed. Did you ever read *Being, Knowing, and Judging*?'

'No,' said Patrick.

'Well, I must give you a copy, then,' said Anne, getting up and going to the bookshelves. She took out what looked to Patrick like a tiresomely thick volume from among half a dozen copies of the same book. He liked slim books which he could slip into his overcoat pocket and leave there unread for months. What was the point of a book if you couldn't carry it around with you as a theoretical defence against boredom?

'It's about identity, is it?' he asked suspiciously.

'All you've ever wanted to know but never dared to formulate precisely,' said Anne.

'Goody,' said Patrick, getting up restlessly. He had to pace, he had to move through space, otherwise the world had a dangerous tendency to flatten itself and he felt like a fly crawling up a windowpane looking for a way out of its translucent prison. Anne, thinking he had come to fetch it, handed him the book.

'Oh, eh, thank you,' he said, leaning over to kiss her quickly, 'I'll read it very soon.'

He tried to stuff the book into his overcoat pocket. He had *known* it wasn't going to fit. It was completely fucking useless. Now he had to carry this stupid fat book round with him everywhere. He felt a wave of violent rage. He stared intensely at a waste-paper basket (once a Somalian water jug) and imagined the book spinning towards it like a Frisbee.

'I really ought to be going now,' he said curtly.

'Really? Won't you stay to say hello to Victor?'

'No, I must go,' he said impatiently.

'OK, but let me give you Samantha's address.'

'What?'

'The party.'

'Oh, yes. I doubt I'll come,' said Patrick.

Anne wrote down the address on a piece of paper and handed it to Patrick. 'There you are.'

'Thank you,' said Patrick abruptly, flicking up the collar of his overcoat. 'I'll call you tomorrow.'

'Or see you tonight.'

'Maybe.'

He turned around and hurried towards the door. He had to get outside. His heart seemed to be about to leap out of his chest, like a jack-in-the-box, and he felt that he could only force the lid down for a few seconds more.

'Goodbye,' he called from the door.

'Goodbye,' said Anne.

Down in the sluggish airless lift, past the fat moronic doorman, and into the street. The shock of standing again under the wide pale sky, completely exposed. This must be what the oyster feels when the lemon juice falls.

Why had he left the shelter of Anne's flat? And so rudely. Now she would hate him forever. Everything he did was wrong.

Patrick looked down the avenue. It was like the opening shot of a documentary on overpopulation. He walked down the street, imagining the severed heads of passers-by rolling into the gutter in his wake.

4

How could he think his way out of the problem when the problem was the way he thought, Patrick wondered, not for the first time, as he slipped reluctantly out of his overcoat and handed it to a brilliantined red-jacketed waiter.

Eating was only a temporary solution. But then all solutions were temporary, even death, and nothing gave him more faith in the existence of an afterlife than the inexorable sarcasm of Fate. No doubt suicide would turn out to be the violent preface to yet another span of nauseating consciousness, of diminishing spirals and tightening nooses, and memories like shrapnel tearing all day long through his flesh. Who could guess what exquisite torments lay ahead in the holiday camps of eternity? It almost made one grateful to be alive.

Only behind a waterfall of brutal and pleasurable sensations, thought Patrick, accepting the leather-clad menu without bothering to glance up, could he hide from the bloodhounds of his conscience. There, in the cool recess of the rock, behind that heavy white veil, he would hear them yelping and snarling confusedly on the river bank, but at least they couldn't tear out his throat with the fury of their reproach. After all, the trail he'd left was not hard to follow. It was littered with the evidence of wasted time and hopeless longing, not to mention those bloodstained shirts, and the syringes whose spikes he had bent in a fit of disgust and then unbent again for one last fix. Patrick drew in his breath sharply and folded his arms over his chest.

'A dry martini. Straight up, with a twist,' he drawled. 'And I'm ready to order.'

A waiter was coming right on over to take his order. Everything was under control.

Most people who were withdrawing and speeding, jet-lagged and cudgelled by Quaaludes, might have lost their interest in food, but Patrick found that all his appetites were operational at all times, even when his loathing of being touched gave his desire for sex a theoretical complexion.

He could remember Johnny Hall saying indignantly of a girlfriend he had recently thrown out, 'She was the kind of girl who came over and ruffled your hair when you'd just had a fix of coke.' Patrick had howled at the horror of such a tactless act. When a man is feeling as empty and fragile as a pane of glass, he does not want to have his hair ruffled. There could be no negotiation between people who thought that cocaine was a vaguely naughty and salacious drug and the intravenous addict who knew that it was an opportunity to experience the arctic landscape of pure terror.

That terror was the price he had to pay for the first heart-breaking wave of pleasure when consciousness seemed to burst out, like white blossoms, along the branches of every nerve. And all his scattered thoughts came rushing together, like loose iron filings as a magnet is held over them and draws them into the shape of a rose. Or – he must stop thinking about it – or like a solution of saturated copper sulphate under the microscope, when it suddenly transforms and crystals break out everywhere on its surface.

He must stop thinking about it – and do it. No! And think about something else. His father's corpse, for instance. Would that be an improvement? It would get rid of the problem of desire, but hatred could be compulsive too.

Ah, here was the dry martini. If not the cavalry, at least some more ammunition. Patrick drained the cold unctuous liquid in one gulp.

'Would you care for another one, sir?'

'Yes,' said Patrick brusquely.

A more senior waiter in a dinner jacket came over to take Patrick's order.

'Tartare de Saumon Cru, followed by the Steak Tartare,' said Patrick, taking an innocent pleasure in saying 'tartare' twice and pleased to be ordering two adult forms of baby food, already cut up and squished together for him.

A third waiter, with a golden bunch of grapes in his lapel, and a large golden wine-tasting cup dangling from a chain around his neck, was only too ready to bring Patrick a bottle of Corton Charlemagne straight away and to open a bottle of Ducru-Beaucaillou for later on. Everything was under control.

No, he mustn't think about it, or indeed about anything, and especially not about heroin, because heroin was the only thing that really worked, the only thing that stopped him scampering around in a hamster's wheel of unanswerable questions. Heroin was the cavalry. Heroin was the missing chair leg, made with such precision that it matched every splinter of the break. Heroin landed purring at the base of his skull, and wrapped itself darkly around his nervous system, like a black cat curling up on its favourite cushion. It was as soft and rich as the throat of a wood pigeon, or the splash of sealing wax onto a page, or a handful of gems slipping from palm to palm.

The way other people felt about love, he felt about heroin, and he felt about love the way other people felt about heroin: that it was a dangerous and incomprehensible waste of time. What could he say to Debbie? 'Although you know that my hatred for my father, and my love for drugs, are the most

175

important relationships in my life, I want you to know that you come in third.' What woman would not be proud to be 'among the medals' in such a contest?

'Oh, for fuck's sake shut up,' mumbled Patrick out loud, drinking his second dry martini with as little restraint as the first. If things went on this way he would have to call Pierre, his truly wonderful New York dealer. No! He wasn't going to do it, he had sworn that he wasn't going to do it. 555–1726. The number might as well have been tattooed on his wrist. He hadn't rung it since September, eight months ago, but he would never forget the bowel-loosening excitement of those seven digits.

Golden Grapes was back, peeling the heavy yellow lead from the neck of the Corton Charlemagne, and cradling the bottle of claret, while Patrick studied the picture of a white chateau under a flat gold sky. Perhaps with these consolations he would not have to score after dinner, thought Patrick sceptically, sucking a sample of Corton Charlemagne into his mouth.

The first taste made him break into a grin of recognition, like a man who has sighted his lover at the end of a crowded platform. Raising the glass again, he took a large gulp of the pale yellow wine, held it in his mouth for a few seconds, and then let it slide down his throat. Yes, it worked, it still worked. Some things never let him down.

He closed his eyes and the taste rippled over him like an hallucination. Cheaper wine would have buried him in fruit, but the grapes he imagined now were mercifully artificial, like earrings of swollen yellow pearls. He pictured the long sinewy shoots of the vine, dragging him down into the heavy reddish soil. Traces of iron and stone and earth and rain flashed across his palate and tantalized him like shooting stars. Sensations long wrapped in a bottle now unfurled like a stolen canvas.

Some things never let him down. It made him want to cry.

'Would you care to taste the Do-crew Bo-ca-u?'

'Yes,' said Patrick.

Golden Grapes poured the red wine into a ludicrously large glass. Even the smell of it made Patrick see things. Glistening granite. Cobwebs. Gothic cellars.

'That's fine,' he said, without bothering to taste it. 'Pour some now, I'll drink it later.'

Patrick sank back in his chair. Now that the wine distraction was over, the same question returned: would he go to his dealer after dinner, or to his hotel? Perhaps he could go to see Pierre socially. Patrick yelped with laughter at the absurdity of this pretext, but at the same time he felt a tremendous sentimental desire to see the demented Frenchman again. In many ways Pierre was the person Patrick felt closest to.

Pierre had spent eight years in a lunatic asylum under the misapprehension that he was an egg. 'For eight fucking years, man,' he would say, speaking very rapidly in a strong French accent, 'I thought I was an egg. *Je croyais que j'étais un œuf* – it's no fucking joke.' During this time his deserted body was fed, moved, washed, and clothed by nurses who had no idea that they were ministering to an egg. Pierre was let free to shoot about the world on unfettered voyages, in a state of enlightenment which did not require the crass mediation of words and senses. 'I understood everything,' he would say, glaring at Patrick defiantly. '*J'avais une conscience totale.*'

On these voyages, Pierre would occasionally stop by his hospital room and hover with pity and contempt over the as yet unhatched egg of his body. However, after eight years he realized that his body was dying of neglect.

'I had to force myself back into my fucking body; it was horrible. *J'avais un dégoût total.*'

Patrick was fascinated. It reminded him of Lucifer's disgust when he had to squeeze himself into the clammy and confining rings of the serpent's body.

One day the nurses came in with their sponges and their baby food, and found Pierre weak but impatient, sitting on the edge of his bed after almost a decade of inertia and silence.

'OK, I go now,' he snapped.

Tests showed that he was perfectly lucid, perhaps too lucid, and so they discharged him from the hospital with relief.

Only a perpetual flow of heroin and cocaine could now sustain a coarse version of his former glorious insanity. He hovered, but not as lightly as before, on the margins between his body and his fatal nostalgia for disembodiment. In his arm a wound like a volcano cone, a scabrous mound of dried blood and scar tissue, rose up from the soft hollow opposite his elbow. It enabled him to drop the thin spike of his insulin syringes vertically into the vein, never digging for a hit, but leaving open this access to his bloodstream, like an emergency runway, always ready for another speedball to relieve the horror of his incarceration in a jaundiced and inhospitable body he could hardly call his own.

Pierre's routine was perfectly regular. He stayed awake for two and a half days and then, after a big shot of heroin, slept or at least rested for eighteen hours. During his waking periods he sold drugs curtly and efficiently, allowing most of his customers no more than ten minutes in his black-and-white apartment. He also saved himself the inconvenience of people dying in his bathroom by banning injections, a prohibition he soon lifted for Patrick. Throughout the last summer Patrick had tried to keep to the same sleep patterns as Pierre. They often stayed up all night, sitting either side of the horizontal mirror Pierre used as a table, stripped to the waist to save themselves the trouble of rolling their sleeves up and down, shooting up every quarter of an hour and, as they poured with chemical-smelling sweat, talking about their favourite subjects: how to achieve perfect disembodiment; how to witness their own deaths; how to stay in the border-lands, undefined by the identities which their histories tried to thrust upon them; how dishonest and shallow all the straight people were; and, of course, how they could give up drugs if they really wanted to, a condition that had not so far afflicted either of them for very long. Fucking hell, thought Patrick, draining his third glass of white wine and immedi-ately reloading it from the dripping bottle. He *must* stop thinking about it.

With a father like his (sob, sob), Authority Figures and Role Models had always been a problem, but in Pierre he had at last found someone whose example he could follow with unqualified enthusiasm, and whose advice he could bear to take. At least until Pierre had tried to limit him to two grams of coke a day instead of the seven Patrick regarded as indispensable.

'You're fucking crazy, man,' Pierre had shouted at him, 'you go for the rush every time. You kill yourself that way.'

This argument had marred the end of the summer, but in any case it had been time to get rid of the inflamed rashes that covered Patrick's entire body and the burning white ulcers that had suddenly sprouted throughout his mouth, throat, and stomach, and so he had returned to England a few days later to check into his favourite clinic.

'*Oh, les beaux jours,*' he sighed, wolfing down his raw salmon in a few breathless mouthfuls. He drank the last of the white wine, indifferent now to its taste.

Who else was in this ghastly restaurant? Extraordinary that he hadn't looked before; or not so extraordinary, in fact. They wouldn't be calling him in to solve the Problem of Other Minds, although of course the people, like Victor, who thought it was a problem in the first place were famous for being entirely absorbed in the workings of their own minds. Strange coincidence.

He swivelled his eyes around the room with reptilian coldness. He hated them all, every single one, especially that incredibly fat man sitting with the blonde. He must have paid her to mask her disgust at being in his company.

'God, you're repulsive,' muttered Patrick. 'Have you ever considered going on a diet? Yes, that's right, a diet, or hasn't it crossed your mind that you're quite appallingly fat?' Patrick felt vindictively and loutishly aggressive. Alcohol is such a crude high, he thought, remembering the sage pronouncement of his first hash dealer from his schooldays, a zonked-out old hippie bore called Barry.

'If I looked like you,' he sneered at the fat man, 'I'd commit suicide. Not that one needs an incentive.' There was no doubt about it, he was a fattist and a sexist and an ageist and a racist and a straightist and a druggist and, naturally, a snob, but of such a virulent character that nobody satisfied his demands. He defied anyone to come up with a minority or a majority that he did not hate for some reason or another.

'Is everything OK, sir?' asked one of the waiters, mistaking Patrick's mutterings for an attempt to order.

'Yes, yes,' said Patrick. Well, not absolutely everything, he thought, you can't seriously expect anyone to agree to that. In fact the idea of everything being OK made him feel dangerously indignant. Affirmation was too rare a commodity to waste on such a ludicrous statement. He felt like calling the waiter back to correct any false impression of happiness he might have created. But here was another waiter – would they never leave him alone? Could he bear it if they did? – bringing his Steak Tartare. He wanted it spicy, very spicy.

A couple of minutes later, his mouth seared with Tabasco

and cayenne pepper, Patrick had already devoured the mound of raw meat and *pommes allumettes* on his plate.

'That's right, dear,' he said in his Nanny voice, 'you get something solid inside you.'

'Yes, Nanny,' he replied obediently. 'Like a bullet, or a needle, eh, Nanny?'

'A bullet, indeed,' he huffed and puffed, 'a needle! Whatever next? You always were a strange boy. No good'll come of it, you mark my words, young man.'

Oh, God, it was starting. The endless voices. The solitary dialogues. The dreadful jabbering that poured out uncontrollably. He gulped down an entire glass of red wine with an eagerness worthy of Lawrence of Arabia, as interpreted by Peter O'Toole, polishing off his glass of lemonade after a thirsty desert crossing. 'We've taken Aqaba,' he said, staring madly into space and twitching his eyebrows expertly.

'Would you care for a dessert, sir?'

At last, a real person with a real question, albeit a rather bizarre question. How was he supposed to 'care for' a dessert? Did he have to visit it on Sundays? Send it a Christmas card? Did he have to feed it?

'Yeah,' said Patrick, smiling wildly, 'I'll have a crème brûlée.'

Patrick stared at his glass. The red wine was definitely beginning to unfold. Pity he had already drunk it all. Yes, it had been beginning to unfold, like a fist opening slowly. And in its palm . . . In its palm, what? A ruby? A grape? A stone? Perhaps similes just shunted the same idea back and forth, lightly disguised, to give the impression of a fruitful trade. Sir Sampson Legend was the only honest suitor who ever sang the praises of a woman. 'Give me your hand, Odd, let me kiss it; 'tis as warm and as soft – as what? Odd, as t'other hand.' Now there was an accurate simile. The tragic

limitations of comparison. The lead in the heart of the sky-
lark. The disappointing curvature of space. The doom of
time.

Christ, he was really quite drunk. Not drunk enough,
though. He poured the stuff in, but it didn't reach the root-
confusions, the accident by the roadside, still trapped in the
buckling metal after all these years. He sighed loudly, ending
in a kind of grunt, and bowing his head hopelessly.

The crème brûlée arrived and he gobbled it down with
the same desperate impatience he showed towards all food,
but now edged with weariness and oppression. His violent
way of eating always left him in a state of speechless sadness
at the end of a meal. After several minutes during which he
could only stare at the foot of his glass, he summoned enough
passion to order some marc de Bourgogne and the bill.

Patrick closed his eyes and let the cigarette smoke drift
out of his mouth and up into his nose and out through his
mouth again. This was recycling at its best. Of course he could
still go to the party Anne had invited him to, but he knew
that he wouldn't. Why did he always refuse? Refuse to participate. Refuse to agree. Refuse to forgive. Once it was too
late he would long to have gone to this party. He glanced at
his watch. Only nine thirty. The time had not yet come, but
the moment it did, refusal would turn into regret. He could
even imagine loving a woman if he had lost her first.

With reading it was the same thing. As soon as he was
deprived of books, his longing to read became insatiable,
whereas if he took the precaution of carrying a book with
him, as he had this evening, slipping *The Myth of Sisyphus*
yet again into his overcoat pocket, then he could be sure that
he would not be troubled by a desire for literature.

Before *The Myth of Sisyphus* he had carried round *The
Unnamable* and *Nightwood* for at least a year, and for
two years before that the ultimate overcoat book, *Heart of*

Darkness. Sometimes, driven on by horror at his own ignorance and a determination to conquer a difficult book, or even a seminal text, he would take a copy of something like *Seven Types of Ambiguity* or *The Decline and Fall of the Roman Empire* out of his bookshelves only to find that its opening pages were already covered in spidery and obscure annotations in his own handwriting. These traces of an earlier civilization would have reassured him if he had any recollection at all of the things he had obviously once read, but this forgetfulness made him panic instead. What was the point of an experience if it eluded him so thoroughly? His past seemed to turn to water in his cupped hands and to slip irretrievably through his nervous fingers.

Patrick heaved himself up and walked across the thick red carpet of the restaurant, his head thrown back precariously and his eyes so nearly closed that the tables were dark blurs through the mesh of his eyelashes.

He had made a big decision. He would telephone Pierre and leave it to fate whether he scored or not. If Pierre was asleep then he would not get any smack, but if he was awake it was worth going round to get just enough for a good night's rest. And a little for the morning so he didn't feel sick.

The barman put a telephone down on the mahogany counter, and beside it a second marc. 5 . . . 5 . . . 5 . . . 1 . . . 7 . . . 2 . . . 6. Patrick's heart rate increased; he suddenly felt alert.

'I cannot come to the phone right now, but if you leave . . .'

Patrick slammed the phone down. It was the fucking machine. What was he doing asleep at ten in the evening? It was absolutely intolerable. He picked the phone up and dialled the number again. Should he leave a message? Something subtly coded like 'Wake up, fuckface, I want to score.'

No, it was hopeless. Fate had spoken and he must accept its judgement.

Outside it was surprisingly warm. Nevertheless, Patrick flicked up the collar of his overcoat, scanning the street for a free cab.

He soon spotted a taxi and stepped into the street to hail it.

'The Pierre Hotel,' he said as he climbed inside.

5

What instrument could he use to set himself free? Disdain? Aggression? Hatred? They were all contaminated by the influence of his father, the very thing he needed to free himself from. And the sadness he felt, if he paused for a second, had he not learned it from his father's descent into paralysing misery?

After his divorce from Eleanor, David had remained in the south of France, only fifteen miles away from the old house in Lacoste. In his new house, which had no exterior windows, only windows looking onto a central weed-choked courtyard, he lay in bed for days on end wheezing and staring at the ceiling fixedly, without even the energy to cross the room and get the copy of *Jorrocks Rides Again* which had once been able to cheer him up in the most unpromising circumstances.

When Patrick, aged eight or nine, and torn between terror and unfathomable loyalty, visited his father, the enormous silences were only broken for David to express a desire to die, and to issue his final instructions.

'I may not be alive for much longer,' he would gasp, 'and we may not see each other again.'

'No, Daddy, don't say that,' Patrick would plead with him.

And then the old exhortations would come out: observe everything . . . trust nobody . . . despise your mother . . .

effort is vulgar . . . things were better in the eighteenth century.

Impressed by the thought, year after year, that these might be his father's last pronouncements on the world, the distillation of all his wisdom and experience, Patrick paid undue attention to this tiresome set of opinions, despite the overwhelming evidence that they had not got his father very far in the pursuit of happiness. But then that was vulgar too. The whole system worked beautifully, like so many others, after the initial leap of faith.

If his father ever managed to get out of bed, things got worse. They would walk down to the village on a shopping expedition, his father dressed in an old pair of green pyjamas, a short blue overcoat with anchors on the buttons, a pair of dark glasses now tied to a coarse string around his neck, and on his feet the heavy lace-up boots favoured by the local tractor-driving peasants. David had also grown a snow-white beard and always carried with him an orange nylon shopping bag with a tarnished gold handle. Patrick was mistaken for his grandson, and he could remember the shame and horror, as well as the defensive pride, with which he accompanied his increasingly eccentric and depressed father into the village.

'I want to die . . . I want to die . . . I want to die,' muttered Patrick rapidly. It was completely unacceptable. He could not be the person who had been that person. The speed was coming back and bringing with it the menace of lucidity and strong emotion.

They were approaching the hotel and Patrick had to make a quick decision. He leaned forward and said to the driver, 'I've changed my mind, take me to Eighth Street between C and D.'

The Chinese driver looked doubtfully in his rear-view mirror. Avenue D was a far cry from the Pierre Hotel. What sort of man would suddenly veer from one to the other? Only a junkie or an ignorant tourist.

'Avenue D bad place,' he said, testing the second theory.

'I'm relying on that,' said Patrick. 'Just take me there.'

The driver carried on down Fifth Avenue, past the turning for the hotel. Patrick sank back, excited and sick and guilty, but masking the feeling, as usual, with a show of languid indifference.

So what if he had changed his mind? Flexibility was an admirable quality. And nobody was more flexible when it came to giving up drugs, nobody more open to the possibility of taking them after all. He hadn't done anything yet. He could still reverse his decision, or rather reverse his revision. He could still go back.

Plummeting from the Upper to the Lower East Side, from Le Veau Gras to the Bargain Grocery Store on Eighth Street, he could not help admiring the way he ranged freely, or perhaps the word was 'inevitably', between luxury and squalor.

The taxi was approaching Tompkins Square, the beginning of the fun district. It was here that Chilly Willy, his street contact for those annoying occasions on which Pierre was asleep, dragged out his life of perpetual withdrawal. Chilly could only ever get enough smack to keep him looking for more; scavenging enough bags to twitch instead of convulsing, to squeal instead of screaming, he walked in little jerky steps with one limp and nerveless arm dangling by his side, like an old flex from the draughty ceiling. With his good hand, Chilly held up the filthy baggy trousers that were always in danger of slipping down over his emaciated waist. Despite being black, he looked pale and his face was speckled with brown liver spots. His teeth, the four or five that still clung heroically to his gums, were either dark yellow or black, chipped or shattered. He was an inspiration to his community and his customers since nobody could imagine looking as ill as him, however recklessly they lived.

The cab crossed Avenue C and carried on down Eighth Street. Here he was among the filthy haunches of the city, thought Patrick contentedly.

'Where you want?' asked the Chinaman.

'I want heroin,' said Patrick.

'Heloin,' repeated the driver anxiously.

'That's right,' said Patrick. 'Stop here, this is good.'

Wired Puerto Ricans were pacing about pugilistically on the corner, and black guys with big hats were leaning in doorways. Patrick lowered the window of the taxi, and new friends crowded in from every side.

'What ju wan, man? What ju looking for?'

'Clear tape . . . red tape . . . yellow tape. What you want?'

'Smack,' said Patrick.

'Shit, man, you from the police. You're a policeman.'

'No, I'm not. I'm an Englishman,' Patrick protested.

'Get out the cab, man, we don't sell you nothin' in the cab.'

'Wait here,' said Patrick to the driver. He got out of the taxi. One of the dealers took him by the arm and started to march him round the corner.

'I'm not going any further,' said Patrick as they were about to lose sight of the taxi.

'How much you want?'

'Give me four dime-bags of clear tape,' said Patrick, carefully unpeeling two twenty-dollar bills. He kept the twenties in the left trouser pocket, tens in the right trouser pocket, fives and ones in the overcoat pockets. The hundreds remained in their envelope in the inside coat pocket. This way he never tempted anybody with a show of cash.

'I'll give you six for fifty, man. You git one extra bag.'

'No, four is fine.'

Patrick pocketed the four little bags of greaseproof paper, turned around and climbed back into the cab.

'We go hotel now,' said the Chinaman eagerly.

'No, just drive me round the block for a bit. Take me to Sixth and B.'

'What you go lound block for?' The driver mumbled a Chinese curse, but moved off in the right direction.

Patrick had to test the smack he had just bought before he left the area altogether. He tore open one of the bags and poured the powder into the hollow formed in the back of his hand by the tendon of his raised thumb. He raised the tiny quantity of white powder to his nose and sniffed it up.

Oh, God! It was vile. Patrick clutched his stinging nose. Fuck, wank, blast, shit, damn.

It was a hideous cocktail of Vim and barbs. The scouring powder gave that touch of genuine bitterness to the mix, and the barbiturates provided a small thud of sedation. There were some advantages, of course. You could take ten of these bags a day and never become a junkie. You could be arrested with them and not be charged with possession of heroin. Thank God he hadn't shot it up, the Vim afterburn would have scorched his veins. What was he doing scoring off the street? He must be mad. He should have tried to get hold of Chilly Willy and sent him round to Loretta's. At least there were some traces of heroin in her little greaseproof packages.

Still, he wouldn't throw away this rubbish until he knew he could get something better. The cab had arrived at Sixth and C.

'Stop here,' said Patrick.

'I no wai' here,' shouted the driver in a sudden burst of vexation.

'Oh, well, fuck off then,' said Patrick, tossing a ten-dollar bill into the passenger seat and getting out of the cab. He slammed the door and stalked off towards Seventh Street.

The taxi screeched away from the kerb. When it had gone, Patrick was conscious of a hush in which his footsteps seemed to ring loudly on the pavement. He was alone. But not for long. On the next corner, a group of about a dozen dealers were standing around outside the Bargain Grocery Store.

Patrick slowed down, and one of the men, spotting him first, detached himself from the group and sauntered across the street with a buoyant and muscular gait. An exceptionally tall black man, he wore a shiny red jacket.

'How you doing?' he asked Patrick. His face was completely smooth, his cheekbones high, and his wide eyes seemingly saturated with indolence.

'Fine,' said Patrick. 'How about you?'

'I'm good. What you looking for?'

'Can you take me to Loretta's?'

'Loretta,' said the black man lazily.

'Sure.' Patrick was frustrated by his slowness and, feeling the book in his overcoat pocket, he imagined whipping it out like a pistol and gunning the dealer down with its ambitious first sentence, 'There is only one really serious philosophical problem: it is suicide.'

'How much you lookin' for?' asked the dealer, reaching nonchalantly behind his back.

'Just fifty dollars' worth,' said Patrick.

There was a sudden commotion on the other side of the street and he saw a half-familiar figure hobbling towards them in an agitated way.

'Don't stick him, don't stick him,' the new character shouted.

Patrick recognized him now: it was Chilly, clutching his trousers. He arrived, stumbling and out of breath. 'Don't stick him,' he repeated, 'he's my man.'

The tall black man smiled as if this was a truly hilarious

incident. 'I was going to stick you,' he said, proudly showing Patrick a small knife. 'I didn't know yuz knew Chilly!'

'What a small world,' said Patrick wearily. He felt totally detached from the threat that this man claimed to represent, and impatient to get on with his business.

'That's right,' said the tall man, ever more ebullient. He offered his hand to Patrick, after removing the knife. 'My name's Mark,' he said. 'You ever need anything, ask for Mark.'

Patrick shook his hand and smiled at him faintly. 'Hello, Chilly,' he said.

'Where you been?' asked Chilly reproachfully.

'Oh, over to England. Let's go to Loretta's.'

Mark waved goodbye and lolloped back across the street. Patrick and Chilly headed downtown.

'Extraordinary man,' drawled Patrick. 'Does he always stab people when he first meets them?'

'He's a bad man,' said Chilly. 'You don't wanna hang around him. Why din't you ask for me?'

'I did,' Patrick lied, 'but of course he said you weren't around. I guess he wanted a free hand to stab me.'

'Yeah, he's a bad man,' repeated Chilly.

The two men turned the corner of Sixth Street and Chilly almost immediately led Patrick down a short flight of steps into the basement of a dilapidated brown-stone building. Patrick was quietly pleased that Chilly was taking him to Loretta's, instead of leaving him to wait on a street corner.

There was only one door in the basement, reinforced with steel and equipped with a brass flap and a small spyglass. Chilly rang the bell and soon after a voice called out suspiciously, 'Who's that?'

'It's Chilly.'

'How much you want?'

Patrick handed Chilly fifty dollars. Chilly counted the

money, opened the brass flap and stuffed it inside. The flap retracted quickly and remained closed for what seemed like a long time.

'You got a bag for me?' asked Chilly, shifting from leg to leg.

'Of course,' replied Patrick magnificently, taking a ten-dollar bill out of his trouser pocket.

'Thanks, man.'

The flap reopened and Patrick clawed out the five little bags. Chilly got one for himself, and the two men left the building with a sense of achievement, counterbalanced by desire.

'Have you got any clean works?' asked Patrick.

'My ole lady got some. You wanna come back to my place?'

'Thanks,' said Patrick, flattered by these multiplying signs of trust and intimacy.

Chilly's place was a room on the second floor of a fire-gutted building. Its walls were blackened by smoke, and the unreliable staircase littered with empty matchbooks, liquor bottles, brown-paper bags, heaps of cornered dust, and balls of old hair. The room itself only contained one piece of furniture, a mustard-coloured armchair covered in burns, with a spring bursting from the centre of the seat, like an obscene tongue.

Mrs Chilly Willy – if that was her correct title, mused Patrick – was sitting on the arm of this chair when the two men came in. She was a large woman, more masculine in build than her skeletal husband.

'Hi, Chilly,' she said dozily, obviously further from withdrawal than he was.

'Hi,' he said, 'you know my man.'

'Hi, honey.'

'Hello,' beamed Patrick charmingly. 'Chilly said you might have a spare syringe.'

'I might,' she said playfully.

'Is it new?'

'Well, it ain't exactly noo, but I boiled it and everythin'.'

Patrick raised one eyebrow with deadly scepticism. 'Is it *very* blunt?' he asked.

She fished a bundle of loo paper out of her voluminous bra and carefully unwrapped the precious package. At its centre was a threateningly large syringe which a zookeeper would have hesitated to use on a sick elephant.

'That's not a needle, it's a bicycle pump,' Patrick protested, holding out his hand.

Intended for intramuscular use, the spike was worryingly thick, and when Patrick detached the green plastic head that held it he could not help noticing a ring of old blood inside. 'Oh, all right,' he said. 'How much do you want for it?'

'Gimme two bags,' urged Mrs Chilly, wrinkling up her nose endearingly.

It was an absurd price, but Patrick never argued about prices. He tossed two bags into her lap. If the stuff was any good he could always get more. Right now he had to shoot up. He asked Chilly to lend him a spoon and a cigarette filter. Since the light in the main room had failed, Chilly offered him the bathroom, a room without a bath in it, but with a black mark on the floor where there might once have been one. A naked bulb cast a dim yellow light on the insanely cracked basin and the seatless old loo.

Patrick trickled some water into the spoon and rested it at the back of the basin. Tearing open the three remaining packages, he wondered what sort of gear it was. Nobody could claim that Chilly looked well on a diet of Loretta's smack, but at least he wasn't dead. If Mr and Mrs Chilly were planning to shoot it up, there was no reason why he shouldn't. He could hear them whispering next door. Chilly was saying something about 'hurting' and was obviously trying to get the second bag out of his wife. Patrick emptied the three packets into the spoon and heated the solution, the flame from his lighter licking the already blackened underside of the spoon. As soon as it started to bubble, he cut off the heat and put the steaming liquid down again. He tore a thin strip off the cigarette filter, dropped it in the spoon, removed the spike from the syringe, and sucked the liquid up through the filter. The barrel was so thick that the solution barely rose a quarter of an inch.

Dropping his overcoat and jacket on the floor, Patrick rolled up his sleeve and tried to make out his veins in the faint light which gave a hepatic glow to every object that was not already black. Luckily, his track marks formed brown and purple threads, as if his veins were gunpowder trails burned along his arm.

Patrick rolled the sleeve of his shirt tight around his bicep and pumped his forearm up and down several times, clenching and unclenching his fist at the same time. He had good veins and, despite a certain shyness that resulted from his savage treatment of them, he was in a better position than many people whose daily search for a vein sometimes took up to an hour of exploratory digging.

He picked up the syringe and rested its point on the widest section of his track marks, slightly sideways to the scar. With such a long spike there was always a danger that it would go through the vein altogether and into the muscle on the other side, a painful experience, and so he approached the arm at a fairly low angle. At this crucial moment the syringe slipped from his hand and landed on a wet patch of the floor beside the loo. He could hardly believe what had happened. He felt vertiginous with horror and disappointment. There was a conspiracy against his having any fun today. He leaned over, desperate with longing, and picked up the works from the damp patch. The spike wasn't bent. Thank God for that. Everything was all right. He quickly wiped the syringe on his trousers.

By now his heart was beating fast and he felt that visceral excitement, a combination of dread and desire, which always preceded a fix. He pushed the painfully blunt tip of the needle under his skin and thought he saw, miracle of miracles, a globule of blood shoot into the barrel. Not wanting to waste any time with such an unwieldy instrument, he put his thumb on the plunger and pushed it straight down.

He felt a violent and alarming swelling in his arm and recognized immediately that the spike had slipped out of his vein and he had squirted the solution under his skin.

'Shit,' he shouted.

Chilly came shuffling through. 'What's happening, man?'

'I missed,' said Patrick through clenched teeth, pushing the hand of his wounded arm up against his shoulder.

'Oh, man,' croaked Chilly sympathetically.

'Can I suggest you invest in a stronger light bulb?' said Patrick pompously, holding his arm as if it had been broken.

'You shoulda used the flashlight,' said Chilly, scratching himself.

'Oh, thanks for telling me about it,' snapped Patrick.

'You wanna go back and score some more?' asked Chilly.

'No,' said Patrick curtly, putting his coat back on. 'I'm leaving.'

By the time he hit the street Patrick was wondering why he hadn't taken up Chilly's offer. 'Temper, temper,' he muttered sarcastically. He felt weary, but too frustrated to sleep. It was eleven thirty; perhaps Pierre had woken up by now. He had better go back to the hotel.

Patrick hailed a cab.

'You live around here?' asked the driver.

'No, I was just trying to score,' Patrick sighed, posting the bags of Vim and barbs out of the window.

'You wanna score?'

'That's right,' sighed Patrick.

'Shee-eet, I know a better place than this.'

'Really?' said Patrick, all ears.

'Yeah, in the South Bronx.'

'Well, let's go.'

'All right,' laughed the driver.

At last a cab driver who was helpful. An experience like this might put him in a good mood. Perhaps he should write a letter to the Yellow Cab Company. 'Dear sir,' murmured Patrick under his breath, 'I wish to commend in the highest possible terms the initiative and courtesy of your splendid young driver, Jefferson E. Parker. After a fruitless and, to be perfectly frank, infuriating expedition to Alphabet City, this knight errant, this, if I may put it thus, Jefferson Nightingale, rescued me from a very tiresome predicament, and took me to score in the South Bronx. If only more of your drivers displayed the same old-fashioned desire to serve. Yours, et cetera, Colonel Melrose.'

Patrick smiled. Everything was under control. He felt elated, almost frivolous. The Bronx was a bit of a worry for someone who had seen *Bronx Warriors* – a film of unremitting nastiness, not to be confused with the beautifully choreographed violence of the more simply, and more generically named *The Warriors* – but he felt invulnerable. People drew knives on him, but they could not touch him, and if they did he would not be there.

As the cab sped over a bridge Patrick had never crossed before, Jefferson turned his head slightly and said, 'We're gonna be in the Bronx soon.'

'I'll wait in the cab, shall I?' asked Patrick.

'You better lie on the floor,' laughed Jefferson, 'they don't like white people here.'

'On the floor?'

'Yeah, outta sight. If they see you, they gonna smash the windows. Shee-eet, I don't want my windows smashed.'

Jefferson stopped the taxi a few blocks beyond the bridge and Patrick sat down on the rubber floor mat with his back against the door.

'How much you want?' asked Jefferson, leaning over the driver's seat.

'Oh, five bags. And get a couple for yourself,' said Patrick, handing over seventy dollars.

'Thanks,' said Jefferson. 'I'm gonna lock the doors now. You stay outta sight, right?'

'Right,' said Patrick, sliding down further and stretching out on the floor. The bolts of all the doors slithered into place. Patrick wriggled around for some time before curling up in a foetal position with his head on the central hump. After a few moments his hip bone was persecuting his liver and he felt hopelessly tangled up in the folds of his overcoat. He twisted around onto his front, rested his head in his hands, and stared at the grooves in the floor mat. There was quite a strong smell of oil down at this level. 'It gives you a whole new perspective on life,' said Patrick, in the voice of a television housewife.

It was intolerable. Everything was intolerable. He was always getting into these *situations*, always ending up with the losers, the dregs, the Chilly Willys of life. Even at school he had been sent every Tuesday and Thursday afternoons, when the other boys joined their teams and played their matches, to remote playing fields with every variety of sporting misfit: the pale and sensitive musicians, the hopelessly fat Greek boys, and the disaffected cigarette-smoking protesters who regarded physical exertion as hopelessly uncool. As a punishment for their unsporting natures, these boys were forced to make their way round an assault course. Mr Pitch, the overwrought pederast in charge of this unwholesome squad, quivered with excitement and malice as each boy crashed myopically, waddled feebly, or tried to beat the system by running around the wall at the beginning of the course. While the Greeks splattered into the mud, and the music scholars lost their spectacles, and the conscientious objectors made their cynical remarks, Mr Pitch rushed about screaming abuse at them about their 'privileged' lives and, if the opportunity arose, kicking them in the bottom.

What the hell was going on? Had Jefferson gone to fetch some friends so they could beat him up together, or was he simply being abandoned while Jefferson went to get stoned?

Yes, thought Patrick, shifting restlessly, he had hung out with nothing but failures. Living in Paris when he was nineteen, he had fallen in with Jim, an Australian heroin smuggler on the run, and Simon, a black American bank robber just out of prison. He could remember Jim saying, as he had searched for a vein among the thick orange hairs of his forearm, 'Australia's so beautiful in the spring, man. All the little lambs frisking about. You can tell they're just so happy to be alive.' He had pushed the plunger down with a whimsical expression on his face.

Simon had tried to rob a bank while he was withdrawing, but he had been forced to surrender to the police after they had fired several volleys at him. 'I didn't wanna look like no Swiss cheese,' he explained.

Patrick heard the merciful sound of the locks opening again.

'I got it,' said Jefferson huskily. 'Goody,' said Patrick, sitting up.

Jefferson was happy and relaxed as he drove to the hotel. When he had snorted three of the bags Patrick could understand why. Here at last was a powder that contained a little heroin.

Jefferson and Patrick parted with the genuine warmth of people who had exploited each other successfully. Back in his hotel room, lying on the bed with his arms spread out, Patrick realized that if he took the other two bags and turned on the television he could probably fall asleep. Once he had taken heroin he could imagine being without it; when he was without it he could only imagine getting more. But just to see if all the evening's trouble had been completely unnecessary, he decided to call Pierre's number.

As the telephone rang he again wondered what kept him from suicide. Was it something as contemptible as sentimentality, or hope, or narcissism? No. It was really the desire to know what would happen next, despite the conviction that it was bound to be horrible: the narrative suspense of it all.

'Hallo?'

'Pierre!'

'Who iz this?'

'Patrick.'

'What do you want?'

'Can I come round?'

'OK. How long?'

'Twenty minutes.'

'OK.'

Patrick raised his fist in triumph and sprinted from the room.

6

'Pierre!'

'*Ça va?*' said Pierre, getting up from his leather office chair. The parched yellow skin of his face was stretched more tautly than ever over the thin nose, high cheekbones, and prominent jaw. He shook hands with Patrick, fixing him with lantern eyes.

The fetid atmosphere of the apartment struck Patrick like the scent of a long-absent lover. The stains of overturned coffee mugs still tattooed the oatmeal carpet in the same places as before, and the familiar pictures of severed heads floating on pieces of jigsaw puzzle, lovingly executed by Pierre with a fine ink pen, made Patrick smile.

'What a relief to see you again!' he exclaimed. 'I can't tell you what a nightmare it is out there, scoring off the streets.'

'You score off the street!' barked Pierre disapprovingly. 'You fucking crazy!'

'But you were asleep.'

'You shoot with tap water?'

'Yes,' admitted Patrick guiltily.

'You crazy,' glared Pierre. 'Come in here, I show you.'

He walked through to his grimy and narrow kitchen. Opening the door of the big old-fashioned fridge, he took out a large jar of water.

'This is tap water,' said Pierre ominously, holding up the jar. 'I leave it one month and look . . .' He pointed to a diffuse brown sediment at the bottom of the jar. 'Rust,' he said, 'it's a fucking killer! I have one friend who shoot with tap water and the rust get in his bloodstream and his heart . . .' Pierre chopped the air with his hand and said, '*Tak:* it stop.'

'That's appalling,' murmured Patrick, wondering when they were going to do business.

'The water come from the mountains,' said Pierre, sitting down in his swivel chair and sucking water from a glass into an enviably slim syringe, 'but the pipes are full of rust.'

'I'm lucky to be alive,' said Patrick without conviction. 'It's nothing but mineral water from now on, I promise.'

'It's the City,' said Pierre darkly; 'they keep the money for new pipes. They kill my friend. What do you want?' he added, opening a package and piling some white powder into a spoon with the corner of a razor blade.

'Um . . . a gram of smack,' said Patrick casually, 'and seven grams of coke.'

'The smack is six hundred. The coke I make you a price: one hundred a gram instead of one-twenty. Total: thirteen hundred dollar.'

Patrick slipped the orange envelope out of his pocket while Pierre piled another white powder into the spoon and stirred it, frowning like a child pretending to make cement.

Was that nine or ten? Patrick started counting again. When he reached thirteen he tapped the notes together like a shuffled deck of cards and tossed them over to Pierre's side of the mirror where they fanned out extravagantly. Pierre wound a length of rubber around his bicep and gripped it in his teeth. Patrick was pleased to see that he still had the use of the volcano cone in the hollow of his arm.

Pierre's pupils dilated for a moment and then contracted again, like the feeding mouth of a sea anemone.

'OK,' he croaked, trying to give the impression that

nothing had happened, but sounding subdued by pleasure, 'I give you what you want.' He refilled the syringe and squirted the contents into a second pinkish glass of water.

Patrick wiped his clammy hands on his trousers. Only the need to make one more tricky negotiation contained his heart-exploding impatience.

'Do you have any spare syringes?' he asked. Pierre could be very awkward about syringes. Their value varied wildly according to how many he had left, and although he was generally helpful to Patrick when he had spent over a thousand dollars, there was always the danger that he would lapse into an indignant lecture on his presumption.

'I give you two,' said Pierre with delinquent generosity.

'Two!' exclaimed Patrick as if he had just witnessed a medieval relic waving from behind its glass case. Pierre took out a pair of pale green scales and measured the quantities Patrick had requested, giving him individual gram packets so that he could keep track of his coke consumption.

'Ever thoughtful, ever kind,' murmured Patrick. The two precious syringes followed across the dusty mirror.

'I get you some water,' said Pierre.

Perhaps he had put more heroin than usual in the speedball. How else could one explain this unaccustomed benevolence?

'Thanks,' said Patrick, slipping hastily out of his overcoat and jacket and rolling up his shirt sleeve. Jesus! There was a black bulge in his skin where he had missed the vein round at Chilly's. He'd better not let Pierre see this sign of his incompetence and desperation. Pierre was such a moral man. Patrick let the sleeve flop down, undid the gold cufflink of his right sleeve, and rolled that up instead. Fixing was the one activity in which he had become truly ambidextrous. Pierre came back with one full and one empty glass, and a spoon.

Patrick unfolded one of the packets of coke. The shiny white paper was imprinted with a pale blue polar bear. Unlike Pierre he preferred to take coke on its own until the tension and fear were unbearable, then he would send in the Praetorian Guard of heroin to save the day from insanity and defeat. He held the packet in a funnel and tapped it gently. Small grains of powder slipped down the narrow valley of paper and tumbled into the spoon. Not too much for the first fix. Not too little either. Nothing was more intolerable than a dissipated, watery rush. He carried on tapping.

'How are you?' asked Pierre, so rapidly that the question seemed like one word.

'Well, my father died the other day and so . . .' Patrick was not sure what to say. He looked at the packet, gave it one more decisive tap, and another flurry of powder joined the small heap already in the spoon. 'And so I'm a little confused at the moment,' he concluded.

'How was he, your father?'

'He was a kitten,' Patrick intoned rhapsodically. 'And he had such artistic hands.' For a moment the water went syrupy and then it dissolved into a clear solution. 'He could have been Prime Minister,' he added.

'He was in politics?' asked Pierre, narrowing his eyes.

'No, no,' Patrick replied, 'it was a sort of joke. In his world – a world of pure imagination – it was better if a person "could have been" Prime Minister than if he *was* Prime Minister: that would have shown vulgar ambition.' There was a faint metallic ringing as he directed the jet of water from his syringe against the side of the spoon.

'*Tu regrettes qu'il est mort?*' asked Pierre shrewdly.

'*Non, absolument pas, je regrette qu'il ait vécu.*'

'*Mais sans lui*, you would not exist.'

'One shouldn't be egotistical about these things,' said Patrick with a smile.

His right arm was relatively unscathed. A few bruises the colour of tobacco stains yellowed his lower forearm, and faded pink puncture marks clustered around the bullseye of his principal vein. He raised the needle and allowed a couple of drops to dribble from its eye. His stomach made a rumbling sound and he felt as nervous and excited as a twelve-year-old in the back of a darkened cinema stretching his arm around a girl's shoulders for the first time.

He aimed the needle at the centre of the existing puncture marks and pushed it almost painlessly under his skin. A thread of blood burst into the barrel and curled around, a private mushroom cloud, luminously red in the clear bitter water. Thank God he had found a vein. His heart rate increased, like the drumbeat of a galley rowing into battle. Holding the barrel firmly between his fingers he pushed the plunger down slowly. Like a film in reverse the blood shot back through the needle towards its source.

Before he felt its effects he smelled the heartbreaking fragrance of the cocaine, and then a few seconds afterward, in a time-lapse frenzy, its cold geometric flowers broke out everywhere and carpeted the surface of his inner vision. Nothing could ever be as pleasurable as this. He clumsily drew back the plunger, filled the barrel with blood, and injected himself a second time. Drunk with pleasure, choking with love, he lurched forward and put the syringe down heavily on the mirror. He would have to flush it out before the blood coagulated, but he couldn't do it straight away. The sensation was too strong. Sound was twisted and amplified until it whistled like the engine of a landing jet.

Patrick sat back and closed his eyes, his lips thrust out like a child waiting for a kiss. Sweat had already broken out high on his forehead, and his armpits dripped every few seconds like defective taps.

Pierre knew exactly what state Patrick was in and disapproved strongly of his unbalanced approach, and the irresponsible way he had put his syringe down without flushing it out. He picked it up and filled it with water so that the mechanism didn't block. Sensing a movement, Patrick opened his eyes and whispered, 'Thank you.'

'You should take smack at the same time,' said Pierre reproachfully; 'it's medicine, man, medicine.'

'I like the rush.'

'But you take too much, you lose control.'

Patrick sat up and looked at Pierre intently. 'I never lose control,' he said, 'I just test its limits.'

'Bullshit,' said Pierre, unimpressed.

'Of course you're right,' smiled Patrick. 'But you know what it's like trying to stay on the edge without falling off it,' he said, appealing to their traditional solidarity.

'I know what it's like,' screeched Pierre, his eyes incandescent with passion. 'For eight years I thought I was an egg, but I had total control, *contrôle total*.'

'I remember,' said Patrick soothingly.

The rush was over, and like a surfer who shoots out of a tube of furling, glistening sea only to peter out and fall among the breaking waves, his thoughts began to scatter before the onset of boundless unease. Only a few minutes after the fix he felt a harrowing nostalgia for the dangerous exhilaration which was already dying out. As if his wings had melted in that burst of light, he felt himself falling towards a sea of unbearable disappointment, and it was this that made him pick up the syringe, finish flushing it out and, despite his shaking hands, begin to prepare another fix.

'Do you think the measure of a perversion is its need to be repeated, its inability to be satisfied?' he asked Pierre. 'I wish my father were around to answer that question,' he added piously.

'Why? He was a junkie?'

'No, no . . .' said Patrick. He wanted to say, 'it was a kind of joke' again, but resisted. 'What sort of man was *your* father?' he asked hastily, in case Pierre followed up his remark.

'He was a *fonctionnaire*,' said Pierre contemptuously, '*Métro, boulot, dodo*. His happiest days were his *service militaire*, and the proudest moment of his life was when the Minister congratulated him for saying nothing. Can you imagine? Each time someone visited the house, which was not often, my father would tell the same story.' Pierre straightened his back, smiled complacently, and wagged his finger. '"*Et Monsieur le Ministre m'a dit, Vous avez eu raison de ne rien dire.*" When he told that story I used to run from the room. It fill me with disgust, *j'avais un dégoût total*.'

'And your mother?' said Patrick, pleased to have got Pierre off his own parental case.

'What is a woman who is not maternal?' snapped Pierre. 'A piece of furniture with breasts!'

'Quite,' said Patrick, sucking a new solution into his syringe. As a concession to Pierre's medical advice, he had decided to take some heroin rather than further delay the onset of serenity with another chilling shot of cocaine.

'You have to leave all that behind,' said Pierre. 'Parents, all that shit. You have to invent yourself again to become an individual.'

'Right on,' said Patrick, knowing it was best not to argue with Pierre's theories.

'The Americans, they talk all the time about individuality, but they don't have an idea unless everybody else is having the same idea at the same time. My American customers, they always fuck me about to show they are individuals, but they always do it in exactly the same way. Now I have no American customers.'

'People think they are individuals because they use the word "I" so often,' Patrick commented.

'When I died in the hospital,' said Pierre, '*j'avais une conscience sans limites*. I knew everything, man, literally *everything*. After that I cannot take seriously the *sociologues et psychologues* who say you are "schizoid" or "paranoid", or "social class two" or "social class three". These people know nothing. They think they know about the human mind, but they know nothing, *absolument rien*.' Pierre glared vehemently at Patrick. 'It's like they put moles in charge of the space programme,' he sneered.

Patrick laughed drily. He had stopped listening to Pierre and started searching for a vein. When he saw a poppy of blood light up the barrel, he administered the injection, and pulled out the syringe, flushing it out efficiently this time.

He was amazed by the strength and smoothness of the heroin. His blood became as heavy as a sack of coins and he sank down appreciatively into his body, resolved again into a single substance after the catapulting exile of the cocaine.

'Exactly,' he whispered, 'like moles . . . God, this is good smack.' He closed his eyelids lingeringly.

'It's pure,' said Pierre. '*Faîtes attention, c'est très fort*.'

'Mm, I can tell.'

'It's medicine, man, medicine,' Pierre reiterated.

'Well, I'm completely cured,' whispered Patrick with a private smile. Everything was going to be all right. A coal fire on a stormy night, rain that could not touch him beating against the windowpane. Streams made of smoke, and smoke that formed into shining pools. Thoughts shimmering on the borders of a languorous hallucination.

He scratched his nose and reopened his eyes. Yes, with the firm base provided by the heroin, he could play high notes of cocaine all night without cracking altogether.

But he'd have to be alone for that. With good drugs, solitude was not just bearable, it was indispensable. 'It's much more subtle than Persian smack,' he croaked. 'A gentle sustained curve . . . like a, like a polished tortoise shell.' He closed his eyes again.

'It's the strongest smack in the world,' said Pierre simply.

'Ya,' drawled Patrick, 'it's such a bore, one can hardly ever get it in England.'

'You should come and live here.'

'Good idea,' said Patrick amiably. 'By the way, what's the time?'

'One forty-seven.'

'Gosh, I'd better go to bed,' said Patrick, putting the syringes carefully into his inside pocket. 'It's been lovely seeing you again. I'll be in touch very soon.'

'OK,' said Pierre. 'I'm awake tonight, tomorrow, and tomorrow night.'

'Perfect,' said Patrick nodding.

He put on his jacket and overcoat. Pierre got up, undid the four security locks, opened the door, and let him out.

7

Patrick slumped back in the chair. The tension was deleted from his chest. For a moment he fell quiet. But soon a new character installed itself in his body, forcing his shoulders back and his stomach out, and launching him into another bout of compulsive mimicry.

The Fat Man (pushing back the chair to accommodate his huge stomach): 'I feel compelled to speak, sir, indeed I do. Compelled, sir, is a mild description of the obligation under which I am placed in this matter. My story is a simple one, the story of a man who loved not wisely but too well.' (Wipes a tear from the corner of his eye.) 'A man who ate not from greed, but from passion. Eating, sir – I do not attempt to disguise it – has been my life. Couched in the ruins of this old body are the traces of some of the most exquisite dishes ever cooked. When horses have collapsed beneath my bulk, their legs shattered or their lungs flooded with their own blood, or I have been forced to renounce the fruitless struggle to intervene between the seat and the steering wheel of a motor car, I have consoled myself with the reflection that my weight has been won, and not merely "put on". Naturally, I have dined in Les Bains and Les Baux, but I have also dined in Quito and Khartoum. And when the ferocious Yanomami offered me a dish of human flesh, I did not allow prudishness to prevent me from requesting a third helping. Indeed I did not, sir.' (Smiles wistfully.)

Nanny (huffing and puffing): 'Human flesh indeed! What-ever next? You always were a strange boy.'

'Oh, shut up,' screamed Patrick silently, as he paced across the faded green carpet and turned around abruptly.

Gary (raising his eyes to heaven with a charming little sigh): 'My name's Gary, I'll be your waiter tonight. Today's specials include a Dish of Human Flesh, and a sodium-free Frisson of Colombian Cocaine nestling on a bed of "Wild Baby" Chinese White Heroin.'

Pete Bloke: 'Haven't you got any Hovis, then?'

Mrs Bloke: 'Yeah, we want Hovis.'

Hovis Voice-over (theme music from *Coronation Street*): 'It were grand when I were young. I'd go round t' dealer's, buy 'alf an ounce o' coke and four grams o' smack, order round a case o' champagne from Berry Bros., take wench out ta Mirabelle, and still 'ave change from a farthing. Them were the days.'

He was dangerously out of control. Every thought or hint of a thought took on a personality stronger than his own. 'Please, please, please make it stop,' muttered Patrick, getting up and pacing about the room.

Mocking Echo: 'Please, please, please make it stop.'

Nanny: 'I know about the aristocracy and their filthy ways.'

Humpo Languid (laughing disarmingly): 'What filthy ways, Nanny?'

Nanny: 'Oh, no, you won't find Nanny telling tales out of school. My lips are sealed. Whatever would Lady Dead-wood think? Rolling stones gather no moss. You mark my words. You always were a strange boy.'

Mrs Garsington: 'Who is in charge here? I wish to speak to the manager immediately.'

Dr McCoy: 'It's life, Jim, but not as we know it.'

Captain Kirk (flicking open his communicator): 'Beam us up, Scotty.'

Patrick opened the packet of heroin and, in too much of a hurry to make another fix, simply tipped some of it onto the glass which protected the surface of the table.

Indignant Eric (knowingly): 'Oh, typical, faced with a problem: take more heroin. Basically, the ultimate self-perpetuating system.'

Pulling a banknote out of his pocket, Patrick sat down and stooped over the table.

Captain Languid: 'I say, Sergeant, shut those fellows up, will you?'

Sergeant: 'Don't worry, sir, we'll bring them under control. They're nothing but a bunch of fuzzywuzzies, black-souled bastards, sir, never seen a Gatling in their miserable, godless lives, sir.'

Captain Languid: 'Well done, Sergeant.'

Patrick sniffed up the powder, threw his head back, and inhaled deeply through his nose.

Sergeant: 'Allow me to take the brunt of the impact, sir.' (Groans, a spear lodged in his chest.)

Captain Languid: 'Oh, thank you . . . um . . .'

Sergeant: 'Wilson, sir.'

Captain Languid: 'Yes, of course. Well done, Wilson.'

Sergeant: 'Only wish I could do the same again, sir. But I'm sorry to say I've been fatally wounded, sir.'

Captain Languid: 'Oh, dear. Well, get that wound seen to, Sergeant.'

Sergeant: 'Thank you, sir, very kind of you. What a wonderful gentleman!'

Captain Languid: 'And if the worst should happen, I'm sure we can get you some sort of posthumous gong. My uncle is the chap in charge of that sort of thing.'

Sergeant (sitting up and saluting, shouts): 'Sir!' (Sinking

back.) 'It'll mean a lot to Mrs Wilson and the toddlers, poor little fatherless mites.' (Groans.) 'What . . . a . . . wonderful gentleman.'

George the Barman (polishing a glass meditatively): 'Oh, yes, that Captain Languid, I remember him well. Used to come in here and always ask for nine oysters. Not half a dozen or a dozen, but nine. What a gentleman! They don't make 'em like that anymore. I remember the Fat Man as well. Oh yes, not likely to forget him. We couldn't have him in the bar towards the end, literally couldn't fit him in. What a gentleman, though! One of the old school, didn't go in for all this dieting, dear me, no.'

The Fat Man (standing in an especially enlarged dock at the Old Bailey): 'It has indeed been my misfortune, sir, to live in an age of diets and regimens.' (Wipes a tear from the corner of his eye.) 'They call me the Fat Man, and I am fat enough to flatter myself that the epithet requires no explanation. I stand accused of unnatural appetites and an unnatural degree of appetite. Can I be blamed, sir, if I have filled my cup to the brim, if I have piled the plate of my life high with the *Moules au Menthe Fraîches* of experience (a dish to wake the dead, sir, a dish to charm a king!)? I have not been one of those timid waifs of modern life, I have not been a poor guest at the Feast. Dead men, sir, do not accept the challenge of the Menu Gastronomique at the Lapin Vert when they have scarcely swallowed the last mouthful of the Petit Déjeuner Médiéval at the Château de l'Enterrement. They do not then have themselves driven by ambulance (the natural transport of the bon viveur, sir, the carriage of a king!) to the Sac d'Argent to launch themselves with grim abandon down the Cresta Run of their Carte Royale.' (The violinist from the Café Florian plays in the background.) 'My last days, last days, sir, for I fear that my liver – oh, it has done me valiant service, but now it has grown tired and

I have grown tired too; but enough of that – my last days have been clouded with calumny.' (Sound of muffled sobbing in the court.) 'But I do not regret the course, or rather the courses' (sad little laugh) 'I have taken in life, indeed I don't.' (Gathers all his dignity.) 'I have eaten, and I have eaten bravely.'

Judge (with thunderous indignation): 'This case is dismissed. It is a grave miscarriage of justice that it was ever brought to trial and, in recognition of that fact, the court awards the Fat Man a dinner for one at the Pig and Whistle.'

Contented Populace: 'Hooray! Hooray!'

Patrick felt limitless dread. The rotten floorboards of his thoughts gave way one after another until the ground itself seemed no fitter than sodden paper to catch his fall. Maybe it would never stop. 'I'm so tired, so tired,' he said, sitting down on the edge of the bed, but immediately getting up again.

Mocking Echo: 'I'm so tired, I'm so tired.'

Greta Garbo (screaming hysterically): 'I don't want to be alone. I'm sick of being alone.'

Patrick slid down the wall. 'I'm so fucking tired,' he wailed.

Mrs Mop: 'You have a nice fix of coke, dear, perk yourself up a bit.'

Dr Death (taking out a syringe): 'I have just the thing for you. We always use it in cases of bereavement.'

Cleopatra: 'Oh, yes.' (Pouting girlishly.) 'My bluest veins to kiss.'

Mrs Mop: 'Go on, dear, do yourself a favour.'

Cleopatra (hoarsely): 'Go on, you bastard, fuck me.'

This time Patrick had to use his tie. He wound it around his bicep several times and gripped it in his teeth, baring his gums like a snarling dog.

Gift o' the Gab O'Connor (draining a glass of Jameson's): 'She took to the leech with rowdy Saxon abandon crying, "I've always wanted to be in two places at once."'

Courtier (excitedly): 'A hit, a palpable hit.'

Captain Kirk: 'Warp factor ten, Mr Sulu.'

Attila the Hun (basso profundo): 'I play football with the heads of my enemies. I ride under triumphal arches, my horse's hooves striking sparks from the cobblestones, the slaves of Rome strewing flowers in my path.'

Patrick fell off the chair and curled up on the floor. The brutality of the rush left him winded and amazed. He shook from the violence of his own heartbeat, like a man cowering under the spinning blades of a helicopter. His limbs were paralysed with tension and he imagined his veins, as thin and brittle as the stems of champagne glasses, snapping if he tried to unbend his arms. Without heroin he would die of a heart attack. 'Just fuck off, the lot of you,' he murmured.

Honest John (shaking his head): 'What a vicious bastard, eh, that Attila. Dear, oh dear. "Wot you staring at?" he said. "Nothing," I said. "Well, don't fucking do it, all right?" he said.' (Shakes his head.) 'Vicious!'

Nanny: 'Nanny says if you don't stop talking in silly voices, the wind will change, and you won't be able to stop.'

Boy (desperately): 'But I want to stop, Nanny.'

Nanny: '"I want" gets nowhere.'

Sergeant: 'Get a grip on yourself, laddie.' (Screaming): 'Quick march! Left, right. Left, right.'

Patrick's legs slid back and forth across the carpet, like a tipped-over wind-up doll.

Short notice in *The Times*' Death Column: 'MELROSE. On 25 May, peacefully, after a happy day in the Pierre Hotel. Patrick, aged 22, loving son of David and Eleanor, will be sadly missed by Attila the Hun, Mrs Mop, Indignant Eric, and his many friends, too numerous to enumerate.'

Gift o' the Gab O'Connor: 'A poor unfortunate soul. If he was not twitching like the severed leg of a galvanized frog, it was only because the mood lay heavy on him, like pennies on the eyelids of the dead.' (Drains a tumbler of Jameson's.)

Nanny (older now, her memory no longer what it was): 'I can't get used to it, he was such a lovely little boy. Always called him "my precious pet", I remember. Always said, "Don't forget that Nanny loves you." '

Gift o' the Gab O'Connor (tears rolling down his cheeks): 'And his poor unfortunate arms fit to make a strong man weep. Covered in wounds they were, like the mouths of hungry goldfish crying out for the only thing that would purchase a little peace for his poor troubled heart.' (Drains a tumbler of Jameson's.)

Captain Languid: 'He was the sort of chap who stayed in his room a good deal. Nothing wrong with that, of course, except that he paced about the whole time. As I like to say, if one's going to be idle, one should be thoroughly idle.' (Smiles charmingly.)

Gift o' the Gab O'Connor (drinking straight from the bottle now, knee deep in tears, his speech grown more slurred): 'And he was troubled in his mind also. Maybe it was the worry of the freedom killed him? In every situation – and he was always getting himself into situations – he saw the choices stretching out crazily, like the broken blood vessels of tired eyes. And with every action he heard the death cry of all the things he had not done. And he saw the chance to get the vertigo, even in a sky-catching puddle, or the gleaming of a drain on the corner of Little Britain Street. Maddened he was by the terror of forgetting and losing the trail of who he was, and turning in circles, like a foxy bloody foxhound in the middle of the bloody wood.'

Honest John: 'What a prannit, eh? Never did an honest day's work in his life. When did you ever see him help an old lady across the road, or buy a bag of sweets for some deprived kiddies? Never. You gotta be honest.'

The Fat Man: 'He was a man, sir, who did not eat enough,

a man who picked at his food, who turned from the cornu-
copia to the pharmacopoeia of life. In short, sir, the worst
kind of scoundrel.'

Gift o' the Gab O'Connor (occasionally surfacing above
a lake of tears): 'And the sight of him . . .' (glug, glug, glug)
'. . . those torn lips that had never learned to love . . .' (glug,
glug, glug) '. . . Those lips that had spoken wild and bitter
words . . .' (glug, glug, glug) '. . . torn open by the fury of it,
and the knowledge that death was upon him' (glug).

Debbie (stammering): 'I wonder what I'm meant to say?'

Kay: 'I saw him the day it happened.'

'Let me not go mad,' shouted Patrick in a voice that started
like his own, but became more like John Gielgud's with the
last two words.

The Vicar (looking down soothingly from the pulpit):
'Some of us remember David Melrose as a paedophile, an
alcoholic, a liar, a rapist, a sadist, and a "thoroughly nasty
piece of work". But, you know, in a situation like that,
what Christ asks us to say, and what he would have said himself in his own words is' (pausing) ' "But that's not the whole
story, is it?"'

Honest John: 'Yes it is.'

The Vicar: 'And that "whole story" idea is one of the most
exciting things about Christianity. When we read a book by
one of our favourite authors, be he Richard Bach or Peter
Mayle, we don't just want to know that it's about a very
special seagull, or that it's set in the lovely *campagne*, to use
a French word, of Provence; we want the satisfaction of
reading all the way to the end.'

Honest John: 'Speak for yourself.'

The Vicar: 'And in very much the same spirit, when we
make judgements about other people (and which one of
us doesn't?) we have to make sure that we have the "whole
story" spread out before us.'

Attila the Hun (basso profundo): 'Die, Christian dog!' (Decapitates the Vicar.)

Vicar's Severed Head (pausing thoughtfully): 'You know, the other day, my young granddaughter came to me and said, "Grandfather, I *like* Christianity." And I said to her (thoroughly puzzled), "Why?" And do you know what she said?'

Honest John: 'Of course we don't, you prannit.'

Vicar's Severed Head: 'She said, "Because it's such a comfort."' (Pauses, and then more slowly and emphatically): '"Because it's such a comfort."'

Patrick opened his eyes and uncurled slowly on the floor. The television stared at him accusingly. Perhaps it could save him or distract him from his own involuntary performance.

Television (snivelling and shivering): 'Turn me on, man. Gimme a turn-on.'

Mr President: 'Ask not what your television can do for you, but what you can do for your television.'

Ecstatic Populace: 'Hooray! Hooray!'

Mr President: 'We shall pay any price, bear any burden, meet any hardship . . .'

Von Trapp Family Singers (ecstatically): 'Climb every mountain!'

Mr President: '. . . support any friend, oppose any foe, to assure the survival and success of television.'

Ecstatic Populace: 'Hooray! Hooray!'

Mr President: 'Let the word go forth from this time and place, that the torch has passed to a new generation of Americans – born in this century, tempered by war, disciplined by a hard and bitter peace, proud of our ancient heritage and unwilling to do anything except watch television.'

'Yes, yes, yes,' thought Patrick, crawling across the floor, 'television.'

Television (shifting restlessly from wheel to wheel): 'Gimme a turn-on, man, I gotta have it.'

Viewer (coolly): 'What you got for me?'

Television (ingratiatingly): 'I got *The Million-Dollar Movie. The Billion-Dollar Man. The Trillion-Dollar Quiz Show.*'

Viewer: 'Yeahyeahyeah, but wot you got *now*?'

Television (guiltily): 'A still of the American flag, and some weirdo in a pale blue nylon suit talkin' about the end of the world. *The Farming Report* should be comin' up real soon.'

Viewer: 'OK, I guess I'll take the flag. But don't push me' (getting out a revolver) 'or I'll blow your fuckin' screen out.'

Television: 'OK, man, just keep cool, OK? The reception isn't too great, but it's a *real* good shot of the flag. I personally guarantee that.'

Patrick switched off the television. When would this dreadful night come to an end? Clambering onto the bed, he collapsed, closed his eyes, and listened intently to the silence.

Ron Zak (his eyes closed, smiling benignly): 'I want you to listen to that silence. Can you hear it?' (Pause.) 'Become part of that silence. That silence is your inner voice.'

Honest John: 'Oh, dear, it's not over yet, eh? Who's this Ron Zak, then? Sounds like a bit of a prannit, to be honest.'

Ron Zak: 'Are you all one with that silence?'

Students: 'We are one with the silence, Ron.'

Ron Zak: 'Good.' (Long pause.) 'Now I want you to use the visualization technique you learned last week to picture a pagoda – that's kind of a Chinese beach house, only in the hills.' (Pause.) 'Good. It's very beautiful, isn't it?'

Students: 'Gee, Ron, it's so neat.'

Ron Zak: 'It's got a beautiful golden roof, and a network of bubbling round pools in the garden. Climb into one of those pools – mm, it feels good – and allow the gatekeepers to wash your body and bring you fresh new robes made of silk and other prestigious fabrics. They feel good, don't they?'

Students: 'Oh, yes, they feel great.'

Ron Zak: 'Good. Now I want you to go into the pagoda.' (Pause.) 'There's somebody in there, isn't there?'

Students: 'Yes, it is the Guide we learned about the week before last.'

Ron Zak (a little irritably): 'No, the Guide is in another room.' (Pause.) 'It's your mum and dad.'

Students (in startled recognition): 'Mum? Dad?'

Ron Zak: 'Now I want you to go over to your mum and say, "Mum, I really love you." '

Students: 'Mum, I really love you.'

Ron Zak: 'Now I want you to embrace her.' (Pause.) 'It feels good, doesn't it?'

Students (they scream, faint, write cheques, embrace each other, burst into tears, and punch pillows): 'It feels so good!'

Ron Zak: 'Now I want you to go over to Dad and say, "You, on the other hand, I cannot forgive." '

Students: 'You, on the other hand, I cannot forgive.'

Ron Zak: 'Take out a revolver and shoot his fuckin' brains out. Bang. Bang. Bang. Bang.'

Students: 'Bang. Bang. Bang. Bang.'

Koenig Spook (terrible creaking of armour): 'Omlet! Ich bin thine Popospook!'

'Oh, for fuck's sake,' shouted Patrick, sitting up and slapping himself across the face, 'stop thinking about it.'

Mocking Echo: 'Stop thinking about it.'

Patrick sat down at the table and picked up the packet of coke. He tapped the packet and an unusually large rock fell into the spoon. Bringing a jet of water down on the cocaine, he heard a silvery ringing where it struck the side of the spoon. The powder flooded and dissolved.

His veins were beginning to shrink from the savage onslaught of the evening but one vein, lower down the forearm, still showed without encouragement. Thick and blue, it snaked its way towards his wrist. The skin was tougher there, and it hurt to break beneath it.

Nanny (singing dreamily to her veins): 'Come out, come out, wherever you are!'

A thread of blood appeared in the barrel.

Cleopatra (gasping): 'Oh, yes, yes, yes, yes, yes.'

Attila the Hun (viciously, through clenched teeth): 'No prisoners!'

Patrick fainted and sank back onto the floor, feeling as if his body had suddenly been filled with wet cement. There was silence as he looked down on his body from the ceiling.

Pierre: 'Look at your body, man, it's fucking rubbish. *Tu as une conscience totale. No limites.*' (Patrick's body accelerates very rapidly. Space turns from blue to dark blue, and from dark blue to black. The clouds are like the pieces of a jigsaw puzzle. Patrick looks down and sees, far below him, the window of his hotel room. Inside the room is a thin white beach surrounded by an intensely blue sea. On the beach children are burying Patrick's body in the sand. Only the head is showing. He thinks he can break the case of sand with a simple movement, but he realizes his mistake when one of the children empties a bucket of wet concrete in his face. He tries to wipe the concrete from his mouth and eyes, but his arms are trapped in a concrete tomb.)

'Jennifer's Diary': 'Patrick Melrose's graveside appeared to be unattended as the coffin was lowered, somewhat roughly, into the ground. However, all was not lost, and in the nick of time, that ever popular, gracious, enchanting, indefatigable couple, Mr and Mrs Chilly Willy, the Alphabet City junkies, on a rare visit uptown, shuffled attractively onto the scene. "Don't sink him, don't sink him, he's my man," cried the inconsolable Chilly Willy. "Where I gonna git a dime bag now?" he wailed. "Did he leave me anything in his will?" asked his grief-stricken wife, who wore a cleverly designed, affordable dress in a superbly colourful floral fabric. Among those who did not attend, claiming that they had never heard of the deceased, were Sir Veridian Gravalaux-Gravalax, Marshal of the Island Kennels, and his cousin the very attractive Miss Rowena Keats-Shelley.'

Honest John: 'I don't think he's going to survive this one, to be honest.'

Indignant Eric (shaking his head incredulously): 'What amazes me is that people think they can come along and, eh, casually, eh, bury people alive.'

Mrs Chronos (carrying a huge hourglass, and wearing a tattered old ball gown): 'Well, I must say, it's nice to be wanted! Not a single part since the fourth act of *The Winter's Tale*' (warmly). 'A play by Bill Shakespeare, of course – a lovely man, by the way, and a close personal friend. As the centuries slipped past I thought, "That's right, just ignore me, I know when I'm not wanted." ' (Folds her arms and nods.) 'People think of me as a character actor, but if there's one thing I can't stand, it's being typecast. Anyway,' (little sigh) 'I suppose it's time to say my lines.' (Pulling a face.) 'Frankly, I find them a little bit old fashioned. People don't seem to appreciate that I'm a modern girl.' (Coy laugh.) 'I just want to say one more thing,' (serious now) 'and that's a big "thank you" to all my fans. You kept me going during the lonely years. Thank you for the sonnets, and the letters and the conversations, they mean a lot, they really do. Think of me sometimes, darlings, when your gums go black, and you can't remember someone's name.' (Blows kisses to the audience. Then composes herself, smooths the folds of her dress, and walks front stage.)

'Since his death cannot be mended,
All our revels now are ended.
Think not harshly of our play

But come again another day.'

Attila the Hun (punches the lid off his coffin, making a sound of growling, snarling, hissing fury, like a leopard being baited through the bars of a cage): 'Raaaarrrrghh!'

Patrick shot bolt upright and banged his head on the leg of the chair. 'Shit, wank, fuck, blast,' he said in his own voice at last.

8

Patrick lay on the bed like a dead thing. He had parted the curtains for a moment and seen the sun rising over the East River, and it had filled him with loathing and self-reproach.

The sun shone, having no alternative, on the nothing new. That was another first sentence.

Other people's words drifted through his mind. Tumbleweed riding through a desert. Had he already thought that? Had he already said it? He felt bloated and empty at the same time.

Traces of the night's possession surfaced now and again in the slowly simmering scum of his thoughts, and the experience of being so thoroughly and often displaced left him bruised and lonely. Besides, he had almost killed himself.

'Let's not go over that again,' he murmured, like a beleaguered lover who is never allowed to forget an indiscretion.

He winced as he stretched out his aching and sticky arm to check the time on the bedside clock. Five forty-five. He could order a selection of cold meats or a plate of smoked salmon straight away, but it would be another three-quarters of an hour before he could organize that brief moment of affirmation when a trolley rattling with wholesome breakfast food was wheeled into the room.

Then the fruit juice would sweat and separate under its cardboard cap; the bacon and egg, too intimidatingly carnal after all, would grow cold and begin to smell, and the single rose, in its narrow glass vase, would drop a petal on the white tablecloth, while he gulped down some sugary tea and continued to ingest the ethereal food of his syringe.

After a sleepless night, he always spent the hours from five thirty to eight cowering from the gathering roar of life. In London, when the pasty light of dawn had stained the ceiling above the curtain pole, he would listen with vampirish panic to the squealing and rumbling of distant juggernauts, and then to the nearby whining of a milkcart, and eventually to the slamming doors of cars bearing children to school, or real men to work in factories and banks.

It was nearly eleven o'clock in England. He could kill the time until breakfast with a few telephone calls. He would ring Johnny Hall, who was bound to sympathize with his state of mind.

But first he had to have a little fix to keep him going. Just as he could only contemplate giving up heroin when he had already taken some, so he could only recover from the ravages of cocaine by taking more.

After a fix of a moderation that impressed him almost as much as it bored him, Patrick propped up some pillows and installed himself comfortably beside the phone.

'Johnny?'

'Yup.' There was a strained whisper at the other end of the line.

'It's Patrick.'

'What time is it?'

'Eleven.'

'I've only had three hours' sleep in that case.'

'Do you want me to ring back?'

'No, the damage is already done. How are you?'

'Oh, fine. I've had a rather heavy night.'

'Nearly dying, et cetera?' gasped Johnny.

'Yup.'

'Me too. I've been shooting some really disreputable speed, made by a failed chemistry graduate with a shaking hand and a bottle of hydrochloric acid. It's the kind that smells of burnt test tubes when you push the plunger down, and then makes you sneeze compulsively, sending your heart into wild arrhythmic flurries reminiscent of the worst passages of Pound's *Cantos*.'

'As long as your Chinese is good you should be all right.'

'I haven't got any.'

'I have. It's medicine, man, medicine.'

'I'm coming over.'

'To New York?'

'New York! I thought the hesitating, whispering quality of your speech was a combination of my auditory hallucinations and your notorious indolence. It's very disappointing to learn that it has a *real* cause. Why are you there?'

'My father died over here, so I've come to collect his remains.'

'Congratulations. You've achieved half-orphan status. Are they refusing to part with his body? Are they making you put an equal weight of gold in the opposite scales to secure the precious cargo?'

'They haven't billed me for it yet, but if there's even a hint of exaggeration, I'll just leave the rotten thing behind.'

'Good thinking. Are you at all upset?'

'I feel rather haunted.'

'Yes. I remember finding that the ground beneath my feet seemed, if possible, more unreliable than usual, and that my desire to die was, if possible, even greater than before.'

'Yes, there's a lot of that. Plus quite a bad pain in my liver, as if a gravedigger had pushed a shovel under my ribs and stepped on it rather hard.'

'That's what your liver's for, didn't you know?'

'How can you ask that?'

'It's true. Forgive me. So when are we two Olympians going to meet?'

'Well, I should be back tomorrow evening. Could you get some gear, and then I'll come straight round to you from the airport, without having to see the appalling Brian.'

'Of course. Talking of appalling people, I wound up in the flat of some truly idiotic Italians the other night, but they did have some pink crystal coke which made a sound like a glockenspiel when it dropped into the spoon. Anyhow, I stole the whole lot and locked myself in the bathroom. As you know it takes a lot to ruffle the moronic tranquillity of those doe-eyed Italian dope fiends, but they seemed really pissed off, banging on the door and shouting, "Come out of there, you fucking man, or I kill you. Alessandro, make him come out!" '

'God, how hilarious.'

'Sadly, I think we've said "Ciao" for the last time, or I'd get you some. It was really the stuff to take before pushing the flaming longship into the grey waters for the last time.'

'You're making me envious.'

'Well, maybe we'll finally kill ourselves tomorrow night.'

'Definitely. Make sure you get a lot.'

'Yup.'

'OK, I'll see you tomorrow evening.'

'Goodbye.'

'Bye now.'

Patrick hung up the phone with a faint smile on his lips. It always cheered one up talking to Johnny. He immediately dialled a new set of numbers and settled back on the pillows.

'Hello?'

'Kay?'

'Baby! How are you? Hang on, I'll just turn down the music.'

The sound of an exasperated solitary cello grew suddenly muted, and Kay returned to the phone. 'So how are you?' she asked again.

'I haven't managed to get very much sleep.'

'I'm not surprised.'

'Neither am I, I've had about four grams of coke.'

'Oh, God, that's awful. You haven't been taking heroin as well, have you?'

'No, no, no. I've given that up. Just a few tranquillizers.'

'Well, that's something, but why the coke? Think of your poor nose. You can't let it just drop off.'

'My nose is going to be fine. I just felt so depressed.'

'Poor baby, I'm sure you did. Your father dying is the worst thing that could have happened to you. You never got a chance to work things out.'

'We never would have.'

'That's what all sons feel.'

'Mmm . . .'

'I don't like to think of you there alone. Are you seeing anybody nice today, or just morticians?'

'Are you implying that morticians can't be nice?' asked Patrick lugubriously.

'Lord, no, I think they do a wonderful job.'

'I don't really know. I have to collect the ashes, otherwise I'm as free as the wind. I wish you were here.'

'So do I, but I'll see you tomorrow, won't I?'

'Absolutely. I'll come round straight from the airport.' Patrick lit a cigarette. 'I've been thinking all night,' he continued rapidly, ' – if you can call that thinking – about whether ideas come from the continual need to talk, relieved occasionally by the paralysing presence of other people, or if we simply realize in speech what we've already thought.' He hoped this was the kind of question that would distract Kay from the exact details of his return.

'That shouldn't have kept you up,' she laughed. 'I'll tell you the answer tomorrow night. What time do you get in?'

'Around ten,' said Patrick, adding a few hours to the arrival time.

'So I'll see you about eleven?'

'Perfect.'

'Bye, baby. Lots of love.'

'You too. Bye now.'

Patrick put down the phone and made himself another little fix of coke to keep him going. The last fix was still too recent and he had to lie on the bed for a while, sweating, before he could make the next call.

'Hello? Debbie?'

'Darling. I didn't dare call you in case you were asleep.'

'That hasn't been my problem.'

'Well, I'm sorry, I didn't know that.'

'I'm not accusing you of anything. There's no need to be so defensive.'

'I'm not being defensive,' laughed Debbie. 'I was just worried about you. This is ridiculous. I only meant that I've been worried all night about how you were.'

'Ridiculous, I suppose.'

'Oh, please don't let's argue. I wasn't saying *you* were ridiculous. I meant that arguing is ridiculous.'

'Well, I was arguing, and if arguing is ridiculous then I was being ridiculous. My case rests.'

'What case? You always think I'm attacking you. We're not in a courtroom. I'm not your opponent or your enemy.'

Silence. Patrick's head pounded from the effort of not contradicting her. 'So what did you do last night?' he asked at last.

'Well, I was trying to get hold of you for a long time, and then I went to Gregory and Rebecca's dinner thing.'

'Suffering takes place while somebody else is eating. Who said that?'

'It could have been almost anyone,' laughed Debbie.

'It just popped into my mind.'

'Mm. You should try editing some of the things that just pop into your mind.'

'Well, never mind last night, what are you doing tomorrow night?'

'We've been asked to China's thing, but I don't suppose you want to eat and suffer at the same time.' Debbie laughed at her own joke, as was her habit, while Patrick pursued his ruthless policy of never laughing at anything she said, without feeling on this occasion the least trace of meanness.

'What a brilliant remark,' he said drily. 'I won't come along, but nothing could persuade me to stop you from going.'

'Don't be ridiculous, I'll cancel.'

'It sounds as if I had better not stop being ridiculous, or you won't recognize me. I was going to come and see you straight from the airport, but I'll come when you get back from China's. At twelve or one.'

'Well, OK, but I'll cancel if you like.'

'No, no, I wouldn't dream of it.'

'I'd better not go or you'll just use it against me later.'

'We're not in a courtroom. I'm not your opponent or your enemy,' Patrick echoed mockingly.

Silence. Debbie waited until she could make a fresh start, trying to ignore Patrick's impossibly contradictory demands.

'Are you in the Pierre?' she asked brightly.

'If you don't know what hotel I'm in, how could you have rung me?'

'I guessed you were in the Pierre, but I couldn't be sure since you didn't see fit to tell me,' sighed Debbie. 'Is the room lovely?'

'I think you would like it. There are lots of sachets in the bathroom and a phone next to the loo, so you needn't miss any important calls – an invitation to dinner at China's, for instance.'

'Why are you being so horrid?'

'Am I?'

'I'm going to cancel tomorrow.'

'No, no, *please* don't. It was only a joke. I feel rather mad at the moment.'

'You always feel rather mad,' laughed Debbie.

'Well, my father happens to have died, which makes me feel especially mad.'

'I know, darling, I'm sorry.'

'Plus, I've taken a huge quantity of coke.'

'Was that a good idea?'

'Of course it wasn't a good idea,' yelped Patrick indignantly.

'Do you think your father's death will make you less like him?' Debbie sighed again.

'I'll have the work of two to do now.'

'God, are you sure you wouldn't rather forget the whole thing?'

'Of course I'd rather forget the whole thing,' snapped Patrick, 'but that's not an option.'

'Well, everyone has their cross to bear.'

'Really? What's yours?'

'You,' laughed Debbie.

'Well, be careful or somebody might steal it from you.'

'They'll have to fight for it,' said Debbie affectionately.

'Sweet,' cooed Patrick, wedging the phone between his shoulder and his ear and sitting on the edge of the bed.

'Oh, darling, why do we always argue?' asked Debbie.

'Because we're so in love,' said Patrick haphazardly, as he opened the packet of heroin over the bedside table. He dipped his little finger in the powder, put it to one of his nostrils and inhaled quietly.

'That would seem a strange explanation from anybody else.'

'Well, I hope you're not getting it from anybody else,' said Patrick babyishly, dipping and sniffing several more times.

'Nobody else would dare give it, if they behaved like you,' laughed Debbie.

'It's just that I need you so much,' whispered Patrick, reclining again on the pillows. 'It's frightening if you're addicted to independence like I am.'

'Oh, that's what you're addicted to, is it?'

'Yes. All the other things are illusions.'

'Am I an illusion?'

'No! That's why we argue so much. Do you see?' It sounded good to him.

'Because I'm a *real* obstacle to your independence?'

'To my foolish and misguided desire for independence,' Patrick corrected her gallantly.

'Well, you certainly know how to pay a girl a compliment,' laughed Debbie.

'I wish you were here,' croaked Patrick, dabbing his finger in the white powder again.

'So do I, you must be having a horrible time. Why don't you go and see Marianne? She'll look after you.'

'What a good idea. I'll give her a ring later on.'

'I'd better go now,' sighed Debbie. 'I've got to be interviewed by some silly magazine.'

'What for?'

'Oh, about people who go to lots of parties. I don't know why I agreed to it.'

'Because you're so kind and helpful,' said Patrick.

'Mm . . . I'll call you later. I think you're being very brave and I love you.'

'I love you too.'

'Bye, darling.'

'Bye now.'

Patrick hung up the phone and glanced at the clock. Six thirty-five. He ordered Canadian bacon, fried eggs, toast, porridge, stewed fruit, orange juice, coffee, and tea.

'Is that breakfast for two?' asked the cheerful sounding woman taking the order.

'No, just for one.'

'Wooh, you're sure having a hearty breakfast, honey,' she giggled.

'It's the best way to start the day, don't you find?'

'Sure is!' she agreed.

9

The smell of decaying food had filled the room surprisingly quickly. Patrick's breakfast was devastated without being eaten. A dent in the grey paste of the porridge contained a half-eaten stewed pear; rashers of bacon hung on the edge of a plate smeared with egg yolk, and in the flooded saucer two cigarette butts lay sodden with coffee. A triangle of abandoned toast bore the semicircular imprint of his teeth, and spilled sugar glistened everywhere on the tablecloth. Only the orange juice and the tea were completely finished.

On the television, the Wile E. Coyote, astride an accelerating rocket, crashed explosively into the side of a mountain, while the Road Runner disappeared into a tunnel, emerged at the other side, and receded in a cloud of dust. Watching the Road Runner and the stylized rotundity of the dust in his wake, Patrick was reminded of the early, innocent days of his drug taking, when he had thought that LSD would reveal to him something other than the tyranny of its own effects on his consciousness.

Thanks to his loathing of air conditioning the room was becoming increasingly muggy. Patrick longed to wheel the trolley outside, but the danger of meeting someone in the corridor made him resigned to the growing stench. He had already overheard a conversation about himself between two maids, and although he accepted, theoretically, that it was a hallucination, his strength of mind would not allow him to test this vein of detachment to the extent of opening the door. After all, had one maid not said to the other, 'I told him, "You gonna die, boy, if you go on takin' that shit."' And hadn't the other one replied, "You gotta call the police for your own protection, can't go on livin' like that." '

Wandering into the bathroom, he rolled his right shoulder to ease the pain that was lodged under the shoulder blade. Sceptically but irresistibly, he approached the mirror and noticed that one of his eyelids was drooping much lower than the other, drooping over an inflamed and watering eye. Pulling the skin down he saw the familiar dark yellow of his eyeballs. His tongue was also yellow and thickly coated. Only the purple trenches under his eyes relieved the deadly whiteness of his complexion.

Thank God his father had died. Without a dead parent there was really no excuse for looking so awful. He thought of one of the guiding mottoes of his father's life: 'Never apologize, never explain.'

'What the fuck else is there to do?' muttered Patrick, turning on the taps of his bath and tearing open one of the sachets with his teeth. As he poured the glutinous green liquid into the swirling water he heard, or thought he heard, the ringing of the telephone. Was it the management warning him that the police were on their way up? Whoever it was, the outside world was crashing into his atmosphere, and it filled him with dread. He turned off the taps and listened to the naked ringing of the phone. Why answer? And yet he couldn't bear not to; maybe he was going to be saved.

Sitting on the loo seat, not trusting his own voice, Patrick picked up the phone and said, 'Hello?'

'Patrick, my dear,' drawled a voice from the other end.

'George!'

'Is this a bad time to call?'

'Not at all.'

'I was wondering if you'd like to have lunch with me. It may be the last thing you want to do, of course. You must be feeling perfectly ghastly. It's a terrible shock, you know, Patrick, we all feel that.'

'I do feel a bit wonky, but I'd love to have lunch.'

'I must warn you, I've asked some other people. Charming people, naturally, the nicest sort of Americans. One or two of them have met your father and liked him very much.'

'It sounds perfect,' said Patrick, raising his eyes to the ceiling and grimacing.

'I'm meeting them at the Key Club. Do you know it?'

'No.'

'I think you'll find it amusing in its way. One comes in from the noise and the pollution of New York, and it's quite suddenly like an English country house of a certain sort. God knows whose family they are – I suppose some of the members must have lent them – but the walls are covered in portraits, and the effect is really quite charming. There are all the usual things one would expect to find, like Gentleman's Relish for instance, and strangely enough some things that are nowadays very hard to find in England, like a good Bullshot. Your father and I agreed that we hadn't had such a good Bullshot in years.'

'It sounds heaven.'

'I've asked Ballantine Morgan. I don't know if you've met him. I'm afraid I'm not sure he isn't the most frightful bore, but Sarah has taken to him in a big way and one gets so used to his popping up everywhere that I've asked him to lunch. Oddly enough, I knew someone called Morgan Ballantine once, perfectly charming man; they must be related in some way, but I've never really got to the bottom of it,' said George wistfully.

'Perhaps we'll find out today,' said Patrick.

'Well, I'm not sure I can ask Ballantine again. I have a

feeling I must have asked him before, but it's very hard to be sure because one has such trouble listening to his answers.'

'What time shall we meet?'

'About quarter to one in the bar.'

'Perfect.'

'Well, goodbye, my dear.'

'Bye now. See you at quarter to one.' Patrick's voice trailed off.

He turned his bath back on and wandered into the bedroom to pour himself a glass of bourbon. A bath without a drink was like – was like a bath without a drink. Was there any need to elaborate or compare?

A voice on the television spoke excitedly about a complete set of prestigious carving knives, accompanied by an incredible wok, a beautiful set of salad bowls, a book of mouth-watering recipes and, as if this wasn't enough, a machine for cutting vegetables into different shapes. Patrick glazed over as he stared at carrots being sliced, diced, shredded, and cubed.

The mound of shaved ice in which his orange juice had arrived turned out to be completely melted and Patrick, suddenly frustrated, kicked the breakfast trolley and sent it thudding into the wall. He was overwhelmed with despair at the prospect of having no ice in his drink. What was the point of going on? Everything was wrong, everything was hopelessly fucked up. He sat down, defenceless and defeated, on the edge of the bed, the bottle of bourbon held loosely in one hand. He had imagined an icy glass of bourbon resting steamily on the side of the bath, had wagered all his hope on it, but finding that the plan was compromised, nothing stood between him and utter bankruptcy. He drank a gulp straight from the bottle and put it down on the bedside table. It stung his throat and made him shudder.

The clock showed eleven twenty. He must get into action

and prepare himself for the business of the day. Now was the time for speed and alcohol. He must leave the coke behind, or he would spend the whole of lunch shooting up in the loo, as usual.

He got up from the bed and suddenly punched the lampshade, sending the lamp crashing to the carpet. With the bottle of bourbon in his hand, he walked back into the bathroom, where he found the water gently overflowing from the side of the bath and flooding the floor. Refusing to panic or show any surprise, he slowly turned off the water and pushed the sodden bathmat around with his foot, spreading the water into the corners it had not yet reached. He undressed, getting his trousers wet, and tossed his clothes through the open door.

The bath was absurdly hot and Patrick had to pull the plug out and run the cold water before he could climb in. Once he was lying in it, it seemed too cold again. He reached for the bottle of bourbon he had put on the floor beside the bath, and for no reason that he could make out he poured the bourbon from the air and sucked it in as it splashed and trickled over his face.

The bottle was soon empty and he held it under the water, watching the bubbles run out of the neck and then moving it around the bottom of the bath like a submarine stalking enemy ships.

Looking down, he caught sight of his arms and drew in his breath sharply and involuntarily. Among the fading yellow bruises, and the pink threads of old scars, a fresh set of purple wounds clustered around his main veins and at odd points along his arm. At the centre of this unhealthy canvas was the black bulge produced by the missed shot of the night before. The thought that this was his own arm ambushed Patrick quite suddenly, and made him want to cry. He closed his eyes and sank under the surface of the water, breathing out violently from his nose. It didn't bear thinking about.

As he surged out of the water, flicking his head from side to side, Patrick was surprised to hear the phone ring again.

He got out of the bath, and picked up the phone beside the loo. These bathroom phones were really quite useful – perhaps it was China asking him to dinner, begging him to reconsider.

'Yes?' he drawled.

'Hey, Patrick?' said an unmistakable voice on the other end.

'Marianne! How sweet of you to ring.'

'I'm so *sorry* to hear about your father,' said Marianne in a voice that was hesitating but deeply self-assured, whispering but husky. It seemed not to be projected from her body into the world, but to draw the world inside her body; she did not speak so much as swallow articulately. Anyone who listened to her was forced to imagine her long smooth throat, and the elegant S of her body, exaggerated by the extraordinary curve of her spine that made her breasts swell further forward and her bottom further back.

Why had he never been to bed with her? The fact that she had never shown any signs of desire for him had played an unhelpful role, but that might be attributed to her friendship with Debbie. How could she resist him after all, thought Patrick, glancing in the mirror.

Fucking hell. He was going to have to rely on her pity.

'Well, you know how it is,' he drawled sarcastically. 'Death, where is thy sting?'

'Of all the evils in the world which are reproached with an evil character, death is the most innocent of its accusation.'

'Bang on in this case,' said Patrick. 'Who said that anyhow?'

'Bishop Taylor in *The Correct Rules for Holy Dying*,' Marianne disclosed.

'Your favourite book?'

'It's *so* great,' she gasped hoarsely; 'I swear to God, it's the most beautiful prose I've ever read.'

She was clever too. It was really intolerable; he had to have her.

'Will you have dinner with me?' Patrick asked.

'Oh, God, I wish . . .' gasped Marianne, 'but I've got to have dinner with my parents. Do you want to come along?'

'That would be wonderful,' said Patrick, annoyed not to have her to himself.

'Good. I'll let my parents know,' she purred. 'Come on over to their apartment around seven o'clock.'

'Perfect,' said Patrick, and then, unguardedly, 'I adore you.'

'Hey!' said Marianne ambiguously. 'See you later.'

Patrick hung up the phone. He had to have her, he definitely had to have her. She was not merely the latest object on which his greedy desire to be saved had fixed itself; no, she was the woman who was going to save him. The woman whose fine intelligence and deep sympathy and divine body, yes, whose divine body would successfully deflect his attention from the gloomy well shaft of his feelings and the contemplation of his past.

If he got her he would give up drugs forever, or at least have someone really attractive to take them with. He giggled wildly, wrapping a towel around himself and striding back into his bedroom with renewed vigour.

He looked like shit, it was true, but everybody knew that what women really valued, apart from a great deal of money, was gentleness and humour. Gentleness was not his speciality, and he wasn't feeling especially funny, but this was a case of destiny: he had to have her or he would die.

It was time to get practical, to take a Black Beauty and

lock the coke in his suitcase. He fished a capsule out of his jacket and swallowed it with impressive efficiency. As he tidied away the coke he could see no reason not to have one last fix. After all, he hadn't had one for almost forty minutes and he would not be having another for a couple of hours. Too lazy to go through the entire ritual, he stuck the needle into an easily accessible vein in the back of his hand and administered the injection.

The effects were certainly growing weaker, he noted, still able to walk around, if a little shakily, with his shoulders hunched high up beside his ears, and his jaw tightly clenched.

It was really unbearable to contemplate being separated from the coke for so long, but he couldn't control himself if he carried supplies with him. The sensible thing to do was to prepare a couple of fixes, one in the rather tired old syringe he had been using all night, its rubber plunger now tending to stick to the sides of the barrel, and the other in the precious untouched syringe. Just as some men wore a handkerchief in their breast pockets to cope with the emergency of a woman's tears, or a sneeze, he often tucked away a couple of syringes into the same pocket to cope with the endlessly renewed emptiness that invaded him. Pip! Pip! Be prepared!

Suffering from yet another aural hallucination, Patrick overheard a conversation between a policeman and a member of the hotel staff.

'Was this guy a regular?'

'Na, he was the holiday-of-a-lifetime type.'

'Ya, ya,' muttered Patrick impatiently. He wasn't that easily intimidated.

He put on a clean white shirt, slipped into his second suit, a dark grey herringbone, stepping into his shoes at the same time as he did up his gold cufflinks. His silver and black tie, unfortunately the only one he had, was flecked with blood, but he managed, by tying it rather too short, to disguise the fact, although he had to tuck the longer strip into his shirt, a practice he despised.

Less easily solved was the problem of his left eye, which had now completely closed, except for an occasional nervous fluttering. He could, with great effort, open it up but only by raising his eyebrows to a position of high indignation. On his way to the Key Club, he would have to go to the pharmacy and get himself an eyepatch.

His breast pocket was deep enough to conceal the raised plungers of the two syringes, and the bag of smack fitted neatly into the ticket pocket of his jacket. Everything was completely under control, except that he was sweating like a stuck pig and couldn't shake off the sense that he had forgotten something crucial.

Patrick took the chain off the door and glanced back nostalgically at the fetid dark chaos he was leaving behind. The curtains were still closed, the bed unmade, pillows and clothes on the floor, the lamp overturned, the trolley of food rotting in the warm atmosphere, the bathroom flooded and the television, where a man was shouting, 'Come to Crazy Eddie's! The prices are insane,' still flickering.

Stepping out into the corridor, Patrick could not help noticing a policeman standing outside the next-door room.

His overcoat! That was what he had forgotten. But if he doubled back wouldn't it look guilty?

He hovered in the doorway, and then muttered loudly, 'Oh yes, I must . . .' drawing the policeman's attention to himself as he strode back appalled into his room. What were the police doing there? Could they tell what he'd been doing?

His overcoat felt heavy and less reassuring than usual. He mustn't take too long or they would wonder what he was up to.

'You're gonna fry in that coat,' said the policeman with a smile.

'It's not a crime, is it?' asked Patrick, more aggressively than he'd intended.

'Normally,' said the policeman with mock seriousness, 'we'd have to arrest ya, but we got our hands full,' he added with a resigned shrug.

'What happened here?' asked Patrick in his MP-with-the-constituent manner.

'Guy died of a heart attack.'

'The party's over,' said Patrick with a private sense of pleasure.

'There was a party here last night?' The policeman was suddenly curious.

'No, no, I just meant . . .' Patrick felt he was coming from too many directions at once.

'You heard no noises, cries, nothing unusual?'

'No, I heard nothing.'

The policeman relaxed, and ran his hand over his largely bald scalp. 'You're from England, right?'

'That's right.'

'I could tell from the accent.'

'They'll make you a detective soon,' said Patrick boisterously. He waved as he set off down the long carpet of gushing pink and green flower-laden urns, with the policeman's imagined eyebeams burning into his back.

10

Patrick sprang up the steps of the Key Club with unaccustomed eagerness, his nerves squirming like a bed of maggots whose protective stone has been flicked aside, exposing them to the assault of the open sky. Wearing an eyepatch, he hurried gratefully into the gloomy hall of the club, his shirt clinging to his sweating back.

The hall porter took his overcoat in silent surprise and led him down a narrow corridor, its walls covered with memorials to remarkable dogs, horses, and servants, and one or two cartoons bearing witness to the feeble and long-forgotten eccentricities of certain dead members. It really was a temple of English virtues as George had promised.

Ushered into a large panelled room full of green and brown leather armchairs of Victorian design, and huge glossy paintings of dogs holding birds in their obedient mouths, Patrick saw George in the corner, already in conversation with another man.

'Patrick, my dear, how are you?'

'Hello, George.'

'Is there something wrong with your eye?'

'Just a little inflammation.'

'Oh, dear, well, I hope it clears up,' said George sincerely. 'Do you know Ballantine Morgan?' he asked, turning to a small man with weak blue eyes, neat white hair, and a well-trimmed moustache.

'Hello, Patrick,' said Ballantine, giving him a firm hand-shake. Patrick noticed that he was wearing a black silk tie and wondered if he was in mourning for some reason.

'I was very sorry to hear about your father,' said Ballantine. 'I didn't know him personally, but from everything George tells me it sounds like he was a great English gentleman.'

Jesus Christ, thought Patrick.

'What have you been telling him?' he asked George reproachfully.

'Only what an exceptional man your father was.'

'Yes, I'm pleased to say that he was exceptional,' said Patrick. 'I've never met anybody quite like him.'

'He refused to compromise,' drawled George. 'What was it he used to say? "Nothing but the best, or go without."'

'Always felt the same way myself,' said Ballantine fatuously.

'Would you like a drink?' asked George.

'I'll have one of those Bullshots you spoke about so passionately this morning.'

'Passionately,' guffawed Ballantine.

'Well, there are some things one feels passionately about,' smiled George, looking at the barman and briefly raising his index finger. 'I shall feel quite bereft without your father,' he continued. 'Oddly enough, it was here that we were supposed to be having lunch on the day that he died. The last time I met him we went to a perfectly extraordinary place that has an arrangement of some sort – I can't believe that it's recip-rocal – with the Travellers in Paris. The portraits were at least four times life size – we laughed about that a good deal – he was on very good form, although, of course, there was always an undercurrent of disappointment with your father. I think he really enjoyed himself on this last visit. You must never forget, Patrick, that he was very proud of you. I'm sure you know that. Really proud.'

Patrick felt sick.

Ballantine looked bored, as people do when someone they don't know is being discussed. He had a very natural desire to talk about himself, but felt that a little pause was in order.

'Yes,' said George to the waiter. 'We'd like two Bullshots and . . .' He leaned enquiringly towards Ballantine.

'I'll have another martini,' said Ballantine. There was a short silence.

'What a lot of faithful gundogs,' said Patrick wearily, glancing around the room.

'I suppose a lot of the members are keen shots,' said George. 'Ballantine is one of the best shots in the world.'

'Whoa, whoa, whoa,' protested Ballantine, '*used* to be the best shot in the world.' He held out his hand to arrest the flow of self-congratulation, but was no more effective than King Canute in the face of another great force of nature. 'What I haven't lost,' he couldn't help pointing out, 'is a gun collection which is probably the greatest in the world.'

The waiter returned with the drinks.

'Would you bring me the book called *The Morgan Gun Collection*?' Ballantine asked him.

'Yes, Mr Morgan,' said the waiter in a voice that suggested he had dealt with this request before.

Patrick tasted the Bullshot and found himself smiling irresistibly. He drank half of it in one gulp, put it down for a moment, picked it up again, and said to George, 'You were right about these Bullshots,' drinking the rest.

'Would you like another one?' asked George.

'I think I will, they're so delicious.'

The waiter weaved his way back to the table with an enormous white volume. On the front cover, visible from some way off, was a photograph of two silver-inlaid pistols.

'Here you are, Mr Morgan,' said the waiter.

'Ahh-aa,' said Ballantine, taking the book.

'And another Bullshot, would you?' said George.

'Yes, sir.'

Ballantine tried to suppress a grin of pride. 'These guns right here,' he said, tapping the front cover of the book, 'are a pair of Spanish seventeenth-century duelling pistols which are the most valuable firearms in the world. If I tell you that the triggers cost over a million dollars to replace, you'll have some idea of what I mean.'

'It's enough to make you wonder if it's worth fighting a duel,' said Patrick.

'The original cleaning brushes alone are worth over a quarter of a million dollars,' chuckled Ballantine, 'so you wouldn't want to fire the pistols too often.'

George looked pained and distant, but Ballantine in his role as the Triumph of Life, performing the valuable task of distracting Patrick from his terrible grief, was unstoppable. He put on a pair of tortoiseshell half-moon spectacles, pushed his head back, and looked condescendingly at his book, while he allowed the pages to flicker past.

'This here,' he said, stopping the flow of pages and holding the book open towards Patrick, 'this is the first Winchester repeating rifle ever manufactured.'

'Amazing,' sighed Patrick.

'When I was shooting in Africa, I brought down a lion with this gun,' admitted Ballantine. 'It took a number of shots – it doesn't have the calibre of a modern weapon.'

'You must have been all the more grateful for the repeating mechanism,' Patrick suggested.

'Oh, I was covered by a couple of reliable hunters,' said Ballantine complacently. 'I describe the incident in the book I wrote about my African hunting trips.'

The waiter returned with Patrick's second Bullshot, and another large book under his arm.

'Harry thought you might want this as well, Mr Morgan.'

'Well, I'll be darned,' said Ballantine with a colloquial twang, craning back in his chair and beaming at the barman. 'I mentioned the book and it falls in my lap. Now that's what I call service!'

He opened the new volume with familiar relish. 'Some of my friends have been kind enough to say that I have an excellent prose style,' he explained in a voice that did not sound as puzzled as it was meant to. 'I don't see it myself, I just put it down as it was. The way I hunted in Africa is a way of life that doesn't exist anymore, and I just told the truth about it, that's all.'

'Yes,' drawled George. 'Journalists and people of that sort write a lot of nonsense about what they call the "Happy Valley Set". Well, I was there a good deal at the time, and I can tell you there was no more unhappiness than usual, no more drunkenness than usual, people behaved just as they did in London or New York.'

George leaned over and picked up an olive. 'We did have dinner in our pyjamas,' he added thoughtfully, 'which I suppose *was* a little unusual. But not because we all wanted to jump into bed with one another, although obviously a good deal of that sort of thing went on, as it always does; it was simply that we had to get up the next day at dawn to go hunting. When we got back in the afternoon, we would have "toasty", which would be a whisky and soda, or whatever you wanted. And then they would say, "Bathy, bwana, bathy time," and run you a bath. After that more "toasty", and then dinner in one's pyjamas. People behaved just as they did anywhere else, although I must say, they did drink a great deal, really a great deal.'

'It sounds like heaven,' said Patrick.

'Well, you know, George, the drinking went with the life-style. You just sweated it all out,' said Ballantine.

'Yes, quite,' said George.

You don't have to go to Africa to sweat too much, thought Patrick.

'This is a photograph of me with a Tanganyikan mountain goat,' said Ballantine, handing Patrick the second book. 'I was told that it was the last potent male of the species, so I can't help having mixed feelings about it.'

God, he's sensitive too, thought Patrick, looking at the photograph of a younger Ballantine, in a khaki hat, kneeling beside the corpse of a goat.

'I took the photographs myself,' said Ballantine casually. 'A number of professional photographers have begged me to tell them my "secret", but I've had to disappoint them – the only secret is to get a fascinating subject and photograph it the best way you know how.'

'Amazing,' mumbled Patrick.

'Sometimes, from a foolish impulse of pride,' Ballantine continued, 'I included myself in the shots and allowed one of the boys to press the trigger – they could do that well enough.'

'Ah,' said George with uncharacteristic verve, 'here's Tom.'

An exceptionally tall man in a blue seersucker suit worked his way through the tables. He had thin but rather chaotic grey hair, and drooping bloodhound eyes.

Ballantine closed the two books and rested them on his knees. The loop of his monstrous vanity was complete. He had been talking about a book in which he wrote about his photographs of the animals he had shot with guns from his own magnificent collection, a collection photographed (alas, not by him) in the second book.

'Tom Charles,' said George, 'Patrick Melrose.'

'I see you've been talking to the Renaissance Man,' said Tom in a dry gravelly voice. 'How are you, Ballantine? Been keeping Mr Melrose up to date on your achievements?'

'Well, I thought he might be interested in the guns,' said Ballantine peevishly.

'The thought he never has, is that somebody might *not* be interested in the guns,' Tom croaked. 'I was sorry to hear about your father, I guess you must be feeling sick at heart.'

'I suppose I am,' said Patrick, caught off balance. 'It's a terrible time for anybody. Whatever you feel, you feel it strongly, and you feel just about everything.'

'Do you want a drink, or do you want to go straight in to lunch?' asked George.

'Let's eat,' said Tom.

The four men got up. Patrick noticed that the two Bullshots had made him feel much more substantial. He could also detect the steady lucid throb of the speed. Perhaps he could allow himself a quick fix before lunch.

'Where are the loos, George?'

'Oh, just through that door in the corner,' said George. 'We'll be in the dining room, up the stairs on the right.'

'I'll see you there.'

Patrick broke away from the group and headed for the door that George had pointed out. On the other side he found a large cool room of black and white marble, shiny chrome fittings, and mahogany doors. At one end of a row of basins was a pile of starched linen with 'Key Club' sewn into the corner in green cotton, and, beside it, a large wicker basket for discarding the used towels.

With sudden efficiency and stealth, he picked up a towel, filled a glass with water, and slipped into one of the mahogany cubicles.

There was no time to waste and Patrick seemed to put

the glass down, drop the towel, and take off his jacket in one gesture.

He sat on the loo seat and put the syringe carefully on the towel in his lap. He rolled his sleeve up tightly on his bicep to act as a makeshift tourniquet and, while he frantically clenched and unclenched his fist, removed the cap of the syringe with the thumb of his other hand.

His veins were becoming quite shy, but a lucky stab in the bicep, just below his rolled-up sleeve, yielded the gratifying spectacle of a red mushroom cloud uncurling in the barrel of the syringe.

He pushed the plunger down hard and unrolled his shirt as fast as he could to allow the solution a free passage through his bloodstream.

Patrick wiped the trickle of blood from his arm and flushed out the syringe, also squirting its pinkish water into the towel.

The rush was disappointing. Although his hands were shaking and his heart was pounding, he had missed that blissful fainting sensation, that heartbreaking moment, as compressed as the autobiography of a drowning man, but as elusive and intimate as the smell of a flower.

What was the fucking point of shooting coke if he wasn't going to get a proper rush? It was intolerable. Indignant and yet anxious about the consequences, Patrick took out the second syringe, sat down on the loo again, and rolled up his sleeve. The strange thing was that the rush seemed to be getting stronger, as if it had been dammed up against his shirt sleeve and had taken unusually long to reach his brain. In any case he was now committed to a second fix and, with a combination of bowel-loosening excitement and dread, he tried to put the spike back in exactly the same spot as before.

As he rolled down his sleeve this time, he realized that he had made a serious mistake. This was too much. Only far too much was enough. But this was more than enough.

Too overwhelmed to flush it out, he only managed to put the cap back on the precious new syringe and drop it on the floor. He slumped against the back wall of the cubicle, his head hanging to one side, gasping and wincing like an athlete who has just crossed the finishing line after losing a race, the prickle of fresh sweat breaking out all over the surface of his skin, and his eyes tightly closed while a rapid succession of scenes flashed across his inner vision: a bee crashing drunkenly into the pollen-laden pistils of a flower; fissures spreading over the concrete of a disintegrating dam; a long blade cutting strips of flesh from the body of a dead whale; a barrel of gouged-out eyes tumbling stickily between the cylinders of a wine press.

He forced his eyes open. His inner life was definitely *in decline* and it would be more cautious to go upstairs and face the confusing effects of other people than sink any further into this pool of discrete and violent imagery.

The aural hallucinations that afflicted Patrick as he groped his way along the wall towards the line of basins were not yet organized into words, but consisted of twisting strands of sound and an eerie sense of space, like amplified breathing.

He mopped his face and emptied the glass of bloody water down the drain. Remembering the second syringe, he quickly tried to clean it out, watching the reflection of the door in the mirror in case somebody came in. His hands shook so badly it was hard to hold the needle under the tap.

It must have been ages since he left the others. They were probably ordering the bill by now. Short of breath, but with insane urgency, he stuffed the wet syringe back into his breast pocket and hurried back through the bar, into the hall, and up the main staircase.

In the dining room he saw George, Tom, and Ballantine still reading the menu. How long had he kept them waiting, politely postponing their lunch? He moved clumsily towards the table, the strands of curving, twisting sound bending the space around him.

George looked up.

'Ziouuu . . . Ziouuu . . . Ziouuu . . .' he asked. 'Chok-chok-chok-chok,' said Ballantine, like a helicopter.

'Aioua. Aioua,' Tom suggested.

What the fuck were they trying to tell him? Patrick sat down and mopped his face with the pale pink napkin.

'Sot,' he said in a long elastic whisper. 'Chok-chok-chok,' Ballantine replied.

George was smiling, but Patrick listened helplessly as the sounds streamed past him like a photograph of brake lights on a wet street.

'Ziou . . . Ziou . . . Ziou . . . Aiou. Aiou. Chok-chok-chok.'

He sat astonished in front of the menu, as if he had never seen one before. There were pages of dead things – cows, shrimps, pigs, oysters, lambs – stretched out like a casualty list, accompanied by a brief description of how they had been treated since they died – skewered, grilled, smoked, and boiled. Christ, if they thought he was going to eat these things they must be mad.

He had seen the dark blood from the neck of a sheep gushing into the dry grass. The busy flies. The stench of offal. He had heard the roots tearing as he eased a carrot out of the ground. Any living man squatted on a mound of corruption, cruelty, filth, and blood.

If only his body would turn into a pane of glass, the flesh-less interval between two spaces, knowing both but belonging to neither, then he would be set free from the gross and savage debt he owed to the rest of nature.

'Ziou . . . Ziou . . . wan?' asked George.

'Um . . . I'll . . . um, eh just,' Patrick felt remote from his own voice, as if it was coming out of his feet. 'I'll . . .

um, eh, have . . . another . . . Bullshot . . . late breakfast . . .
eh . . . not really hungry.'

The effort of saying these few words left him breathless.

'Chok-chok-chok-chok,' objected Ballantine. 'Aioua sure.
Aioua ziou?' asked Tom.

What was he saying 'Ziou' for? The fugue was growing
more complicated. Before long George would be saying
'Chok' or 'Aioua', and then where would he stand? Where
would any of them stand?

'Justanothershot,' gasped Patrick, 'really.' Mopping his
brow again, he stared fixedly at the stem of his wineglass
which, caught by the sun, cast a fractured bone of light onto
the white tablecloth, like an X-ray of a broken finger. The
twisting echoing sounds around him had started to die down
to the faint hiss of an untuned television. It was no longer
incomprehension but a kind of sadness, like an enormously
amplified postcoital gloom, that cut him off from what
was happening around him. 'Martha Boeing,' Ballantine was
saying, 'told me that she was experiencing dizzy spells on the
drive up to Newport and that her doctor told her to take
along these small French cheeses to eat on the journey –
evidently it was some kind of protein deprivation.'

'I can't imagine that Martha's malnutrition is too severe,'
said Tom.

'Well,' remarked George diplomatically, 'not everybody
has to be driven to Newport as often as she does.'

'I mention it because I,' said Ballantine with some pride,
'was getting the same symptoms.'

'On the same journey?' asked Tom.

'The exact same journey,' Ballantine confirmed.

'Well, that's Newport for you,' said Tom; 'sucks the
protein right out of you. Only sporting types can make it
there without medical assistance.'

'But *my* doctor,' said Ballantine patiently, 'recommended

peanut butter. Martha was sorta doubtful about it, and said that these French cheeses were so great because you could just peel them off and pop them in your mouth. She wanted to know how you were supposed to eat the peanut butter. "With a spoon," I said, "like caviar."' Ballantine chuckled. 'Well, she had no answer to that,' he concluded triumphantly, 'and I believe she's going to be switching to peanut butter.'

'Somebody ought to warn Sun-Pat,' said Tom.

'Yes, you must be careful,' drawled George, 'or you'll start a run on this butter of yours. Once these Newport people take to something, there's really no stopping them. I remember Brooke Rivers asking me where I had my shirts made, and the next time I ordered some they told me there was a two-year waiting list. They told me there had been a perfectly extraordinary surge in American orders. Well, of course, I knew who that was.'

A waiter came to take the orders and George asked Patrick if he was absolutely sure that he didn't want 'something solid'.

'Absolutely. Nothing solid,' Patrick replied.

'I never knew your father to lose his appetite,' said George.

'No, it was the one thing about him that was reliable.'

'Oh, I wouldn't go that far,' protested George. 'He was an awfully good pianist. Used to keep one up all night,' he explained to the others, 'playing the most spellbinding music.'

Pastiche and parody and hands twisted like old vine stumps, thought Patrick.

'Yes, he could be very impressive at the piano,' he said out loud.

'And in conversation,' George added.

'Mm . . .' said Patrick. 'It depends what you find impressive. Some people don't like uninterrupted rudeness, or so I'm told.'

'Who *are* these people?' asked Tom, looking around the room with mock alarm.

'It is true,' said George, 'that I once or twice had to tell him to stop being quite so argumentative.'

'And what did he do?' asked Ballantine, thrusting his chin forward to get more of his neck out of its tight collar.

'Told me to bugger off,' replied George tersely.

'Hell,' said Ballantine, seeing an opportunity for wisdom and diplomacy. 'You know, people argue about the darnedest things. Why, I spent an entire weekend trying to persuade my wife to dine in Mortimer's the evening we got back to New York. "I'm all Mortimered out," she kept saying, "can't we go someplace else?" Of course she couldn't say where.'

'Of course she couldn't,' said Tom, 'she hasn't seen the inside of another restaurant in fifteen years.'

'All Mortimered out,' repeated Ballantine, his indignation tinged with a certain pride at having married such an original woman.

A lobster, some smoked salmon, a crab salad, and a Bullshot arrived. Patrick lifted the drink greedily to his lips and then froze, hearing the hysterical bellowing of a cow, loud as an abattoir in the muddy liquid of his glass.

'Fuck it,' he murmured, taking a large gulp.

His defiance was soon rewarded with the vivid fantasy that a hoof was trying to kick its way out of his stomach. He remembered, when he was eighteen, writing to his father from a psychiatric ward, trying to explain his reasons for being there, and receiving a short note in reply. Written in Italian, which his father knew he could not understand, it turned out, after some research, to be a quotation from Dante's *Inferno*: 'Consider your descent / You were not made to live among beasts / But to pursue virtue and knowledge.' What had seemed a frustratingly sublime response at the time, struck him with a fresh sense of relevance now that he was listening to the sound of howling, snuffling cattle and felt, or thought he felt, another blow on the inner wall of his stomach.

As his heart rate increased again and a new wave of sweat prickled his skin, Patrick realized that he was going to be sick.

'Excuse me,' he said, getting up abruptly.

'Are you all right, my dear?' said George.

'I feel rather sick.'

'Perhaps we should get you a doctor.'

'I have the best doctor in New York,' said Ballantine. 'Just mention my name and . . .'

Patrick tasted a bitter surge of bile from his stomach. He swallowed stubbornly and, without time to thank Ballantine for his kind offer, hurried out of the dining room.

On the stairs Patrick forced down a second mouthful of vomit, more solid than the first. Time was running out. Wave after wave of nausea heaved the contents of his stomach into his mouth with increasing velocity. Feeling dizzy, his vision blurred by watering eyes, he fumbled down the corridor, knocking one of the hunting prints askew with his shoulder. By the time he reached the cool marble sanctuary of the lavatories, his cheeks were as swollen as a trumpeter's. A member of the club, admiring himself with that earnestness reserved for mirrors, found that the ordinary annoyance of being interrupted was soon replaced by alarm at being so close to a man who was obviously about to vomit.

Patrick, despairing of reaching the loo, threw up in the basin next to him, turning the taps on at the same time.

'Jesus,' said the member, 'you could have done that in the john.'

'Too far,' said Patrick, throwing up a second time.

'Jesus,' repeated the man, leaving hastily.

Patrick recognized traces of last night's dinner and, with

his stomach already empty, knew that he would soon be bringing up that sour yellow bile which gives vomiting its bad name.

To encourage the faster disappearance of the vomit he twirled his finger in the plughole and increased the flow of water with his other hand. He longed to gain the privacy of one of the cubicles before he was sick again. Feeling queasy and hot, he abandoned the not yet entirely clean basin and staggered over to one of the mahogany cubicles. He hardly had time to slide the brass lock closed before he was stooped over the bowl of the loo convulsing fruitlessly. Unable to breathe or to swallow, he found himself trying to vomit with even more conviction than he had tried to avoid vomiting a few minutes earlier.

Just when he was about to faint from lack of air he managed to bring up a globule of that yellow bile he had been anticipating with such dread.

'Fucking hell,' he cursed, sliding down the wall. However often he did it, being sick never lost its power to surprise him.

Shaken by coming so close to choking, he lit a cigarette and smoked it through the bitter slime that coated his mouth. The question now, of course, was whether to take some heroin to help him calm down.

The risk was that it would make him feel even more nauseous.

Wiping the sweat from his hands, he gingerly opened the packet of heroin over his lap, dipped his little finger into it, and sniffed through both nostrils. Not feeling any immediate ill effects, he repeated the dose.

Peace at last. He closed his eyes and sighed. The others could just fuck off. He wasn't going back. He was going to fold his wings and (he took another sniff) relax. Where he took his smack was his home, and more often than not that was in some stranger's bog.

He was so tired; he really must get some sleep. Get some sleep. Fold his wings. But what if George and the others sent somebody to look for him and they found the sick-spattered basin and hammered on the door of the cubicle? Was there no peace, no resting place? Of course there wasn't. What an absurd question.

'I'm here to collect the remains of David Melrose,' said Patrick to the grinning young man with the big jaw and the mop of shiny chestnut hair.

'Mr . . . David . . . Melrose,' he mused, as he turned the pages of a large leather register.

Patrick leaned over the edge of the counter, more like a grounded pulpit than a desk, and saw, next to the register, a cheap exercise book marked 'Almost Dead'. That was the file to get on; might as well apply straight away.

Escaping from the Key Club had left him strangely elated. After passing out for an hour in the loo, he had woken refreshed but unable to face the others. Bolting past the doorman like a criminal, he had dashed round the corner to a bar, and then walked on to the funeral parlour. Later he would have to apologize to George. Lie and apologize as he always did or wanted to do after any contact with another human being.

'Yes, sir,' said the receptionist brightly, finding the page. 'Mr David Melrose.'

'I have come not to praise him, but to bury him,' Patrick declared, thumping the table theatrically.

'Bu-ry him?' stammered the receptionist. 'We understood that party was to be cremated.'

'I was speaking metaphorically.'

'Metaphorically,' repeated the young man, not quite

reassured. Did that mean the customer was going to sue or not?

'Where are the ashes?' asked Patrick.

'I'll go fetch them for you, sir,' said the receptionist. 'We have you down for a box,' he added, no longer as confident as he'd sounded at first.

'That's right,' said Patrick. 'No point in wasting money on an urn. The ashes are going to be scattered anyway.'

'Right,' said the receptionist with uncertain cheerfulness. Glancing sideways he quickly rectified his tone. 'I'll attend to that right away, sir,' he said in an unctuous and artificially loud singsong, setting off promptly towards a door concealed in the panelling.

Patrick looked over his shoulder to find out what had provoked this new eagerness. He saw a tall figure he recognized without immediately being able to place him.

'We're in an industry where the supply and the demand are *bound* to be identical,' quipped this half-familiar man.

Behind him stood the bald, moustachioed director who had led Patrick to his father's corpse the previous afternoon. He seemed to wince and smile at the same time.

'We've got the one resource that's never going to run out,' said the tall man, obviously enjoying himself.

The director raised his eyebrows and flickered his eyes in Patrick's direction.

Of course, thought Patrick, it was that ghastly man he'd met on the plane.

'Goddamn,' whispered Earl Hammer, 'I guess I still got something to learn about PR.' Recognizing Patrick, he shouted 'Bobby!' across the chequered marble hall.

'Patrick,' said Patrick.

'Paddy! Of course. That eyepatch was unfamiliar to me. What happened to you anyway? Some lady give you a black eye?' Earl guffawed, pounding over to Patrick's side.

'Just a little inflammation,' said Patrick. 'Can't see properly out of that eye.'

'That's too bad,' said Earl. 'What are you doing here anyhow? When I told you on the plane that I had been diversifying my business interests, I bet you never guessed that I was in the process of acquiring New York's premier funeral parlour.'

'I hadn't guessed that,' confessed Patrick. 'And I don't suppose you guessed that I was coming to collect my father's remains from New York's premier funeral parlour.'

'Hell,' said Earl, 'I'm sorry to hear that. I'll bet he was a fine man.'

'He was perfect in his way,' said Patrick.

'My condolences,' said Earl, with that abrupt solemnity that Patrick recognized from the discussion about Miss Hammer's volleyball prospects.

The receptionist returned with a simple wooden box about a foot long and eight inches high.

'It's so much more compact than a coffin, don't you think?' commented Patrick.

'There's no way of denying that,' Earl replied.

'Do you have a bag?' Patrick asked the receptionist.

'A bag?'

'Yes, a carrier bag, a brown-paper bag, that sort of thing.'

'I'll go check that, sir.'

'Paddy,' said Earl, as if he had been giving the matter some thought, 'I want you to have a ten per cent discount.'

'Thank you,' said Patrick, genuinely pleased.

'Don't mention it,' said Earl.

The receptionist returned with a brown-paper bag that was already a little crumpled, and Patrick imagined that he'd had to empty out his groceries hastily in order not to fail in front of his employer.

'Perfect,' said Patrick.

'Do we charge for these bags?' asked Earl, and then, before the receptionist could answer, he added, 'Because this one's on me.'

'Earl, I don't know what to say.'

'It's nothing,' said Earl. 'I have a meeting right now, but I would be honoured if you would have a drink with me later.'

'Can I bring my father?' asked Patrick, raising the bag.

'Hell, yes,' said Earl, laughing.

'Seriously, though, I'm afraid I can't. I'm going out to dinner tonight and I have to fly back to England tomorrow.'

'That's too bad.'

'Well, it's a great regret to me,' said Patrick with a wan smile, as he headed quickly for the door.

'Goodbye, old friend,' said Earl, with a big wave.

'Bye now,' said Patrick, flicking up the collar of his overcoat before he ventured into the rush hour street.

In the black-lacquered hall, opposite the opening doors of the elevator, an African mask gawked from a marble-topped console table. The gilded aviary of a Chippendale mirror gave Patrick a last chance to glance with horror at his fabulously ill-looking face before turning to Mrs Banks, Marianne's emaciated mother, who stood vampirishly in the elegant gloom.

Opening her arms so that her black silk dress stretched from her wrists to her knees, like bat's wings, she cocked her head a little to one side, and exclaimed with excrutiated sympathy, 'Oh, Patrick, we were so sorry to hear your news.'

'Well,' said Patrick, tapping the casket he held under his arm, 'you know how it is: ashes to ashes, dust to dust. What the Lord giveth he taketh away. After what I regard, in this case, as an unnaturally long delay.'

'Is that . . . ?' asked Mrs Banks, staring round-eyed at the brown-paper bag.

'My father,' confirmed Patrick.

'I must tell Ogilvy we'll be one more for dinner,' she said with peals of chic laughter. That was Nancy Banks all over, as magazines often pointed out after photographing her drawing room, so daring but so *right*.

'Banquo doesn't eat meat,' said Patrick, putting the box down firmly on the hall table.

Why had he said Banquo? Nancy wondered, in her husky inner voice which, even in the deepest intimacy of her own thoughts, was turned to address a large and fascinated audience. Could he, in some crazy way, feel responsible for his father's death? Because he had wished for it so often in fantasy? God, she had become good at this after seventeen years of analysis. After all, as Dr Morris had said when they were talking through their affair, what was an analyst but a former patient who couldn't think of anything better to do? Sometimes she missed Jeffrey. He had let her call him Jeffrey during the 'letting-go process' that had been brought to such an abrupt close by his suicide. Without even a note! Was she really meeting the challenges of life, as Jeffrey had promised? Maybe she was 'incompletely analysed'. It was too dreadful to contemplate.

'Marianne's dying to see you,' she murmured consolingly as she led Patrick into the empty drawing room. He stared at a baroque escritoire cascading with crapulous putti.

'She got a phone call the moment you arrived and couldn't get out of answering it,' she added.

'We have the whole evening . . .' said Patrick. And the whole night, he thought optimistically. The drawing room was a sea of pink lilies, their shining pistils accusing him of lust. He was dangerously obsessed, dangerously obsessed. And his thoughts, like a bobsleigh walled with ice, would not change their course until he had crashed or achieved his end. He wiped his hands sweatily on his trousers, amazed to have found a preoccupation stronger than drugs. 'Ah, there's Eddy,' exclaimed Nancy.

Mr Banks strode into the room in a chequered lumber-jack shirt and a pair of baggy trousers. 'Hello,' he said with his rapid little blur, 'I was tho thorry to hear about your fawther. Marianne says that he was a wemarkable man.'

'You should have heard the remarks,' said Patrick.

'Did you have a very difficult relationship with him?' asked Nancy encouragingly.

'Yup,' Patrick replied.

'When did the twouble stawt?' asked Eddy, settling down on the faded orange velvet of a bow-legged marquise.

'Oh, June the ninth, nineteen-o-six, the day he was born.'

'That early?' smiled Nancy.

'Well, we're not g^— resolve the question of whether his pr... were congenital or not, at least not before dinner; but even if they weren't, he didn't delay in acquiring them. By all accounts, the moment he could speak he dedi-cated his new skill to hurting people. By the age of ten he was banned from his grandfather's house because he used to set everyone against each other, cause accidents, force people to do things they didn't want to.'

'You make him sound evil in a rather old-fashioned way. The satanic child,' said Nancy sceptically.

'It's a point of view,' said Patrick. 'When he was around, people were always falling off rocks, or nearly drowning, or bursting into tears. His life consisted of acquiring more and more victims for his malevolence and then losing them again.'

'He must have been charming as well,' said Nancy.

'He was a kitten,' said Patrick.

'But wouldn't we now say that he was just wery dis-turbed?' asked Eddy.

'So what if we did? When the effect somebody has is destructive enough the cause becomes a theoretical curiosity. There are some very nasty people in the world and it is a pity if one of them is your father.'

'I don't think that people noo so much about how to bring up kids in those days. A lot of parents in your fawther's generation just didn't know how to express their love.'

'Cruelty is the opposite of love,' said Patrick, 'not just some inarticulate version of it.'

'Sounds right to me,' said a husky voice from the door-way.

'Oh, hi,' said Patrick, swivelling around in his chair, suddenly self-conscious in Marianne's presence.

Marianne sailed towards him across the dim drawing room, its floorboards creaking underfoot, and her body tipped forward at a dangerous angle like the figurehead on the prow of a ship.

Patrick rose and wrapped his arms around her with greed and desperation.

'Hey, Patrick,' she said, hugging him warmly. 'Hey,' she repeated soothingly when he seemed reluctant to let go. 'I'm so sorry. Really, really sorry.'

Oh, God, thought Patrick, this is where I want to be buried.

'We were just tawking about how parents sometimes don't know how to express their love,' lisped Eddy.

'Well, I guess I wouldn't know about that,' said Marianne with a cute smile.

Her back as curved as a negress's, she walked towards the drinks tray with awkward and hesitating grace, as if she were a mermaid only recently equipped with human legs, and helped herself to a glass of champagne.

'Does anybody wanna a glass of this,' she stammered,

craning her neck forward and frowning slightly, as if the question might contain hidden depths.

Nancy declined. She preferred cocaine. Whatever you said about it, it wasn't fattening. Eddy accepted and Patrick said he wanted whisky.

'Eddy hasn't really gotten over *his* father's death,' said Nancy to nudge the conversation on a little.

'I never really told my fawther how I felt,' explained Eddy, smiling at Marianne as she handed him a glass of champagne.

'Neither did I,' said Patrick. 'Probably just as well in my case.'

'What would you have said?' asked Marianne, fixing him intently with her dark blue eyes.

'I would have said . . . I can't say . . .' Patrick was bewildered and annoyed by having taken the question seriously. 'Never mind,' he mumbled, and poured himself some whisky.

Nancy reflected that Patrick was not really pulling his weight in this conversation.

'They fuck you up. They don't mean to but they do,' she sighed.

'Who says they don't mean to?' growled Patrick.

'Philip Larkin,' said Nancy, with a glassy little laugh.

'But what was it about your father that you couldn't get over?' Patrick asked Eddy politely.

'He was kind of a hero to me. He always noo what to do in any situation, or at least what he wanted to do. He knew how to handle money and women; and when he hooked a three-hundred-pound marlin, the marlin always lost. And when he bid for a picture at auction, he always got it.'

'And when *you* wanted to sell it again you always succeeded,' said Nancy humorously.

'Well, you're *my* hero,' stammered Marianne to her father, 'and I don't want to get over it.'

Fucking hell, thought Patrick, what do these people do

all day, write scripts for *The Brady Bunch*? He hated happy families with their mutual encouragement, and their demonstrative affection, and the impression they gave of valuing each other more than other people. It was utterly disgusting.

'Are we going out to dinner together?' Patrick asked Marianne abruptly.

'We could have dinner here.' She swallowed, a little frown clouding her face.

'Would it be frightfully rude to go out?' he insisted. 'I'd like to talk.'

The answer was clearly yes, as far as Nancy was concerned, it would be frightfully rude. Consuela was preparing the scallops this very minute. But in life, as in entertaining, one had to be flexible and graceful and, in this case, some allowances should be made for Patrick's bereavement. It was hard not to be insulted by the implication that she was handling it badly, until one considered that his state of mind was akin to temporary insanity.

'Of course not,' she purred.

'Where shall we go?' asked Patrick.

'Ah . . . there's a small Armenian restaurant I really really like,' Marianne suggested.

'A small Armenian restaurant,' Patrick repeated flatly.

'It's so great,' gulped Marianne.

12

Under a cerulean dome dotted with dull-gold stars Marianne and Patrick, in a blue velveteen booth of their own, read the plastic-coated menus of the Byzantium Grill. The muffled rumble of a subway train shuddered underfoot and the iced water, always so redundant and so quick to arrive, trembled in the stout ribbed glasses. Everything was shaking, thought Patrick, molecules dancing in the tabletop, electrons spinning, signals and soundwaves undulating through his cells, cells shimmering with country music and police radios, roaring garbage trucks and shattering bottles; his cranium shuddering like a drilled wall, and each sensation Tabasco-flicked onto his soft grey flesh.

A passing waiter kicked Patrick's box of ashes, looked round and apologized. Patrick refused his offer to 'check that for you' and slid the box further under the table with his feet.

Death should express the deeper being rather than represent the occasion for a new role. Who had said that? The terror of forgetting. And yet here was his father being kicked around by a waiter. A new role, definitely a new role.

Perhaps Marianne's body would enable him to forget his father's corpse, perhaps it contained a junction where his obsession with his father's death and his own dying could switch tracks and hurtle towards its new erotic destination with all of its old morbid élan. What should he say? What could he say?

Angels, of course, made love without obstruction of limb or joint, but in the sobbing frustration of human love-making, the exasperating substitution of ticklishness for interfusion, and the ever-renewed drive to pass beyond the mouth of the river to the calm lake where we were conceived, there would have been, thought Patrick, as he pretended to read the menu but in fact fixed his eyes on the green velvet that barely contained Marianne's breasts, an adequate expression of the failure of words to convey the confusion and intensity he felt in the wake of his father's death.

Besides, not having fucked Marianne was like not having read the *Iliad* – something else he had been meaning to do for a long time.

Like a sleeve caught in some implacable and uncomprehending machine, his need to be understood had become lodged in her blissful but dangerously indifferent body. He would be dragged through a crushing obsession and spat out the other end without her pulse flickering or her thoughts wandering from their chosen paths.

Instead of her body saving him from his father's corpse, their secrets would become intertwined; half the horizon formed by his broken lip, half by her unbroken lips. And this vertiginous horizon, like an encircling waterfall, would suck him away from safety, as if he stood on a narrow column of rock watching the dragging water turn smooth around him, seeming still as it turned to fall, falling everywhere.

Jesus, thought Marianne, why had she agreed to have dinner with this guy? He read the menu like he was staring at a ravine from a high bridge. She couldn't bear to ask him another question about his father, but it seemed wrong to make him talk about anything else.

The whole evening could turn into a major drag. He was

in some drooling state between loathing and desire. It was enough to make a girl feel guilty about being so attractive. She tried to avoid it, but she had spent too much of her life sitting opposite hangdog men she had nothing in common with, their eyes burning with reproach, and the conversation long congealed and mouldy, like something from way way *way* back in the icebox, something you must have been crazy to have bought in the first place.

Vine leaves and hummus, grilled lamb, rice, and red wine. At least she could eat. The food here was really good. Simon had brought her here first. He had a gift for finding the best Armenian restaurants in any city in the world. Simon was so so clever. He wrote poems about swans and ice and stars, and it was tough to know what he was trying to say, because they were so indirect without really being very suggestive. But he was a genius of savoir faire, especially in the Armenian-restaurant department. One day Simon had said to her in his faintly Brooklyn stammer, 'Some people have certain emotions. I don't.' Just like that. No swans, no ice, no stars, nothing.

They had made love once and she had tried to absorb the essence of his impudent, elusive genius, but when it was over he had gone into the bathroom to write a poem, and she'd lain in bed feeling like an ex-swan. Of course it was wrong to want to change people, but what else could you possibly want to do with them?

Patrick aroused a reforming zeal akin to carpet bombing. Those slit eyes and curling lips, that arrogant way he arched one of his eyebrows, the stooped, near-foetal posture, the stupid self-destructive melodrama of his life – which of these could not be cheerfully cast aside? But then what would be left if you threw out the rotten stuff? It was like trying to imagine bread without the dough.

There he was, drooling at her again. The green velvet

dress was obviously a big hit. It made her angry to think of Debbie, who was ragged and crazy with love of this sleaze-ball (Marianne had made the mistake of calling him a 'temporary aberration' at the beginning, but Debbie had forgiven her now that she wished it was true), of Debbie being rewarded with this would-be infidelity, no doubt as generalized as his insatiable appetite for drugs.

The trouble with doing something you didn't like was that it made you conscious of all the things that you should be doing instead. Even going to the movies for the first performance of the afternoon failed to provoke the sense of burning urgency she felt right now. The untaken photographs, the call of the dark room, the sting of unwritten thank-you letters which had left her untroubled until now, all crowded in and gave an even more desperate air to the conversation she was having with Patrick.

Condemned to the routine of dismissing men, she sometimes wished (especially tonight) that she didn't arouse emotions she could do nothing to satisfy. Naturally a *tiny* part of her wanted to save them, or at least stop them trying so hard.

Patrick had to acknowledge that the conversation was going pretty badly. Every line he threw to the quayside slipped back heavily into the filthy harbour. She might as well have had her back turned to him, but then nothing excited him more than a turned back. Each mute appeal, disguised by a language as banal as it was possible to imagine, made him more conscious of how little experience he had of saying what he meant. If he could speak to her in another voice, or with another intention – to deceive or to ridicule, for example – then he could wake from this tongue-tied nightmare.

Thick, black and sweet, the coffee arrived. Time was running out. Couldn't she see what was going on? Couldn't she read between the lines? And so what if she could? Perhaps she liked to see him suffer. Perhaps she didn't even like that about him.

Marianne yawned and complained of tiredness. All the signs are good at this point, thought Patrick sarcastically. She's dying for it, *dying* for it. Yes means yes, maybe means yes, perhaps means yes, and no of course means yes as well. He knew how to read women like an open book.

Outside in the street, Marianne kissed him goodbye, sent her love to Debbie, and grabbed a cab.

Patrick stormed down Madison Avenue with his father on his arm. The brown-paper bag occasionally crashed into a passer-by who was unwise enough not to get out of the way.

By the time he reached Sixty-first Street, Patrick realized that it was the first time he had been alone with his father for more than ten minutes without being buggered, hit, or insulted. The poor man had had to confine himself to blows and insults for the last fourteen years, and insults alone for the last six.

The tragedy of old age, when a man is too weak to hit his own child. No wonder he had died. Even his rudeness had been flagging towards the end, and he had been forced to introduce a note of repulsive self-pity to ward off any counter-attack.

'Your trouble,' snarled Patrick, as he swept past the doorman of his hotel, 'is that you're mentally ill.'

'You mustn't say those things to your poor old father,' he murmured, shaking imaginary heart pills into a bunched and twisted palm.

Bastard. Nobody should do that to anybody else.

Never mind, never tell.

Stop thinking about it right now.

'Right now,' said Patrick out loud.

Death and destruction. Buildings swallowed by flame as

he passed. Windows shattering at a glance. An inaudible jugular-bursting scream. No prisoners.

'Death and destruction,' he muttered. Christ, he was really anxious now, really very *fucking anxious*.

Patrick imagined sliding a chainsaw through the neck of the lift operator. Wave after wave of shame and violence, ungovernable shame and violence.

If thy head offend thee, cut it off. Incinerate it and trample it into ash. No prisoners, no pity. Tamburlaine's black tent. My favourite colour! It's so chic.

'Which floor, sir?'

What are you staring at, fuckface?

'Thirty-nine.'

Steps. Over-associative. Over-accelerated. Sedation. Scalpel. Patrick flicked out his hand. Anaesthetic first, surely, Doctor?

Surely: the adverb of a man without an argument. Scalpel first, anaesthetic afterward. The Dr Death Method. You know it makes sense.

Whose idea was it to put him on the thirty-ninth floor? What were they trying to do? Drive him mad? Hide under the sofa. Must hide under the sofa.

Nobody can find me there. What if nobody finds me there? What if they do?

Patrick burst into the room, dropped the brown-paper bag, and threw himself onto the floor. He rolled over towards the sofa, lay on his back, and tried to squirm underneath the skirt of the sofa.

What was he doing? He was going mad. Can't get under the sofa anymore. Too big now. Six foot two. No longer a child.

Fuck that. He lifted the sofa into the air and insinuated his body underneath it, lowering it again onto his chest.

And he lay there in his overcoat and his eyepatch, with

the sofa covering him up to his neck, like a coffin built for a smaller man.

Dr Death: 'This is just the sort of episode we had hoped to avoid. Scalpel. Anaesthetic.' Patrick flicked out his hand.

Not that again. Quickly, quickly, a fix of smack. More of the speed capsules must be dissolving in his stomach. There was an explanation for everything.

'There isn't a bin in the world that wouldn't take you for free,' he sighed in the voice of an affectionate but dishonest hospital matron, as he wriggled from under the sofa and got up slowly to his knees.

He slipped out of his now rather crumpled and fluff-covered overcoat and crawled towards the box of ashes on all fours, watching it carefully as if it might pounce.

How could he get into the box? Get into the box, take out the ashes and empty them down the loo. What better resting place could there be for his father than a New York sewer, among the albino wildlife and tons of shit?

He examined the bevelled cedarwood for a gap or a screw which would enable him to pry the casket open, but only found a thin gold plaque taped to the seamless base in a tiny plastic bag.

In fury and frustration, Patrick leaped to his feet and jumped up and down on the box. It was made of sturdier wood than he had imagined and withstood the assault without a creak. Could he order a chainsaw from room service? He remembered no mention of it on the menu.

Drop it out of the window and watch it shatter on the pavement? He would probably kill someone without denting the box.

With one last effort Patrick kicked the impregnable casket across the floor, where it hit the metal waste-paper basket with a hollow clang and came to a rest.

With admirable swiftness and efficiency, Patrick prepared

and administered an injection of heroin. His eyelids clicked closed. And half opened again, cool and inert.

If only it could always be like this, the calm of the initial hit. But even in this voluptuous Caribbean tranquillity there were too many snapped trees and flayed roofs to let him relax. There was always an argument to win, or a feeling to fight off. He glanced at the box. Observe Everything. Always think for yourself. Never let other people make important decisions for you.

Patrick scratched himself lazily. Well, at least he didn't care so much.

13

Patrick had tried to sleep, but tattered rags of speed still trailed through his consciousness and kept him charging forward. He rubbed his eye compulsively, obsessed with the stye that tickled his eyeball with each blink. The jelly they had given him at the pharmacy was of course completely useless. Nevertheless, he squirted a large amount into his eye and his vision blurred like a greased camera. The eyepatch had left a diagonal dent across his forehead, and he only stopped rubbing his eye to scratch the dent with the same desperate irritation. He wanted to scratch out his eye and peel off his face to end the terrible itchiness that had erupted from his failed attempt to sleep, but knew that it was only the surface play of a more fundamental unease: itching powder in the first pair of nappies, sniggering faces around the hospital cot.

He rolled off the bed, loosening his tie. The room was stiflingly hot, but he loathed the meat-locker cold of the air conditioning. What was he, a carcass on a hook? A corpse in a morgue? Better not to ask.

It was time to check his drugs, to review his troops and see what chance he had of making it through another night and getting onto the plane the next morning at nine thirty.

He sat down at the desk, taking the heroin and pills out of his coat pockets and the coke from an envelope in his suitcase. He had about one and a half out of the seven grams of coke, about a fifth of a gram of heroin, one Quaalude, and one Black Beauty. If he wasn't going to sleep but abandon himself to shooting coke, then there was only enough for two or three hours. It was eleven o'clock now and even with exemplary self-restraint, whatever that was, he would be left with the agony of the come-down in the deadest part of the night. There was enough heroin, just. He was still OK from the fix he'd had after dinner. If he had one at three in the morning and one just before getting on the plane, he'd be able to last until he got to Johnny Hall's. Thank God for Concorde. On the other hand, more coke meant more smack to control the danger of heart attack and insanity, and so he should try to avoid scoring again, or he'd be too out of it for Customs.

The sensible thing to do was to try to divide the coke into two halves, taking the first now and the second after he had gone out to a nightclub or bar. He would try to stay out until three and take the amphetamines just before returning, so that the lift from the speed would cushion the coke come-down after the second bout of fixing. The Black Beauty had about a fifteen-hour life, or maybe a twelve-hour life on the second day, which meant that the effect would be wearing off at about three in the afternoon New York time – eight o'clock London time: just when he could expect to arrive at Johnny's and get some more gear.

Brilliant! He really ought to be in charge of a multinational company or a wartime army to find an outlet for these planning skills. The Quaalude was a freefloating agent. He could use it to cope with the boredom of the plane flight, or give it to some chick in the Mudd Club so as to get her into bed. The incident with Marianne had left him bruised, like a bad dry martini. He wanted to strike back at the female sex and also to satisfy the desires that Marianne had inflamed.

So, he could have a fix of coke now. Yes, yes, yes. He

wiped his clammy hands on his trousers, and began to prepare the solution. His bowels loosened at the thought, and all the longing that a man bestows on a woman who is betraying him, and whose betrayal deepens his longing and enslaves him as her fidelity never could, all the impatience and desperation of waiting while flowers wither in his hands, assailed him. It was love, there was no other word for it.

Like an incompetent bullfighter who cannot find the angle for a kill, Patrick stabbed at his veins without bringing blood into the barrel. Trying to calm himself down, he breathed deeply and reintroduced the needle into his arm, moving it slowly clockwise to find an angle that would break the wall of the vein without going through the other side. As he made this arc, he teased the plunger upward with his thumb.

At last a small thread of blood galloped into the barrel and circled round. Patrick held the syringe as still as possible and pushed down the plunger. The mechanism was stiff and he immediately pulled the plunger back. He felt a sharp pain in his arm. He had lost the vein! He had lost the fucking vein. He was in the muscle. There was only about twenty seconds before the blood coagulated and then he would be shooting a heart-arresting clot into his bloodstream. But if he didn't shoot it up the fix would be ruined. Heat could miraculously reliquify the blood in a solution of heroin, but it would spoil the coke. Almost weeping with frustration, Patrick didn't know whether to push deeper or withdraw the needle. Taking a gamble, he retracted the syringe slightly and flattened it at the same time. More blood curled into the barrel and, with hysterical gratitude, he pushed the plunger down as hard as he could. It was insane to shoot up so quickly, but he couldn't take the risk of the blood coagulating. When he tried to draw the plunger back a second time to make sure he got all the coke that was still lurking in the barrel, he found the mechanism stuck and realized that he had slipped out of the vein again.

He whipped the spike out of his arm and, struggling against a flood of promiscuous lucidity, tried to fill the barrel with water before the blood dried. His hands shook so badly that the syringe clinked on the side of the glass. Jesus, it was strong. Once he had sucked in the water, he put the syringe down, too high to flush it out.

Clasping his arm so that the fist was couched under his chin, he rocked back and forth on the edge of his chair and tried to disperse the pain. But he could not shake off the sense of intimate violation that came with every botched fix. The walls of his veins were perforated again and again by the thin steel he had stuck into them, torturing his body to gratify his mind.

The coke was marauding through his system, like a pack of white wolves, spreading terror and destruction. Even the brief euphoria of the rush had been eclipsed by the fear that he had shot up a blood clot. Next time he would inject himself in the back of his hand where he could still see the veins clearly. The good old-fashioned pain of puncturing that tough skin and probing the tiny delicate bones was less spooky than the horror of missed invisible veins. At least he wasn't fixing in his groin. Gouging around unsuccessfully among those elusive veins could make one question the whole intravenous method of absorbing drugs.

In fact, it was at times like this, in the wake of missed veins, overdoses, minor heart attacks, and fainting fits, that his vicious addiction to needles, quite apart from drugs, made him want to bend spikes and post syringes down drains. It was only the certainty that these quarrels were always lost and merely committed him to the tedious search for new works, or the humiliation of fishing the old ones out from under the wet Kleenexes, slimy yogurt pots, and limp potato peel of the bin liner, that prevented Patrick from destroying his syringes straight away.

This needle fever had a psychological life of its own. What better way to be at once the fucker and the fucked, the subject and the object, the scientist and the experiment, trying to set the spirit free by enslaving the body? What other form of self-division was more expressive than the androgynous embrace of an injection, one arm locking the needle into the other, enlisting pain into the service of pleasure and forcing pleasure back into the service of pain?

He had injected whisky, watching his burned vein turn black under the skin, just to satisfy the needle fever. He had dissolved cocaine in Perrier because the tap was too far away for his imperious desire. Brain like a bowl of Rice Krispies – snap! crackle! pop! – and a disturbing effervescence in the valves of his heart. He had woken up after passing out for thirty hours, the syringe, still half full of smack, hanging loosely from his arm, and started again, with that cold annihilating will, the ritual that had nearly killed him.

Patrick could not help wondering, after his failure to capture Marianne, if a syringe would not have been a better intermediary than his conversation. It made him sentimental to think of Natasha saying in her hoarse whisper, 'Baby, you're so good, you always hit the vein,' a trickle of dark blood flowing from her pale arm as it dangled over the edge of the chair.

He'd shot her up the first time they'd met. She had sat on the sofa with her knees raised, and proffered her arm trustingly. He sat beside her on the floor, and when he gave her the fix, her knees fell open, gathering light in the heavy folds of her black silk trousers, and he was overwhelmed with tenderness as she fell back and sighed, her eyes closed and her face glowing, 'Too much . . . pleasure . . . too much.'

What was sex next to this compassionate violence? Only

this violence could break open a world constrained by the hidden cameras of conscience and vanity.

After that, their relationship had decayed from injection to intercourse, from dazzled recognition to chat. Still, thought Patrick, dazed by the solid-looking objects around him, as he got up from his chair and out of his trance, he had to believe that somewhere out there was a girl willing to trade her body for a couple of drinks and a Quaalude. And he was going to begin his search at the Mudd Club. After one more quick fix.

An hour later, Patrick managed with some difficulty to leave the hotel. He sprawled in the back of the cab as it rumbled downtown. Those pencils of steel, chrome fans, and crystal towers that seemed to burst like pure soprano notes from a prima donna's hideous, pockmarked face, were muffled by darkness. Crossword puzzles of lit and unlit offices slipped by cluelessly. Two lit offices down – call it 'no' – and five across. Five-letter word beginning with 'o'. Oran . . . one . . . order. Call it order. No order. The building disappeared in the back window. Did everyone play this game? The land of the free and the home of the brave, where people only did something if everyone else did too. Had he already thought that? Had he already said that?

As usual, there was a crowd outside the Mudd Club. Patrick slipped to the front where two black men and a fat, bearded white man stood behind a twisted red cord and decided who to let in. He greeted the bouncers in a tired drawl. They always let him in. Perhaps it was because he assumed that they would; or because he didn't really care if they did; or, of course, because he looked rich and likely to order a lot of drinks.

Patrick went straight upstairs where, instead of the live music that was blaring from a small stage on the ground floor, tapes played continuously while videos of spectacular but familiar events – time-lapse flowers suddenly blossoming, Hitler thumping the podium at Nuremberg and then embracing himself in an ecstasy of approval, early attempts at human flight crashing, disintegrating and plummeting from bridges – radiated from a dozen television screens into every angle of the dark room. Just before he stepped inside, a slim sulky girl with short white hair and violet contact lenses slipped past him down the stairs. Dressed all in black, her white make-up and discontented but symmetrical features made her look like a junkie doll. She even had a black silk tourniquet around her thin bicep. Sweet! He watched her. She was not leaving, just switching rooms. He would check her out later.

The Talking Heads pulsed from every speaker. 'The centre is missing,' gasped David Byrne, and Patrick could not help agreeing with him. How did they know exactly what he was feeling? It was spooky.

A shot of a cheetah chasing an antelope through the African bush flickered onto all the screens at once. Patrick pressed himself against the wall as if he had been thrown back by the centrifugal force of a spinning room. He felt waves of weakness and exhaustion when the real state of his body broke through the guard of drugs. The last fix of coke had petered out on the journey down and he might have to take that Black Beauty sooner than scheduled.

The antelope was brought down in a cloud of dust. Its legs twitched for a while as the cheetah ate into its neck. At first the event seemed to shatter and dissipate among all the screens, and then, as the shot closed in, the kill multiplied and gathered force. The room still seemed to Patrick to be throwing him backward, as if rejection and exclusion, the companions of any social contact, had been turned into a physical force. Sometimes the startling contentment of a smack rush caused him to believe that the universe was in-different rather than hostile, but such a touching faith was bound to be betrayed and seemed especially remote now, as he rested with flattened palms against the wall of the room.

Naturally, he still thought of himself in the third person, as a character in a book or a movie, but at least it was still the third person singular. 'They' hadn't come to get him yet tonight, the bacteria of voices that had taken over the night before. In the presence of the absence, in the absence of the presence, Tweedledee and Tweedledum. Life imitating bad literary criticism. Dis/inte/gration. Exhausted and febrile. Business as usual. Funny business as usual.

Like a man in the spinning barrel of a funfair, Patrick unglued himself laboriously from the wall. Under the shim-mering blue light of the televisions, cool customers sprawled uncomfortably on the bench of soft grey cushions that ran around the edge of the room. Patrick walked towards the bar with the care of a driver trying to convince a policeman that he is sober.

'Doctor said his liver looked like a relief map of the Rockies,' said a thick-necked, jocular man leaning on the bar.

Patrick winced and immediately felt a needle-sharp twinge in his side. Absurdly suggestible, must try to calm down. In a parody of detachment, he swivelled his eyes around the room with the small staccato movements of a predatory lizard.

Sprawling on the cushion nearest to the bar was a guy in a red and yellow kilt, a studded belt, army boots, a black leather jacket, and thunderbolt earrings. He looked as if he'd had too many Tuinals. Patrick thought of the black flash of the Tuinal rush, burning the arm like scouring powder; strictly an emergency measure. The look struck him as outmoded; after all, it was six years since the punk summer of '76 when he'd sat on the fire escape at school in the sweltering heat, smoking joints, listening to 'White Riot', and shouting 'destroy' over the rooftops. Next to the kilted punk were two nervous New Jersey secretaries perched on the edge of their seats in tight trousers that cut into their soft bellies. They transferred red lipstick to their all-white cigarette butts with promising zeal, but were too hideous to be considered for the task of consoling him for Marianne's indifference. With his back slightly turned to them, a commodity broker in a dark suit (or was he an art dealer?) was talking to a man who compensated for his near-baldness with a long wispy curtain of grey hair emerging from the last productive follicles at the back of his skull. They looked as if they were keeping in touch with the desperate state of youth, checking out the new-wave kids, spotting the latest inflections of rebellious fashion.

On the other side of the room, a pretty girl with the ever-popular poor look, a black sweater over a simple second-hand skirt, held hands with a man in a T-shirt and jeans. They stared obediently at one of the TV screens, two glasses of beer at their feet. Beyond them, a group of three people talked excitedly. One man in a cobalt-blue suit and thin tie, and another in a primary-red suit and thin tie, bracketed a hook-nosed girl with long black hair and a pair of leather jodhpurs. From the far reaches of the room, Patrick could make out the gleam of chains.

Hopeless, completely hopeless. The only remotely pretty girl in the room was physically linked to another man. They weren't even having an argument. It was disgusting.

He checked his pockets again, crossing himself devoutly. The smack, the speed, the cash, and the Quaalude. One could never be too paranoid – or could one? The coke was back in the hotel with the credit cards. He ordered a bourbon on the rocks, fished out the Black Beauty, and swallowed it with the first gulp. Two hours ahead of schedule, but never mind. Rules were made to be broken. Which meant, if that was a rule, that sometimes they should be observed. Mind sputtering on. Circular thinking. So tired.

A shot of David Bowie sitting drunkenly in front of a serried bank of television screens flickered onto the club's television screens, only to be replaced by the famous shot of Orson Welles walking through the hall of mirrors in Charles Foster Kane's Floridian castle. Multiplying images of multiplication.

'I suppose you think that's clever,' sighed Patrick, like a disappointed schoolmaster.

'I'm sorry?'

Patrick turned around. It was the man with the curtain of long grey hair.

'Just talking to myself,' muttered Patrick. 'I was thinking that the images on the screen were empty and out of control.'

'Maybe they are intended to be images about emptiness,' said the man solemnly. 'I think that's something the kids are very much in touch with right now.'

'How can you be in touch with emptiness?' asked Patrick.

'By the way, my name's Alan. Two Beck's,' he said to the waiter. 'What's yours?'

'Bourbon.'

'I mean your name.'

'Oh, eh, Patrick.'

'Hi.' Alan extended his hand. Patrick shook it reluctantly. 'What are headlights flaring on the road?' asked Alan as if it were a riddle.

Patrick shrugged his shoulders.

'Headlights flaring on the road,' Alan replied with admirable calm.

'That's a relief,' said Patrick.

'Everything in life is a symbol of itself.'

'That's what I was afraid of,' said Patrick, 'but luckily words are too slippery to communicate that.'

'They must communicate that,' Alan affirmed. 'It's like when you're screwing you gotta think of the person you're with.'

'I suppose so,' said Patrick sceptically, 'as long as you put them in a different situation.'

'If the screens here show other ways of making images, other screens, mirrors, cameras, you can call that self-reflection emptiness or you can call it honesty. It announces that it can only announce itself.'

'But what about Batman?' said Patrick. 'That's not about the nature of the television medium.'

'At some level it is.'

'Somewhere below the Batcave.'

'That's right,' said Alan encouragingly, 'somewhere below the Batcave. That's what a lot of the kids feel: the cultural emptiness.'

'I'll take your word for it,' said Patrick.

'*I* happen to think that there's still news of Being worth telling,' said Alan, picking up the bottles of Beck's. 'Whitman's love is more precious than money,' he beamed.

Fucking hell, thought Patrick.

'Do you want to join us?'

'No, in fact I was just going,' said Patrick. 'Frightfully bad jet lag.'

'OK,' said Alan unperturbed.

'So long.'

'Bye now.'

Patrick drained his glass of bourbon to convince Alan that he was really leaving, and headed for the downstairs room.

He really wasn't doing too well. Not only had he failed to pick up a chick, but he'd had to ward off this loony faggot.

What a pickup line, 'Whitman's love is more precious than money.' Patrick let out a short burst of laughter on the stairs. At least down here he might be able to track down that violet-eyed punk. He had to have her. She was definitely the lucky woman destined to share his hotel bed for the last few hours before he left the country.

The atmosphere downstairs was very different from the carpeted bar above. On the stage, musicians in black T-shirts and torn jeans produced a heavily strumming wall of sound which the lead singer's voice tried unsuccessfully to scale. The long bare room, once a warehouse, had no decorations or fancy lights, only a heroic sense of its own rawness. In this loud darkness, Patrick made out blue and pink spiked hair, zebra, leopard and tiger prints, tight black trousers and pointy shoes, exotics and tramps leaning against the walls sniffing powders, solitary dancers with closed eyes and nodding heads, robotic couples, and small groups of jumping and crashing bodies nearer the stage.

Patrick stood on tiptoe trying to find the violet-eyed junkie doll. She was nowhere to be seen, but he soon became distracted by the back of a blonde girl in a homemade chiffon dress and a black leather jacket. Wandering casually past her he glanced around. 'You must be fucking joking,' he muttered vehemently. He felt angry and betrayed, as if her face were a broken promise.

How could he have been so disloyal? He was after the violet-eyed junkie doll. Debbie had once screamed at him in the middle of an argument, 'Do you know what love is, Patrick? Do you have the faintest idea?' And he'd said wearily, 'How many guesses do I get?'

Patrick doubled back and, checking from side to side, weaved his way across the room, and took up a position against the wall.

There she was! With her back to a column and her hands behind her, as if she were tied to a stake, she looked up at the musicians with reverent curiosity. Patrick concentrated madly and imagined her sliding across the floor towards the magnetic field of his chest and stomach. Frowning ferociously, he cast a neurone net over her body and hauled her in like a heavy catch. He whipped mental lassoes around the column she stood beside, and brought her staggering across the floor like a bound slave. Finally, he closed his eyes, took flight, and projected his desire through the room, covering her neck and breasts with kisses.

When he opened his eyes she was gone. Maybe he should have tried conversation. He looked around him indignantly. Where the hell was she? His psychic powers were failing, even though the resurgence of the speed was giving his incompetence a renewed intensity.

He must have her. He must have her, or someone else. He needed contact, skin to skin, muscle to muscle. Above all, he needed the oblivious moment of penetration when, for a second, he could stop thinking about himself. Unless, as too often happened, the appearance of intimacy unleashed a further disembodiment and a deeper privacy. Never mind that. Even if sex sentenced him to an exile which, on top of the usual melancholy, contained the additional irritation of another person's dumb reproach, the conquest was bound to be exhilarating. Or was it? Who was left to him? Beautiful women were always with someone, unless you happened to catch them in the split second between inconsolable loss and consolation, or in the taxi that was taking them from their principal lover to one of the secondary ones. And if you had a beautiful woman, they always kept you waiting, kept you doubting, because it was the only time they could be sure that you were thinking about them.

Having worked himself up into a state of some bitterness, Patrick strode over to the bar.

'Jack Daniel's on the rocks,' he said to the barman. As he drew back, Patrick checked the girl to his left. She was slightly plump, dark-haired, and marginally pretty. She looked back at him steadily, a good sign.

'Aren't you hot in that coat?' she asked. 'It is May, you know.'

'Incredibly hot,' Patrick admitted with a half-smile, 'but I'd feel flayed without it.'

'It's like a defence mechanism,' said the girl.

'Yes,' drawled Patrick, feeling that she had not captured the full subtlety and poignancy of his overcoat. 'What's your name?' he asked as casually as possible.

'Rachel.'

'Mine's Patrick. Can I offer you a drink?' Christ, he sounded like a parody of someone making conversation. Everything had taken on a threatening or facetious aspect that made it harder than ever to climb down from the position of an observer. Perhaps she would experience the crushing dullness as a reassuring ritual.

'Sure. I'd like a beer. A Dos Equis.'

'Fine,' said Patrick, catching the barman's attention. 'So what kind of work do you do?' he went on, practically vomiting at the effort of making ordinary conversation and feigning an interest in somebody else.

'I work in a gallery.'

'Really?' said Patrick, hoping he sounded impressed. He seemed to have lost all control over his voice.

'Yeah, but I really wanna start a gallery of my own.'

Here we go again, thought Patrick. The waiter who thinks he's an actor, the actor who thinks he's a director, the taxi driver who thinks he's a philosopher. All the signs are good at this point, the deal is about to happen, there's a lot of interest from the record companies . . . a city full of phoney aggressive fantasists and, of course, a few genuinely unpleasant people with power.

'Only, I need the financial backing,' she sighed.

'Why do you want to start out on your own?' he asked, concerned and yet encouraging.

'I don't know if you're familiar with Neo-Objective art, but I think it's going to be really major,' said Rachel. 'I know a lot of the artists and I'd like to get their careers started while everybody else is still ignoring them.'

'I'm sure that won't be for long.'

'That's why I gotta move quickly.'

'I'd love to see some Neo-Objective art,' said Patrick earnestly.

'I could arrange that,' said Rachel, looking at him in a new light. Was this the financial backing she had been waiting for? His overcoat might be weird, but it looked expensive. It might be kinda cool to have an eccentric English backer who wasn't going to breathe down her neck.

'I do a little collecting,' Patrick lied. 'By the way, would you like a Quaalude?'

'I don't really do drugs,' said Rachel, wrinkling her nose.

'Neither do I,' said Patrick. 'I just happen to have one floating around. Somebody gave it to me ages ago.'

'I don't need to get high to have fun,' said Rachel coolly.

She's on for it, she's definitely on for it, thought Patrick. 'You're so right,' he said, 'it spoils the magic – makes people unreal.' His heartbeat accelerated; he'd better clinch the deal. 'Do you want to come back to my hotel? I'm staying at the Pierre.'

The Pierre, thought Rachel; all the signs were good. 'Sure,' she smiled.

14

Two thirty according to the clock next to the St Christopher medallion. That gave him about five hours. More than enough, more than a lifetime's worth of conversation with Rachel. He smiled at her vaguely. What could he tell her? That his father had just died? That he was a drug addict? That he was leaving for the airport in five hours? That his girlfriend really wouldn't mind? He certainly didn't want to ask her any more questions about herself. Nor did he want to hear her views on Nicaragua.

'I'm feeling kinda hungry,' said Rachel uneasily.

'Hungry?'

'Yeah, I got this craving for chilli.'

'Well, I'm sure we can get you some on room service,' said Patrick, who knew perfectly well that there was no chilli on the Pierre's all-night menu and would have disapproved if there had been.

'But there's this diner where they make like the greatest chilli in the entire world,' said Rachel, sitting up eagerly. 'I *really* wanna go there.'

'Right,' said Patrick patiently. 'What's the address?'

'Eleventh Avenue and Thirty-eighth.'

'I'm sorry about this,' said Patrick to the driver, 'we've changed our minds. Could we go to Eleventh Avenue and Thirty-eighth Street instead?'

'Eleventh and Thirty-eighth?' repeated the driver.

'Yup.'

The diner was a ribbed silver caravan with TRY OUR FAMOUS CHILI AND TACOS in red neon outside. It was an offer that Rachel could not resist. A green neon chilli flashed cutely next to a yellow sombrero.

When the giant oval plate arrived loaded with chilli-flavoured minced meat, refried beans, guacamole, and sour cream, topped with bright orange Cheddar and accompanied by speckled ochre tortilla shells, Patrick lit a cigarette in the hope of drawing a veil of thin blue smoke over the pungent heap of spicy food. He took another sip of insipid coffee and sat back as far as possible in the corner of the red plastic bench. Rachel was clearly a nervous overeater, stuffing herself before he stuffed her, or perhaps, very persuasively, trying to put him off sex altogether by wreaking havoc on her digestive system, and saturating her breath with the torrid stench of cheese and chilli.

'Uh-hum,' said Rachel appreciatively, 'I love this food.'

Patrick raised an eyebrow slightly but made no comment.

She piled the chilli into the tortilla, smeared some guacamole on top, and patted down the sour cream with the back of her fork. Finally, she took a pinch of Cheddar between her fingers and sprinkled it on top.

The tortilla flopped open and chilli flooded onto her chin. Giggling, she lifted it with her index finger and forced it back into her mouth.

'Delicioso,' she commented.

'It looks disgusting,' said Patrick sullenly.

'You should try some.'

She stooped over the plate and found ingenious angles from which to snap at the collapsing tortilla. Patrick rubbed his eye. It was itching wildly again. He stared out of the window but was drawn back into the arena of its reflections. The tulip-red bar stools on their chrome stems, the hatch into the kitchen, the old man hunched over a cup of coffee and, of course, Rachel like a pig in a trough. It reminded him of the famous painting by whatshisname. Memory getting burned out. The terror of forgetting everything. Hooper . . . Hopper. Got it. Life in the old dog.

'Finished?' asked Patrick.

'They make a great banana split here,' said Rachel saucily, still chomping her last mouthful of chilli.

'Well, don't restrain yourself,' said Patrick. 'Will one be enough?'

'Don't you want one too?'

'No, I do not,' said Patrick pompously.

Soon a long glass dish arrived on which scoops of chocolate, vanilla, and strawberry ice cream were bracketed by the two halves of a banana, buried under rippling waves of whipped cream and decorated with beads of pink and green candy. Red maraschino cherries ran down the centre like a row of clown's buttons.

Patrick's leg twitched up and down involuntarily as he watched Rachel exhume bits of banana from the mound of brightly coloured creams.

'I've given up dairy products,' she said, 'but I allow myself these binges sometimes.'

'So it seems,' said Patrick stiffly.

He was overcome with loathing and contempt. The girl was completely out of control. Whereas drugs were at least amenable to advertising: life on the edge, exploring the inner Congo, the heart of darkness, outstaring death, returning with the scars and medals of a haunting knowledge, Coleridge, Baudelaire, Leary . . . ; and even if this advertising seemed horribly false to anyone who had taken drugs at all seriously, it wasn't possible even to pretend that there was anything heroic about an eating problem. And yet there was something unsettlingly familiar about Rachel's obsessive greed and ridiculous dishonesty.

'Can we go now?' snapped Patrick.

'Yeah, OK,' said Rachel timidly.

He ordered the check, threw down a twenty-dollar bill before it arrived, and wriggled out of the booth. Another fucking taxi drive, he thought.

'I feel kinda nau-tious,' complained Rachel, as they went up in the hotel elevator.

'I'm not surprised,' said Patrick severely, 'I feel nauseous and I was only watching.'

'Hey, you're pretty hos-tel.'

'I'm sorry,' said Patrick, 'I'm awfully tired.' Better not lose her now.

'Me too,' said Rachel.

Patrick unlocked the door, and switched on the lights. 'Sorry about the mess.'

'You should see my apartment.'

'Maybe I will,' said Patrick, 'and all that Neo-Objective art.'

'Definitely,' said Rachel. 'Can I use the bathroom?'

'Of course.'

Time to mix a quick fix, thought Patrick, as he heard the lock slide closed on the bathroom door. He fished the coke from his suitcase and the smack from his inner left pocket, took the spoon from the back of the bottom drawer, and retrieved the half-bottle of Evian he had hidden, with unnecessary caution, behind the curtain. There might not be many more opportunities, and he'd better make a strong speedball to reduce the number of fixes to a minimum. He mixed the smack and coke together, dissolved them and drew the solution into the syringe.

He was ready, but how long did he have before Rachel

emerged from the bathroom? With his hearing strained, like a man listening to his footsteps on a creaking staircase, he concentrated on the sounds coming from the bathroom. The muffled noise of vomiting, followed by a little rasping cough, reassured him that there would be time for a fix.

Taking no risks, he stuck the spike into a thick vein in the back of his hand. The smell of cocaine assailed him and he felt his nerves stretching like piano wires. The heroin followed in a soft rain of felt hammers playing up his spine and rumbling into his skull.

He groaned contentedly and scratched his nose. It was so pleasurable, so fucking pleasurable. How could he ever give up? It was love. It was coming home. It was Ithaca, the end of all his storm-tossed wanderings. He dropped the syringe into the top drawer, staggered across the room, and sprawled on the bed.

Peace at last. The mingling lashes of half-closed eyes, the slow reluctant flutter of folding wings; his body pounded by felt hammers, pulses dancing like sand on a drum; love and poison evacuating his breath in a long slow exhalation, fading into a privacy he could never quite remember, nor for a moment forget. His thoughts shimmered like a hesitating stream, gathering into pools of discrete and vivid imagery.

He pictured his feet walking through a damp London square, his shoes sealing wet leaves darkly to the pavement. In the square, the heat from a heap of smouldering leaves syruped the air, and billows of yellow smoke skewed the sunlight like a broken wheel, its spokes scattered among the balding plane trees. The lawn was littered with dead branches, and from the railings he watched the sad and acrid ceremony, his eyes irritated by the smoke.

Patrick blinked back into the present, scratching his eye. He focused on the painting of a Normandy beach that hung above his desk. Why didn't the women in long dresses and the straw-hatted men walk into the sea? Was it the sheer gaiety of the parasols that detained them on the beach, or a sentence they must complete before disrobing their flesh in the indifferent water?

Everything was dying, every lifted stone revealed its bed of blind white maggots. He must leave the dank rotting earth and the all-consuming sea, and head for the mountains. 'I hail you, great mountains!' he chanted under his breath. 'Lofty! Alone! Serene! Good for jumping off!'

Patrick giggled feebly. The coke had already sputtered out. He was really beginning to feel rather ghastly. There was only enough for two more good fixes of coke and then he would be condemned to an accelerating agony of disappointment. The speed was perhaps only temporarily eclipsed by the heroin, but even so its performance was bound to be enormously reduced after he'd been awake for so long. The sensible thing to do in a situation like this, when one's body was a battleground strewn with the carnage of internarcotic wars, was to take the last Quaalude that Rachel had so high-mindedly refused, and try to have a nap on the plane. There was definitely an argument for getting some sleep; namely, that when he woke up the impact of the drugs would be stronger.

As usual, his liver ached as if he'd had a rugby ball kicked under his ribcage. His desire for drugs, like the fox hidden under the Spartan's tunic, gnawed at his entrails. The double vision which afflicted him if he didn't blink constantly had grown worse, and the two images of each object were drifting further apart.

These complaints and the general feeling that his body was held together with paper clips and safety pins and would tear apart at the slightest strain, filled him with remorse and terror. It was always now, on the dawn of the third day, that he was filled with a disgusted desire to stop taking drugs, but he knew that the first hints of lucidity and withdrawal would bring an even greater horror of their absence.

Patrick was surprised to see Rachel standing miserably at the end of his bed. She had faded quickly from his memory while she threw up in the bathroom, losing her individuality and simply becoming Other People, someone who might interrupt his fix, or his contemplation of the rush.

'I feel so bloated,' she complained, clasping her stomach.

'Why don't you lie down?' croaked Patrick.

Rachel sank onto the bed and crawled to the far end, groaning as she collapsed on the pillows.

'Come here,' said Patrick in what he hoped was a tender voice.

Rachel rolled over slightly and lay sideways. He leaned towards her, hoping she had brushed her teeth and wondering when he had last brushed his own, and kissed her. The difficult angle meant that their noses clashed and then, in their haste to overcome this awkwardness, their teeth clashed too.

'Jesus, it's like being twelve years old,' said Patrick.

'I'm sorry,' said Rachel.

He sat back with his head in one hand and ran the other hand over Rachel's knitted white dress. She looked drained and nervous. There was a bulge in her lower abdomen which had not been visible when she was standing up. Patrick skirted the bulge and brushed the back of his fingers gently over her hip and thigh.

'I'm sorry,' Rachel repeated, 'I can't go through with this, I'm too nervous. Maybe we can spend some time together, get to know each other.'

Patrick disengaged his hand and flopped back onto the bed.

'Of course,' he said flatly, glancing at the bedside clock. Four fifty. They had about two hours and forty minutes to 'get to know each other'.

'When I was younger I used to fall into bed with anyone,' Rachel whined, 'but it always left me feeling empty.'

'Even after a plate of chilli and a banana split?' said Patrick. If he wasn't going to fuck her, he might as well torment her.

'You're a really hos-tel person,' said Rachel, 'do you know that? Do you have a problem with women?'

'Men, women, dogs: I don't discriminate,' said Patrick, 'they all piss me off.'

He rolled off the bed and went over to the desk. Why had he brought this tiresome lump of lard back to his room? It was intolerable, everything was intolerable.

'Look, I don't want to argue with you,' said Rachel. 'I know you're disappointed, I just need you to help me relax.'

'Relaxing isn't my speciality,' said Patrick, putting the coke and spoon into his trouser pocket and reaching to the back of the drawer to find the second syringe.

Rachel got off the bed and came over to Patrick's side.

'We're both real tired,' she said; 'let's go to bed and get some sleep. Maybe in the morning things'll seem different,' she said coyly.

'Will they?' asked Patrick. Her hand was burning into his back. He didn't want to be touched by her or by anybody else. He wriggled away, waiting for the opportunity to leave her.

'What's in this box?' asked Rachel, with a renewed effort at cheerfulness, touching the casket on top of the television.

'My father's ashes.'

'Your father's ashes.' She gulped, retracting her hand. 'That makes me feel weird.'

'I wouldn't worry about it,' said Patrick. 'I think it counts as hand luggage, don't you?'

'I guess,' said Rachel, puzzled by this line of argument.

'God, I mean, I really feel weird about this. Your father is in the room with us. Maybe I sensed that before.'

'Who knows? Anyway, he can keep you company while I'm in the bathroom. I may be some time.'

'This is heavy,' said Rachel, round-eyed.

'Don't be alarmed. He was a charming man, everybody said so.'

Patrick left Rachel in the bedroom and locked the bathroom door behind him. She sat on the edge of the bed, looking anxiously at the casket, as if she expected it to move. She took this golden opportunity to use the breathing exercises she dimly remembered from her two yoga classes, but after a couple of minutes she grew bored and still wanted to leave. The trouble was that she lived way over in Brooklyn. The cab ride was going to be ten–twelve dollars, and she would only arrive a couple of hours before she had to struggle to the gallery on the subway. If she stayed here she might get some sleep and some breakfast. She snuggled up with the breakfast menu and, after the initial excitement and guilt of seeing how many wonderful things there were to eat, she was overcome by tiredness.

Patrick lay in the bathtub, one leg dangling over the edge of the bath, blood trickling from his arm. He'd put all the coke in one last fix and, blasted by the rush, had fallen off the edge of the bath. Now he stared at the chrome shower rail and the glossy white ceiling, drawing shallow breaths through his gritted teeth, as if a girder had collapsed on his chest. Dark patches of sweat stained his shirt, and his nostrils were powdered with heroin. He had pressed the packet straight to his nose, and now it lay crumpled and empty on his neck.

With his left hand he ground the spike of the syringe against the side of the bath. He had to stop shooting up – especially now that he had run out of gear.

All the harm he'd done crowded in on him at once, like a troupe of fallen angels in a medieval painting, goading him towards hell with red-hot pitchforks, their sniggering and malicious faces surrounding him with ugliness and despair. He felt the irresistible desire to make an eternal resolution, to make the devout and impossible promise never to take a drug again. If he survived now, if he was allowed to survive, he would never shoot up again.

In this grave predicament, his fervour outweighed the knowledge of his dishonesty, even though he already detected, like distant gunfire, the disturbing feeling that something was missing. He had run out of gear. One syringe was destroyed and the other blocked with blood. It was just as well, but it was infinitely sad. Soon enough, his synapses would be screaming like starving children, and every cell in his body tugging pathetically at his sleeve.

Patrick moved his leg down tentatively and hoisted himself upright. Nearly died again. Always a shock to the system. Better take that Quaalude. He heaved himself up, nearly fainted and, leaning heavily on the wall like an old man, stepped carefully out of the bath. His coat was lying on the floor (he'd often thought of asking his tailor to put flaps in the sleeves) and he very slowly picked it up, very slowly took out the Quaalude, put it in his mouth, and washed it down with a little water.

Dazed, Patrick sat down on the loo and unhooked the phone. 555–1726.

'I cannot come to the phone right now, but if you leave . . .' Fuck, he wasn't in.

'Pierre, it's Patrick. I just rang to say goodbye,' he lied. 'I'll be in touch the *moment* I get back to New York. Bye now.'

Next, he rang Johnny Hall in London to make sure there would at least be something waiting for him when he arrived.

The phone rang a few times. Maybe Johnny could meet him at the airport. It rang a few more times. Jesus Christ, he wasn't in either. It was intolerable.

Patrick tried to hook the phone back, missing several times before he got it on the receiver. He was as weak as a child. Noticing that the syringe was still in the bath he picked it up wearily, wrapped it in loo paper and threw it in the waste-paper basket under the basin.

In the bedroom, Patrick found Rachel stranded on the bed, snoring erratically. If he were in love, he thought. But couldn't finish. The flame play of disturbed water under a bridge's arch, a muffled echo, a kiss. Snow sliding from his boots in front of the stove, blood swelling back into his fingertips. If he were in love.

As it was, white-bellied and heavy breathing, she looked to Patrick like a beached whale.

Packing was easy if you rolled everything into one ball, stuffed it in the suitcase, sat on it, and did up the zip. He had to undo the zip again to squeeze Victor's book in. 'I think I'm an egg, therefore I am an egg,' he squealed in Pierre's French accent. Putting on his last clean shirt, he went back into the bathroom to call the reception.

'Hello?' he drawled.

'Yes, sir, how may I help you?'

'I'd like a limo at seven thirty, please. A big one with black windows,' he added childishly.

'I'll arrange that for you, sir.'

'And prepare my bill, will you?'

'Yes, sir. Shall I send a bellboy to collect your baggage?'

'In about quarter of an hour, thank you.' Everything was under control. He finished dressing, put on his eye-patch, and sat in the armchair waiting for the man to collect his bag. Should he leave a note for Rachel? 'I do not think I shall ever forget our evening together', or 'Let's do this again sometime soon'. Sometimes silence was more eloquent.

There was a faint knock on the door. The bellboy was about sixty, small, bald, and dressed in the hotel's plainest grey uniform.

'There's only one bag.'

'Roight, sir,' he said in an Irish accent.

They walked down the corridor, Patrick a little stooped to protect his liver, and lopsided from the pain in his back.

'Life's not just a bag of shit,' said Patrick conversationally, 'but a leaky one. You can't help being touched by it, don't you find?'

'I believe dat's what a lot of people feel about it,' the other man replied in a lilting and agreeable tone. And then he came to a halt and put Patrick's bag down.

'And there will be rivers of blood. And de wicked shall be drowned,' he intoned. 'Nor shall de high places be spared.'

'One of your own prophecies?' asked Patrick suavely.

'It's in de Boible,' said the bellboy. 'And de bridges shall be swept away,' he promised, pointing to the ceiling and then swatting an invisible fly. 'And men shall say that de end of de world cometh upon them.'

'And they shall have a point,' said Patrick, 'but I really must be going.'

'Roight you are,' said the bellboy, still excited. 'I'll be meeting you at the reception.' He scuttled off towards the service elevator. Try as one might to live on the edge, thought Patrick, getting into the other lift, there was no point in competing with people who believed what they saw on television.

The bill for two thousand one hundred and fifty-three dollars was larger than even Patrick had expected. He was secretly pleased. Capital erosion was another way to waste his substance, to become as thin and hollow as he felt, to lighten the burden of undeserved good fortune, and commit a symbolic suicide while he still dithered about the real one. He also nursed the opposite fantasy that when he became penniless he would discover some incandescent purpose born of his need to make money. On top of the hotel bill, he must have spent another two or two and a half thousand on taxis, drugs, and restaurants, plus six thousand for the air tickets. That brought the total to over ten thousand dollars, and the funeral expenses were on their way. He felt like a gameshow winner. How irritating if it had been eight and a half or nine. Ten thousand in two days. Nobody could say he didn't know how to have fun.

Patrick tossed his American Express card onto the counter without bothering to verify the bill.

'Oh, by the way,' he yawned, 'I'll sign the form, but could you leave the total open? A friend of mine is still in the room. She may want breakfast; in fact, I'm sure she will. She can order anything she likes,' he added munificently.

'O-kay.' The receptionist hesitated, wondering whether to make an issue of the double occupancy. 'She'll be leaving the room by noon, will she?'

'I suppose so. She works, you see,' said Patrick as if this were rather exceptional. He signed the credit-card form.

'We'll send a copy of the total to your home address.'

'Oh, I wouldn't bother to do that,' said Patrick, yawning again. He noticed the bellboy standing nearby with his bag. 'Hello,' he smiled. 'Rivers of blood, eh?'

The bellboy looked at him with servile incomprehension. Maybe he'd imagined the whole thing. Might be a good idea to get some sleep.

'I hope you enjoyed your stay with us,' said the receptionist, handing Patrick a copy of the bill in an envelope.

'Enjoyed isn't the word,' said Patrick with his most charming smile, 'I loved it.' He refused the envelope with a little frown. 'Oh my God,' he suddenly exclaimed, 'I've forgotten something in the room.' He turned to the bellboy. 'There's a wooden box on top of the television; you couldn't go and fetch it for me, could you? And the brown-paper bag would be very useful too.'

How could he have forgotten the box? No need to call Vienna for an interpretation. What would they have done on the bleak Cornish estuary where his father had asked to have his ashes scattered? He would have had to bribe a local crematorium to give him some of their spare sweepings.

The bellboy returned ten minutes later. Patrick stubbed out his cigarette and took the brown-paper bag from him. The two of them walked together towards the revolving doors.

'The young lady was wondering where you were going,' said the bellboy.

'What did you say?'

'I said I thought it was de airport.'

'And what did she say?'

'I wouldn't loik to repeat it, sir,' said the bellboy respectfully.

So much for that, thought Patrick, spinning through the doors. Slash. Burn. Move on. Out into the scintillating light, under a paler wider sky, his eyeballs drilled like a Roman statue.

Across the street he saw a man, his left arm severed at the wrist, a slight rawness where the bone was most prominent, a four days' unshaven, bitter face, yellow lenses, curling lip, lank hair, stained raincoat. The stump twitched upward in brisk involuntary jerks. Heavy smoker. Hater of the world. *Mon semblable*. Other people's words.

Still, there were some important differences. Patrick distributed banknotes to the doorman and the bellboy. The driver opened the door for him and he climbed into the back with his brown-paper bag. He sprawled across the black leather seat, closed his eyes, and pretended to sleep.

SOME HOPE

For my mother, and my sister

1

Patrick woke up knowing he had dreamed but unable to remember the contents of his dream. He felt the familiar ache of trying to track something that had just disappeared off the edge of consciousness but could still be inferred from its absence, like a whirlwind of scrap paper left by the passage of a fast car.

The obscure fragments of his dream, which seemed to have taken place beside a lake, were confused with the production of *Measure for Measure* he had seen the night before with Johnny Hall. Despite the director's choice of a bus depot as the setting for the play, nothing could diminish the shock of hearing the word 'mercy' so many times in one evening.

Perhaps all his problems arose from using the wrong vocabulary, he thought, with a brief flush of excitement that enabled him to throw aside the bedcovers and contemplate getting up. He moved in a world in which the word 'charity', like a beautiful woman shadowed by her jealous husband, was invariably qualified by the words 'lunch', 'committee', or 'ball'. 'Compassion' nobody had any time for, whereas 'leniency' made frequent appearances in the form of complaints about short prison sentences. Still, he knew that his difficulties were more fundamental than that.

He was worn out by his lifelong need to be in two places at once: in his body and out of his body, on the bed and on the curtain pole, in the vein and in the barrel, one eye behind the eyepatch and one eye looking at the eyepatch, trying to stop observing by becoming unconscious, and then forced to observe the fringes of unconsciousness and make darkness visible; cancelling every effort, but spoiling apathy with restlessness; drawn to puns but repelled by the virus of ambiguity; inclined to divide sentences in half, pivoting them on the qualification of a 'but', but longing to unwind his coiled tongue like a gecko's and catch a distant fly with unwavering skill; desperate to escape the self-subversion of irony and say what he really meant, but really meaning what only irony could convey.

Not to mention, thought Patrick, as he swung his feet out of bed, the two places he wanted to be tonight: at Bridget's party and *not* at Bridget's party. And he wasn't in the mood to dine with people called Bossington-Lane. He would ring Johnny and arrange to have dinner with him alone. He dialled the number but immediately hung up, deciding to call again after he had made some tea. He had scarcely replaced the receiver when the phone rang. Nicholas Pratt was ringing to chastise him for not answering his invitation to Cheatley.

'No need to thank me,' said Nicholas Pratt, 'for getting you invited to this glittering occasion tonight. I owe it to your dear Papa to see that you get into the swim of things.'

'I'm drowning in it,' said Patrick. 'Anyhow, you prepared the way for my invitation to Cheatley by bringing Bridget down to Lacoste when I was five. Even then one could tell she was destined to command the heights of society.'

'You were much too badly behaved to notice anything as important as *that*,' said Nicholas. 'I remember you once in Victoria Road giving me a very sharp kick in the shins. I hobbled through the hall, trying to hide my agony so as not to upset your sainted mother. How is she, by the way? One never sees her these days.'

'It's amazing, isn't it? She seems to think there are better things to do than going to parties.'

'I always thought she was a little peculiar,' said Nicholas wisely.

'As far as I know she's driving a consignment of ten thousand syringes to Poland. People say it's marvellous of her, but I still think that charity begins at home. She could have saved herself the journey by bringing them round to my flat,' said Patrick.

'I thought you'd put all that behind you,' said Nicholas.

'Behind me, in front of me. It's hard to tell, here in the Grey Zone.'

'That's rather a melodramatic way to talk at thirty.'

'Well, you see,' sighed Patrick, 'I've given up everything, but taken nothing up instead.'

'You could make a start by taking my daughter up to Cheatley.'

'I'm afraid I can't,' lied Patrick, who couldn't bear Amanda Pratt. 'I'm getting a lift from someone else.'

'Oh, well, you'll see her at the Bossington-Lancs',' said Nicholas. 'And we'll see each other at the party.'

Patrick had been reluctant to accept his invitation to Cheatley for several reasons. One was that Debbie was going to be there. After years of trying to thrust her away, he was bewildered by his sudden success. She, on the other hand, seemed to enjoy falling out of love with him more than anything else about their long affair. How could he blame her? He ached with unspoken apologies.

In the eight years since his father's death, Patrick's youth had slipped away without being replaced by any signs of maturity, unless the tendency for sadness and exhaustion to eclipse hatred and insanity could be called 'mature'. The sense of multiplying alternatives and bifurcating paths had been replaced by a quayside desolation, contemplating the long list of missed boats. He had been weaned from his drug addiction in several clinics, leaving promiscuity and party-going to soldier on uncertainly, like troops which have lost their commander. His money, eroded by extravagance and medical bills, kept him from poverty without enabling him to buy his way out of boredom. Quite recently, to his horror, he had realized he would have to get a job. He was therefore studying to become a barrister, in the hope that he would find some pleasure in keeping as many criminals as possible at large.

His decision to study the law had got him as far as hiring *Twelve Angry Men* from a video shop. He had spent several days pacing up and down, demolishing imaginary witnesses with withering remarks, or suddenly leaning on furniture and saying with mounting contempt, 'I put it to you that on the night of . . .' until he recoiled, and, turning into the victim of his own cross-examination, collapsed in a fit of histrionic sobs. He had also bought some books, like *The Concept of Law*, *Street on Tort*, and *Charlesworth on Negligence*, and this pile of law books now competed for his attention with old favourites like *Twilight of the Idols* and *The Myth of Sisyphus*.

As the drugs had worn off, a couple of years earlier, he had started to realize what it must be like to be lucid all the time, an unpunctuated stretch of consciousness, a white tunnel, hollow and dim, like a bone with the marrow sucked out. 'I want to die, I want to die, I want to die,' he found himself muttering in the middle of the most ordinary task, swept away by a landslide of regret as the kettle boiled or the toast popped up.

At the same time, his past lay before him like a corpse waiting to be embalmed. He was woken every night by savage nightmares; too frightened to sleep, he climbed out of his sweat-soaked sheets and smoked cigarettes until the dawn crept into the sky, pale and dirty as the gills of a poisonous mushroom. His flat in Ennismore Gardens was strewn with violent videos which were a shadowy expression of the endless reel of violence that played in his head. Constantly on the verge of hallucination, he walked on ground that undulated softly, like a swallowing throat.

Worst of all, as his struggle against drugs grew more successful, he saw how it had masked a struggle not to become like his father. The claim that every man kills the thing he loves seemed to him a wild guess compared with the near certainty of a man turning into the thing he hates. There were of course people who didn't hate anything, but they were too remote from Patrick for him to imagine their fate. The memory of his father still hypnotized him and drew him like a sleepwalker towards a precipice of unwilling emulation. Sarcasm, snobbery, cruelty, and betrayal seemed less nauseating than the terrors that brought them into existence. What could he do but become a machine for turning terror into contempt? How could he relax his guard when beams of neurotic energy, like searchlights weaving about a prison compound, allowed no thought to escape, no remark to go unchecked.

The pursuit of sex, the fascination with one body or another, the little rush of an orgasm, so much feebler and more laborious than the rush of drugs, but like an injection, constantly repeated because its role was essentially palliative – all this was compulsive enough, but its social complications were paramount: the treachery, the danger of pregnancy, of infection, of discovery, the pleasures of theft, the tensions that arose in what might otherwise have been very tedious circumstances; and the way that sex merged with the penetration of ever more self-assured social circles where, perhaps, he would find a resting place, a living equivalent to the intimacy and reassurance offered by the octopus embrace of narcotics.

As Patrick reached for his cigarettes, the phone rang again.

'So, how are you?' said Johnny.

'I'm stuck in one of those argumentative daydreams,' said Patrick. 'I don't know why I think intelligence consists of proving that I can have a row all on my own, but it would be nice just to grasp something for a change.'

'*Measure for Measure* is a very argumentative play,' said Johnny.

'I know,' said Patrick. 'I ended up theoretically accepting that people have to forgive on a "judge not that ye be not judged" basis, but there isn't any emotional authority for it, at least not in that play.'

'Exactly,' said Johnny. 'If behaving badly was a good enough reason to forgive bad behaviour, we'd all be oozing with magnanimity.'

'But what is a good enough reason?' asked Patrick.

'Search me. I'm more and more convinced that things just happen, or don't just happen, and there's not much you can do to hurry them along.' Johnny had only just thought of this idea and was not convinced of it at all.

'Ripeness is all,' groaned Patrick.

'Yes, exactly, another play altogether,' said Johnny.

'It's important to decide which play you're in before you get out of bed,' said Patrick.

'I don't think anyone's heard of the one we're in tonight. Who are the Bossington-Lanes?'

'Are they having you for dinner too?' asked Patrick. 'I think we're going to have to break down on the motorway, don't you? Have dinner in the hotel. It's so hard facing strangers without drugs.'

Patrick and Johnny, although they now fed on grilled food

and mineral water, had a well-established nostalgia for their former existence.

'But when we took gear at parties, all we saw was the inside of the loos,' Johnny pointed out.

'I know,' said Patrick. 'Nowadays when I go into the loos I say to myself, "What are you doing here? You don't take drugs anymore!" It's only after I've stormed out that I realize I wanted to have a piss. By the way, shall we drive down to Cheatley together?'

'Sure, but I have to go to an NA meeting at three o'clock.'

'I don't know how you put up with those meetings,' said Patrick. 'Aren't they full of ghastly people?'

'Of course they are, but so is any crowded room,' said Johnny.

'But at least I'm not required to believe in God to go to this party tonight.'

'I'm sure if you were you'd find a way,' laughed Johnny. 'What is a strain is being forced into the lobster pot of good behaviour while being forced to sing its praises.'

'Doesn't the hypocrisy get you down?'

'Luckily, they have a slogan for that: "Fake it to make it."'

Patrick made a vomiting sound. 'I don't think that dressing the Ancient Mariner as a wedding guest is the solution to the problem, do you?'

'It's not like that, more like a roomful of Ancient Mariners deciding to have a party of their own.'

'Christ!' said Patrick. 'It's worse than I thought.'

'You're the one who wants to dress as a wedding guest,' said Johnny. 'Didn't you tell me that the last time you were banging your head against the wall and begging to be released from the torment of your addiction, you couldn't get that sentence about Henry James out of your mind: "He was an inveterate diner-out and admitted to accepting one hundred and fifty invitations in the winter of 1878," or something like that?'

'Hmm,' said Patrick.

'Anyhow, don't you find it hard not to take drugs?' asked Johnny.

'Of course it's hard, it's a fucking nightmare,' said Patrick. Since he was representing stoicism against therapy, he wasn't going to lose the chance to exaggerate the strain he was under.

'Either I wake up in the Grey Zone,' he whispered, 'and I've forgotten how to breathe, and my feet are so far away I'm not sure I can afford the air fare; or it's the endless reel of lazy decapitations, and kneecaps stolen by passing traffic, and dogs fighting over the liver I quite want back. If they made a film of my inner life, it would be more than the public could take. Mothers would scream, "Bring back *The Texas Chainsaw Massacre*, so we can have some decent family entertainment!" And all these joys accompanied by the fear that I'll forget everything that's ever happened to me, and all the things I've seen will be lost, as the Replicant says at the end of *Blade Runner*, "like tears in rain".'

'Yeah, yeah,' said Johnny, who'd often heard Patrick rehearse fragments of this speech. 'So why don't you just go ahead?'

'Some combination of pride and terror,' said Patrick, and then, changing the subject quickly, he asked when Johnny's meeting ended. They agreed to leave from Patrick's flat at five o'clock.

Patrick lit another cigarette. The conversation with Johnny had made him nervous. Why had he said, 'Some combination of pride and terror'? Did he still think it was uncool to admit to any enthusiasm, even in front of his greatest friend? Why did he muzzle new feelings with old habits of speech? It might not have been obvious to anyone else, but he longed to stop thinking about himself, to stop strip-mining his memories, to stop the introspective and retrospective drift of his thoughts. He wanted to break into a wider world, to learn something, to make a difference. Above all, he wanted to stop being a child without using the cheap disguise of becoming a parent.

'Not that there's much danger of that,' muttered Patrick, finally getting out of bed and putting on a pair of trousers. The days when he was drawn to the sort of girl who whispered, 'Be careful, I'm not wearing any contraception,' as you came inside her, were almost completely over. He could remember one of them speaking warmly of abortion clinics. 'It's quite luxurious while you're there. A comfortable bed, good food, and you can tell all your secrets to the other girls because you know you're not going to meet them again. Even the operation is rather exciting. It's only afterwards that you get really depressed.'

Patrick ground his cigarette into the ashtray and walked through to the kitchen.

And why did he have to attack Johnny's meetings? They were simply places to confess. Why did he have to make everything so harsh and difficult? On the other hand, what was the point of going somewhere to confess if you weren't going to say the one thing that mattered? There were things he'd never told anyone and never would.

2

Nicholas Pratt, still wearing his pyjamas, waddled back to the bedroom of his house in Clabon Mews, squeezing the letters he had just collected from the doormat and scrutinizing the handwriting on the envelopes to see how many 'serious' invitations they might contain. At sixty-seven his body was as 'well preserved' as his memoirs were 'long awaited'. He had met 'everybody', and had a 'fund of marvellous stories', but discretion had placed its gallant finger on his half-opened lips and he had never started the book which he was widely known to be working on. It was not unusual in what he called the 'big world', namely among the two or three thousand rich people who recognized his name, to hear anxious men and women 'dreading to think' how they had turned out in 'Nicholas's book'.

Collapsing on his bed, where he nowadays slept alone, he was about to test his theory that he had only received three letters that were really worth opening, when he was interrupted by the ringing of the phone.

'Hello,' he yawned.

'Ni-ko-la?' said a brisk woman's voice, pronouncing the name as if it were French. 'It's Jacqueline d'Alantour.'

'*Quel honneur*,' simpered Nicholas in his appalling French accent.

'How are you, darling? I r-ring because Jacques and I are

staying at Cheet-lai for Sonny's birthday, and I thought you might be going there too.'

'Of course I am,' said Nicholas sternly. 'In fact, as the patron saint of Bridget's social triumph, I'm meant to be there already. It was I, after all, who introduced little Miss Watson-Scott, as she was then, into the beau monde, as *it* was then, and she has not forgotten her debt to Uncle Nicholas.'

'R-remind me,' said Jacqueline, 'was she one of the ladies you married?'

'Don't be absurd,' said Nicholas, pretending to take offence. 'Just because I've had six failed marriages, there's no need to invent more.'

'But Ni-ko-la, seriously, I r-ring in case you want to come with us in the car. We have a driver from the embassy. It will be more fun – no? – to go down together, or up together – this English "up" and "down" *c'est vraiment* too much.'

Nicholas was enough of a man of the world to know that the French ambassador's wife was not being entirely altruistic. She was offering him a lift so as to arrive at Cheatley with an intimate friend of Bridget's. Nicholas, for his part, would bring fresh glamour to that intimacy by arriving with the Alantours. They would enhance each other's glory.

'Up or down,' said Nicholas, 'I'd adore to come with you.'

Sonny Gravesend sat in the library at Cheatley dialling the familiar digits of Peter Porlock's number on his radio telephone. The mystical equation between property and person which had so long propped up Sonny's dim personality was worshipped nowhere more ardently than at Cheatley. Peter, George Watford's eldest son, was Sonny's best friend and the only person he really trusted when he wanted sound advice about farming or sex. Sonny sat back in his chair and waited for Peter to wade through the vast rooms of Richfield to the nearest telephone. He looked at the fireplace, above which hung the painting that Robin Parker was taking so long to authenticate as a Poussin. It had been a Poussin when the fourth Earl bought it and, as far as Sonny was concerned, it still was. Nevertheless, one had to get an 'expert opinion'.

'Sonny?' bawled Peter.

'Peter!' Sonny shouted back. 'Sorry to interrupt you again.'

'Quite the opposite, old boy, you've saved me from showing round the Gay London Bikers my old housemaster sent down to gawp at the ceilings.'

'Slaving away as usual,' said Sonny. 'Makes it all the more annoying when one reads the sort of rubbish they put in the papers this morning: "ten thousand acres . . . five hundred guests . . . Princess Margaret . . . party of the year." Sounds as if we're *made* of money, whereas the reality, as nobody knows better than you, with your Gay London Bikers, is that we never stop slaving to keep the rain out.'

'Do you know what one of my tenants said to me the other day after my famous appearance on the box?' Peter adopted his standard yokel accent. '"Saw you on the television, m'lord, pleading poverty, as usual." Damned cheek!'

'It's quite funny, actually.'

'Well, he's really a splendid fellow,' said Peter. 'His family have been tenants of ours for three hundred years.'

'We've got some like that. One lot have been with us for twenty generations.'

'Shows an amazing lack of initiative when you think of the conditions we keep them in,' said Peter mischievously.

Both men guffawed, and agreed that that was just the sort of thing one shouldn't say during one's famous television appearances.

'What I really rang about,' said Sonny, more seriously, 'is this business with Cindy. Bridget, of course, wouldn't have her, on the grounds that we didn't know her, but I've spoken to David Windfall this morning and, since his wife's ill, he's agreed to bring Cindy along. I hope he'll be discreet.'

'David Windfall? You must be joking!' said Peter.

'Well, I know, but I made out that I was longing to meet her, rather than the truth, namely that all my Historic Houses Association and Preservation of Rural England meetings have been one long thrash in the sack with Cindy.'

'I'm glad you didn't tell him that,' said Peter wisely.

'The thing is, and I need hardly tell you to keep this under your hat, the thing is, Cindy's pregnant.'

'Are you sure it's yours?'

'Apparently there's no doubt about it,' said Sonny.

'I suppose she's blackmailing you,' said Peter loyally.

'No, no, no, that's not it at all,' said Sonny, rather put out. 'The thing is, I haven't had "conjugal relations" with Bridget for some time, and I'm not sure anyway, given her age, that it would be a good idea to try and have another child. But, as you know, I'm very keen to have a son, and I thought that if Cindy has a boy . . .' Sonny trailed off, uncertain of Peter's reaction.

'Golly,' said Peter, 'but you'd have to marry her if he was going to inherit. It's one of the penalties of being a peer,' he added with a note of noble stoicism.

'Well, I know it sounds awfully mercenary to chuck Bridget at this stage of the game,' Sonny admitted, 'and of course it's bound to be misrepresented as a sexual infatuation, but one does feel some responsibility towards Cheatley.'

'But think of the expense,' said Peter, who had grave doubts that the divorce could be achieved in time. 'And, besides, is Cindy the right girl for Cheaters?'

'She'll be a breath of fresh air,' said Sonny breezily, 'and, as you know, all the things are in trust.'

'I think,' said Peter with the measured authority of a

consultant advising his patient to have surgery, 'we'd better have lunch in Buck's next week.'

'Good idea,' said Sonny. 'See you tonight.'

'Very much looking forward to it,' said Peter. 'Oh, and, by the way, happy birthday.'

Kitty Harrow, at home in the country, lay in bed propped up by a multitude of pillows, her King Charles spaniels hidden in the troughs of her undulating bedspread, and a ravaged breakfast tray abandoned beside her like an exhausted lover. Under a pink satin lampshade, bottles of contradictory medicines crowded the inlaid surface of her bedside table. Her hand rested on the telephone she used ceaselessly every morning between eleven o'clock and lunchtime, or, as on this occasion, until the hairdresser arrived at twelve thirty to rebuild those cliffs of grey hair against which so many upstarts had dashed themselves in vain. When she had found Robin Parker's name in the large red leather address book that was spread open on her lap, she dialled his number and waited impatiently.

'Hello,' said a rather peevish voice.

'Robin, my darling,' warbled Kitty, 'why aren't you here already? Bridget has unloaded some perfectly ghastly people on me, and you, my only ally, are still in London.'

'I had to go to a drinks party last night,' simpered Robin.

'A party in London on a Friday night!' protested Kitty. 'It's the most antisocial thing I've ever heard. I do think people are inconsiderate, not to say cruel. I practically never go to London these days,' she added with a real note of pathos, 'and so I rely terribly on my weekends.'

'Well, I'm coming to the rescue,' said Robin. 'I ought to be leaving for Paddington in five minutes.'

'Thank God,' she continued, 'you'll be here to protect me. I had an obscene telephone call last night.'

'Not again,' sighed Robin.

'He made the most perfectly revolting suggestions,' confided Kitty. 'And so before putting the phone down I said to him, "Young man, I should have to see your face before I allowed you to do any of those things!" He seemed to think I was encouraging him, and rang back the very next minute. I insist on answering the phone myself in the evenings: it's not fair on the servants.'

'It's not fair on you either,' Robin warned her.

'I've been haunted,' growled Kitty, 'by what you told me about those cocks the prudish Popes snapped off the classical statues and stored in the Vatican cellars. I'm not sure *that* wasn't an obscene phone call.'

'That was history of art,' giggled Robin.

'You know how fascinated I am by people's families,' said Kitty. 'Well, now, whenever I think about them, and the dark secrets they all have lurking under the surface, I can't help picturing those crates hidden in the Vatican cellars. You've corrupted my imagination,' she declared. 'Did you know what a dreadful effect you have on people?'

'My conversation will be completely chaste this evening,' threatened Robin. 'But I really ought to be going to the station now.'

'Goodbye,' cooed Kitty, but her need to talk was so imperious that she added conspiratorially, 'Do you know what George Watford told me last night? – he at least was a familiar face. He said that three-quarters of the people in his address book are dead. I told him not to be so morbid. Anyway, what could be more natural at his age: he's well into his eighties.'

'My dear, I'm going to miss my train,' said Robin.

'I used to suffer terribly from train fever,' said Kitty considerately, 'until my wonderful doctor gave me a magic pill, and now I just float on board.'

'Well, I'm going to have to sprint on board,' squealed Robin.

'Goodbye, my dear,' said Kitty, 'I won't delay you a moment longer. Hurry, hurry, hurry.'

Laura Broghlie felt her existence threatened by solitude. Her mind became 'literally blank', as she had told Patrick Melrose during their week-long affair. Five minutes alone, or off the telephone, unless it was spent in the company of a mirror and a great deal of make-up, was more literal blankness than she could stand.

It had taken her ages to get over Patrick's defection. It was not that she had liked him particularly – it never occurred to her to like people while she was using them, and when she had finished using them, it would clearly have been absurd to start liking them – but it was such a *bore* getting a new lover. Being married put some people off, until she made it clear that it was no impediment from her point of view. Laura was married to Angus Broghlie, who was entitled by ancient Scottish custom to call himself 'The Broghlie'. Laura, by the same token, could call herself 'Madame Broghlie', a right she seldom exercised.

Eventually, after a whole fortnight without a lover, she had managed to seduce Johnny Hall, Patrick's best friend. Johnny wasn't as good as Patrick because he worked during the day. Still, as a journalist he could often 'work on a story at home', which was when they could spend the whole day in bed.

Some subtle questioning had established that Johnny didn't yet know about her affair with Patrick, and she had sworn Johnny to secrecy about their own affair. She didn't know whether to be insulted by Patrick's silence or not, but she intended to let Patrick know about Johnny whenever it would cause maximum confusion. She knew that Patrick still found her sexy, even if he had reservations about her personality. Even she had reservations about her personality.

When the phone rang, Laura raised her head and wriggled across the bed.

'Don't answer it,' moaned Johnny, but he knew he was in a weak position, having left the room earlier to talk to Patrick. He lit a cigarette.

Laura turned to him and stuck her tongue out, hooking her hair behind her ear as she picked up the phone. 'Hello,' she said, suddenly serious.

'Hi.'

'China! God, your party was *so* great,' gasped Laura, pinching her nose with her thumb and index finger and raising her eyes to the ceiling. She had already analysed with Johnny what a failure it had been.

'Did you really think it was a success?' China asked sceptically.

'Of course it was, darling, everybody loved it,' said Laura, grinning at Johnny.

'But everybody got stuck in the downstairs room,' China whined. 'I really hated it.'

'One always hates one's own parties,' said Laura sympathetically, rolling onto her back and stifling a yawn.

'But you really did like it,' pleaded China. 'Promise.'

'Promise,' said Laura, crossing her fingers, her legs, and finally her eyes. Suddenly convulsed with silent giggles, she raised her feet in the air and rocked on the bed.

Johnny watched, amazed by her childishness, faintly contemptuous of the mocking conspiracy into which he was being drawn, but charmed by the contortions of her naked body. He sank back against the pillows, scanning the details which might explain, but only confirmed the mystery of his obsession: the small dark mole on the inner slope of her hip bone, the surprisingly thick golden hair on her forearm, the high arch of her pale feet.

'Is Angus with you?' sighed China.

'No, he's going straight from Scotland to the party. I have to collect him in Cheltenham. It's such a bore, I don't see why he can't get a taxi.'

'Save, save, save,' said China.

'He looked so good on paper,' said Laura, 'but when it comes down to it, he's completely obsessed with whether a cheap day-return is refundable if you don't use the second half, and other fascinating problems of that kind. It makes one long for an extravagant lover.' She allowed one of her knees to flop sideways on the bed.

Johnny took a long drag on his cigarette and smiled at her.

China hesitated and then, spurred on by the thought that Laura's praise of her party might not have been entirely sincere, she said, 'You know there's a rumour going around that you're having an affair with Patrick Melrose.'

'Patrick Melrose,' said Laura, as if she were repeating the name of a fatal disease, 'you must be joking.' She raised her eyebrows at Johnny and putting her hand over the mouthpiece whispered, 'Apparently I'm having an affair with Patrick.'

He flicked up one of his eyebrows and stubbed out his cigarette.

'Who on earth told you that?' she asked China.

'I shouldn't really tell you, but it was Alexander Politsky.'

'Him, I don't even know him.'

'Well, he thinks he knows about you.'

'How pathetic,' said Laura. 'He just wants to get in with you by pretending he knows all about your friends.' Johnny knelt in front of Laura and, catching both her feet, eased her legs apart.

'He said he found out from Ali Montague,' China insisted.

Laura drew in her breath sharply. 'Well, that just proves it's a lie,' she sighed. 'Anyway, I don't even fancy Patrick Melrose,' she added, digging her nails into Johnny's arms.

'Oh, well, you know better than me whether you're having an affair with him or not,' China concluded. 'I'm glad you're not, because personally I find him really tricky . . .'

Laura held the phone in the air so Johnny could hear. 'And,' continued China, 'I can't stand the way he treated Debbie.'

Laura put the phone back to her ear. 'It was disgusting, wasn't it?' she said, grinning at Johnny, who leaned down to bite her neck. 'But who are you going to the party with?' she asked, knowing that China was going alone.

'I'm not going with anybody, but there's someone called Morgan Ballantine,' China put on an unconvincing American accent to pronounce his name, 'who is going to be there, and I'm quite keen on him. He's supposed to have just inherited two hundred and forty million dollars and an amazing gun collection,' she added casually, 'but that's not really the point, I mean, he's *really* sweet.'

'He may be worth two hundred and forty million dollars, but is he going to spend it?' asked Laura, who had bitter experience of how misleading these figures could be. 'That's the real question,' she said, propping herself up on one elbow and effortlessly ignoring the caresses she had found so breathtaking moments before. Johnny stopped and leaned over, partly from curiosity, but also to disguise the fact that his sexual efforts could not compete with the mention of such a large sum of money.

'He did say something rather sinister the other day,' China admitted.

'What?' asked Laura eagerly.

'Well, he said, "I'm too rich to lend money." A friend of his had gone bankrupt, or something.'

'Don't touch him,' said Laura, in her special serious voice. 'That's the kind of thing Angus says. You think it's all going to be private planes, and the next thing you know he's asking for a doggy bag in a restaurant, or implying that *you* ought to be doing the cooking. It's a complete nightmare.'

'That reminds me,' said China, rather annoyed that she had given so much away. 'We played a wonderful game after you left last night. Everybody had to think of the things people were least likely to say, and someone came up with one for Angus: "Are you sure you won't have the lobster?" '

'Very funny,' said Laura drily.

'By the way, where are you staying?' asked China.

'With some people called Bossington-Lane.'

'Me too,' exclaimed China. 'Can I have a lift?'

'Of course. Come here about twelve thirty and we can go out to lunch.'

'Perfect,' said China. 'See you later.'

'Bye, darling,' Laura trilled. 'Stupid cow,' she said, putting the phone down.

All her life men had rushed around Cindy, like the citizens of Lilliput with their balls of string, trying to tie her down so she wouldn't wreck their little lives, but now she was thinking of tying herself down voluntarily.

'Hello?' she purred in her soft Californian accent. 'Can I speak with David Windfall, please?'

'Speaking,' said David.

'Hi there, I'm Cindy Smith. I guess Sonny already talked to you about tonight.'

'He certainly did,' said David, flushing to a deeper shade of raspberry than usual.

'I hope you've got your Sonny and Bridget invitation,

'cause I sure don't have one,' said Cindy with disarming candour.

'I've got mine in the bank,' said David. 'One can't be too careful.'

'I know,' said Cindy, 'that's a valuable item.'

'You realize you'll have to pretend to be my wife,' said David.

'How far am I meant to go?'

David, quivering, sweating, and blushing at the same time, took refuge in the bluffness for which he was well known. 'Only until we get past the security people,' he said.

'Anything you say,' Cindy replied meekly. 'You're the boss.'

'Where shall we meet?' asked David.

'I've got a suite in the Little Soddington House Hotel. That's in Gloucestershire, right?'

'I certainly hope so, unless it's moved,' said David, more pompously than he'd intended.

Cindy giggled. 'Sonny didn't tell me you were so funny,' she said. 'We could have dinner together at my hotel, if you'd like.'

'Splendid,' said David, already scheming to get out of the dinner party Bridget had put him in. 'About eight?'

Tom Charles had ordered a car to take him down to the country. It was extravagant, but he was too old to fool around with trains and suitcases. He was staying at Claridge's, as usual, and one of the nicest things about it was the wood fire that was subsiding brightly in the grate while he finished his frugal breakfast of tea and grapefruit juice.

He was on his way to stay with Harold Greene, an old friend from the IMF days. Harold had said to bring a dinner jacket because they were going to a neighbour's birthday party. He'd got the low-down on the neighbour, but all Tom could remember was that he was one of those Englishmen with plenty of 'background' and not a hell of a lot going on in the foreground. If you weren't unduly impressed by these 'background' types they said you were 'chippy', but in fact nothing could make you feel less 'chippy' than contemplating a lifetime wasted in gossip, booze, and sexual intrigue.

Harold was not like that at all; he was a mover and shaker. He was on the Christmas-card list of grateful presidents and friendly senators – as was Tom – but like everybody else on this rainy island he liked the 'background' types too much.

Tom picked up the phone to ring Anne Eisen. Anne was an old friend and he was looking forward to driving down with her to Harold's, but he had to know what time to send the car to collect her. Her number was engaged and so Tom hung up crisply and continued reading the pile of English and American newspapers he'd ordered with his breakfast.

3

Tony Fowles was what Bridget called an 'absolute genius' when it came to colours and fabrics. He confessed to 'having a crush on ash colours at the moment,' and she had agreed to have the interior of the tent done in grey. Her initial misgivings about this bold idea were swept aside by Tony's remark that Jacqueline d'Alantour, the French Ambassador's wife, was 'so correct that she's never really *right*'.

Bridget wondered how far one could be incorrect without being wrong, and it was in this grey area that Tony had become her guide, increasing her dependency on him until she could hardly light a cigarette without his assistance, and had already had a row with Sonny about wanting to have him at her side during dinner.

'That appalling little man shouldn't be coming at all,' said Sonny, 'let alone sitting next to you. I need hardly remind you that we're having Princess Margaret for dinner and that every one of the men has a better claim to be by your side than that . . .' Sonny spluttered, 'that popinjay.'

What was a popinjay anyway? Whatever it was, it was so unfair, because Tony was her guru and her jester. People who knew how funny he was – and one only had to hear his story about hurrying through the streets of Lima clutching bolts of fabric during a bread riot to practically die laughing – didn't perhaps realize how wise he was also.

But where was Tony? He was supposed to meet her at

eleven o'clock. One could worship him for all sorts of things, but punctuality wasn't one of them. Bridget looked around at the wastes of grey velvet that lined the inside of the tent; without Tony, her confidence faltered. One end of the tent was dominated by a hideous white stage on which a forty-piece band, flown over from America, would later play the 'traditional New Orleans jazz' favoured by Sonny. The industrial heaters that roared in every corner still left the atmosphere numbingly cold.

'Obviously, I'd rather that my birthday was in June instead of gloomy old February,' Sonny was fond of saying, 'but one can't choose when one's born.'

The shock of not having planned his own birth had given Sonny a fanatical desire to plan everything else. Bridget had tried to keep him out of the tent on the grounds that it should be a 'surprise', but since this word was for him roughly equivalent to 'terrorist outrage', she had failed. She had, on the other hand, managed to keep secret the astonishing cost of the velvet, communicated to her by a honking Sloane with a laugh like a death rattle, who had said that it came to 'forty thousand, plus the dreaded'. Bridget had thought 'the dreaded' was a technical decorating term until Tony explained that it was VAT.

He had also said that the orange lilies would make a 'riot of colour' against the soft grey background, but now that they were being arranged by a team of busy ladies in chequered blue overalls, Bridget could not help thinking they looked more like dying embers in a huge heap of ash.

Just as this heretical thought was entering her mind, Tony swept into the tent dressed in a baggy earth, ash, and grape sweater, a pair of beautifully ironed jeans, white socks, and brown moccasins with surprisingly thick soles. He had wrapped a white silk scarf around his throat after he felt, or thought he felt, a tickle. 'Tony! At last,' Bridget dared to point out.

'I'm sorry,' croaked Tony, laying his hand on his chest and frowning pathetically. 'I think I'm coming down with something.'

'Oh, dear,' said Bridget, 'I hope you won't be too ill for tonight.'

'Even if they had to wheel me in on a life-support machine,' he replied, 'I wouldn't miss it for the world. I know the artist is supposed to stand outside his creation, paring his fingernails,' he said, looking down at his fingernails with affected indifference, 'but I don't feel my creation is finished until it's filled with living fabric.'

He paused and stared at Bridget with hypnotic intensity, like Rasputin about to inform the Tsarina of his latest inspiration. 'Now, I know what you're thinking,' he assured her. 'Not enough colour!'

Bridget felt a searchlight shining into the recesses of her soul. 'The flowers haven't changed it as much as I thought they would,' she confessed.

'And that's why I've brought you these,' said Tony, pointing to a group of assistants who had been waiting meekly until they were called forward. They were surrounded by large cardboard boxes.

'What are they?' asked Bridget, apprehensive.

The assistants started to open the tops of the boxes. 'I thought tents, I thought poles, I thought ribbons,' said Tony, who was always ready to explain his imaginative processes. 'And so I had these specially made. It's a sort of regimental-maypole theme,' he explained, no longer able to contain his excitement. 'It'll look stunning against the pearly texture of the ash.'

Bridget knew that 'specially made' meant extremely expensive. 'They look like ties,' she said, peering into a box.

'Exactly,' said Tony triumphantly. 'I saw Sonny wearing a rather thrilling green and orange tie. He told me it was a regimental tie and I thought, that's it: the orange will pick up the lilies and lift the whole room.' Tony's hands flowed upward and outward. 'We'll tie the ribbons to the top of the pole and bring them over to the sides of the tent.' This time his hands flowed outwards and downward.

These graceful balletic gestures were enough to convince Bridget that she had no choice.

'It sounds wonderful,' she said. 'But put them up quickly, we haven't much time.'

'Leave it to me,' said Tony serenely.

A maid came to tell Bridget that there was a phone call for her. Bridget waved goodbye to Tony, and hurried out of the tent through the red-carpeted tunnel that led back to the house. Smiling florists arranged wreaths of ivy around the green metal hoops that supported the canvas.

It was strange, in February, not to give the party in the house, but Sonny was convinced that his 'things' would be imperilled by what he called 'Bridget's London friends'. He was haunted by his grandfather's complaint that his grandmother had filled the house with 'spongers, buggers, and Jews', and, while he recognized the impossibility of giving an amusing party without samples from all these categories, he wasn't about to trust them with his 'things'.

Bridget walked across the denuded drawing room, and picked up the phone.

'Hello?'

'Darling, how are you?'

'Aurora! Thank God it's you. I was dreading another virtual stranger begging to bring their entire family to the party.'

'Aren't people *awful*?' said Aurora Donne in that condescending voice for which she was famous. Her large liquid eyes and creamy complexion gave her the soft beauty of a

Charolais cow, but her sniggering laughter, reserved for her own remarks, was more reminiscent of a hyena. She had become Bridget's best friend, instilling her with a grim and precarious confidence in exchange for Bridget's lavish hospitality.

'It's been a nightmare,' said Bridget, settling down in the spindly caterer's chair that had replaced one of Sonny's things. 'I can't believe the cheek of some of these people.'

'You don't have to tell me,' said Aurora. 'I hope you've got good security.'

'Yes,' said Bridget. 'Sonny's got the police, who were supposed to be at a football match this afternoon, to come here instead and check everything. It makes a nice change for them. They're going to form a ring around the house. Plus, we've got the usual people at the door, in fact, someone called "Gresham Security" has left his walkie-talkie by the phone.'

'They make such a fuss about royalty,' said Aurora.

'*Don't*,' groaned Bridget. 'We've had to give up two of our precious rooms to the private detective and the lady-in-waiting. It's such a waste of space.'

Bridget was interrupted by the sound of screaming in the hall.

'You're a filthy little girl! And nothing but a burden to your parents!' shouted a woman with a strong Scottish accent. 'What would the Princess say if she knew that you dirtied your dress? You filthy child!'

'Oh dear,' said Bridget to Aurora, 'I do wish Nanny wasn't quite so horrid to Belinda. It's rather terrible, but I never dare say anything to her.'

'I know,' said Aurora sympathetically, 'I'm absolutely terrified of Lucy's nanny. I think it's because she reminds one of one's own nanny.'

Bridget, who had not had a 'proper' nanny, wasn't about to reveal this fact by disagreeing. She had made a special effort, by way of compensation, to get a proper old-fashioned nanny for seven-year-old Belinda. The agency had been delighted when they found such a good position for the vicious old bag who'd been on their books for years.

'The other thing I dread is my mother coming tonight,' said Bridget.

'Mothers can be so critical, can't they?' said Aurora.

'Exactly,' said Bridget, who in fact found her mother tiresomely eager to please. 'I suppose I ought to go off and be nice to Belinda,' she added with a dutiful sigh.

'Sweet!' cooed Aurora.

'I'll see you tonight, darling.' Bridget was grateful to get rid of Aurora. She had a million and one things to do and besides, instead of giving her those transfusions of self-confidence for which she was, well, almost employed (she didn't have a bean), Aurora had recently taken to implying that she would have handled the arrangements for the party better than Bridget.

Given that she had no intention of going up to see Belinda it was quite naughty to have used her as an excuse to end the conversation. Bridget seldom found the time to see her daughter. She could not forgive her for being a girl and burdening Sonny with the anxiety of having no heir. After spending her early twenties having abortions, Bridget had spent the next ten years having miscarriages. Successfully giving birth had been complicated enough without having a child of the wrong gender. The doctor had told her that it would be dangerous to try again, and at forty-two she was becoming resigned to having one child, especially in view of Sonny's reluctance to go to bed with her.

Her looks had certainly deteriorated over the last sixteen years of marriage. The clear blue eyes had clouded over, the candlelit glow of her skin had sputtered out and could only be partially rekindled with tinted creams, and the lines of her body, which had shaped so many obsessions in their time, were now deformed by accumulations of stubborn fat. Unwilling to betray Sonny, and unable to attract him, Bridget had allowed herself to go into a mawkish physical decline, spending more and more time thinking of other ways to please her husband – or rather not to displease him, since he took her efforts for granted but lavished his attention on the slightest failure.

She ought to get on with the arrangements, which, in her case, meant worrying, since all the work had been delegated to somebody else. The first thing she decided to worry about was the walkie-talkie on the table beside her. It had clearly been lost by some hopeless security man. Bridget picked the machine up and, curious, switched it on. There was a loud hissing sound and then the whinings of an untuned radio.

Interested to see if she could make anything intelligible emerge from this melee of sound, Bridget got up and walked around the room. The noises grew louder and fainter, and sometimes intensified into squeals, but as she moved towards the windows, darkened by the side of the marquee that reared up wet and white under the dull winter sky, she heard, or thought she heard, a voice. Pressing her ear close to the walkie-talkie she could make out a crackling, whispering conversation.

'The thing is, I haven't had conjugal relations with Bridget for some time . . .' said the voice at the other end, and faded again. Bridget shook the walkie-talkie desperately, and moved closer to the window. She couldn't understand what was going on. How could it be Sonny she was listening to? But who else could claim that he hadn't had 'conjugal relations' with her for some time?

She could make out words again, and pressed the walkie-talkie to her ear with renewed curiosity and dread.

'To chuck Bridget at this . . . it's bound to be . . . but one does feel some responsibility towards . . .' Interference drowned the conversation again. A prickling wave of heat rushed over her body. She must hear what they were saying, what monstrous plan they were hatching. Who was Sonny talking to? It must be Peter. But what if it wasn't? What if he talked like this to everyone, everyone except her?

'All the things are in trust,' she heard, and then another voice saying: 'Lunch . . . next week.' Yes, it was Peter. There was more crackling, and then, 'Happy birthday.'

Bridget sank down in the window seat. She raised her arm and almost flung the walkie-talkie against the wall, but then lowered it again slowly until it hung loosely by her side.

4

Johnny Hall had been going to Narcotics Anonymous meetings for over a year. In a fit of enthusiasm and humility he found hard to explain, he had volunteered to make the tea and coffee at the Saturday three o'clock meeting. He recognized many of the people who took one of the white plastic cups he had filled with a tea bag or a few granules of instant coffee, and struggled to remember their names, embarrassed that so many of them remembered his.

After making the tea Johnny took a seat in the back row, as usual, although he knew that it would make it harder for him to speak, or 'share', as he was urged to say in meetings. He enjoyed the obscurity of sitting as far away as possible from the addict who was 'giving the chair'. The 'preamble' – a ritual reading of selections from 'the literature', explaining the nature of addiction and NA – washed over Johnny almost unnoticed. He tried to see if the girl sitting in the front row was pretty, but couldn't see enough of her profile to judge.

A woman called Angie had been asked by the secretary to do the chair. Her stumpy legs were clad in a black leotard, and her hair hid two-thirds of her raddled and exhausted face. She had been invited down from Kilburn to add a touch of grit to a Chelsea meeting which dwelt all too often on the shame of burgling one's parents' house, or the difficulty of finding a parking space.

Angie said she had started 'using', by which she meant

taking drugs, in the sixties, because it was 'a gas'. She didn't want to dwell on the 'bad old days', but she had to tell the group a little bit about her using to put them in the picture. Half an hour later, she was still describing her wild twenties, and yet there was clearly some time to go before her listeners could enjoy the insight that she had gleaned from her regular attendance of meetings over the last two years. She rounded off her chair with some self-deprecating remarks about still being 'riddled with defects'. Thanks to the meetings she had discovered that she was totally insane and completely addicted to everything. She was also 'rampantly co-dependent', and urgently needed individual counselling in order to deal with lots of 'childhood stuff'. Her 'relationship', by which she meant her boyfriend, had discovered that living with an addict could create a lot of extra hassles, and so the two of them had decided to attend 'couples counselling'. This was the latest excitement in a life already packed with therapeutic drama, and she was very hopeful about the benefits.

The secretary was very grateful to Angie. A lot of what she had shared, he said, was relevant for him too. He'd 'identified one hundred per cent', not with her using because his had been very different – he had never used needles or been addicted to heroin or cocaine – but with 'the feelings'. Johnny could not remember Angie describing any feelings, but tried to silence the scepticism which made it so difficult for him to participate in the meetings, even after the break-through of volunteering to make the tea. The secretary went on to say that a lot of childhood stuff had been coming up for him too, and he had recently discovered that although nothing unpleasant had happened to him in childhood, he'd found himself smothered by his parents' kindness and that breaking away from their understanding and generosity had become a real issue for him.

With these resonant words the secretary threw the meeting

open, a moment that Johnny always found upsetting because it put him under pressure to 'share'. The problem, apart from his acute self-consciousness and his resistance to the language of 'recovery', was that sharing was supposed to be based on 'identification' with something that the person who was doing the chair had said, and it was very rare for Johnny to have any clear recollection of what had been said. He decided to wait until somebody else's identification identified for him the details of Angie's chair. This was a hazardous procedure because most of the time people identified with something that had not in fact been said in the chair.

The first person to speak from the floor said that he'd had to nurture himself by 'parenting the child within'. He hoped that with God's help – a reference that always made Johnny wince – and the help of the Fellowship, the child within would grow up in a 'safe environment'. He said that he too was having problems with his relationship, by which he meant his girlfriend, but that hopefully, if he worked his Step Three and 'handed it over', everything would be all right in the end. He wasn't in charge of the results, only the 'footwork'.

The second speaker identified one hundred per cent with what Angie had said about her veins being 'the envy of Kilburn', because his veins had been the envy of Wimbledon. There was general merriment. And yet, the speaker went on to say, when he had to go to the doctor nowadays for a proper medical reason, they couldn't find a vein anywhere on his body. He had been doing a Step Four, 'a fearless and searching moral inventory', and it had brought up a lot of stuff that needed looking at. He had heard someone in a meeting saying that she had a fear of success and he thought that maybe this was his problem too. He was in a lot of pain at the moment because he was realizing that a lot of his 'relationship problems' were the result of his 'dysfunctional family'. He felt unlovable and consequently he was unloving, he concluded, and his neighbour, who recognized that he was in the presence of feelings, rubbed his back consolingly.

Johnny looked up at the fluorescent lights and the white polystyrene ceiling of the dingy church-hall basement. He longed to hear someone talk about their experiences in ordinary language, and not in this obscure and fatuous slang. He was entering the stage of the meeting when he gave up daydreaming and became increasingly anxious about whether to speak. He constructed opening sentences, imagined elegant ways of linking what had been said to what he wanted to say, and then, with a thumping heart, failed to announce his name quickly enough to win the right to speak. He was particularly restless after the show of coolness he always felt he had to put on in front of Patrick. Talking to Patrick had exacerbated his rebellion against the foolish vocabulary of NA, while increasing his need for the peace of mind that others seemed to glean from using it. He regretted agreeing to have dinner alone with Patrick, whose corrosive criticism and drug nostalgia and stylized despair often left Johnny feeling agitated and confused.

The current speaker was saying that he'd read somewhere in the literature that the difference between 'being willing' and 'being ready' was that you could sit in an armchair and be willing to leave the house, but you weren't entirely ready until you had on your hat and overcoat. Johnny knew that the speaker must be finishing, because he was using Fellowship platitudes, trying to finish on a 'positive' note, as was the custom of the obedient recovering addict, who always claimed to bear in mind 'newcomers' and their need to hear positive notes.

He must do it, he must break in now, and say his piece.

'My name's Johnny,' he blurted out, almost before the previous speaker had finished. 'I'm an addict.'

'Hi, Johnny,' chorused the rest of the group.

'I have to speak,' he said boldly, 'because I'm going to a party this evening, and I know there'll be a lot of drugs around. It's a big party and I just feel under threat, I suppose. I just wanted to come to this meeting to reaffirm my desire to stay clean today. Thanks.'

'Thanks, Johnny,' the group echoed.

He'd done it, he'd said what was really troubling him. He hadn't managed to say anything funny, clever, or interesting, but he knew that somehow, however ridiculous and boring these meetings were, having taken part in one would give him the strength not to take drugs at the party tonight and that he would be able to enjoy himself a little bit more.

Glowing with goodwill after speaking, Johnny listened to Pete, the next speaker, with more sympathy than he'd been able to muster at the beginning of the meeting.

Someone had described recovery to Pete as 'putting your tie around your neck instead of your arm'. There was subdued laughter. When he was using, Pete had found it easy to cross the road because he didn't care whether he was run over or not, but in early recovery he'd become fucking terrified of the traffic (subdued laughter) and walked for miles and miles to find a zebra crossing. He'd also spent his early recovery making lines out of Coleman's mustard powder and wondering if he'd put too much in the spoon (one isolated cackle). He was 'in bits' at the moment because he had broken up with his relationship. She'd wanted him to be some kind of trout fisherman, and he'd wanted her to be a psychiatric nurse. When she'd left she'd said that she still thought he was the 'best thing on two legs'. It had worried him that she'd fallen in love with a pig (laughter). Or a centipede (more laughter). Talk about pushing his shame buttons! He'd been on a 'Step Twelve Call' the other day, by which he meant a visit to an active addict who had rung the NA office, and the guy was in a dreadful state, but frankly, Pete admitted, he had wanted what the other guy had more than the other guy wanted what he had. That was the insanity of the disease! 'I came to this programme on my knees,' concluded Pete in a more pious tone, 'and it's been suggested that I remain on them' (knowing grunts, and an appreciative, 'Thanks, Pete').

The American girl who spoke after Pete was called Sally. 'Sleeping at night and staying awake during the day' had been 'a real concept' for her when she 'first came round'. What she wanted from the programme was 'wall-to-wall freedom', and she knew she could achieve that with the help of a 'Loving Higher Power'. At Christmas she'd been to a pantomime to 'celebrate her inner child'. Since then she'd been travelling with another member of the Fellowship because, like they said in the States, 'When you're sick together, you stick together.'

After the group had thanked Sally, the secretary said that they were in 'Newcomer's Time' and that he would appreciate it if people would respect that. This announcement was almost always followed by a brief silence for the Newcomer who either didn't exist, or was too terrified to speak. The last five minutes would then be hogged by some old hand who was 'in bits' or 'just wanted to feel part of the meeting'. On this occasion, however, there was a genuine Newcomer in the room, and he dared to open his mouth.

Dave, as he was called, was at his first meeting and he didn't see how it was supposed to stop him taking drugs. He'd been about to go, actually, and then someone had said about the mustard and the spoon and making lines, and like he'd thought he was the only person to have ever done that, and it was funny hearing someone else say it. He didn't have any money, and he couldn't go out because he owed money everywhere: the only reason he wasn't stoned was that he didn't have the energy to steal anymore. He still had his TV, but he had this thing that he was controlling it, and he was afraid of watching it now because last night he'd been worried that he'd been putting the bloke on TV off by staring at him. He couldn't think what else to say.

The secretary thanked him in the especially coaxing voice he used for Newcomers whose distress formed his own spiritual nourishment, an invaluable opportunity to 'give it away' and 'pass on the message'. He advised Dave to stick around after the meeting and get some phone numbers. Dave said his phone had been cut off. The secretary, afraid that magical 'sharing' might degenerate into mere conversation, smiled firmly at Dave and asked if there were any more Newcomers.

Johnny, somewhat to his surprise, found himself caring about what happened to Dave. In fact, he really hoped that these people, people like him who had been hopelessly dependent on drugs, obsessed with them, and unable to think about anything else for years, would get their lives together. If they had to use this obscure slang in order to do so, then that was a pity but not a reason to hope that they would fail.

The secretary said that unless there was somebody who urgently needed to share, they were out of time. Nobody spoke, and so he stood up and asked Angie to help him close the meeting. Everybody else stood up as well and held hands.

'Will you join me in the Serenity Prayer,' asked Angie, 'using the word "God" as you understand him, her, or it. God,' she said to kickstart the prayer, and then when everyone was ready to join in, repeated, 'God, grant me the serenity to accept the things I cannot change, The courage to change the things I can, And the wisdom to know the difference.'

Johnny wondered as usual to whom he was addressing this prayer. Sometimes when he got chatting to his 'fellow addicts' he would admit to being 'stuck on Step Three'. Step

Three made the bold suggestion that he hand his will and his life over to God 'as he understood him'.

At the end of the meeting, Amanda Pratt, whom he hadn't noticed until then, came up to him. Amanda was the twenty-two-year-old daughter of Nicholas Pratt by his most sensible wife, the general's daughter with the blue woolly and the simple string of pearls he used to dream gloomily of marrying when he was going out with Bridget.

Johnny did not know Amanda well, but he somehow knew this story about her parents. She was eight years younger than him, and to Johnny she was not a drug addict at all, just one of those neurotic girls who had taken a bit of coke or speed to help her dieting, and a few sleeping pills to help her sleep, and, worst of all, when these pitiful abuses had started to become unpleasant, she had stopped them. Johnny, who had wasted his entire twenties repeating the same mistakes, took a very condescending view of anybody who came to the end of their tether before him, or for less good reasons.

'It was so funny,' Amanda was saying rather louder than Johnny would have liked, 'when you were sharing about going to a big party tonight, I knew it was Cheatley.'

'Are you going?' asked Johnny, already knowing the answer.

'Oh, ya,' said Amanda. 'Bridget's practically a stepmother, because she went out with Daddy just before he married Mummy.'

Johnny looked at Amanda and marvelled again at the phenomenon of pretty girls who were not at all sexy. Something empty and clinging about her, a missing centre, prevented her from being attractive.

'Well, we'll see each other tonight,' said Johnny, hoping to end the conversation.

'You're a friend of Patrick Melrose, aren't you?' asked Amanda, immune to the finality of his tone.

'Yes,' said Johnny.

'Well, I gather he spends a lot of time slagging off the Fellowship,' said Amanda indignantly.

'Can you blame him?' sighed Johnny, looking over Amanda's shoulder to see if Dave was still in the room.

'Yes, I do blame him,' said Amanda. 'I think it's rather pathetic, actually, and it just shows how sick he is: if he wasn't sick, he wouldn't need to slag off the Fellowship.'

'You're probably right,' said Johnny, resigned to the familiar tautologies of 'recovery'. 'But listen, I have to go now, or I'll miss my lift down to the country.'

'See you tonight,' said Amanda cheerfully. 'I may need you for an emergency meeting!'

'Umm,' said Johnny. 'It's nice to know you'll be there.'

5

Robin Parker was horrified to see, through the pebble spectacles which helped him to distinguish fake Poussins from
real ones, but could not, alas, make him a safe driver, that
an old woman had moved into 'his' compartment during the
ordeal he had just undergone of fetching a miniature gin and
tonic from the squalid buffet. Everything about the train
offended him: the plastic 'glass', the purple-and-turquoise
upholstery, the smell of diesel and dead skin, and now the
invasion of his compartment by an unglamorous personage
wearing an overcoat that only the Queen could have hoped
to get away with. He pursed his lips as he squeezed past an
impossible pale-blue nanny's suitcase that the old woman
had left cluttering the floor. Picking up his copy of the
Spectator, a Perseus's shield against the Medusa of modernity, as he'd said more than once, he lapsed into a daydream
in which he was flown *privately* into Gloucestershire from
Zurich or possibly Deauville, with someone really glamorous.
And as he pretended to read, passing through Charlbury and
Moreton-in-Marsh, he imagined the clever and subtle things
he would have said about the Ben Nicholsons on the wall
of the cabin.

Virginia Watson-Scott glanced nervously at her suitcase,
knowing it was in everybody's way. The last time she'd been
on a train, a kind young man had hoisted it into the luggage
rack without sparing a thought for how she was going to

get it down again. She'd been too polite to say anything, but she could remember tottering under the weight as the train drew in to Paddington. Even so, the funny-looking gentleman opposite might at least have offered.

In the end she'd decided not to pack the burgundy velvet dress she'd bought for the party. She had lost her nerve, something that would never have happened when Roddy was alive, and fallen back on an old favourite that Sonny and Bridget had seen a hundred times before, or would have seen a hundred times if they asked her to Cheatley more often.

She knew what it was, of course: Bridget was embarrassed by her. Sonny was somehow gallant and rude at the same time, full of old-fashioned courtesies that failed to disguise his underlying contempt. She didn't care about him, but it did hurt to think that her daughter didn't want her around. Old people were always saying that they didn't want to be a burden. Well, she *did* want to be a burden. It wasn't as if she would be taking the last spare room, just one of Sonny's cottages. He was always boasting about how many he had and what a terrible responsibility they were.

Bridget had been such a nice little girl. It was that horrible Nicholas Pratt who had changed her. It was hard to describe, but she had started to criticize everything at home, and look down her nose at people she'd known all her life. Virginia had only met Nicholas once, thank goodness, when he had taken her and Roddy to the opera. She had said to Roddy afterwards that Nicholas wasn't her cup of tea at all, but Roddy had said that Bridget was a sensible girl and she was old enough now to make her own decisions.

'Oh, do come on,' said Caroline Porlock. 'We promised to arrive early and lend moral support.'

Moral support, thought Peter Porlock, still dazed from

his conversation with Sonny that morning, was certainly what Cheatley needed.

They headed down the drive past placid deer and old oaks. Peter reflected that he was one of those Englishmen who could truly claim that his home was his castle, and wondered whether that was the sort of thing to say during one's famous television appearances. On balance, he decided, as Caroline whizzed the Subaru through the honey-coloured gateposts, probably not.

Nicholas Pratt lounged in the back of the Alantours' car. This is how the world should be seen, he thought: through the glass partition of a limousine.

The rack of lamb had been excellent, the cheeses flown in from France that morning, delicious, and the 1970 Haut Brion, '*très buvable*,' as the ambassador had modestly remarked.

'*Et la comtesse, est-elle bien née?*' asked Jacqueline, returning to the subject of Bridget, so that her husband could savour the details of her background.

'*Pas du tout*,' answered Nicholas in a strong English accent.

'Not quite from the top basket!' exclaimed Jacques d'Alantour, who prided himself on his command of colloquial English.

Jacqueline was not quite from the top basket herself, reflected Nicholas, which was what gave that rather hungry quality to her fascination with social standing. Her mother had been the daughter of a Lebanese arms dealer, and had married Phillipe du Tant, a penniless and obscure baron who had neither been able to spoil her like her father, nor to save her from being spoilt. Jacqueline had not been born so much as numbered, somewhere in the Union des Banques Suisses. With the slightly sallow complexion and downturned mouth she had inherited from her mother, she could have done without the frighteningly prominent nose that her father had settled on her; but already famous as an heiress from an early age, she appeared to most people as a photograph come to life, a name made flesh, a bank account personified.

'Is that why you didn't marry her?' teased Jacqueline.

'I'm quite *bien né* enough for two,' replied Nicholas grandly. 'But, you know, I'm not the snob I used to be.'

The ambassador raised his finger in judgement. 'You are a better snob!' he declared, with a witty expression on his face.

'There are so many varieties of snobbism,' said Jacqueline, 'one cannot admire all of them.'

'Snobbery is one of the things one should be most discriminating about,' said Nicholas.

'Some things, like not tolerating stupid people, or not having pigs at one's table, are not snobbish at all, they are simply common sense,' said Jacqueline.

'And yet,' said the wily ambassador, 'sometimes it is necessary to have pigs at one's table.'

Diplomats, thought Nicholas, long made redundant by telephones, still preserved the mannerisms of men who were dealing with great matters of state. He had once seen Jacques d'Alantour fold his overcoat on a banister and declare with all the emphasis of a man refusing to compromise over the Spanish Succession, 'I shall put my coat *here*.' He had then placed his hat on a nearby chair and added with an air of infinite subtlety, 'But my hat I shall put *here*. Otherwise it may fall!' as if he were hinting that on the other hand some arrangement could be reached over the exact terms of the marriage.

'If they are at one's table,' concluded Jacqueline tolerantly, 'they are no longer pigs.'

*

Obeying the law that people always loathe those they have wronged, Sonny found himself especially allergic to Bridget after his conversation with Peter Porlock, and went as far as the nursery to avoid her.

'Dada! What are you doing here?' asked Belinda.

'I've come to see my favourite girl,' boomed Sonny.

'What a lucky girl you are,' cooed Nanny, 'a busy man like your father coming to see you on a day like this!'

'That's all right, Nanny,' said Sonny. 'I'll take over.'

'Yes, sir,' said Nanny unctuously.

'Well,' said Sonny, rubbing his hands together, 'what have you been up to?'

'We were reading a book!'

'What's the story about?' asked Sonny.

'It's a school trip,' said Belinda rather shyly.

'And where do they go?'

'To the wax museum.'

'Madame Tussaud's?'

'Yes, and Tim and Jane are very naughty and they stay behind and hide, and when it's night-time all the wax people come to life, and then they start to dance with each other like real people, and they make friends with the children. Will you read it to me, Dada, please?'

'But you've just read it,' said Sonny, puzzled.

'It's my favourite story, and it's better if you read it. *Please*,' pleaded Belinda.

'Of course I will. I'd be delighted,' said Sonny with a little bow, as if he'd been asked to address an agricultural fair. Since he was in the nursery he might as well create a good impression. Besides, he was jolly fond of Belinda and there was no harm in underlining the fact. It was awful to think this way, but one had to be practical and plan ahead and think of Cheatley. Nanny would be a useful character witness if there was a fuss about custody. One could be sure that this unexpected swoop into the nursery would be branded on her memory. Sonny installed himself in an old battered armchair and Belinda, hardly believing her luck, sat in his lap and rested her head against the soft cashmere of his bright red sweater.

'All the children in Tim and Jane's class were very excited,' boomed Sonny. 'They were going on a trip to London . . .'

'It's too bad your not being able to come,' said David Wind-fall to his wife, slipping a couple of condoms into the inside pocket of his dinner jacket, just in case.

'Have fun, darling,' gasped Jane, longing for him to leave.

'It won't be fun without you,' said David, wondering whether two condoms were enough.

'Don't be silly, darling, you'll forget about me on the motorway.'

David couldn't be bothered to contradict the truth of this assertion.

'I hope you feel better tomorrow,' he said instead. 'I'll call you first thing.'

'You're an angel,' said his wife. 'Drive carefully.'

Johnny had called to say that he would take his own car after all, and so Patrick left London alone, relieved to get away before it was dark. He marvelled at the feverish excitement he had once been able to put into partygoing. It had been based on the hope, never yet fulfilled, that he would stop worrying and stop feeling pointless once the movie of his life took on the appearance of flawless glamour. For this to work, though, he would have had to allow the perspective of a stranger leafing through the filled pages of his diary to eclipse his own point of view, and he would have had to believe, which was far from being the case, that if he got enough reflected glory he could be spared the trouble of seeking out any of his own. Without this snobbish fever he was stranded under the revolving ceiling fan of his own consciousness, taking shallow breaths to get as little oxygen as possible into a brain apparently unable to manufacture anything but dread and regret.

Patrick rewound Iggy Pop's 'The Passenger' for the third time. His car shot down the hill towards the viaduct suspended between the factories and houses of High Wycombe. Released from the trance of the music, a fragment of the dream he'd forgotten that morning came back to him. He could picture an obese Alsatian flinging itself against a padlocked gate, the rattling of the gate. He'd been walking along the path next to a garden, and the dog had been barking at him through the green chicken wire that so often marks the boundary of a French suburban garden.

His car swept up the hill on the other side of the viaduct while the introductory notes of the song strummed through the speakers. Patrick contorted his face, preparing to sing along with Iggy, starting to shout out the familiar words half a beat too early. The smoke-filled car sped tunelessly on into the gathering darkness.

One of the reservations Laura had about her personality was that she sometimes got this thing about leaving her flat. She couldn't get through the door, or if she did she had to double back, she just *had* to. Lost and forgotten objects surfaced in her bag the moment she stepped back inside. It had grown worse since her cat died. Making sure the cat had water and food before she went out, and making sure it didn't follow her into the corridor, had helped a lot.

She had just sent China off to fetch the car with the excuse that the bags were too bulky to carry far, but really so that China didn't witness the propitiatory ritual that enabled

Laura to get out of the flat. She had to walk out backwards – it was ridiculous, she knew it was ridiculous – and touch the top of the door frame as she went through. There was always the danger of one of her neighbours finding her reversing out of her flat on tiptoe with her arms outstretched, and so she glanced down the corridor first to check that it was clear.

'We could play a game in the car,' China had said. 'The person you'd least like to sit next to at dinner.'

'We've played that before,' Laura had complained.

'But we could play it from other people's point of view.'

'Oh, I hadn't thought of that,' Laura had said.

Anyhow, thought Laura as she locked her front door, Johnny was China's ex-boyfriend and so at least she could have some fun on the drive down, asking about his habits and about how much China missed him.

Alexander Politsky, whose extreme Englishness derived from his being Russian, was perhaps the last man in England to use the term 'old bean' sincerely. He was also widely acknowledged to have the best collection of shoes in the country. A pair of pre-First World War Lobb riding boots given to him by 'a marvellous old boulevardier and *screaming* queen who was rather a friend of my father's' were only brought out on special occasions when the subject of boots or shoes arose spontaneously in the conversation.

He was driving Ali Montague down to the Bossington-Lanes', where they were both staying. Ali, who had known Bill Bossington-Lane for forty years, had described him and his wife as 'the sort of people one never sees in London. They just don't travel well.'

Someone once asked Bill if he still had his beautiful manor house. 'Beautiful manor house?' he said. 'We've still got the old dump, if that's what you mean.' 'By the way,' Ali continued, 'did you see that thing in Dempster about tonight? After all the usual rubbish about the best shoot in England, and ten thousand acres and Princess Margaret, there was Bridget saying, "I'm just having a few people round to celebrate my husband's birthday." She just can't get it right, can she?'

'Ugh,' groaned Alexander, 'I can't stand that woman. I mean, I almost don't mind being patronized by Princess Margaret, and no doubt will be tonight—'

'You should be so lucky,' interjected Ali. 'Do you know, I think I *prefer* parties given by people I don't like.'

'But,' Alexander continued, unperturbed, 'I won't be patronized by Bridget Gravesend, née Watson-Spot or whatever it was.'

'Watson-Spot,' laughed Ali. 'Oddly enough I knew the father *slightly* in another lifetime. He was called Roddy Watson-Scott, frightfully stupid and jolly and rather used-car salesman, but nice. As you know I'm *not* a snob, but you didn't have to be a snob to drop that man.'

'Well, there you are,' said Politsky. 'I don't want to be patronized by the daughter of a used-car salesman. After all, my family used to be able to walk from Moscow to Kiev on their own land.'

'It's no use telling me about these foreign places,' said Ali. 'I'm afraid I just don't know where Kiev is.'

'All you need to know is that it's a very long way from Moscow,' said Alexander curtly. 'Anyway, it sounds as if Bridget'll get her comeuppance with this Cindy Smith affair.'

'What I can't understand is why Cindy's gone for Sonny,' said Ali.

'He's the key to the world she wants to penetrate.'

'Or be penetrated *by*,' said Ali.

Both men smiled.

'By the way, are you wearing pumps this evening?' asked Alexander casually.

With her fist, Anne Eisen rubbed the Jaguar's back window and got nowhere; the dirty fog on the other side stood its ground.

The driver glanced in the rear-view mirror disapprovingly.

'Do you know where we are?' asked Tom.

'Sure,' said Anne. 'We're out of our minds.' She spaced the words slowly and evenly. 'That's where we are. We're on our way to see a lot of museum pieces, arrogant snobs, air-heads, and feudal boondockers . . .'

'Harold tells me that Princess Margaret is coming.'

'And thick Krauts.' Anne added this last item to her list with satisfaction.

The Jaguar turned left and crept down to the end of a long drive where the lights of an Elizabethan manor glowed through the fog. They had arrived at Harold Greene's, their host for the weekend.

'Wow!' said Anne. 'Get a load of this: fifty rooms, and I'll bet all of them are haunted.'

Tom, picking up a battered leather case from the floor, was not impressed. 'It's a Harold-type house,' he said, 'I'll give you that. He had one just like it years ago in Arlington, when we were young and saving the world.'

6

Bridget had told her mother to get a taxi at the station and not to worry because she would pay, but when Virginia Watson-Scott arrived at Cheatley she was too embarrassed to ask and so she paid herself, although seventeen pounds plus a pound for the driver was no small sum.

'If orchids could write novels,' Tony Fowles was saying when Virginia was shown into Bridget's little sitting room, 'they would write novels like Isabel's.'

'Oh, hello, Mummy,' sighed Bridget, getting up from the sofa where she'd been drinking in Tony's words. The Valium had helped to muffle the impact of overhearing Sonny's telephone call, and Bridget was slightly shocked but pleased by her ability to enter into the trance of habit and to be distracted by Tony's witty conversation. Nevertheless the presence of her mother struck her as an additional and unfair burden.

'I thought I was so well organized,' she explained to her mother, 'but I've still got a million and one things to do. Do you know Tony Fowles?'

Tony got up and shook hands. 'Pleased to meet you,' he said.

'It's nice to be in proper countryside,' said Virginia, nervous of silence. 'It's become so built-up around me.'

'I know,' said Tony. 'I love seeing cows, don't you? They're so natural.'

'Oh yes,' said Virginia, 'cows are nice.'

'My trouble,' Tony confessed, 'is that I'm so aesthetic. I want to rush into the field and arrange them. Then I'd have them glued to the spot so they looked perfect from the house.'

'Poor cows,' said Virginia, 'I don't think they'd like that. Where's Belinda?' she asked Bridget.

'In the nursery, I imagine,' said Bridget. 'It's a bit early, but would you like some tea?'

'I'd rather see Belinda first,' Virginia replied, remembering that Bridget had asked her to come at teatime.

'All right, we'll go and have tea in the nursery,' said Bridget. 'I'm afraid your room is on the nursery floor anyhow – we're so crowded with Princess Margaret and everything – so I can show you your room at the same time.'

'Righty-ho,' said Virginia. It was a phrase Roddy had always used, and it drove Bridget mad.

'Oh,' she couldn't help groaning, 'please don't use that expression.'

'I must have caught it from Roddy!'

'I know,' said Bridget. She could picture her father in his blazer and his cavalry twills saying 'righty-ho' as he put on his driving gloves. He had always been kind to her, but once she had learned to be embarrassed by him she had never stopped, even after he died.

'Let's go up, then,' sighed Bridget. 'You'll come with us, won't you?' she pleaded with Tony.

'Aye-aye,' said Tony, saluting, 'or aren't I allowed to say that?'

Bridget led the way to the nursery. Nanny, who had been in the middle of scolding Belinda for being 'overexcited', set off to make tea in the nursery kitchen, muttering, 'Both parents in one day,' with a mixture of awe and resentment.

'Granny!' said Belinda, who liked her grandmother. 'I didn't know you were coming!'

'Didn't anyone tell you?' asked Virginia, too pleased with Belinda to dwell on this oversight.

Tony and Bridget moved over to the tattered old sofa at the far end of the room.

'Roses,' said Tony reproachfully, sitting down.

'Aren't they sweet together?' asked Bridget, watching Belinda on Virginia's knee, peering into her grandmother's bag to see if there were sweets in it. For a moment Bridget could remember being in the same position and feeling happy.

'Sweet,' confirmed Tony, 'or sweets anyway.'

'You old cynic,' said Bridget.

Tony put on an expression of wounded innocence. 'I'm not a cynic,' he moaned. 'Is it my fault that most people are motivated by greed and envy?'

'What motivates you?' asked Bridget.

'Style,' said Tony bashfully. 'And love for my friends,' he added, softly patting Bridget's wrist.

'Don't try to butter me up,' said Bridget.

'Who's being a cynic now?' gasped Tony.

'Look what Granny brought me,' said Belinda, holding out a bag of lemon sherbets, her favourite sweets.

'Would you like one?' she asked her mother.

'You mustn't give her sweets,' said Bridget to Virginia. 'They're frightfully bad for her teeth.'

'I only bought a quarter of a pound,' said Virginia. 'You used to like them too as a girl.'

'Nanny disapproves terribly, don't you, Nanny?' asked Bridget, taking advantage of the reappearance of Nanny with a tea tray.

'Oh yes,' said Nanny, who hadn't in fact heard what was being discussed.

'Sweets rot little girls' teeth,' said Bridget.

'Sweets!' cried Nanny, able to focus on the enemy at last. 'No sweets in the nursery except on Sundays!' she thundered.

Belinda ran through the nursery door and out into the corridor. 'I'm not in the nursery anymore,' she chanted.

Virginia put her hand over her mouth to make a show of concealing her laughter. 'I didn't want to cause any trouble,' she said.

'Oh, she's a lively one,' said Nanny cunningly, seeing that Bridget secretly admired Belinda's rebelliousness.

Virginia followed Belinda out into the corridor. Tony looked critically at the old tweed skirt she wore. Stylish it was not. He felt licensed by Bridget's attitude to despise Virginia, without forgoing the pleasure of despising Bridget for not being more loyal to her mother, or stylish enough to rise above her.

'You should take your mum shopping for a new skirt,' he suggested.

'Don't be so rude,' said Bridget.

Tony could smell the weakness in her indignation. 'That maroon check gives me a headache,' he insisted.

'It is ghastly,' admitted Bridget.

Nanny brought over two cups of tea, and a plate of Jaffa Cakes.

'Granny's going to keep the sweets for me,' said Belinda, coming back into the nursery. 'And I have to ask her if I want one.'

'It seemed to us like a good compromise,' Virginia explained.

'And she's going to read me a story before dinner,' said Belinda.

'Oh, I meant to tell you,' said Bridget absently, 'you've been asked to dinner at the Bossington-Lanes'. I couldn't refuse, they made such a fuss about needing extra women. It'll be so stuffy here with Princess Margaret, you'll be much more at home over there. They're neighbours of ours, frightfully nice.'

'Oh,' said Virginia. 'Well, if I'm needed I suppose . . .'

'You don't *mind*, do you?' asked Bridget.

'Oh no,' said Virginia.

'I mean, I thought it would be nicer for you, more relaxed.'

'Yes, I'm sure I'll be more relaxed,' said Virginia.

'I mean, if you really don't want to go I could still cancel them I suppose, although they'll be frightfully angry at this stage.'

'No, no,' said Virginia. 'I'd love to go, you mustn't cancel them now. They sound very nice. Will you excuse me a moment?' she added, getting up and opening the door that led to the other rooms on the nursery floor.

'Did I handle that all right?' Bridget asked Tony.

'You deserve an Oscar.'

'You don't think it was unkind of me? It's just that I don't think I can handle P.M. and Sonny *and* my mother all at once.'

'You did the right thing,' Tony reassured her. 'After all, you couldn't very well send either of *those* two to the Bossington-Lanes'.'

'I know, but I mean, I was thinking of her too.'

'I'm sure she'll be happier there,' said Tony. 'She seems a nice woman but she's not very . . .' he searched for the right word, ' . . . social, is she?'

'No,' said Bridget. 'I know the whole P.M. thing would make her terribly tense.'

'Is Granny upset?' asked Belinda, coming to sit down next to her mother.

'What on earth makes you ask that?'

'She looked sad when she left.'

'That's just the way she looks when her face relaxes,' said Bridget inventively.

Virginia came back into the nursery, stuffing her handkerchief up the sleeve of her cardigan.

'I went into one of the rooms for a moment and saw my suitcase there,' she said cheerfully. 'Is that where I'm sleeping?'

'Hmm,' said Bridget, picking up her cup of tea and sipping it slowly. 'I'm sorry it's rather poky, but after all it's only for one night.'

'Just for one night,' echoed Virginia, who'd been hoping to stay for two or three.

'The house is incredibly full,' said Bridget. 'It's such a strain on . . . on everybody.' She tactfully swallowed the word 'servants' in Nanny's presence. 'Anyhow, I thought you'd like to be near Belinda.'

'Oh, of course,' said Virginia. 'We can have a midnight feast.'

'A midnight feast,' spluttered Nanny who could contain herself no longer. 'Not in *my* nursery!'

'I thought it was Belinda's nursery,' said Tony waspishly.

'I'm in charge,' gasped Nanny, 'and I can't have midnight feasts.'

Bridget could remember the midnight feast her mother had made to cheer her up on the night before she went to boarding school. Her mother had pretended that they had to hide from her father, but Bridget later found out that he had known all about it and had even gone to buy the cakes himself. She suppressed this sentimental memory with a sigh and got up when she heard the noise of cars at the front of the house. She craned out of one of the small windows in the corner of the nursery.

'Oh God, it's the Alantours,' she said. 'I suppose I have to go down and say hello to them. Tony, will you be an angel and help me?' she asked.

'As long as you leave me time to put on my ball gown for Princess Margaret,' said Tony.

'Can I do anything?' asked Virginia.

'No, thanks. You stay here and unpack. I'll order you a

taxi to go to the Bossington-Lanes'. At about seven thirty,' said Bridget calculating that Princess Margaret would not yet have come down for a drink. 'My treat, of course,' she added.

Oh, dear, thought Virginia, more money down the drain.

7

Patrick had booked his room late and so had been put in the annexe of the Little Soddington House Hotel. With the letter confirming his reservation the management had enclosed a brochure featuring a vast room with a four-poster bed, a tall marble fireplace, and a bay window opening onto wide views of the ravishing Cotswolds. The room Patrick was shown into, with its severely pitched ceiling and view onto the kitchen yard, boasted a full complement of tea-making facilities, instant-coffee sachets, and tiny pots of longlife milk. The miniature floral pattern on its matching waste-paper basket, curtains, bedspread, cushions, and Kleenex dispenser seemed to shift and shimmer.

Patrick unpacked his dinner jacket and threw it onto the bed, throwing himself down after it. A notice under the glass of the bedside table said: 'To avoid disappointment, residents are advised to book in the restaurant in advance.' Patrick, who had been trying to avoid disappointment all his life, cursed himself for not discovering this formula earlier.

Was there no other way he could stop being disappointed? How could he find any firm ground when his identity seemed to begin with disintegration and go on to disintegrate further? But perhaps this whole model of identity was mis-conceived. Perhaps identity was not a building for which one had to find foundations, but rather a series of impersonations held together by a central intelligence, an intelligence that knew the history of the impersonations and eliminated the distinction between action and acting.

'Impersonation, sir,' grunted Patrick, thrusting out his stomach and waddling towards the bathroom, as if he were the Fat Man himself, 'is a habit of which I cannot approve, it was the ruination of Monsieur Escoffier . . .' He stopped.

The self-disgust that afflicted him these days had the stagnancy of a malarial swamp, and he sometimes missed the cast of jeering characters that had accompanied the more dramatic disintegrations of his early twenties. Although he could conjure up some of these characters, they seemed to have lost their energy, just as he had soon forgotten the agony of being a ventriloquist's dummy and replaced it with a sense of nostalgia for a period that had made up for some of its unpleasantness with its intensity.

'Be absolute for death', a strange phrase from *Measure for Measure*, returned to him while he bared his teeth to rip open a sachet of bath gel. Perhaps there was something in this half-shallow, half-profound idea that one had to despair of life in order to grasp its real value. Then again, perhaps there wasn't. But in any case, he pondered, squeezing the green slime from the sachet and trying to get back to his earlier line of thought, what was this central intelligence, and just how intelligent was it? What was the thread that held together the scattered beads of experience if not the pressure of interpretation? The meaning of life was whatever meaning one could thrust down its reluctant throat.

Where was Victor Eisen, the great philosopher, when he needed him most? How could he have left the doubtless splendid *Being, Knowing, and Judging* (or was it *Thinking, Knowing, and Judging*?) behind in New York when Anne Eisen had generously given him a copy during his corpse-collecting trip?

On his most recent visit to New York, he'd been back to

the funeral parlour where, years before, he had seen his father's body. The building was not as he remembered it at all. Instead of the grey stone facade, he saw soft brown brick. The building was much smaller than he expected and when he was driven inside by curiosity he found that there was no chequered black-and-white marble floor, and no reception desk where he expected to see one. Perhaps it had been changed, but even so, the scale was wrong, like places remembered from childhood and dwarfed by the passage of time.

The strange thing was that Patrick refused to alter his memory of the funeral parlour. He found the picture he had evolved over the years more compelling than the facts with which he was presented on revisiting the place. This picture was more suitable to the events that had occurred within the disappointing building. What he must remain true to was the effort of interpretation, the thread on which he tried to hang the scattered beads.

Even involuntary memory was only the resurfacing of an old story, something that had definitely once been a story. Impressions that were too fleeting to be called stories yielded no meaning. On the same visit to New York he had passed a red-and-white funnel next to some roadworks, spewing steam into the cold air. It felt nostalgic and significant, but left him in a state of nebulous intensity, not knowing whether he was remembering an image from a film, a book, or his own life. On the same walk he had dropped into a sleazy hotel in which he had once lived and found that it was no longer a hotel. The thing he was remembering no longer existed but, blind to the refurbished lobby, he continued to imagine the Italian with the scimitar tie-pin accusing him of trying to install his girlfriend Natasha as a prostitute, and to imagine the frenetic wallpaper covered in scratchy red lines like the frayed blood vessels of exhausted eyes.

What could he do but accept the disturbing extent to

which memory was fictional and hope that the fiction lay at the service of a truth less richly represented by the original facts?

The house in Lacoste, where Patrick had spent most of his childhood, was now separated by only a few vines from a nasty suburb. Its old furniture had been sold and the redundant well filled in and sealed. Even the tree frogs, bright green and smooth against the smooth grey bark of the fig trees had gone, poisoned, or deprived of their breeding ground. Standing on the cracked terrace, listening to the whining of a new motorway, Patrick would try to hallucinate the faces that used to emerge from the smoky fluidity of the limestone crags, but they remained stubbornly hidden. On the other hand, geckos still flickered over the ceilings and under the eaves of the roof, and a tremor of unresolved violence always disturbed the easy atmosphere of holidays, like the churning of an engine setting the gin trembling on a distant deck. Some things never let him down.

The phone rang, and Patrick picked it up hastily, grateful for the interruption. It was Johnny saying that he'd arrived, and suggesting that they meet in the bar at eight thirty. Patrick agreed and, released from the hamster's wheel of his thoughts, got up to turn off the bathwater.

David Windfall, florid and hot from his bath, squeezed into dinner jacket trousers that seemed to strain like sausage skins from the pressure of his thighs. Beads of sweat broke out continually on his upper lip and forehead. He wiped them away, glancing at himself in the mirror; although he looked like a hippopotamus with hypertension he was well satisfied.

He was going to have dinner with Cindy Smith. She was world-famously sexy and glamorous, but David was not intimidated because he was charming and sophisticated and, well, English. The Windfalls had been making their influence felt in Cumbria for centuries before Miss Smith popped onto the scene, he reassured himself as he buttoned up the over-tight shirt on his already sweating neck. His wife was in the habit of buying him seventeen-and-a-half-inch collars in the hope that he would grow thin enough to wear them. This trick made him so indignant that he decided that she deserved to be ill and absent and, if everything went well, betrayed.

He still hadn't told Mrs Bossington-Lane that he wouldn't be going to her dinner. He decided, as he choked himself on his bow tie, that the best way to handle it was to seek her out at the party and claim that his car had broken down. He just hoped that nobody else he knew would be having dinner in the hotel. He might try to use this fear to persuade Cindy to dine in his room. His thoughts panted on opti-mistically.

It was Cindy Smith who occupied the magnificent bedroom advertised in the brochure of the hotel. They'd told her it was a suite, but it was just a semi-large bedroom without a separate seating area. These old English houses were so uncomfortable. She'd only seen a photograph of Cheatley from the outside, and it looked real big, but there'd better be underfloor heating and a whole lot of private bathrooms, or she couldn't even face her own plan to become the inde-pendently wealthy ex-Countess of Gravesend.

She was taking a long-term view and looking ahead two or three years. Looks didn't last forever and she wasn't ready for religion yet. Money was kind of a good compromise, staked up somewhere between cosmetics and eternity. Besides, she liked Sonny, she really did. He was cute, not to look at, God no, but aristocratic cute, old-fashioned out-of-a-movie cute.

Last year in Paris all the other models had come back to her suite in the Lotti – now there was a real suite – and each one of them, except a couple who chickened out, had done her fake orgasm, and Cindy's was voted Best Fake Orgasm. They'd pretended the champagne bottle was an Oscar and she'd made an acceptance speech thanking all the men without whom it wouldn't have been possible. Too bad she'd mentioned Sonny, seeing how she was going to marry him. Whoops!

She'd drunk a bit too much and put her father on the list also, which was probably a mistake 'cause all the other girls fell silent and things weren't so much fun after that.

Patrick arrived downstairs before Johnny, and ordered a glass of Perrier at the bar. Two middle-aged couples sat together at a nearby table. The only other person in the bar, a florid man in a dinner jacket, obviously going to Sonny's party, sat with folded arms, looking towards the door.

Patrick took his drink over to a small book-lined alcove in the corner of the room. Scanning the shelves, his eye fell on a volume called *The Journal of a Disappointed Man*, and next to it a second volume called *More Journals of a Disappointed Man*, and finally, by the same author, a third volume entitled *Enjoying Life*. How could a man who had made such a promising start to his career have ended up writing a book called *Enjoying Life*? Patrick took the offending volume from the shelf and read the first sentence that he saw: 'Verily, the flight of a gull is as magnificent as the Andes!'

'Verily,' murmured Patrick.

'Hi.'

'Hello, Johnny,' said Patrick, looking up from the page. 'I've just found a book called *Enjoying Life*.'

'Intriguing,' said Johnny, sitting down on the other side of the alcove.

'I'm going to take it to my room and read it tomorrow. It might save my life. Mind you, I don't know why people get so fixated on happiness, which always eludes them, when there are so many other invigorating experiences available, like rage, jealousy, disgust, and so forth.'

'Don't you want to be happy?' asked Johnny.

'Well, when you put it like *that*,' smiled Patrick.

'Really you're just like everyone else.'

'Don't push your luck,' Patrick warned him.

'Will you be dining with us this evening, gentlemen?' asked a waiter.

'Yes,' replied Johnny, taking a menu, and passing one on to Patrick who was too deep in the alcove for the waiter to reach.

'I thought he said, "Will you be dying with us?"' admitted Patrick, who was feeling increasingly uneasy about his decision to tell Johnny the facts he had kept secret for thirty years.

'Maybe he did,' said Johnny. 'We haven't read the menu yet.'

'I suppose "the young" will be taking drugs tonight,' sighed Patrick, scanning the menu.

'Ecstasy: the non-addictive high,' said Johnny.

'Call me old fashioned,' blustered Patrick, 'but I don't like the sound of a non-addictive drug.'

Johnny felt frustratingly engulfed in his old style of banter with Patrick. These were just the sort of 'old associations' that he was supposed to sever, but what could he do? Patrick was a great friend and he wanted him to be less miserable.

'Why do you think we're so discontented?' asked Johnny, settling for the smoked salmon.

'I don't know,' lied Patrick. 'I can't decide between the onion soup and the traditional English goat's cheese salad. An analyst once told me I was suffering from a "depression on top of a depression".'

'Well, at least you got on top of the first depression,' said Johnny, closing the menu.

'Exactly,' smiled Patrick. 'I don't think one can improve on the traitor of Strasbourg whose last request was that he give the order to the firing squad himself. Christ! Look at that girl!' he burst out in a half-mournful surge of excitement.

'It's whatshername, the model.'

'Oh, yeah. Well, at least now I can get obsessed with an unobtainable fuck,' said Patrick. 'Obsession dispels depression: the third law of psychodynamics.'

'What are the others?'

'That people loathe those they've wronged, and that they despise the victims of misfortune, and . . . I'll think of some more over dinner.'

'I don't despise the victims of misfortune,' said Johnny. 'I am worried that misfortune is contagious, but I'm not secretly convinced that it's deserved.'

'Look at her,' said Patrick, 'pacing around the cage of her Valentino dress, longing to be released into her natural habitat.'

'Calm down,' said Johnny, 'she's probably frigid.'

'Just as well if she is,' said Patrick. 'I haven't had sex for so long I can't remember what it's like, except that it takes place in that distant grey zone beneath the neck.'

'It's not grey.'

'Well, there you are, I can't even remember what it looks like, but I sometimes think it would be nice to have a relationship with my body which wasn't based on illness or addiction.'

'What about work and love?' asked Johnny.

'You know it's not fair to ask me about work,' said Patrick reproachfully, 'but my experience of love is that you get excited thinking that someone can mend your broken heart, and then you get angry when you realize that they can't. A certain economy creeps into the process and the jewelled daggers that used to pierce one's heart are replaced by ever-blunter penknives.'

'Did you expect Debbie to mend your broken heart?'

'Of course, but we were like two people taking turns with a bandage – I'm afraid to say that her turns tended to be a great deal shorter. I don't blame anyone anymore – I always mostly and rightly blamed myself . . .' Patrick stopped. 'It's just sad to spend so long getting to know someone and explaining yourself to them, and then having no use for the knowledge.'

'Do you prefer being sad to being bitter?' asked Johnny.

'Marginally,' said Patrick. 'It took me some time to get bitter. I used to think I saw things clearly when we were going out. I thought, she's a mess and I'm a mess, but at least I know what kind of mess I am.'

'Big deal,' said Johnny.

'Quite,' sighed Patrick. 'One seldom knows whether perseverance is noble or stupid until it's too late. Most people either feel regret at staying with someone for too long, or regret at losing them too easily. I manage to feel both ways at the same time about the same object.'

'Congratulations,' said Johnny.

Patrick raised his hands, as if trying to quiet the roar of applause.

'But why is your heart broken?' asked Johnny, struck by Patrick's unguarded manner.

'Some women,' said Patrick, ignoring the question, 'provide you with anaesthetic, if you're lucky, or a mirror in which you can watch yourself making clumsy incisions, but most of them spend their time tearing open old wounds.' Patrick took a gulp of Perrier. 'Listen,' he said, 'there's something I want to tell you.'

'Your table is ready, gentlemen,' a waiter announced with gusto. 'If you'd care to follow me into the dining room.'

Johnny and Patrick got up and followed him into a brown-carpeted dining room decorated with portraits of sunlit salmon and bonneted squires' wives, each table flickering with the light of a single pink candle.

Patrick loosened his bow tie and undid the top button of his shirt. How could he tell Johnny? How could he tell anyone? But if he told no one, he would stay endlessly isolated and divided against himself. He knew that under the tall grass of an apparently untamed future the steel rails of fear and habit were already laid. What he suddenly couldn't bear, with every cell in his body, was to act out the destiny prepared for him by his past, and slide obediently along those rails, contemplating bitterly all the routes he would rather have taken.

But which words could he use? All his life he'd used words to distract attention from this deep inarticulacy, this unspeakable emotion which he would now have to use words to describe. How could they avoid being noisy and tactless, like a gaggle of children laughing under the bedroom window of a dying man? And wouldn't he rather tell a woman, and be engulfed in maternal solicitude, or scorched by sexual frenzy? Yes, yes, yes. Or a psychiatrist, to whom he would be almost obliged to make such an offering, although he had resisted the temptation often enough. Or his mother, that Mrs Jellyby whose telescopic philanthropy had saved so many Ethiopian orphans while her own child fell into the fire. And yet Patrick wanted to tell an unpaid witness, without money, without sex, and without blame, just another human being. Perhaps he should tell the waiter: at least he wouldn't be seeing him again.

'There's something I have to tell you,' he repeated, after they had sat down and ordered their food. Johnny paused expectantly, putting down his glass of water from an intuition that he had better not be gulping or munching during the next few minutes.

'It's not that I'm embarrassed,' Patrick mumbled. 'It's more a question of not wanting to burden you with something you can't really be expected to do anything about.'

'Go ahead,' said Johnny.

'I know that I've told you about my parents' divorce and the drunkenness and the violence and the fecklessness . . . That's not really the point at all. What I was skirting around and not saying is that when I was five—'

'Here we are, gentlemen,' said the waiter, bringing the first courses with a flourish.

'Thank you,' said Johnny. 'Go on.'

Patrick waited for the waiter to slip away. He must try to be as simple as he could.

'When I was five, my father "abused" me, as we're invited to call it these days—' Patrick suddenly broke off in silence, unable to sustain the casualness he'd been labouring to achieve. Switchblades of memory that had flashed open all his life reappeared and silenced him.

'How do you mean "abused"?' asked Johnny uncertainly. The answer somehow became clear as he formulated the question.

'I . . .' Patrick couldn't speak. The crumpled bedspread with the blue phoenixes, the pool of cold slime at the base of his spine, scuttling off over the tiles. These were memories he was not prepared to talk about.

He picked up his fork and stuck the prongs discreetly but very hard into the underside of his wrist, trying to force

himself back into the present and the conversational respon-
sibilities he was neglecting.

'It was . . .' he sighed, concussed by memory.

After having watched Patrick drawl his way fluently
through every crisis, Johnny was shocked at seeing him unable
to speak, and he found his eyes glazed with a film of tears.
'I'm so sorry,' he murmured.

'Nobody should do that to anybody else,' said Patrick,
almost whispering.

'Is everything to your satisfaction, gentlemen?' said the
chirpy waiter.

'Look, do you think you could leave us alone for five
minutes so we can have a conversation?' snapped Patrick,
suddenly regaining his voice.

'I'm sorry, sir,' said the waiter archly.

'I can't stand this fucking music,' said Patrick, glancing around the dining room aggressively. Subdued Chopin
teetered familiarly on the edge of hearing.

'Why don't they turn the fucking thing off, or turn it
up?' he snarled. 'What do I mean by abused?' he added impatiently. 'I mean sexually abused.'

'God, I'm sorry,' said Johnny. 'I'd always wondered why
you hated your father quite so much.'

'Well, now you know. The first incident masqueraded as
a punishment. It had a certain Kafkaesque charm: the crime
was never named and therefore took on great generality and
intensity.'

'Did this go on?' asked Johnny.

'Yes, yes,' said Patrick hastily.

'What a bastard,' said Johnny.

'That's what I've been saying for years,' said Patrick. 'But
now I'm exhausted by hating him. I can't go on. The hatred
binds me to those events and I don't want to be a child

anymore.' Patrick was back in the vein again, released from silence by the habits of analysis and speculation.

'It must have split the world in half for you,' said Johnny.

Patrick was taken aback by the precision of this comment.

'Yes. Yes, I think that's exactly what happened. How did you know?'

'It seemed pretty obvious.'

'It's strange to hear someone say that it's obvious. It always seemed to me so secret and complicated.' Patrick paused. He felt that although what he was saying mattered to him enormously, there was a core of inarticulacy that he hadn't attacked at all. His intellect could only generate more distinctions or define the distinctions better.

'I always thought the truth would set me free,' he said, 'but the truth just drives you mad.'

'Telling the truth might set you free.'

'Maybe. But self-knowledge on its own is useless.'

'Well, it enables you to suffer more lucidly,' argued Johnny.

'Oh, ya, I wouldn't miss that for the world.'

'In the end perhaps the only way to alleviate misery is to become more detached about yourself and more attached to something else,' said Johnny.

'Are you suggesting I take up a hobby?' laughed Patrick. 'Weaving baskets or sewing mailbags?'

'Well, actually, I was trying to think of a way to avoid those two particular occupations,' said Johnny.

'But if I were released from my bitter and unpleasant state of mind,' protested Patrick, 'what would be left?'

'Nothing much,' admitted Johnny, 'but think what you could put there instead.'

'You're making me dizzy . . . Oddly enough there was something about hearing the word mercy in *Measure for Measure* last night that made me imagine there might be a course that is neither bitter nor false, something that lies beyond argument. But if there is I can't grasp it; all I know is that I'm tired of having these steel brushes whirring around the inside of my skull.'

Both men paused while the waiter silently cleared away their plates. Patrick was puzzled by how easy it had been to tell another person the most shameful and secret truth about his life. And yet he felt dissatisfied; the catharsis of confession eluded him. Perhaps he had been too abstract. His 'father' had become the codename for a set of his own psychological difficulties and he had forgotten the real man, with his grey curls and his wheezing chest and his proud face, who had made such clumsy efforts in his closing years to endear himself to those he had betrayed.

When Eleanor had finally gathered the courage to divorce David, he had gone into a decline. Like a disgraced torturer whose victim has died, he cursed himself for not pacing his cruelty better, guilt and self-pity competing for mastery of his mood. David had the further frustration of being defied by Patrick who, at the age of eight, inspired by his parents' separation, refused one day to give in to his father's sexual assaults. Patrick's transformation of himself from a toy into a person shattered his father, who realized that Patrick must have known what was being done to him.

During this difficult time, David went to visit Nicholas Pratt in Sister Agnes, where he was recovering from a painful operation on his intestine following the failure of his fourth marriage. David, reeling from the prospect of his own divorce, found Nicholas lying in bed drinking champagne smuggled in by loyal friends, and only too ready to discuss how one should never trust a bloody woman.

'I want someone to design me a fortress,' said David, for whom Eleanor was proposing to build a small house surprisingly close to her own house in Lacoste. 'I don't want to look out on the fucking world again.'

'Completely understand,' slurred Nicholas, whose speech had become at once thicker and more staccato in his post-operative haze. 'Only trouble with the bloody world is the bloody people in it,' he said. 'Give me that writing paper, would you?'

While David paced up and down the room, flouting the hospital rules by smoking a cigar, Nicholas, who liked to surprise his friends with his amateur draughtsmanship, made a sketch worthy of David's misanthropic ecstasy.

'Keep the buggers out,' he said when he had finished, tossing the page across the bedclothes.

David picked it up and saw a pentagonal house with no windows on the outside and a central courtyard in which Nicholas had poetically planted a cypress tree, flaring above the low roof like a black flame.

The architect who was given this sketch took pity on David and introduced a single window into the exterior wall of the drawing room. David locked the shutters and stuffed crunched-up copies of *The Times* into the aperture, cursing himself for not sacking the architect when he first visited him in his disastrously converted farmhouse near Aix, with its algae-choked swimming pool. He pressed the window closed on the newspaper and then sealed it with the thick black tape favoured by those who wish to gas themselves efficiently. Finally a curtain was drawn across the window and only reopened by rare visitors who were soon made aware of their error by David's rage.

The cypress tree never flourished and its twisted trunk and grey peeling bark writhed in a dismal parody of Nicholas's noble vision. Nicholas himself, after designing the house, was too busy ever to accept an invitation. 'One doesn't have fun with David Melrose these days,' he would tell people in London. This was a polite way to describe the state of mental illness into which David had degenerated. Woken every night by his own screaming nightmares, he lay in bed almost continuously for seven years, wearing those yellow-and-white flannel pyjamas, now worn through at the elbows, which were the only things he had inherited from his father, thanks to the generous intervention of his mother who had refused to see him leave the funeral empty-handed. The most enthusiastic thing he could do was to smoke a cigar, a habit his father had first encouraged in him, and one he had passed on to Patrick, among so many other disadvantages, like a baton thrust from one wheezing generation to the next. If David left his house he was dressed like a tramp, muttering to himself in giant supermarkets on the outskirts of Marseilles. Sometimes in winter he wandered about the house in dark glasses, trailing a Japanese dressing gown, and clutching a glass of pastis, checking again and again that the heating was off so that he didn't waste any money. The contempt that saved him from complete madness drove him almost completely mad. When he emerged from his depression he was a ghost, not improved but diminished, trying to tempt people to stay in the house that had been designed to repel their unlikely invasion.

Patrick stayed in this house during his adolescence, sitting in the courtyard, shooting olive stones over the roof so that they at least could be free. His arguments with his father, or rather his one interminable argument, reached a crucial point when Patrick said something more fundamentally insulting to David than David had just said to him, and David, conscious that he was growing slower and weaker while his son grew faster and nastier, reached into his pocket for his heart pills and, shaking them into his tortured rheumatic hands, said with a melancholy whisper, 'You mustn't say those things to your old Dad.'

Patrick's triumph was tainted by the guilty conviction that his father was about to die of a heart attack. Still, things were not the same after that, especially when Patrick was able to patronize his disinherited father with a small income, and cheapen him with his money as Eleanor had once cheapened him with hers. During those closing years Patrick's terror had largely been eclipsed by pity, and also by boredom in the company of his 'poor old Dad'. He had sometimes dreamed that they might have an honest conversation, but a moment in his father's company made it clear that this would never happen. And yet Patrick felt there was something missing, something he wasn't admitting to himself, let alone telling Johnny.

Respecting Patrick's silence, Johnny had eaten his way through most of his corn-fed chicken by the time Patrick spoke again.

'So, what can one say about a man who rapes his own child?'

'I suppose it might help if you could see him as sick rather than evil,' Johnny suggested limply. 'I can't get over this,' he added, 'it's really awful.'

'I've tried what you suggest,' said Patrick, 'but then, what is evil if not sickness celebrating itself? While my father had any power he showed no remorse or restraint, and when he was poor and abandoned he only showed contempt and morbidity.'

'Maybe you can see his actions as evil, but see *him* as sick. Maybe one can't condemn another person, only their actions . . .' Johnny hesitated, reluctant to take on the role of the defence. 'Maybe he couldn't stop himself any more than you could stop yourself taking drugs.'

'Maybe, maybe, maybe,' said Patrick, 'but I didn't harm anyone else by taking drugs.'

'Really? What about Debbie?'

'She was a grown-up, she could choose. I certainly gave her a hard time,' Patrick admitted. 'I don't know, I try to negotiate truces of one sort or another, but then I run up against this unnegotiable rage.' Patrick pushed his plate back and lit a cigarette. 'I don't want any pudding, do you?'

'No, just coffee.'

'Two coffees, please,' said Patrick to the waiter who was now theatrically tight-lipped. 'I'm sorry I snapped at you earlier, I was in the middle of trying to say something rather tricky.'

'I was only trying to do my job,' said the waiter.

'Of course,' said Patrick.

'Do you think there's any way you can forgive him?' asked Johnny.

'Oh, yes,' said the waiter, 'it wasn't that bad.'

'No, not you,' laughed Johnny.

'Sorry I spoke,' said the waiter, going off to fetch the coffee.

'Your father, I mean.'

'Well, if that absurd waiter can forgive me, who knows what chain reaction of absolution might not be set in motion?' said Patrick. 'But then neither revenge nor forgiveness change what happened. They're sideshows, of which forgiveness is the less attractive because it represents a collaboration with one's persecutors. I don't suppose that forgiveness was uppermost in the minds of people who were being nailed to a cross until Jesus, if not the first man with a Christ complex still the most successful, wafted onto the scene. Presumably those who enjoyed inflicting cruelty could hardly believe their luck and set about popularizing the superstition that their victims could only achieve peace of mind by forgiving them.'

'You don't think it might be a profound spiritual truth?' asked Johnny.

Patrick puffed out his cheeks. 'I suppose it might be, but as far as I'm concerned, what is meant to show the spiritual advantages of forgiveness in fact shows the psychological advantages of thinking you're the son of God.'

'So how do you get free?' asked Johnny.

'Search me,' said Patrick. 'Obviously, or I wouldn't have told you, I think it has something to do with telling the truth. I'm only at the beginning, but presumably there comes a point when you grow bored of telling it, and that point coincides with your "freedom".'

'So rather than forgive you're going to try and talk it out.'

'Yes, narrative fatigue is what I'm going for. If the talk cure is our modern religion then narrative fatigue must be its apotheosis,' said Patrick suavely.

'But the truth includes an understanding of your father.'

'I couldn't understand my father better and I still don't like what he did.'

'Of course you don't. Perhaps there is nothing to say except, "What a bastard." I was only groping for an alternative because you said you were exhausted by hatred.'

'I am, but at the moment I can't imagine any kind of liberation except eventual indifference.'

'Or detachment,' said Johnny. 'I don't suppose you'll ever be indifferent.'

'Yes, detachment,' said Patrick, who didn't mind having his vocabulary corrected on this occasion. 'Indifference just sounded cooler.'

The two men drank their coffee, Johnny feeling that he had been drawn too far away from Patrick's original revelation to ask, 'What actually happened?'

Patrick, for his part, suspected that he had left the soil of his own experience, where wasps still gnawed at the gaping figs and he stared down madly onto his own five-year-old head, in order to avoid an uneasiness that lay even deeper than the uneasiness of his confession. The roots of his

imagination were in the Pagan South and the unseemly liberation it had engendered in his father, but the discussion had
somehow remained in the Cotswolds being dripped on by
the ghosts of England's rude elms. The opportunity to make
a grand gesture and say, 'This thing of darkness I acknowledge mine,' had somehow petered out into ethical debate.

'Thanks for telling me what you've told me,' said Johnny.

'No need to get Californian about it, I'm sure it's nothing
but a burden.'

'No need to be so English,' said Johnny. 'I *am* honoured.
Any time you want to talk about it I'm available.'

Patrick felt disarmed and infinitely sad for a moment.
'Shall we head off to this wretched party?' he said.

They walked out of the dining room together, passing
David Windfall and Cindy Smith.

'There was an unexpected fluctuation in the exchange
rate,' David was explaining. 'Everyone panicked like mad,
except for me, the reason being that I was having a tremendously boozy lunch with Sonny in his club. At the end of the
day I'd made a huge amount of money from doing absolutely
nothing while everybody else had been very badly stung. My
boss was absolutely livid.'

'Do you get on well with your boss?' asked Cindy who
really couldn't have cared less.

'Of course I do,' said David. 'You Americans call it
"internal networking", we just call it good manners.'

'Gee,' said Cindy.

'We'd better go in separate cars,' said Patrick, as he walked
through the bar with Johnny, 'I might want to leave early.'

'Right,' said Johnny, 'see you there.'

8

Sonny's inner circle, the forty guests who were dining at Cheatley before the party, hung about in the Yellow Room, unable to sit down before Princess Margaret chose to.

'Do you believe in God, Nicholas?' asked Bridget, introducing Nicholas Pratt into the conversation she was having with Princess Margaret.

Nicholas rolled his eyeballs wearily, as if someone had tried to revive a tired old piece of scandal.

'What intrigues me, my dear, is whether he still believes in *us*. Or have we given the supreme schoolmaster a nervous breakdown? In any case, I think it was one of the Bibescos who said, "To a man of the world, the universe is a suburb."'

'I don't like the sound of your friend Bibesco,' said Princess Margaret, wrinkling her nose. 'How can the universe be a suburb? It's too silly.'

'What I think he meant, ma'am,' replied Nicholas, 'is that sometimes the largest questions are the most trivial, because they cannot be answered, while the seemingly trivial ones, like where one sits at dinner,' he gave this example while raising his eyebrows at Bridget, 'are the most fascinating.'

'Aren't people funny? I don't find where one sits at dinner fascinating at all,' lied the Princess. 'Besides, as you know,' she went on, 'my sister is the head of the Church of England, and I don't like listening to atheistic views. People think they're being so clever, but it just shows a lack of humility.'

Silencing Nicholas and Bridget with her disapproval, the Princess took a gulp from her glass of whisky. 'Apparently it's on the increase,' she said enigmatically.

'What is, ma'am?' asked Nicholas.

'Child abuse,' said the Princess. 'I was at a concert for the NSPCC last weekend, and they told me it's on the increase.'

'Perhaps it's just that people are more inclined to wash their dirty linen in public nowadays,' said Nicholas. 'Frankly I find *that* tendency much more worrying than all this fuss about child abuse. Children probably didn't realize they were being abused until they had to watch it on television every night. I believe in America they've started suing their parents for bringing them up badly.'

'Really?' giggled the Princess. 'I must tell Mummy, she'll be fascinated.'

Nicholas burst out laughing. 'But seriously, ma'am, the thing that worries me isn't all this child abuse, but the appalling way that people spoil their children these days.'

'Isn't it dreadful?' gasped the Princess. 'I see more and more children with absolutely no discipline at all. It's frightening.'

'Terrifying,' Nicholas confirmed.

'But I don't think that the NSPCC were talking about *our* world,' said the Princess, generously extending to Nicholas the circle of light that radiated from her presence. 'What it really shows is the emptiness of the socialist dream. They thought that every problem could be solved by throwing money at it, but it simply isn't true. People may have been poor, but they were happy because they lived in real communities. My mother says that when she visited the East End during the Blitz she met more people there with real dignity than you could hope to find in the entire corps diplomatique.'

*

'What I find with beautiful women,' said Peter Porlock to Robin Parker as they drifted towards the dining room, 'is that, after one's waited around for ages, they all arrive at once, as buses are supposed to do. Not that I've ever waited around for a bus, except at that British Heritage thing in Washington. Do you remember?'

'Yes, of course,' said Robin Parker, his eyes swimming in and out of focus, like pale blue goldfish, behind the thick lenses of his glasses. ' They hired a double-decker London bus for us.'

'Some people said "coals to Newcastle",' said Peter, 'but I was jolly pleased to see what I'd been missing all these years.'

Tony Fowles was full of amusing and frivolous ideas. Just as there were boxes at the opera where you could hear the music but not see the action, he said that there should be soundproof boxes where you could neither hear the music nor see the action, but just look at the other people with very powerful binoculars.

The Princess laughed merrily. Something about Tony's effete silliness made her feel relaxed, but all too soon she was separated from him and placed next to Sonny at the far end of the table.

'Ideally, the number of guests at a private dinner party,' said Jacques d'Alantour, raising a judicious index finger, 'should be more than the graces and less than the muses! But this,' he said, spreading his hands out and closing his eyes as if words were about to fail him, 'this is something absolutely extraordinary.'

Few people were more used than the ambassador to looking at a dinner table set for forty, but Bridget smiled radiantly at him, while trying to remember how many muses there were supposed to be.

'Do you have any politics?' Princess Margaret asked Sonny.

'Conservative, ma'am,' said Sonny proudly.

'So I assumed. But are you *involved* in politics? For myself I don't mind who's in government so long as they're good at governing. What we must avoid at all costs is these windscreen wipers: left, right, left, right.'

Sonny laughed immoderately at the thought of political windscreen wipers.

'I'm afraid I'm only involved at a very local level, ma'am,' he replied. 'The Little Soddington bypass, that sort of thing. Trying to make sure that footpaths don't spring up all over the place. People seem to think that the countryside is just an enormous park for factory workers to drop their sweet papers in. Well, those of us who live here feel rather differently about it.'

'One needs someone responsible keeping an eye on things at a local level,' said Princess Margaret reassuringly. 'So many of the things that get ruined are little out-of-the-way places that one only notices once they've already been ruined. One drives past thinking how nice they must have once been.'

'You're absolutely right, ma'am,' agreed Sonny.

'Is it venison?' asked the Princess. 'It's hard to tell under this murky sauce.'

'Yes, it is venison,' said Sonny nervously. 'I'm awfully sorry about the sauce. As you say, it's perfectly disgusting.' He could remember checking with her private secretary that the Princess liked venison.

She pushed her plate away and picked up her cigarette lighter. 'I get sent fallow deer from Richmond Park,' she said smugly. 'You have to be on the list. The Queen said to me, "Put yourself on the list," so I did.'

'How very sensible, ma'am,' simpered Sonny.

'Venison is the one meat I rr-eally don't like,' Jacques d'Alantour admitted to Caroline Porlock, 'but I don't want to create a diplomatic incident, and so . . .' He popped a piece of meat into his mouth, wearing a theatrically martyred expression which Caroline later described as being 'a bit much'.

'Do you like it? It's venison,' said Princess Margaret leaning over slightly towards Monsieur d'Alantour, who was sitting on her right.

'Really, it is something absolutely marvellous, ma'am,' said the ambassador. 'I did not know one could find such cooking in your country. The sauce is extremely subtle.' He narrowed his eyes to give an impression of subtlety.

The Princess allowed her views about the sauce to be eclipsed by the gratification of hearing England described as 'your country', which she took to be an acknowledgement of her own feeling that it belonged, if not legally, then in some much more profound sense, to her own family.

In his anxiety to show his love for the venison of merry old England, the ambassador raised his fork with such an extravagant gesture of appreciation that he flicked glistening brown globules over the front of the Princess's blue tulle dress.

'I am prostrated with horr-rror!' he exclaimed, feeling that he was on the verge of a diplomatic incident.

The Princess compressed her lips and turned down the corners of her mouth, but said nothing. Putting down the cigarette holder into which she had been screwing a cigarette, she pinched her napkin between her fingers and handed it over to Monsieur d'Alantour.

'Wipe!' she said with terrifying simplicity.

The ambassador pushed back his chair and sank to his knees obediently, first dipping the corner of the napkin in a glass of water. While he rubbed at the spots of sauce on her dress, the Princess lit her cigarette and turned to Sonny.

'I thought I couldn't dislike the sauce more when it was on my plate,' she said archly.

'The sauce has been a disaster,' said Sonny, whose face was now maroon with extra blood. 'I can't apologize enough, ma'am.'

'There's no need for *you* to apologize,' she said.

Jacqueline d'Alantour, fearing that her husband might be performing an act inconsistent with the dignity of France, had risen and walked around the table. Half the guests were pretending not to have noticed what was going on and the other half were not bothering to pretend.

'What I admire about P.M.,' said Nicholas Pratt, who sat on Bridget's left at the other end of the table, 'is the way she puts everyone at their ease.'

George Watford, who sat on Bridget's other side, decided to ignore Pratt's interruption and to carry on trying to explain to his hostess the purpose of the Commonwealth.

'I'm afraid the Commonwealth is completely ineffectual,' he said sadly. 'We have nothing in common, except our poverty. Still, it gives the Queen some pleasure,' he added, glancing down the table at Princess Margaret, 'and that is reason enough to keep it.'

Jacqueline, still unclear about what had happened, was amazed to find that her husband had sunk even deeper under the table and was rubbing furiously at the Princess's dress.

'*Mais tu es complètement cinglé,*' hissed Jacqueline. The sweating ambassador, like a groom in the Augean stables, had no time to look up.

'I have done something unpardonable!' he declared. 'I have splashed this wonder-fool sauce on Her Royal Highness's dress.'

'Ah, ma'am,' said Jacqueline to the Princess, girl to girl, 'he's so clumsy! Let me help you.'

'I'm quite happy to have your husband do it,' said the Princess. 'He spilled it, he should wipe it up! In fact, one feels he might have had a great career in dry cleaning if he hadn't been blown off course,' she said nastily.

'You must allow us to give you a new dress, ma'am,' purred Jacqueline, who could feel claws sprouting from her fingertips. '*Allez*, Jacques, it's enough!' She laughed.

'There's still a spot here,' said Princess Margaret bossily, pointing to a small stain on the upper edge of her lap.

The ambassador hesitated.

'Go on, wipe it up!'

Jacques dipped the corner of the napkin back into his glass of water, and attacked the spot with rapid little strokes.

'*Ah, non, mais c'est vraiment insupportable*,' snapped Jacqueline.

'What is "*insupportable*",' said the Princess in a nasal French accent, 'is to be showered in this revolting sauce. I needn't remind you that your husband is Ambassador to the Court of St James's,' she said as if this were somehow equivalent to being her personal maid.

Jacqueline bobbed briefly and walked back to her place, but only to grab her bag and stride out of the room.

By this time the table had fallen silent.

'Oh, a silence,' declared Princess Margaret. 'I don't approve of silences. If Noël were here,' she said, turning to Sonny, 'he'd have us all in stitches.'

'Nole, ma'am?' asked Sonny, too paralysed with terror to think clearly.

'Coward, you silly,' replied the Princess. 'He could make

one laugh for hours on end. It's the people who could make one laugh,' she said, puffing sensitively on her cigarette, 'whom one really misses.'

Sonny, already mortified by the presence of venison at his table, was now exasperated by the absence of Noël. The fact that Noël was long dead did nothing to mitigate Sonny's sense of failure, and he would have sunk into speechless gloom had he not been saved by the Princess, who found herself in a thoroughly good mood after asserting her dignity and establishing in such a spectacular fashion that she was the most important person in the room.

'Remind me, Sonny,' she said chattily, 'do you have any children?'

'Yes, indeed, ma'am, I have a daughter.'

'How old is she?' asked the Princess brightly.

'It's hard to believe,' said Sonny, 'but she must be seven by now. It won't be long before she's at the blue-jean stage,' he added ominously.

'Oh,' groaned the Princess, making a disagreeable face, a muscular contraction that cost her little effort, 'aren't they dreadful? They're a sort of uniform. And so scratchy. I can't imagine why one would want to look like everyone else. I know I don't.'

'Absolutely, ma'am,' said Sonny.

'When my children got to that stage,' confided the Princess, 'I said, "For goodness' sake, don't get those dreadful blue jeans," and they very sensibly went out and bought themselves some green trousers.'

'Very sensible,' echoed Sonny, who was hysterically grateful that the Princess had decided to be so friendly.

Jacqueline returned after five minutes, hoping to give the impression that she had only absented herself because, as one mistress of modern manners has put it, 'certain bodily functions are best performed in private'. In fact she had paced about her bedroom furiously until she came to the reluctant conclusion that a show of levity would in the end be less humiliating than a show of indignation. Knowing also that what her husband feared most, and had spent his career nimbly avoiding, was a diplomatic incident, she hastily applied some fresh lipstick and breezed back into the dining room.

Seeing Jacqueline return, Sonny experienced a fresh wave of anxiety, but the Princess ignored her completely and started telling him one of her stories about 'the ordinary people of this country' in whom she had 'enormous faith' based on a combination of complete ignorance about their lives and complete confidence in their royalist sympathies.

'I was in a taxi once,' she began in a tone that invited Sonny to marvel at her audacity. He duly raised his eyebrows with what he hoped was a tactful combination of surprise and admiration. 'And Tony said to the driver, "Take us to the Royal Garden Hotel," which, as you know, is at the bottom of our drive. And the driver said – ' the Princess leaned forward to deliver the punch line with a rough little jerk of her head, in what might have been mistaken by a Chinaman for a Cockney accent – '"I know where *she* lives."' She grinned at Sonny. 'Aren't they wonderful people?' she squawked. 'Aren't they marvellous people?'

Sonny threw back his head and roared with laughter. 'What a splendid story, ma'am,' he gasped. 'What wonderful people.'

The Princess sat back in her chair well satisfied; she had charmed her host and lent a golden touch to the evening. As to the clumsy Frenchman on her other side, she wasn't going to let him off the hook so easily. After all, it was no small matter to make a mistake in the presence of the Queen's sister. The constitution itself rested on respect for the Crown, and it was her duty (oh, how she sometimes wished she could lay it all aside! How, in fact, she sometimes did, only to scold more severely those who thought she was serious), yes, it was her *duty* to maintain that respect. It was the price she had to pay for what other people foolishly regarded as her great privileges.

Next to her the ambassador appeared to be in a kind of trance, but under his dumb surface he was composing, with the fluency of an habitual dispatch writer, his report for the Quai d'Orsay. The glory of France had not been diminished by his little gaffe. Indeed, he had turned what might have been an awkward incident into a triumphant display of gallantry and wit. It was here that the ambassador paused for a while to think of something clever he might have said at the time.

While Alantour pondered, the door of the dining room opened slowly, and Belinda, barefooted, in a white nightdress, peered around the edge of the door.

'Oh, look, it's a little person who can't sleep,' boomed Nicholas.

Bridget swivelled around and saw her daughter looking pleadingly into the room.

'Who is it?' the Princess asked Sonny.

'I'm afraid it's my daughter, ma'am,' replied Sonny, glaring at Bridget.

'Still up? She should be in bed. Go on, tuck her up immediately!' she snapped.

Something about the way she had said 'tuck her up' made Sonny momentarily forget his courtly graces and feel protective towards his daughter. He tried again to catch Bridget's eye, but Belinda had already come into the room and approached her mother.

'Why are you still up, darling?' asked Bridget.

'I couldn't sleep,' said Belinda. 'I was lonely because everyone else is down here.'

'But this is a dinner for grown-ups.'

'Which one's Princess Margaret?' asked Belinda, ignoring her mother's explanation.

'Why don't you get your mother to present you to her?' suggested Nicholas suavely. 'And then you can go to bed like a good little girl.'

'OK,' said Belinda. 'Can someone read me a story?'

'Not tonight, darling,' said her mother. 'But I'll introduce you to Princess Margaret.' She got up and walked the length of the table to Princess Margaret's side. Leaning over a little, she asked if she could present her daughter.

'No, not now, I don't think it's right,' said the Princess. 'She ought to be in bed, and she'll just get overexcited.'

'You're quite right, of course,' said Sonny. 'Honestly, darling, you must scold Nanny for letting her escape.'

'I'll take her upstairs myself,' said Bridget coldly.

'Good girl,' said Sonny, extremely angry that Nanny, who after all cost one an absolute bomb, should have shown him up in front of the Princess.

'I'm very pleased to hear that you've got the Bishop of Cheltenham for us tomorrow,' said the Princess, grinning at her host, once the door was firmly closed on his wife and daughter.

'Yes,' said Sonny. 'He seemed very nice on the phone.'

'Do you mean you don't know him?' asked the Princess.

'Not as well as I'd like to,' said Sonny, reeling from the prospect of more royal disapproval.

'He's a saint,' said the Princess warmly. 'I really think he's a saint. And a wonderful scholar: I'm told he's happier speaking in Greek than in English. Isn't it marvellous?'

'I'm afraid my Greek's a bit rusty for that sort of thing,' said Sonny.

'Don't worry,' said the Princess, 'he's the most modest man in the world, he wouldn't dream of showing you up;

he just gets into these Greek trances. In his mind, you see, he's still chatting away to the apostles, and it takes him a while to notice his surroundings. Isn't it fascinating?'

'Extraordinary,' murmured Sonny.

'There won't be any hymns, of course,' said the Princess.

'But we can have some if you like,' protested Sonny.

'It's Holy Communion, silly. Otherwise I'd have you all singing hymns to see which ones I liked best. People always seem to enjoy it, it gives one something to do after dinner on Saturday.'

'We couldn't have managed that tonight in any case,' said Sonny.

'Oh, I don't know,' said the Princess, 'we might have gone off to the library in a small group.' She beamed at Sonny, conscious of the honour she was bestowing on him by this suggestion of deeper intimacy. There was no doubt about it: when she put her mind to it she could be the most charming woman in the world.

'One had such fun practising hymns with Noël,' she went on. 'He would make up new words and one would die laughing. Yes, it might have been rather cosy in the library. I do so *hate* big parties.'

9

Patrick slammed the car door and glanced up at the stars, gleaming through a break in the clouds like fresh track marks in the dark blue limbs of the night. It was a humbling experience, he thought, making one's own medical problems seem so insignificant.

An avenue of candles, planted on either side of the drive, marked the way from the car park to the wide circle of gravel in front of the house. Its grey porticoed facade was theatrically flattened by floodlights, and looked like wet cardboard, stained by the sleet that had fallen earlier in the afternoon.

In the denuded drawing room, the fireplace was loaded with crackling wood. The champagne being poured by a flushed barman surged over the sides of glasses and subsided again to a drop. As Patrick headed down the hooped canvas tunnel that led to the tent, he heard the swell of voices rising, and sometimes laughter, like the top of a wave caught by the wind, splashing over the whole room. A room, he decided, full of uncertain fools, waiting for an amorous complication or a practical joke to release them from their awkward wanderings. Walking into the tent, he saw George Watford sitting on a chair immediately to the right of the entrance.

'George!'

'My dear, what a nice surprise,' said George, wincing as he clambered to his feet. 'I'm sitting here because I can't hear anything these days when there's a lot of noise about.'

'I thought people were supposed to lead lives of *quiet* desperation,' Patrick shouted.

'Not quiet enough,' George shouted back with a wan smile.

'Oh look, there's Nicholas Pratt,' said Patrick, sitting down next to George.

'So it is,' said George. 'With him one has to take the smooth with the smooth. I must say I never really shared your father's enthusiasm for him. I miss your father, you know, Patrick. He was a very brilliant man, but never happy, I think.'

'I hardly ever think of him these days,' said Patrick.

'Have you found something you enjoy doing?' asked George.

'Yes, but nothing one could make a career out of,' said Patrick.

'One really has to try to make a contribution,' said George. 'I can look back with reasonable satisfaction on one or two pieces of legislation that I helped steer through the House of Lords. I've also helped to keep Richfield going for the next generation. Those are the sorts of things one is left hanging on to when all the fun and games have slipped away. No man is an island – although one's known a surprising number who own one. Really a surprising number, and not just in Scotland. But one really must try to make a contribution.'

'Of course you're right,' sighed Patrick. He was rather intimidated by George's sincerity. It reminded him of the disconcerting occasion when his father had clasped his arm, and said to him, apparently without any hostile intention, 'If you have a talent, use it. Or you'll be miserable all your life.'

'Oh, look, it's Tom Charles, over there taking a drink from the waiter. He has a jolly nice island in Maine. Tom!' George called out. 'I wonder if he's spotted us. He was head

398

of the IMF at one time, made the best of a frightfully hard job.'

'I met him in New York,' said Patrick. 'You introduced us at that club we went to after my father died.'

'Oh, yes. We all rather wondered what had happened to you,' said George. 'You left us in the lurch with that frightful bore Ballantine Morgan.'

'I was overwhelmed with emotion,' said Patrick.

'I should think it was dread at having to listen to another of Ballantine's stories. His son is here tonight. I'm afraid he's a chip off the old block, as they say. Tom!' George called out again.

Tom Charles looked around, uncertain whether he'd heard his name being called. George waved at him again. Tom spotted them, and the three men greeted each other. Patrick recognized Tom's bloodhound features. He had one of those faces that ages prematurely but then goes on looking the same forever. He might even look young in another twenty years.

'I heard about your dinner,' said Tom. 'It sounds like quite something.'

'Yes,' said George. 'I think it demonstrates again that the junior members of the royal family should pull their socks up and we should all be praying for the Queen during these difficult times.'

Patrick realized he was not joking.

'How was your dinner at Harold's?' asked George. 'Harold Greene was born in Germany,' he went on to explain to Patrick. 'As a boy he wanted to join the Hitler Youth – smashing windows and wearing all those thrilling uniforms: it's any boy's dream – but his father told him he couldn't because he was Jewish. Harold never got over the disappointment, and he's really an anti-Semite with a veneer of Zionism.'

'Oh, I don't think that's fair,' said Tom.

'Well, I don't suppose it is,' said George, 'but what is the point of reaching this idiotically advanced age if one can't be unfair?'

'There was a lot of talk at dinner about Chancellor Kohl's claim that he was "very shocked" when war broke out in the Gulf.'

'I suppose it was shocking for the poor Germans not to have started the war themselves,' George interjected.

'Harold was saying over dinner,' continued Tom, 'that he's surprised there isn't a United Nations Organisation called UNUC because "when it comes down to it they're no bloody use at all".'

'What I want to know,' said George, thrusting out his chin, 'is what chance we have against the Japanese when we live in a country where "industrial action" means going on strike. I'm afraid I've lived for too long. I can still remember when this country counted for something. I was just saying to Patrick,' he added, politely drawing him back into the conversation, 'that one has to make a contribution in life. There are too many people in this room who are just hanging around waiting for their relations to die so that they can go on more expensive holidays. Sadly, I count my daughter-in-law among them.'

'Bunch of vultures,' growled Tom. 'They'd better take those holidays soon. I don't see the banking system holding up, except on some kind of religious basis.'

'Currency always rested on blind faith,' said George.

'But it's never been like this before,' said Tom. 'Never has so much been owed by so many to so few.'

'I'm too old to care anymore,' said George. 'Do you know, I was thinking that if I go to heaven, and I don't see why I shouldn't, I hope that King, my old butler, will be there.'

'To do your unpacking?' suggested Patrick.

'Oh, no,' said George. 'I think he's done quite enough of that sort of thing down here. In any case, I don't think one takes any luggage to heaven, do you? It must be like a perfect weekend, with no luggage.'

Like a rock in the middle of a harbour, Sonny stood stoutly near the entrance of the tent putting his guests under an obligation to greet him as they came in.

'But this is something absolutely marvellous,' said Jacques d'Alantour in a confidential tone, spreading his hands to encompass the whole tent. As if responding to this gesture the big jazz band at the far end of the room struck up simultaneously.

'Well, we try our best,' said Sonny smugly.

'I think it was Henry James,' said the ambassador, who knew perfectly well that it was and had rehearsed the quotation, unearthed for him by his secretary, many times before leaving Paris, 'who said: "this richly complex English world, where the present is always seen, as it were in profile, and the past presents a full face." '

'It's no use quoting these French authors to me,' said Sonny. 'All goes over my head. But, yes, English life is rich and complex – although not as rich as it used to be with all these taxes gnawing away at the very fabric of one's house.'

'Ah,' sighed Monsieur d'Alantour sympathetically. 'But you are putting on a "brave face" tonight.'

'We've had our tricky moments,' Sonny confessed. 'Bridget went through a mad phase of thinking we knew nobody, and invited all sorts of odds and sods. Take that little Indian chap over there, for instance. He's writing a biography of Jonathan Croyden. I'd never set eyes on him before he came down to look at some letters Croyden wrote to my father, and blow me down, Bridget asked him to the party over lunch. I'm afraid I lost my temper with her afterwards, but it really was a bit much.'

'Hello, my dear,' said Nicholas to Ali Montague. 'How was your dinner?'

'Very *county*,' said Ali.

'Oh, dear. Well, ours was really *tous ce qu'il y a de plus chic*, except that Princess Margaret rapped me over the knuckles for expressing "atheistic views".'

'Even I might have a religious conversion under those circumstances,' said Ali, 'but it would be so hypocritical I'd be sent straight to hell.'

'One thing I am sure of is that if God didn't exist, nobody would notice the difference,' said Nicholas suavely.

'Oh, I thought of you a moment ago,' said Ali. 'I overheard a couple of old men who both looked as if they'd had several riding accidents. One of them said, "I'm thinking of writing a book," and the other one replied, "Jolly good idea." "They say everyone has a book in them," said the would-be author. "Hmm, perhaps I'll write one as well," his friend replied. "Now you're stealing my idea," said the first one, really quite angrily. So naturally I wondered how your book was getting along. I suppose it must be almost finished by now.'

'It's very difficult to finish an autobiography when you're leading as thrilling a life as I am,' said Nicholas sarcastically. 'One constantly finds some new nugget that has to be put in, like a sample of your conversation, my dear.'

'There's always an element of cooperation in incest,' said Kitty Harrow knowingly. 'I know it's supposed to be fearfully taboo, but of course it's always gone on, sometimes in the very best families,' she added complacently, touching the cliff of blue-grey hair that towered over her small forehead. 'I remember my own father standing outside my bedroom door hissing, "You're completely hopeless, you've got no sexual imagination." '

'Good God!' said Robin Parker.

'My father was a marvellous man, very magnetic.' Kitty rolled her shoulders as she said this. 'Everybody adored him. So, you see, I *know* what I'm talking about. Children give off the most enormous sexual feeling; they set out to seduce their parents. It's all in Freud, I'm told, although I haven't read his books myself. I remember my son always showing me his little erection. I don't think parents should take advantage of these situations, but I can quite see how they get swept along, especially in crowded conditions with everybody living on top of each other.'

'Is your son here?' asked Robin Parker.

'No, he's in Australia,' Kitty replied sadly. 'I begged him to take over running the farm here, but he's mad about Australian sheep. I've been to see him twice, but I really can't manage the plane flight. And when I get there I'm not at all keen on that way of life, standing in a cloud of barbecue smoke being bored to death by a sheepshearer's wife – one doesn't even get the sheepshearer. Fergus took me to the coast and *forced* me to go snorkelling. All I can say is that the Great Barrier Reef is the most vulgar thing I've ever seen. It's one's worst nightmare, full of frightful loud colours, peacock blues, and impossible oranges all higgledy-piggledy while one's mask floods.'

'The Queen was saying only the other day that London property prices are so high that she doesn't know how she'd cope without Buckingham Palace,' Princess Margaret explained to a sympathetic Peter Porlock.

'How are you?' Nicholas asked Patrick.

'Dying for a drink,' said Patrick.

'Well you have all my sympathy,' yawned Nicholas. 'I've never been addicted to heroin, but I had to give up smoking cigarettes, which was quite bad enough for me. Oh, look, there's Princess Margaret. One has to be so careful not to trip over her. I suppose you've already heard what happened at dinner.'

'The diplomatic incident.'

'Yes.'

'Very shocking,' said Patrick solemnly.

'I must say, I rather admire P.M.,' said Nicholas, glancing over at her condescendingly. 'She used a minor accident to screw the maximum amount of humiliation out of the ambassador. Somebody has to uphold our national pride during its Alzheimer years, and there's no one who does it with more conviction. Mind you,' said Nicholas in a more withering tone, '*entre nous*, since I'm relying on them to give me a lift back to London, I don't think France has been so heroically represented since the Vichy government. You should have seen the way Alantour slid to his knees. Although I'm absolutely devoted to his wife who, behind all that phoney chic, is a genuinely malicious person with whom one can have the greatest fun, I've always thought Jacques was a bit of a fool.'

'You can tell him yourself,' said Patrick as he saw the ambassador approaching from behind.

'*Mon cher* Jacques,' said Nicholas, spinning lightly round, 'I thought you were absolutely brilliant! The way you handled that tiresome woman was faultless: by giving in to her ridiculous demands you showed just how ridiculous they were. Do you know my young friend Patrick Melrose? His father was a very good friend of mine.'

'René Bollinger was such heaven,' sighed the Princess. 'He was a really great ambassador, we all absolutely adored him. It makes it all the harder to put up with the mediocrity of these two,' she added, waving her cigarette holder towards the Alantours, to whom Patrick was saying goodbye.

'I hope we didn't dr-rive away your young friend,' said Jacqueline. 'He seemed very nervous.'

'We can do without him even if I am a great advocate of diversity,' said Nicholas.

'You?' laughed Jacqueline.

'Absolutely, my dear,' Nicholas replied. 'I firmly believe that one should have the widest possible range of acquaintances, from monarchs right down to the humblest baronet in the land. With, of course, a sprinkling of superstars,' he added, like a great chef introducing a rare but pungent spice into his stew, 'before they turn, as they inevitably do, into black holes.'

'*Mais il est vraiment* too much,' said Jacqueline, delighted by Nicholas's performance.

'One's better off with a title than a mere name,' Nicholas continued. 'Proust, as I'm sure you're aware, writes very beautifully on this subject, saying that even the most fashionable commoner is bound to be forgotten very quickly, whereas the bearer of a great title is certain of immortality, at least in the eyes of his descendants.'

'Still,' said Jacqueline a little limply, 'there have been some very amusing people without titles.'

'My dear,' said Nicholas, clasping her forearm, 'what would we do without them?'

They laughed the innocent laughter of two snobs taking a holiday from that need to appear tolerant and open-minded which marred what Nicholas still called 'modern life', although he had never known any other kind.

'I feel the royal presence bearing down on us,' said Jacques uncomfortably. 'I think the diplomatic course is to explore the depths of the party.'

'My dear fellow, you are the depths of the party,' said Nicholas. 'But I quite agree, you shouldn't expose yourself to any more petulance from that absurd woman.'

'*Au revoir*,' whispered Jacqueline.

'*A bientôt*,' said Jacques, and the Alantours withdrew and separated, taking the burden of their glamour to different parts of the room.

Nicholas had hardly recovered from the loss of the Alantours when Princess Margaret and Kitty Harrow came over to his side.

'Consorting with the enemy,' scowled the Princess.

'They came to me for sympathy, ma'am,' said Nicholas indignantly, 'but I told them they'd come to the wrong place. I pointed out to him that he was a clumsy fool. And as to his absurd wife, I said that we'd had quite enough of her petulance for one evening.'

'Oh, did you?' said the Princess, smiling graciously.

'Good for you,' chipped in Kitty.

'As you saw,' boasted Nicholas, 'they slunk off with their tails between their legs. "I'd better keep a low profile," the ambassador said to me. "You've got a low enough profile already," I replied.'

'Oh, how marvellous,' said the Princess. 'Putting your sharp tongue to good use, I approve of that.'

'I suppose this'll go straight into your book,' said Kitty. 'We're all terrified, ma'am, by what Nicholas is going to say about us in his book.'

'Am I in it?' asked the Princess.

'I wouldn't dream of putting you in, ma'am,' protested Nicholas. 'I'm far too discreet.'

'You're allowed to put me in it as long as you say something nice,' said the Princess.

*

'I remember you when you were five years old,' said Bridget. 'You were so sweet, but rather standoffish.'

'I can't imagine why,' said Patrick. 'I remember seeing you kneeling down on the terrace just after you arrived. I was watching from behind the trees.'

'Oh God,' squealed Bridget. 'I'd forgotten that.'

'I couldn't work out what you were doing.'

'It was very shocking.'

'I'm unshockable,' said Patrick.

'Well, if you really want to know, Nicholas had told me it was something your parents did: your father making your mother eat figs off the ground, and I was rather naughtily acting out what he'd told me. He got frightfully angry with me.'

'It's nice to think of my parents having fun,' said Patrick.

'I think it was a power thing,' said Bridget, who seldom dabbled in deep psychology.

'Sounds plausible,' said Patrick.

'Oh God, there's Mummy, looking terribly lost,' said Bridget. 'You wouldn't be an angel and talk to her for a second, would you?'

'Of course,' said Patrick.

Bridget left Patrick with Virginia, congratulating herself on solving her mother problem so neatly.

'So how was your dinner here?' said Patrick, trying to open the conversation on safe ground. 'I gather Princess Margaret got showered in brown sauce. It must have been a thrilling moment.'

'I wouldn't have found it thrilling,' said Virginia. 'I know how upsetting it can be getting a stain on your dress.'

'So you didn't actually see it,' said Patrick.

'No, I was having dinner with the Bossington-Lanes,' said Virginia.

'Really? I was supposed to be there. How was it?'

'We got lost on the way there,' sighed Virginia. 'All the cars were busy collecting people from the station, so I had to go by taxi. We stopped at a cottage that turned out to be just at the bottom of their drive and asked the way. When I said to Mr Bossington-Lane, "We had to ask the way from your neighbour in the cottage with the blue windows," he said to me, "That's not a neighbour, that's a tenant, and what's more he's a sitting tenant and a damned nuisance."'

'Neighbours are people you can ask to dinner,' said Patrick.

'That makes me his neighbour, then,' laughed Virginia. 'And I live in Kent. I don't know why my daughter told me they needed spare ladies, there were nothing but spare ladies. Mrs Bossington-Lane told me just now that she's had apologies from all four gentlemen who didn't turn up, and they all said they'd broken down on the motorway. She was very put out, after all the trouble she'd been to, but I said, "You've got to keep your sense of humour."'

'I thought she looked unconvinced when I told her I'd broken down on the motorway,' said Patrick.

'Oh,' said Virginia, clapping her hand over her mouth. 'You must have been one of them. I'd forgotten you said you were supposed to have dinner there.'

'Don't worry,' smiled Patrick. 'I just wish we'd compared stories before all telling her the same one.'

Virginia laughed. 'You've got to keep your sense of humour,' she repeated.

'What is it, darling?' asked Aurora Donne. 'You look as if you've seen a ghost.'

'Oh, I don't know,' sighed Bridget. 'I just saw Cindy Smith with Sonny – and I remember saying that we couldn't ask her because we didn't know her, and thinking it was odd of

Sonny to make a thing of it – and now she's here and there was something familiar about the way they stood together, but I'm probably just being paranoid.'

Aurora, presented with the choice of telling a friend a painful truth which could do her no possible good, or reassuring her, felt no hesitation in taking the first course for the sake of 'honesty', and the pleasure of seeing Bridget's enjoyment of her expensive life, which Aurora had often told herself she would have handled better, spoiled.

'I don't know whether I should tell you this,' said Aurora. 'I probably shouldn't.' She frowned, glancing at Bridget.

'What?' Bridget implored her. 'You've got to tell me.'

'No,' said Aurora. 'It'll only upset you. It was stupid of me to mention it.'

'You *have* to tell me now,' said Bridget desperately.

'Well, of course you're the last to know – one always is in these situations, but it's been fairly common knowledge . . .' Aurora lingered suggestively on the word 'common' which she had always been fond of, 'that Sonny and Miss Smith have been having an affair for some time.'

'God,' said Bridget. 'So that's who it is. I knew something was going on . . .' She suddenly felt very tired and sad, and looked as if she was going to cry.

'Oh, darling, don't,' said Aurora. 'Chin up,' she added consolingly.

But Bridget was overwhelmed and went up with Aurora to her bedroom and told her all about the telephone call she'd overheard that morning, swearing her to a secrecy to which Aurora swore several other people before the evening was out. Bridget's friend advised her to 'go on the warpath', thinking this was the policy likely to yield the largest number of amusing anecdotes.

*

'Oh, do come and help us,' said China who was sitting with Angus Broghlie and Amanda Pratt. It was not a group that Patrick had any appetite to join.

'We're making a list of all the people whose fathers aren't really their fathers,' she explained.

'Hmm, I'd do anything to be on it,' groaned Patrick. 'Anyway, it would take far too long to do in one evening.'

David Windfall, driven by a fanatical desire to exonerate himself from the blame of bringing Cindy Smith and making his hostess angry, rushed up to his fellow guests to explain that he had just been obeying orders, and it wasn't really his idea. He was about to make the same speech to Peter Porlock when he realized that Peter, as Sonny's best friend, might view it as faint-hearted, and so he checked himself and remarked instead on 'that dreadful christening' where they had last met.

'Dreadful,' confirmed Peter. 'What's the vestry for, if it isn't to dump babies along with one's umbrella and so forth? But of course the vicar wanted all the children in the church. He's a sort of flower child who believes in swinging services, but the purpose of the Church of England is to be the Church of England. It's a force of social cohesion. If it's going to get evangelical we don't want anything to do with it.'

'Hear, hear,' said David. 'I gather Bridget's very upset about my bringing Cindy Smith,' he added, unable to keep away from the subject.

'Absolutely furious,' laughed Peter. 'She had a blazing row with Sonny in the library, I'm told: audible above the band and the din, apparently. Poor Sonny, he's been locked in there all evening,' grinned Peter, nodding his head towards the door. 'Stole in there to have a *tête-à-tête*, or rather a *jambe-à-jambe*, I should imagine, with Miss Smith, then the blazing row, and now he's stuck with Robin Parker trying to cheer himself up by having his Poussin authenticated. The thing is for you to stick to your story. You met Cindy, wife couldn't come, asked her instead, foolishly didn't check, nothing to do with Sonny. Something along those lines.'

'Of course,' said David who had already told a dozen people the opposite story.

'Bridget didn't actually see them at it, and you know how women are in these situations: they believe what they want to believe.'

'Hmm,' said David, who'd already told Bridget he was just obeying orders. He winced as he saw Sonny emerging from the library nearby. Did Sonny know that he'd told Bridget?

'Sonny!' squealed David, his voice slipping into falsetto.

Sonny ignored him and boomed, 'It is a Poussin!' to Peter.

'Oh, well done,' said Peter, as if Sonny had painted it himself. 'Best possible birthday present to find that it's the real thing and not just a "school of"—'

'The trees,' said Robin, slipping his hand inside his dinner jacket for a moment, 'are unmistakable.'

'Will you excuse us?' Sonny asked Robin, still ignoring David. 'I have to have a word with Peter in private.' Sonny and Peter went into the library and closed the door.

'I've been a bloody fool,' said Sonny. 'Not least for trusting David Windfall. That's the last time I'm having him under my roof. And now I've got a wife crisis on my hands.'

'Don't be too hard on yourself,' said Peter needlessly.

'Well, you know, I was driven to it,' said Sonny, immediately taking up Peter's suggestion. 'I mean, Bridget's not having a son and everything has been frightfully hard. But when it comes to the crunch I'm not sure I'd like life here without the old girl running the place. Cindy has got some very peculiar ideas. I'm not sure what they are, but I can sense it.'

'The trouble is it's all become so complicated,' said Peter. 'One doesn't really know where one stands with women. I mean, I was reading about this sixteenth-century Russian marriage-guidance thing, and it advises you to beat your wife lovingly so as not to render her permanently blind or deaf. If you said that sort of thing nowadays they'd string you up. But, you know, there's a lot in it, obviously in a slightly milder form. It's like the old adage about native bearers: "Beat them for no reason and they won't give you a reason to beat them."'

Sonny looked a little bewildered. As he later told some of his friends, 'When it was all hands on deck with the Bridget crisis, I'm afraid Peter didn't really pull his weight. He just waffled on about sixteenth-century Russian pamphlets.'

'It was that lovely judge Melford Stevens,' said Kitty, 'who said to a rapist, "I shall not send you to prison but back to the Midlands, which is punishment enough." I know one isn't meant to say that sort of thing, but it is rather marvellous, isn't it? I mean England used to be full of that sort of wonderfully eccentric character, but now everybody is so grey and goody-goody.'

'I frightfully dislike this bit,' said Sonny, struggling to keep up the appearance of a jovial host. 'Why does the band leader introduce the musicians, as if anyone wanted to know their names? I mean, one's given up announcing one's own guests, so why should these chaps get themselves announced?'

'Couldn't agree with you more, old bean,' said Alexander Politsky. 'In Russia, the grand families had their own estate band, and there was no more question of introducing them than there was of presenting your scullion to a grand duke. When we went shooting and there was a cold river to cross, the beaters would lie in the water and form a sort of bridge. Nobody felt they had to know their names in order to walk over their heads.'

'I think that's going a bit far,' said Sonny. 'I mean, walking over their heads. But, you see, that's why we didn't have a revolution.'

'The reason you didn't have a revolution, old bean,' said Alexander, 'is because you had two of them: the Civil War and the Glorious one.'

'And on cornet,' said Joe Martin, the band leader, '"Chilly Willy" Watson!'

Patrick, who had been paying almost no attention to the introductions, was intrigued by the sound of a familiar name. It certainly couldn't be the Chilly Willy he'd known in New York. He must be dead by now. Patrick glanced round anyway to have a look at the man who was standing up in the front row to play his brief solo. With his bulging cheeks and his dinner jacket he couldn't have been less reminiscent of the street junkie whom Patrick had scored from in Alphabet City. Chilly Willy had been a toothless, hollow-cheeked scavenger, shuffling about on the edge of oblivion, clutching on to a pair of trousers too baggy for his cadaverous frame. This jazz musician was vigorous and talented, and definitely black, whereas Chilly, with his jaundice and his pallor, although obviously a black man, had managed to look yellow.

Patrick moved towards the edge of the bandstand to have a closer look. There were probably thousands of Chilly Willys and it was absurd to think that this one was 'his'. Chilly had sat down again after playing his solo and Patrick stood in front of him frowning curiously, like a child at the zoo, feeling that talking was a barrier he couldn't cross.

'Hi,' said Chilly Willy, over the sound of a trumpet solo.

'Nice solo,' said Patrick.

'Thanks.'

'You're not . . . I knew someone in New York called Chilly Willy!'

'Where'd he live?'

'Eighth Street.'

'Uh-huh,' said Chilly. 'What did he do?'

'Well, he . . . sold . . . he lived on the streets really . . . that's why I knew it couldn't be you. Anyway, he was older.'

'I remember you!' laughed Chilly. 'You're the English guy with the coat, right?'

'That's right!' said Patrick. 'It is you! Christ, you look well. I practically didn't recognize you. You play really well too.'

'Thanks. I was always a musician, then I . . .' Chilly made a diving motion with his hand, glancing sideways at his fellow musicians.

'What happened to your wife?'

'She OD'd,' said Chilly sadly.

'Oh, I'm sorry,' said Patrick, remembering the horse syringe she had carefully unwrapped from the loo paper and charged him twenty dollars for. 'Well, it's a miracle you're alive,' he added.

'Yeah, everything's a miracle, man,' said Chilly. 'It's a fuckin' miracle we don't melt in the bath like a piece of soap.'

'The Herberts have always had a weakness for low life,' said Kitty Harrow. 'Look at Shakespeare.'

'They were certainly scraping the barrel with him,' said Nicholas. 'Society used to consist of a few hundred families all of whom knew each other. Now it just consists of one: the Guinnesses. I don't know why they don't make an address book with an especially enlarged G spot.'

Kitty giggled.

'Oh, well, I can see that you're an entrepreneur *manqué*,' said Ali to Nicholas.

'That dinner at the Bossington-Lanes' was beyond anything,' said Ali Montague to Laura and China. 'I knew we were in trouble when our host said, "The great thing about having daughters is that you can get them to fag for you." And when that great horsy girl of his came back she said, "You can't argue with Daddy, he used to have exactly the same vital statistics as Muhammad Ali, except he was a foot and a half shorter."'

Laura and China laughed. Ali was such a good mimic.

'The mother's absolutely terrified,' said Laura, 'because some friend of Charlotte's went up to "the Metrop" to share a flat with a couple of other county gals, and the first week she fell in with someone called "Evil John"!'

They all howled with laughter.

'What really terrifies Mr Bossington-Lane,' said Ali, 'is Charlotte getting an education.'

'Fat chance,' said Laura.

'He was complaining about a neighbour's daughter who had "a practically unheard of number of Os".'

'What, three?' suggested China.

'I think it was five and she was going on to do an A level in history of art. I asked him if there was any money in art, just to get him going.'

'And what did he say?' asked China.

Ali thrust out his chin and pushed a hand into his dinner jacket pocket with a thumb resting over the edge.

'"Money?" he boomed. "Not for most of them. But you know, one's dealing with people who are too busy struggling with the meaning of life to worry about that sort of thing. Not that one isn't struggling a bit oneself!" I said I thought the meaning of life included a large income. "And capital," he said.'

'The daughter is impossible,' grinned Laura. 'She told me a really boring story that I couldn't be bothered to listen to, and then ended it by saying, "Can you imagine anything worse than having your barbecue sausage stolen?" I said,

"Yes, easily." And she made a dreadful honking sound and said, "Well, obviously, I didn't mean *literally*."'

'Still, it's nice of them to have us to stay,' said China provocatively.

'Do you know how many of those horrid porcelain knick-knacks I counted in my room?' Ali asked with a supercilious expression on his face to exaggerate the shock of the answer he was about to give.

'How many?' asked Laura.

'One hundred and thirty-seven.'

'A hundred and thirty-seven,' gasped China.

'And, apparently, if one of them moves, she knows about it,' said Ali.

'She once had everyone's luggage searched because one of the knick-knacks had been taken from the bedroom to the bathroom or the bathroom to the bedroom, and she thought it was stolen.'

'It's quite tempting to try and smuggle one out,' said Laura.

'Do you know what's rather fascinating?' said Ali, hurrying on to his next insight. 'That old woman with the nice face and the ghastly blue dress was Bridget's mother.'

'No!' said Laura. 'Why wasn't she at dinner here?'

'Embarrassed,' said Ali.

'How awful,' said China.

'Mind you, I do see what she means,' said Ali. 'The mother *is* rather Surrey Pines.'

'I saw Debbie,' said Johnny.

'Really? How was she looking?' asked Patrick.

'Beautiful.'

'She always looked beautiful at big parties,' said Patrick. 'I must talk to her one of these days. It's easy to forget that she's just another human being, with a body and a face and almost certainly a cigarette, and that she may well no longer be the same person that I knew.'

'How have you been feeling since dinner?' asked Johnny.

'Pretty weird to begin with, but I'm glad we talked.'

'Good,' said Johnny. He felt awkward not knowing what more to say about their earlier conversation, but not wanting to pretend it had never happened. 'Oh, I thought of you during my meeting,' he said with artificial brightness. 'There was this man who had to switch off his television last night because he thought he was putting the presenters off.'

'Oh, I used to get that,' said Patrick. 'When my father died in New York one of the longest conversations I had (if I is the right pronoun in this case) was with the television set.'

'I remember you telling me,' said Johnny.

The two men fell silent and stared at the throng that struggled under wastes of grey velvet with the same frantic but restricted motion as bacteria multiplying under a microscope.

'It takes about a hundred of these ghosts to precipitate one flickering and disreputable sense of identity,' said Patrick. 'These are the sort of people who were around during my childhood: hard dull people who seemed quite sophisticated but were in fact as ignorant as swans.'

'They're the last Marxists,' said Johnny unexpectedly. 'The last people who believe that class is a total explanation. Long after that doctrine has been abandoned in Moscow and Peking it will continue to flourish under the marquees of England. Although most of them have the courage of a half-eaten worm,' he continued, warming to his theme, 'and the intellectual vigour of dead sheep, they are the true heirs to Marx and Lenin.'

'You'd better go and tell them,' said Patrick. 'I think most of them were expecting to inherit a bit of Gloucestershire instead.'

*

'Every man has his price,' said Sonny tartly. 'Wouldn't you agree, Robin?'

'Oh, yes,' said Robin, 'but he must make sure that his price isn't too low.'

'I'm sure most people are very careful to do that,' said Sonny, wondering what would happen if Robin blackmailed him.

'But it's not just money that corrupts people,' said Jacqueline d'Alantour. 'We had the most wonder-fool driver called Albert. He was a very sweet, gentle man who used to tell the most touching story you could imagine about operating on his goldfish. One day, when Jacques was going shooting, his loader fell ill and so he said, "I'll have to take Albert." I said, "But you can't, it will kill him, he adores animals, he won't be able to bear the sight of all that blood." But Jacques insisted, and he's a very stubborn man, so there was nothing I could do. When the first few birds were shot, poor Albert was in agony,' Jacqueline covered her eyes theatrically, 'but then he started to get interested,' she parted her fingers and peeped out between them. 'And now,' she said, flinging her hands down, 'he subscribes to the *Shooting Times*, and has every kind of gun magazine you can possibly imagine. It's become quite dangerous to drive around with him because every time there's a pigeon, which in London is every two metres, he says, "Monsieur d'Alantour would get that one." When we go through Trafalgar Square, he doesn't look at the road at all, he just stares at the sky, and makes shooting noises.'

'I shouldn't think you could eat a London pigeon,' said Sonny sceptically.

'Patrick Melrose? You're not David Melrose's son, by any chance?' asked Bunny Warren, a figure Patrick could hardly remember, but a name that had floated around his childhood at a time when his parents still had a social life, before their divorce.

'Yes.'

Bunny's creased face, like an animated sultana, raced through half a dozen expressions of surprise and delight. 'I remember you as a child, you used to take a running kick at my balls each time I came to Victoria Road for a drink.'

'I'm sorry about that,' said Patrick. 'Oddly enough, Nicholas Pratt was complaining about the same sort of thing this morning.'

'Oh, well, in his case . . .' said Bunny with a mischievous laugh.

'I used to get to the right velocity,' Patrick explained, 'by starting on the landing and running down the first flight of stairs. By the time I reached the hall I could manage a really good kick.'

'You don't have to tell me,' said Bunny. 'Do you know, it's a funny thing,' he went on in a more serious tone, 'hardly a day passes without my thinking of your father.'

'Same here,' said Patrick, 'but I've got a good excuse.'

'So have I,' said Bunny. 'He helped me at a time when I was in an extremely wobbly state.'

'He helped to put me *into* an extremely wobbly state,' said Patrick.

'I know a lot of people found him difficult,' admitted Bunny, 'and he may have been at his most difficult with his children – people usually are – but I saw another side of his personality. After Lucy died, at a time when I really couldn't cope at all, he took care of me and stopped me drinking myself to death, listened with enormous intelligence to hours of black despair, and never used what I told him against me.'

'The fact that you mention his not using anything you said against you is sinister enough.'

'You can say what you like,' said Bunny bluntly, 'but your

father probably saved my life.' He made an inaudible excuse and moved away abruptly.

Alone in the press of the party, Patrick was suddenly anxious to avoid another conversation, and left the tent, preoccupied by what Bunny had said about his father. As he hurried into the now-crowded drawing room, he was spotted by Laura, who stood with China and a man Patrick did not recognize.

'Hello, darling,' said Laura.

'Hi,' said Patrick, who didn't want to be waylaid.

'Have you met Ballantine Morgan?' said China.

'Hello,' said Patrick.

'Hello,' said Ballantine, giving Patrick an annoyingly firm handshake. 'I was just saying,' he continued, 'that I've been lucky enough to inherit what is probably the greatest gun collection in the world.'

'Well, I think,' said Patrick, 'I was lucky enough to see a book about it shown to me by your father.'

'Oh, so you've read *The Morgan Gun Collection*,' said Ballantine.

'Well, not from cover to cover, but enough to know how extraordinary it was to own the greatest gun collection in the world and be such a good shot, as well as write about the whole thing in such beautiful prose.'

'My father was also a very fine photographer,' said Ballantine.

'Oh, yes, I knew I'd forgotten something,' said Patrick.

'He was certainly a multitalented individual,' said Ballantine.

'When did he die?' asked Patrick.

'He died of cancer last year,' said Ballantine. 'When a man of my father's wealth dies of cancer, you know they haven't found a cure,' he added with justifiable pride.

'It does you great credit that you're such a fine curator of his memory,' said Patrick wearily.

'Honour thy father and thy mother all thy days,' said Ballantine.

'That's certainly been my policy,' Patrick affirmed.

China, who felt that even Ballantine's gargantuan income might be eclipsed by his fatuous behaviour, suggested that they dance.

'I'd be pleased to,' said Ballantine. 'Excuse us,' he added to Laura and Patrick.

'What a ghastly man,' said Laura.

'You should have met his father,' said Patrick.

'If he could get that silver spoon out of his mouth—'

'He would be even more pointless than he already is,' said Patrick.

'How are you, anyway, darling?' Laura asked. 'I'm pleased to see you. This party is really getting on my nerves. Men used to tell me how they used butter for sex, now they tell me how they've eliminated it from their diet.'

Patrick smiled. 'You certainly have to kick a lot of bodies out there before you find a live one,' he said. 'There's a blast of palpable stupidity that comes from our host, like opening the door of a sauna. The best way to contradict him is to let him speak.'

'We could go upstairs,' said Laura.

'What on earth for?' smiled Patrick.

'We could just fuck. No strings.'

'Well, it's something to do,' said Patrick.

'Thanks,' said Laura.

'No, no, I'm really keen,' said Patrick. 'Although I can't help thinking it's a terrible idea. Aren't we going to get confused?'

'No strings, remember?' said Laura, marching him towards the hall.

A security guard stood at the foot of the staircase. 'I'm sorry, no one goes upstairs,' he said.

'We're staying here,' said Laura, and something indefinably arrogant about her tone made the security man step aside.

Patrick and Laura kissed, leaning against the wall of the attic room they had found.

'Guess who I'm having an affair with?' asked Laura as she detached herself.

'I dread to think. Anyhow, why do you want to discuss it just now?' Patrick mumbled as he bit her neck.

'He's someone you know.'

'I give up,' sighed Patrick who could feel his erection dwindling.

'Johnny.'

'Well, that's put me right off,' said Patrick.

'I thought you might want to steal me back.'

'I'd rather stay friends with Johnny. I don't want more irony and more tension. You never really understood that, did you?'

'You love irony and tension, what are you talking about?'

'You just go round imagining everybody's like you.'

'Oh, fuck off,' said Laura. 'Or as Lawrence Harvey says in *Darling*, "Put away your Penguin Freud."'

'Look, we'd better just part now, don't you think?' said Patrick. 'Before we have a row.'

'God, you're a pain,' said Laura.

'Let's go down separately,' said Patrick. The flickering flame of his lighter cast a dim wobbling light over the room. The lighter went out, but Patrick found the brass doorknob and, opening the door cautiously, allowed a wedge of light to cross the dusty floorboards.

'You go first,' he whispered, brushing the dust from the back of her dress.

'Bye,' she said curtly.

10

Patrick closed the door gratefully and lit a cigarette. Since his conversation with Bunny there'd been no time to think, but now the disturbing quality of Bunny's remarks caught up with him and kept him in the attic.

Even when he had gone to New York to collect his ashes, Patrick had not been completely convinced by the simple solution of loathing his father. Bunny's loyalty to David made Patrick realize that his real difficulty might be in acknowledging the same feelings in himself.

What had there been to admire about his father? The music he had refused to take the risk of recording? And yet it had sometimes broken Patrick's heart to hear it. The psychological insight he had habitually used to torment his friends and family, but which Bunny claimed had saved his life? All of David's virtues and talents had been double-edged, but however vile he had been he had not been deluded, most of the time, and had accepted with some stoicism his well-deserved suffering.

It was not admiration that would reconcile him to his father, or even the famously stubborn love of children for their parents, able to survive far worse fates than Patrick's. The greenish faces of those drowning figures clinging to the edge of the *Medusa*'s raft haunted his imagination, and he did not always picture them *from* the raft, but often as enviably closer to it than he was. How many choked cursing?

How many slipped under silently? How many survived a little longer by pressing on the shoulders of their drowning neighbours?

Something more practical made him rummage about for a reason to make peace. Most of Patrick's strengths, or what he imagined were his strengths, derived from his struggle against his father, and only by becoming detached from their tainted origin could he make any use of them.

And yet he could never lose his indignation at the way his father had cheated him of any peace of mind, and he knew that however much trouble he put into repairing himself, like a once-broken vase that looks whole on its patterned surface but reveals in its pale interior the thin dark lines of its restoration, he could only produce an illusion of wholeness.

All Patrick's attempts at generosity ran up against his choking indignation while, on the other hand, his hatred ran up against those puzzling moments, fleeting and always spoiled, when his father had seemed to be in love with life and to take pleasure in any expression of freedom, or playfulness, or brilliance. Perhaps he would have to settle for the idea that it must have been even worse being his father than being someone his father had attempted to destroy.

Simplification was dangerous and would later take its revenge. Only when he could hold in balance his hatred and his stunted love, looking on his father with neither pity nor terror but as another human being who had not handled his personality especially well; only when he could live with the ambivalence of never forgiving his father for his crimes but allowing himself to be touched by the unhappiness that had produced them as well as the unhappiness they had produced, could he be released, perhaps, into a new life that would enable him to live instead of merely surviving. He might even enjoy himself.

Patrick grunted nervously. Enjoy himself? He mustn't let his optimism run away with him. His eyes had adjusted to the dark and he could now make out the chests and boxes that surrounded the small patch of floor he had been pacing around. A narrow half window giving onto the roof and gutter caught the murky brown glow of the floodlights at the front of the house. He lit another cigarette and smoked it, leaning against the windowsill. He felt the usual panic about needing to be elsewhere, in this case downstairs where he couldn't help imagining the carpets being hoovered and the caterers' vans loaded, although it had only been about one thirty when he came upstairs with Laura. But he stayed in the attic, intrigued by the slightest chance of release from the doldrums in which his soul had lain breathless for so long.

Patrick opened the window to throw his cigarette onto the damp roof. Taking a last gulp of smoke, he smiled at the thought that David probably would have shared his point of view about their relationship. It was the kind of trick that had made him a subtle enemy, but now it might help to end their battle. Yes, his father would have applauded Patrick's defiance and understood his efforts to escape the maze into which he had placed him. The thought that he would have wanted him to succeed made Patrick want to cry.

Beyond bitterness and despair there was something poignant, something he found harder to admit than the facts about his father's cruelty, the thing he had not been able to say to Johnny: that his father had wanted, through the brief interludes of his depression, to love him, and that he had wanted to be able to love his father, although he never would.

And why, while he was at it, continue to punish his mother? She had not done anything so much as failed to do anything, but he had put himself beyond her reach, clinging on to the adolescent bravado of pretending that she was a person he had nothing in common with at all, who just happened to have given birth to him; that their relationship was a geographical accident, like that of being someone's neighbour. She had frustrated her husband by refusing to go to bed with him, but Patrick would be the last person to blame her for that. It would probably be better if women arrested in their own childhood didn't have children with tormented misogynist homosexual paedophiles, but nothing was perfect in this sublunary world, thought Patrick, glancing up devoutly at the moon which was of course hidden, like the rest of the sky during an English winter, by a low swab of dirty cloud. His mother was really a good person, but like almost everybody she had found her compass spinning in the magnetic field of intimacy.

He really must go downstairs now. Obsessed by punctuality and dogged by a heart-compressing sense of urgency, Patrick was still incapable of keeping a watch. A watch might have soothed him by challenging his hysteria and pessimism. He would definitely get a watch on Monday. If he was not going to have an epiphany to take with him from the attic, the promise of a watch might at least represent a shimmering of hope. Wasn't there a single German word meaning 'shimmering of hope'? There was probably a single German word meaning, 'Regeneration through Punctuality, Shimmering of Hope, and Taking Pleasure in the Misfortune of Others'. If only he knew what it was.

Could one have a time-release epiphany, an epiphany without realizing it had happened? Or were they always trumpeted by angels and preceded by temporary blindness, Patrick wondered, as he walked down the corridor in the wrong direction.

Turning the corner, he saw that he was in a part of the house he had never seen before. A threadbare brown carpet stretched down a corridor that ended in darkness.

'How the fuck do you get out of this fucking house?' he cursed.

'You're going the wrong way.'

Patrick looked to his right and saw a girl in a white nightie sitting on a short flight of stairs.

'I didn't mean to swear,' he said. 'Or rather, I did mean to, but I didn't know you'd overhear me.'

'It's all right,' she said, 'Daddy swears all the time.'

'Are you Sonny and Bridget's daughter?'

'Yes. I'm Belinda.'

'Can't you get to sleep?' asked Patrick, sitting down on the stairs next to her. She shook her head. 'Why not?'

'Because of the party. Nanny said if I said my prayers properly I'd go to sleep, but I didn't.'

'Do you believe in God?' asked Patrick.

'I don't know,' said Belinda. 'But if there is a God he's not very good at it.'

Patrick laughed. 'But why aren't you at the party?' he asked.

'I'm not allowed. I'm meant to go to bed at nine.'

'How mean,' said Patrick. 'Do you want me to smuggle you down?'

'Mummy would see me. And Princess Margaret said I had to go to bed.'

'In that case we must definitely smuggle you down. Or I could read you a story.'

'Oh, that would be nice,' said Belinda, and then she put her fingers to her lips and said, 'Shh, there's someone coming.'

At that moment Bridget rounded the corner of the corridor and saw Patrick and Belinda together on the stairs.

'What are you doing here?' she asked Patrick.

'I was just trying to find my way back to the party and I ran into Belinda.'

'But what were you doing here in the first place?'

427

'Hello, Mummy,' interrupted Belinda.

'Hello, darling,' said Bridget, holding out her hand.

'I came up here with a girl,' Patrick explained.

'Oh God, you're making me feel very old,' said Bridget. 'So much for the security.'

'I was just going to read Belinda a story.'

'Sweet,' said Bridget. 'I should have been doing that years ago.' She picked Belinda up in her arms. 'You're so heavy, nowadays,' she groaned, smiling at Patrick firmly, but dismissively.

'Well, good night,' said Patrick, getting up from the stairs.

'Night,' yawned Belinda.

'I've got something I have to tell you,' said Bridget, as she started to carry Belinda down the corridor. 'Mummy is going to stay at Granny's tonight, and we'd like you to come along as well. There won't be any room for Nanny, though.'

'Oh good, I hate Nanny.'

'I know, darling,' said Bridget.

'But why are we going to Granny's?'

Patrick could no longer hear what they were saying as they went round the corner of the corridor.

Johnny Hall had been curious to meet Peter Porlock ever since Laura told him that Peter had needlessly paid for one of her abortions. When Laura introduced them, Peter wasted no time in swearing Johnny to secrecy about this 'dreadful Cindy and Sonny thing'.

'Of course I've known about it for ages,' he began.

'Whereas I had no idea,' David Windfall chipped in, 'even when Sonny asked me to bring her.'

'That's funny,' said Laura, 'I thought everybody knew.'

'Some people may have suspected, but nobody knew the details,' said Peter proudly.

'Not even Sonny and Cindy,' mocked Laura.

David, who was already apprised of Peter's superior knowledge, drifted off and Laura followed.

Left alone with Johnny, Peter tried to correct any impression of frivolity he might have given by saying how worried he was about his 'ailing papa' to whom he had not bothered to address a word all evening. 'Are your parentals still alive?' he asked.

'And kicking,' said Johnny. 'My mother would have managed to give an impression of mild disappointment if I'd become the youngest Prime Minister of England, so you can imagine what she feels about a moderately successful journalist. She reminds me of a story about Henry Miller visiting his dying mother with a pilot friend of his called Vincent. The old woman looked at her son and then at Vincent and said, "If only I could have a son like you, Vincent." '

'Look here, you won't leak anything I've said to the press, will you?' asked Peter.

'Alas, the editorial pages of *The Times* aren't yet given over entirely to love-nest scandals,' said Johnny contemptuously.

'Oh, *The Times*,' murmured Peter. 'Well, I know it's frightfully unfashionable, but I still think one should practise filial loyalty. It's been frightfully easy for me: my mother was a saint and my father's the most decent chap you could hope to meet.'

Johnny smiled vaguely, wishing Laura had charged Peter double.

'Peter!' said a concerned Princess Margaret.

'Oh, ma'am, I didn't see you,' said Peter, bowing his head briefly.

'I think you should go to the hall. I'm afraid your father isn't at all well, and he's being taken off by ambulance.'

'Good God,' said Peter. 'Please excuse me, ma'am, I'll go immediately.'

The Princess, who had announced in the hall that she would tell Peter herself, and forced her lady-in-waiting to intercept other well-wishers on the same mission, was thoroughly impressed by her own goodness.

'And who are you?' she asked Johnny in the most gracious possible manner.

'Johnny Hall,' said Johnny, extending a hand.

The republican omission of ma'am, and the thrusting and unacceptable invitation to a handshake, were enough to convince the Princess that Johnny was a man of no importance.

'It must be funny having the same name as so many other people,' she speculated. 'I suppose there are hundreds of John Halls up and down the country.'

'It teaches one to look for distinction elsewhere and not to rely on an accident of birth,' said Johnny casually.

'That's where people go wrong,' said the Princess, compressing her lips, 'there is no accident in birth.'

She swept on before Johnny had a chance to reply.

Patrick walked down towards the first floor, the hubbub of the party growing louder as he descended past portraits by Lely and Lawrence and even a pair, dominating the first-floor landing, by Reynolds. The prodigious complacency which the Gravesend genes had carried from generation to generation, without the usual interludes of madness, diffidence or distinction, had defied the skills of all these painters, and, despite their celebrity, none of them had been able to make anything appealing out of the drooping eyelids and idiotically arrogant expressions of their sitters.

Thinking about Belinda, Patrick started half-consciously to walk down the stairs as he had in moments of stress when he was her age, leading with one foot and bringing the other down firmly beside it on the same step. As he approached the hall he felt an overwhelming urge to cast himself forward onto the stone floor, but stopped instead and held on to the banister, intrigued by this strange impulse, which he could not immediately explain.

Yvette had told him many times about the day he had fallen down the stairs at Lacoste and cut his hand. The story of his screams and the broken glass and Yvette's fear that he had cut a tendon had installed themselves in his picture of childhood as an accepted anecdote, but now Patrick could feel the revival of the memory itself: he could remember imagining the frames of the pictures flying down the corridor and embedding themselves in his father's chest, and decapitating Nicholas Pratt. He could feel the despairing urge to jump down the stairs to hide his guilt at snapping the stem of the glass by squeezing it so tightly. He stood on the stairs and remembered everything.

The security guard looked at him sceptically. He'd been worried ever since he allowed Patrick and Laura to go upstairs. Laura's coming down on her own and claiming that Patrick was still in their room had strengthened his suspicions. Now Patrick was behaving very eccentrically, trailing one leg as he came down the stairs, staring at the ground. He must be on drugs, thought the security guard angrily. If he had his way he'd arrest Patrick and all the other rich cunts who thought they were above the law.

Patrick, noticing the expression of hostility on the security guard's face, surfaced into the present, smiled weakly, and walked down the final steps. Across the hall, through the windows on either side of the open front door, he could see a flashing blue light.

'Are the police here?' Patrick asked.

'No, it's not the police,' said the security guard sadly. 'Ambulance.'

'What happened?'

'One of the guests had a heart attack.'

'Do you know who it was?' said Patrick.

'Don't know his name, no. White-haired gentleman.' Cold air swept into the hall through the open door. Snow was falling outside. Noticing Tom Charles standing in the doorway, Patrick went over to his side.

'It's George,' said Tom. 'I think he had a stroke. He was very weak, but he could still talk, so I hope he'll be all right.'

'So do I,' said Patrick, who had known George all his life and suddenly realized that he would miss him if he died. George had always been friendly to him, and he urgently wanted to thank him. 'Do you know which hospital they're taking him to?'

'Cheltenham Hospital for tonight,' answered Tom. 'Sonny wants to move him to a clinic, but this ambulance is from the hospital, and I guess the priority is to keep him alive rather than to get him a more expensive room.'

'Quite,' said Patrick. 'Well, I hope King won't be unpacking for him tonight,' he added.

'Don't forget he's travelling light,' said Tom. 'Heaven is the ideal country weekend without any luggage.'

Patrick smiled. 'Let's go and see him tomorrow before lunch.'

'Good idea,' said Tom. 'Where are you staying?'

'The Little Soddington House Hotel,' said Patrick. 'Do you want me to write it down?'

'No,' said Tom, 'with a name like that I may never shake it off.'

'I think it was Talleyrand,' suggested Jacques d'Alantour, pouting a little before his favourite quotation, 'who said,' he paused, '"Doing and saying nothing are great powers, but they should not be abused."'

'Well, nobody could accuse you of doing and saying nothing this evening,' said Bridget.

'Nevertheless,' he continued, 'I shall speak to the Princess about this matter, which I hope will not become known as *"l'affaire Alantour"*.' He chuckled. 'And I hope we can get the bull out of the china shop.'

'Do what you like,' said Bridget. 'I'm past caring.'

Monsieur d'Alantour, too pleased with his new plan to notice his hostess's indifference, bowed and turned on his heels.

'When the Queen's away, I become regent and head of the Privy Council,' Princess Margaret was explaining with satisfaction to Kitty Harrow.

'Ma'am,' said Monsieur d'Alantour, who after considerable thought had worked out the perfect formula for his apology.

'Oh, are you still here,' said the Princess.

'As you can see . . .' said the ambassador.

'Well, shouldn't you be setting off now? You've got a very long journey ahead of you.'

'But I'm staying in the house,' he protested.

'In that case we shall see quite enough of each other tomorrow without spending the whole evening chattering,' said the Princess, turning her back on him.

'Who's that man over there?' she asked Kitty.

'Ali Montague, ma'am,' said Kitty.

'Oh, yes, I recognize the name. You can present him to me,' said Princess Margaret, heading off in Ali's direction.

The ambassador stood in consternation and silence while Kitty presented Ali Montague to Princess Margaret. He was wondering whether he was facing another diplomatic incident or merely the extension of the previous diplomatic incident.

'Oh,' said Ali Montague boldly, 'I love the French. They're treacherous, cunning, two-faced – I don't have to make an effort there, I just fit in. And further down in Italy, they're cowards as well, so I get on even better.'

The Princess looked at him mischievously. She was in a good mood again and had decided that Ali was being amusing.

Alexander Politsky later sought out Ali to congratulate him on 'handling P.M. so well'.

'Oh, I've had my fair share of royalty,' said Ali suavely. 'Mind you, I didn't do nearly so well with that dreadful Amanda Pratt. You know how ghastly all those people become when they're "on the programme" and go to all those meetings. Of course, they do save people's lives.'

Alexander sniffed and looked languidly into the middle distance. 'I've been to them myself,' he admitted.

'But you never had a drink problem,' protested Ali.

'I like heroin, cocaine, nice houses, good furniture, and pretty girls,' said Alexander, 'and I've had all of them in large quantities. But you know, they never made me happy.'

'My word, you're hard to please, aren't you?'

'Frankly, when I first went along I thought I'd stick out like a pair of jeans on a Gainsborough, but I've found more genuine love and kindness in those meetings than I've seen in all the fashionable drawing rooms of London.'

'Well, that's not saying much,' said Ali. 'You could say the same thing about Billingsgate fish market.'

'There isn't one of them,' said Alexander, throwing his shoulders back and closing his eyelids, 'from the tattooed butcher upward, whom I wouldn't drive to Inverness at three in the morning to help.'

'To Inverness? From where?' asked Ali.

'London.'

'Good God,' exclaimed Ali. 'Perhaps I should try one of those meetings, next time I have a spare evening. But the point is, would you ask your tattooed butcher to dinner?'

'Of course not,' said Alexander. 'But only because he wouldn't enjoy it.'

'Anne!' said Patrick. 'I didn't expect to see you here.'

'I know,' said Anne Eisen, kissing him warmly. 'It's not my kind of scene. I get nervous in the English countryside with everybody talking about killing animals.'

'I'm sure there isn't any of that sort of thing in Sonny's part of the world,' said Patrick.

'You mean, there isn't anything alive for miles around,' said Anne. 'I'm here because Sonny's father was a *relatively* civilized man – he noticed that there was a library in the house as well as a boot room and a cellar. He was a sort of friend of Victor's, and used to ask us to stay for weekends sometimes. Sonny was just a kid in those days but even then he was a pompous creep. Jesus,' sighed Anne, surveying the room, 'what a grim bunch. Do you think they keep them in the deep freeze at Central Casting and thaw them out for big occasions?'

'If only,' said Patrick. 'Unfortunately I think they own most of the country.'

'They've only just got the edge on an ant colony,' said Anne, 'except that they don't do anything useful. You remember those ants in Lacoste, they were always tidying up the terrace for you. Talking of doing something useful, what are you planning to do with your life?'

'Hmm,' said Patrick.

'Jesus Christ!' said Anne. 'You're guilty of the worst sin of all.'

'What's that?'

'Wasting time,' she replied.

'I know,' said Patrick. 'It was a terrible shock to me when I realized I was getting too old to die young anymore.'

Exasperated, Anne changed the subject. 'Are you going to Lacoste this year?' she asked.

'I don't know. The more time passes the more I dislike that place.'

'I've always meant to apologize to you,' said Anne, 'but you used to be too stoned to appreciate it. I've felt guilty for years for not doing anything when you were waiting on the stairs one evening during one of your parents' godawful dinner parties, and I said I'd get your mother for you, but I couldn't, and I should have gone back, or stood up to David, or something. I always felt I'd failed you.'

'Not at all,' said Patrick. 'On the contrary, I remember your being kind. When you're young it makes a difference to meet people who are kind, however rarely. You'd imagine they're buried under the routine of horror, but in fact incidents of kindness get thrown into sharp relief.'

'Have you forgiven your father?' asked Anne.

'Oddly enough you've caught me on the right evening. A week ago I would have lied or said something dismissive, but I was just describing over dinner exactly what I had to forgive my father.'

'And?'

'Well,' said Patrick, 'over dinner I was rather against forgiveness, and I still think that it's detachment rather than appeasement that will set me free, but if I could imagine a mercy that was purely human, and not one that rested on the Greatest Story Ever Told, I might extend it to my father for being so unhappy. I just can't do it out of piety. I've had enough near-death experiences to last me a lifetime, and not *once* was I greeted by a white-robed figure at the end of a tunnel – or only once and he turned out to be an exhausted junior doctor in the emergency ward of the Charing Cross Hospital. There may be something to this idea that you have to be broken in order to be renewed, but renewal doesn't have to consist of a lot of phoney reconciliations!'

'What about some genuine ones?' said Anne.

'What impresses me more than the repulsive superstition that I should turn the other cheek, is the intense unhappiness my father lived with. I ran across a diary his mother wrote during the First World War. After pages of gossip and a long passage about how marvellously they'd managed to keep up the standards at some large country house, defying the Kaiser with the perfection of their cucumber sandwiches, there are two short sentences: "Geoffrey wounded again", about her husband in the trenches, and "David has rickets", about her son at his prep school. Presumably he was not just suffering from malnutrition, but being assaulted by paedophiliac schoolmasters and beaten by older boys. This very traditional combination of maternal coldness and official perversion helped to make him the splendid man he turned into, but to forgive someone, one would have to be convinced that they'd made some effort to change the disastrous course that genetics, class, or upbringing proposed for them.'

'If he'd changed the course he wouldn't need forgiving,' said Anne. 'That's the whole deal with forgiving. Anyhow, I don't say you're wrong not to forgive him, but you can't stay stuck with this hatred.'

'There's no point in staying stuck,' Patrick agreed. 'But there's even less point in pretending to be free. I feel on the verge of a great transformation, which may be as simple as becoming interested in other things.'

'What?' said Anne. 'No more father-bashing? No more drugs? No more snobbery?'

'Steady on,' gasped Patrick. 'Mind you, this evening I had a brief hallucination that the world was real . . .'

'"An hallucination that the world was real" – you oughta be Pope.'

'Real,' Patrick continued, 'and not just composed of a series of effects – the orange lights on a wet pavement, a leaf clinging to the windscreen, the sucking sound of a taxi's tyres on a rainy street.'

'Very wintery effects,' said Anne.

'Well, it is February,' said Patrick. 'Anyway, for a moment the world seemed to be solid and out there and made up of things.'

'That's progress,' said Anne. 'You used to belong to the the-world-is-a-private-movie school.'

'You can only give things up once they start to let you down. I gave up drugs when the pleasure and the pain became simultaneous and I might as well have been shooting up a vial of my own tears. As to the naive faith that rich people are more interesting than poor ones, or titled people more interesting than untitled ones, it would be impossible to sustain if people didn't also believe that they became more interesting by association. I can feel the death throes of that particular delusion, especially as I patrol this room full of photo opportunities and feel my mind seizing up with boredom.'

'That's your own fault.'

'As to my "father-bashing",' said Patrick, ignoring Anne's comment, 'I thought of him this evening without thinking about his influence on me, just as a tired old man who'd fucked up his life, wheezing away his last years in that faded blue shirt he wore in the summer. I pictured him sitting in the courtyard of that horrible house, doing *The Times*' crossword, and he struck me as more pathetic and more *ordinary*, and in the end less worthy of attention.'

'That's what I feel about my dreadful old mother,' said Anne. 'During the Depression, which for some of us never ended, she used to collect stray cats and feed them and look after them. The house would be full of cats. I was just a kid, so naturally I'd get to love them, and play with them, but then in the autumn my crazy old mother would start muttering, "They'll never make it through the winter, they'll never make it through the winter." The only reason they weren't going to make it through the winter was that she'd soak a towel in ether and drop it in the old brass washing machine and pile the cats in afterward, and when they'd "fallen asleep" she'd turn on the washing machine and drown the poor buggers. Our whole garden was a cat cemetery, and you couldn't dig a hole or play a game without little cat skeletons turning up. There was a terrible scratching sound as they tried to get out of the washing machine. I can remember standing by the kitchen table – I was only as high as the kitchen table – while my mother loaded them in and I'd say, "Don't, please don't," and she'd be muttering, "They'll never make it through the winter." She was ghastly and quite mad, but when I grew up I figured that her worst punishment was to be herself and I didn't have to do anything more.'

'No wonder you get nervous in the English countryside when people start talking about killing animals. Perhaps that's all identity is: seeing the logic of your own experience and being true to it. If only Victor was with us now!'

'Oh, yes, poor Victor,' said Anne. 'But he was looking for a non-psychological approach to identity,' she reminded Patrick with a wry smile.

'That always puzzled me,' he admitted. 'It seemed like insisting on an overland route from England to America.'

'If you're a philosopher, there is an overland route from England to America,' said Anne.

'Oh, by the way, did you hear that George Watford had a stroke?'

'Yeah, I'm sorry to hear that. I remember meeting him at your parents.'

'It's the end of an era,' said Patrick.

'It's the end of a party as well,' said Anne. 'Look, the band is going home.'

When Robin Parker asked Sonny if they could have 'a private word' in the library, Sonny not only felt that he'd spent his entire birthday party having difficult interviews in that wretched room, but also that, as he'd suspected (and he couldn't help pausing here to congratulate himself on his perspicacity), Robin was going to blackmail him for more money.

'Well, what is it,' he said gruffly, once again sitting at his library desk.

'It isn't a Poussin,' said Robin, 'so I really don't want to authenticate it. Other people, including experts, might think it was, but I *know* it isn't.' Robin sighed. 'I'd like my letter back and of course I'll return the . . . fee,' he said, placing two thick envelopes on the table.

'What are you blathering about?' asked Sonny, confused.

'I'm not blathering,' said Robin. 'It's not fair on Poussin, that's all,' he added with unexpected passion.

'What's Poussin got to do with it?' thundered Sonny.

'Nothing, that's just what I object to.'

'I suppose you want more money.'

'You're wrong,' said Robin. 'I just want some part of my life not to be compromised.' He held out his hand for the certificate of authentication.

Furious, Sonny took a key out of his pocket and opened the top drawer of his desk, and tossed the letter over to Robin. Robin thanked him and left the room.

'Tiresome little man,' muttered Sonny. It really wasn't his day. He'd lost his wife, his mistress, and his Poussin. Buck up, old boy, he thought to himself, but he had to admit that he felt decidedly wobbly.

*

Virginia was sitting on a frail gold chair by the drawing-room door, waiting anxiously for her daughter and grand-daughter to come downstairs and start the long drive back to Kent. Kent was ever such a long way, but she completely understood Bridget's wanting to get out of this bad atmos-phere, and she'd encouraged her to bring Belinda along. She couldn't hide from herself, although she felt a little guilty about it, that she quite liked being *needed*, and having Bridget close to her again, even if it took a crisis like this one. She'd already got her overcoat and her essentials; it didn't matter about her suitcase, Bridget had said they could send for that later. She didn't want to draw attention to herself: the over-coat was suspicious enough.

The party was thinning out and it was important to leave before there were too few people, or Sonny might start badgering Bridget. Bridget's nerves had never been strong, she'd always been a little frightened as a girl, never wanted to put her head under water, that sort of thing, things only a mother could know. Bridget might be intimidated and lose her resolve if Sonny was there booming at her, but she knew that what her daughter needed, after this Cindy Smith affair, was a good rest and a good think. She'd already asked Bridget if she wanted her old room back – it was a marvel how the human mind worked, as Roddy had been fond of remarking – but it had only seemed to annoy Bridget, who'd said, 'Hon-estly, Mummy, I don't know, we'll think about that later.' On reflection, it was probably better to give that room to Belinda, and put Bridget in the nice spare room with the bathroom en suite. There was plenty of room now that she was alone.

Sometimes a crisis was good for a marriage, not all the time of course, or it wouldn't really be a crisis. There'd been that one time with Roddy. She hadn't said anything, but Roddy had known she knew, and she'd known he knew she knew, and that had been enough to end it. He'd bought her that ring and said it was their second engagement ring. He was such an old softie, really. Oh dear, there was a man bearing down on her. She had no idea who he was but he was obviously going to talk to her. That was the last thing she needed.

Jacques d'Alantour was too tormented to go to sleep and, although Jacqueline had warned him that he'd had enough to drink, too melancholy to resist another glass of champagne.

Charm was his speciality, everyone knew that, but since '*l'affaire Alantour*', as he now called it, he had entered a diplomatic labyrinth which seemed to require more charm and tact than it was reasonable to ask of a single human being. Virginia, who was, after all, his hostess's mother, played a relatively clear role in the campaign he was launching to regain Princess Margaret's favour.

'Good evening, dear lady,' he said with a deep bow.

Foreign manners, thought Virginia. What Roddy used to call 'a hand-kissing sell-your-own-mother type'.

'Am I right in assuming that you are the mother of our charming hostess?'

'Yes,' said Virginia.

'I am Jacques d'Alantour.'

'Oh, hello,' said Virginia.

'May I get you a glass of champagne?' asked the ambassador.

'No, thank you, I don't like to have more than two. Anyway, I'm on a diet.'

'A diet?' asked Monsieur d'Alantour, seeing an opportunity to prove to the world that his diplomatic skills were not dead. 'A diet?' he repeated with bewilderment and incredulity. 'But w-h-y?' he lingered on the word, to emphasize his astonishment.

'The same reason as everyone else, I suppose,' said Virginia drily.

Monsieur d'Alantour sat down next to her, grateful to get the weight off his legs. Jacqueline was right, he'd drunk too much champagne. But the campaign must continue!

'When a lady tells me she is on a diet,' he said, his gallantry a little slurred, but his fluency, from years of making the same speech (which had been a great success with the German Ambassador's wife in Paris) undiminished, 'I always clasp her breast so,' he held his cupped hand threateningly close to Virginia's alarmed bosom, 'and say, "But now I think you are exactly the right weight!" If I were to do this to you,' he continued, 'you would not be shocked, would you?'

'Shocked,' gulped Virginia, 'isn't the word. I'd be—'

'You see,' Monsieur d'Alantour interrupted, 'it's the most natural thing in the world!'

'Oh, goodness,' said Virginia, 'there's my daughter.'

'Come on, Mummy,' said Bridget, 'Belinda's already in the car, and I'd rather not run into Sonny.'

'I know, darling, I'm just coming. I can't say it's been a pleasure,' she said to the ambassador stiffly, hurrying after her daughter.

Monsieur d'Alantour was too slow to catch up with the hastening women, but stood mumbling, 'I can't express sufficiently . . . my deepest sentiments . . . a most distinguished gathering.'

Bridget moved so much faster than her guests that they had no time to compliment her or waylay her. Some thought that she was following George Watford to hospital, everyone could tell that she was on important business.

When she got into the car, a four-wheel-drive Subaru that Caroline Porlock had persuaded her to buy, and saw Belinda asleep and seatbelted in the back, and her mother sitting beside her with a warm and reassuring smile, Bridget felt a wave of relief and remorse.

'I've treated you dreadfully sometimes,' she suddenly said to her mother. 'Snobbishly.'

'Oh no, darling, I understand,' said her mother, moved but practical.

'I don't know what came over me sending you to dinner with those dreadful people. Everything gets turned upside down. I've been so anxious to fit in with Sonny's stupid, pompous life that everything else got squeezed out. Anyway, I'm glad the three of us are together.'

Virginia glanced back at Belinda to make sure she was asleep.

'We can have a good long talk tomorrow,' she said, squeezing Bridget's hand, 'but we should probably get started now, we've got a long way to go.'

'You're right,' said Bridget who suddenly felt like crying but busied herself with starting the car and joining the queue of departing guests who choked up her drive.

There was still a gentle snowfall as Patrick left the house behind him, steaming breath twisting around the upturned collar of his overcoat. Footprints crisscrossed his path, and the gravel's black and brown chips shone wetly among the bright patches of snow. Patrick's ears rang from the noise of the party and his eyes, bloodshot from smoke and tiredness, watered in the cold air, but when he reached his car he wanted to go on walking a little longer, and so he climbed over a nearby gate and jumped into a field of unbroken snow. A pewter-coloured ornamental lake lay at the end of the field, its far bank lost in a thick fog.

His thin shoes grew wet as he crunched across the field and his feet soon felt cold, but with the compelling and opaque logic of a dream the lake drew him to its shore.

As he stood in front of the reeds which pierced the first few yards of water, shivering and wondering whether to have his last cigarette, he heard the sound of beating wings emerging from the other side of the lake. A pair of swans rose out of the fog, concentrating its whiteness and giving it shape, the clamour of their wings muffled by the falling snow, like white gloves on applauding hands.

Vicious creatures, thought Patrick.

The swans, indifferent to his thoughts, flew over fields renewed and silenced by the snow, curved back over the shore of the lake, spread their webbed feet, and settled confidently onto the water.

Standing in sodden shoes Patrick smoked his last cigarette. Despite his tiredness and the absolute stillness of the air, he felt his soul, which he could only characterize as the part of his mind that was not dominated by the need to talk, surging and writhing like a kite longing to be let go. Without thinking about it he picked up the dead branch at his feet and sent it spinning as far as he could into the dull grey eye of the lake. A faint ripple disturbed the reeds.

After their useless journey the swans drifted majestically back into the fog. Nearer and noisier, a group of gulls circled overhead, their squawks evoking wilder water and wider shores.

Patrick flicked his cigarette into the snow, and not quite knowing what had happened, headed back to his car with a strange feeling of elation.